ORACLES OF KURNUGI

Also by Gama Ray Martinez

Goblin Star

Nova Dragon

Runestone Fleet

Pharim War

Shadowguard

Veilspeaker

Beastwalker

Lightgiver

Darkmask

Lifebringer

Shadeslayer

Nylean Chronicles

Child of the Wilde

Child of the Stars

Lords of the Wilde

ORACLES OF
KURNUGI

GAMA RAY MARTINEZ

Delphi © 2014 by Gamaliel Martinez

Stepmother's Mirror © 2014 by Gamaliel Martinez

Mimir's Well © 2015 by Gamaliel Martinez

All rights reserved.

ISBN: 1-944091-16-5

ISBN-13: 978-1-944091-16-3

Thanks to Rudder Writing who first published these books.

Contents

Delphi

ONE

You, imaginary boy. Wait for me!"

Henry didn't know why he stopped and turned around. The guy running towards him wore torn jeans and a plain white t-shirt. He had to be at least six feet tall with curly black hair. Henry almost did a double take. This guy ran in sandals. For a second, Henry could've sworn he saw dust trailing behind him. He was running so fast Henry leaped off the sidewalk and into the lawn, sure the guy wouldn't be able to stop in time, but it wasn't necessary. He didn't slow down. One moment he was running full speed, and the next, he stopped right in front of where Henry had stood. Henry grumbled as he picked himself up. His clothes felt damp from the sprinkler-watered grass. The guy wasn't even breathing hard. Though he towered over Henry, he thought they might be the same age. His pale blue eyes almost made Henry shiver.

"You new?" Henry asked. "I don't know where you're from, but Twain doesn't allow torn jeans."

"What?" the stranger asked. He looked down at his clothes. "Oh, no, I don't go to your school. I'm here on a job." He reached into his pocket and pulled out an envelope, which he held it out to Henry.

"What's this?"

"A letter."

"I can see that."

"Then, why'd you ask?"

Henry rolled his eyes. "I didn't know there were any couriers in Trenton."

"I'm not from around here."

"Look, I'm late for school." Henry tried to step around him. "I need to be going."

The stranger didn't move. He was just standing in front of Henry again.

"And I need to deliver this message, imaginary boy. Just take it."

"I'm not imaginary," Henry said.

"You were imaginary first." He looked down at his watch. Who wore watches anymore? "Look, you're late. I'm late. Just take the message, and we can both be on our way. Oh, and you may want to keep quiet about this."

"Fine," Henry said as he snatched the letter and shoved it in his pocket.

He pulled out his phone to check the time. Even at a dead run, he'd never make it to school before the first bell. If only his mom hadn't forced him to eat breakfast. He looked up when he heard the sound of flapping. For a moment, he thought they must've scared a nearby bird, but there wasn't one. Even the agitated messenger had vanished. Henry didn't waste time trying to figure it out. He just bolted.

By the time he reached Mark Twain High School, his chest

burned from the effort, and his shoulders ached from the weight of his backpack. The security guard at the entrance grunted as Henry passed. His footsteps echoed through the empty hallways. When he reached Mr. Adams's history class, the lecture was already in full swing. The balding man stopped in midsentence.

"Mr. Gideon," the teacher said in the thick southern accent he only spoke in when he was upset. "So good of you to join us."

Henry glanced at the wall clock. "It's only five minutes."

He took in a sharp breath and wondered why his mouth always spoke without checking with him first. The class laughed, but Mr. Adams's nostrils flared.

"After you take your seat, why don't you tell me the cause of the Civil War?"

Henry slumped into his chair in the back row. "Um, slaves?"

Mr. Adams glared at him, and the class laughed again. Henry tried to disappear into his chair. Mr. Adams scribbled something in his notebook and called on Matthew, who gave a much more thought out answer about economy and politics.

Henry rolled his eyes. "Great, how stupid am I that even the football player is smarter than me?"

Of course, Matthew, while not the smartest student, hardly fit the description of the dumb jock. It annoyed Henry to no end. Matthew would probably have colleges knocking down his door with football scholarships by the time he started his senior year. The least he could do is have the decency to be dumb.

His friend, Daniel, leaned over from the desk next to him. "Dude, Adams spent the last five minutes explaining why slaves weren't the cause."

"It's not my fault," Henry said. "This weird guy stopped me on the street, and I couldn't get away."

The letter jabbed at Henry through his pocket. He almost

pulled it out, but the last time Mr. Adams caught someone passing notes, he made them read it to the class. Henry didn't know what the letter was about or who it was from, and the messenger's warning nagged at him. The last thing Henry wanted was to read it aloud.

The lesson went on for another hour, but Henry hardly heard it. His mind kept drifting back to the messenger. There was something eerily familiar about him. The bell rang, and the students shuffled to the door.

"Mr. Gideon, a moment of your time," Mr. Adams said as he wrote something in his notebook.

Henry groaned. He walked to the teacher's desk. Mr. Adams looked up.

"Would you care to explain your remark?"

"I'm sorry," Henry said. "I wasn't thinking."

"Obviously," the old man said. "Why were you late?"

"It's my mom. She made this big breakfast to celebrate. She wouldn't let me leave until I'd finished. Last night, she found out she's pregnant."

"My congratulations," the teacher said in a flat voice.

"Whatever," Henry mumbled.

Mr. Adams raised an eyebrow but didn't give any other sign he'd heard Henry. "See that it doesn't happen again. You can go. I wouldn't want you to be late for your next class."

Henry shrugged and walked out. Daniel was waiting for him in the hall.

"He come down on you?"

"No, he let me off easy. Isn't your next class on the other side of the school?"

Daniel made a face. "Yeah, but it's algebra."

"You still have to go."

"Yeah, but I don't have to like it. Check you later."

TWO

As Daniel padded down the hall, Henry walked across the hall to his next class, Classical Literature, and sat down near the front. The teacher, Mr. Bulfinch, wasn't the same one who wrote the book on mythology, but Henry liked to think they were related. He smiled at Henry as the rest of the class trickled in. Most of the other students were seniors who wanted to be English or mythology majors and wanted something that stood out on their transcript. According to Mr. Bulfinch, Henry was the only freshmen to ever sign up for his class.

Henry still had a few minutes before the second bell rang, so he pulled out the envelope. Other than the golden hourglass sticker holding it shut, the envelope didn't have any visible markings. Henry stared at the sticker, and for a second, he thought sand flowed from one side of the hourglass to the other, but it had to be his imagination. He pulled it up, and for a moment, he remembered playing as a kid. He'd put a pot on his head and used a broom to fight off an imaginary dragon. He could almost see it in front of him. He could feel its breath. Henry shook his head to clear his mind.

"That was weird," he said under his breath.

He pulled out the note. It looked thicker than normal paper, and when he ran his fingers along it, he felt a rough texture. The pale brown sheet looked old. He unfolded it, half expecting it to fall apart in his hands. Whoever had written this used some kind of calligraphy. He could imagine someone writing this with a quill and ink. Henry almost laughed at the idea before reading the letter.

Henry Alexander Gideon,

We regret we must contact you under these circumstances, but it is unavoidable. Certain rules bind us, and unlike you, we cannot simply choose to ignore them. They say we must contact you like this, and so we do. Certain events have transpired and we require the services of a singular individual, such as yourself. The job we have for you will benefit all of us, and many others besides. This may take you away from your home for a long time, but we assure you, the cause is just. If you wish to hear more, call the messenger, and he will give you the information required to see us in person. We look forward to hearing from you.

"Wow, are they sending internet scams through couriers now?" Henry asked.

He turned the letter over in his hands, but the back was blank. Henry smirked. It wasn't even a good scam. Even if he wanted to call the messenger, they hadn't bothered to write down a number.

"What was that, Henry?" Mr. Bulfinch asked.

"Nothing," he said. "Just some junk mail."

Henry crumpled up the letter. He almost threw it at the trashcan on the other side of the class, but Mr. Bulfinch was looking at him, so he just shoved it in his pocket. Just then, the bell rang, and the twelve-person class went silent.

"Who is generally considered the greatest hero in Greek antiquity?" the teacher asked.

"Hercules," Henry said without thinking.

A snicker rippled through the class, and he felt his face go red.

"I said Greek, Henry, not Roman." Mr. Bulfinch smiled.

"Sorry. Heracles."

"Good. Fathered by a god like so many others, who was his mother?"

His gaze stayed on Henry, so the rest of the class kept silent. Henry wracked his brain. He knew the name. It was on the tip of his tongue.

"Alcmene?"

"Good, and her father?"

Henry stared at him blankly. "I have no idea."

"Anyone else? Diana?"

"Electryon," the petite girl said without hesitation. She was one of those who wanted to major in mythology.

"And his parents?"

"Perseus and Andromeda."

"Perseus, of course, was also a son of Zeus, so to call Heracles a half god is not entirely accurate. Zeus fathered two children in that line."

"Three if you go back to Lacedaemon, not to mention Poseidon on Andromeda's side," Diana piped up.

"True enough, though that's going a little farther afield than I'd intended. The point is Heracles was more god than man. As Diana has been kind enough to point out, so was Perseus. Most heroes were. You'd be hard pressed to find one who wasn't at least partially god. Why is that? Anyone?" Diana raised her hand. "Someone besides our resident expert?"

Henry laughed. Diana turned to glare at him, and he tried to maintain a straight face. It only lasted for a few seconds. Mr. Bulfinch either didn't see or he ignored them.

"The problems faced by the people of that time were thought to be the works of gods and monsters. A man cannot challenge a storm, much less the power behind the storm, so they created heroes who were more than men to face what they feared. These heroes needed something else, something to set them above mortal man. Since the greatest power these people knew was that of the gods, it made sense for their heroes to be at least partially god."

"You're saying they couldn't handle their own problems, so they let some figment of their imagination handle them so they could feel better about themselves," Henry said.

"Don't underestimate the trials they faced, Henry," Mr. Bulfinch said. "Remember, in those times a single bad season could wipe out a village. In a situation like that, the idea of the hero is incredibly powerful."

"But the hero isn't real," Henry said.

"Maybe. Maybe not," Mr. Bulfinch said. "It's possible some of these mythologies are exaggerated tales of the deeds of real people, but that's not really the point. The hero is larger than the person, regardless of whether or not the hero is real."

The discussion went on for the rest of the hour, and when the bell rang, Henry was sorry to see it end. He liked Mr. Bulfinch's class. It always made him think in a way the rest of his classes didn't. He went to his science class but only halfway listened. His mind kept wandering back to the messenger. There was something about the guy Henry should recognize, but he couldn't put his finger on what.

He went to the cafeteria and picked up a halfway edible burger and fries that tasted more like rubber than potatoes. When Daniel joined him a few minutes later, he was flipping through his Classical Literature textbook.

"Dude, I know you like that class, but you know the rules. There's no thinking allowed at lunch."

"Very funny," Henry rolled his eyes. "I just need to find something. If I don't, it'll bug me all day."

He flipped to a section describing the Greek gods and ran his finger down the page. The hairs on the back of his neck stood up when he reached the description of Hermes. The book described the messenger of the gods as a young-looking god with a beard. Henry's mouth went dry as he looked at the picture next to the description. The statue it showed was the exact likeness of the messenger who'd given him the letter.

THREE

"Y"ou all right? You look like you've just seen a ghost," Daniel said.

"Or a god."

"What?"

Henry slid the book across the table and tapped the statue of Hermes.

"You remember the weird guy I told you about? This was him."

Daniel looked at the picture and laughed. "You're getting too into this stuff. They're just stories."

"No, it was him."

"Next, you're going to tell me you saw the seven dwarves."

"Hermes isn't some fairytale," Henry said louder than he intended. People turned to stare at him and he lowered his voice. "People believed in him for hundreds of years. Isn't it possible they based those stories on someone real?"

Daniel raised his hands in mock surrender. "You know more

about this stuff than I do, but even if you're right, that would make him what? A million years old?"

Henry calmed down. "A couple of thousand."

"Okay, so this guy the stories were based on from a couple of thousand years ago came and made you late for class. I can buy that."

Henry almost told him about the note, but he could practically hear the stranger's voice in his head telling him not to. Besides, that would only give Daniel more ammunition. Instead, he mumbled something that might have been taken as an agreement. He was about to take another bite out of his burger when he noticed Diana sitting alone at the next table. He glanced at the lunch line and saw her best friend, Vanessa, a good ways back in the line. She would be at least a few minutes.

"Be right back," he said as he got up.

He walked over to Diana, feeling a little stupid as he did.

"Hey, got a second?" he asked.

She looked up and smiled. "Sure. What's up?"

"What do you know about Hermes?"

"He was the messenger of the gods." She brushed a strand of hair out of her eye.

Henry narrowed his eyes. "I know that."

"I just figured I'd start at the beginning. Let's see. He held dominion over boundaries and commerce. His parents were Zeus and Maia. He conducted souls to the afterlife. Aesop claimed Hermes gave him the fables. Was there anything specific you wanted to know?"

Henry nodded, but he thought about it. What was he looking for? Some confirmation that the guy he'd met on the streets was really the messenger of the gods? Diana would probably laugh if he told her that, and he could hardly blame her.

"No, I think that's enough to get me started. Thanks."

"No problem."

He walked back to his seat. Daniel was grinning at him.

"Shut up," Henry said.

"I didn't say anything."

"You didn't have to. You were thinking it so loud I could hear it across the room."

"I'm just saying if you keep talking like that, people are going to start thinking you're crazy."

"I said shut up."

After lunch, Henry went to his art history class. As the teacher droned on, Henry wished he could be anywhere else. Rather than listening, he flipped through his book and glanced at the pictures. He stopped at a section illustrating various depictions of Saint George and the Dragon. One, painted by Gustav Moreau, caught his eye. Saint George wore black armor. His white horse reared at a dragon so small it almost looked like an ugly dog. Like almost every picture depicting Catholic saints, a halo surrounded George's head. It shone like it was done in gold paint. Henry had gone through this book a dozen times, and he knew he'd looked at this picture before. He couldn't remember it ever looking like that, though. He ran his hand over it. When it passed over George's face, his fingers sunk into the page and touched warm skin. The knight turned and looked at him, and the dragon breathed fire. The flames grazed his fingers, and Henry yelped in pain. He jumped up, pushing the book away. It flew off his desk and banged on the floor. The teacher stopped talking, and everyone looked at him.

"It was the book," Henry said. "The knight. He looked at me."

Mrs. Cornell's brow wrinkled. "Henry, are you feeling okay?"

"It was the book," Henry said again.

"I think you need to see the nurse," she said as she picked up a pad of hall passes.

His heart pounded, and sweat ran down his face. He hadn't imagined it. He knew it. He walked over to the book and picked it up. He flipped to the page he'd been on, but the halo around George's head was in plain yellow ink. He touched it but felt only paper. It had been real, hadn't it?

Everyone was still staring when Mrs. Cornell finished writing out the pass and a note to the nurse. He took them without saying a word. As he walked down the hall, he tried to convince himself he had imagined it, but his finger still ached from the dragon's fire.

"Hello," the nurse said. "What can I do for you?"

He didn't even know what to say. He handed her the note and plopped down on a chair while she read it. That smell that always hung around hospitals and nurse's offices made him wonder if there was a cure for crazy. When the nurse looked up, he felt like she knew what he was thinking. She stuck an electric thermometer in his ear and waited for it to beep.

"You don't have a fever," she said. "Did you fall asleep in class?"

"No, it was the book. It burned my finger."

"Let me see."

He held it up to her. She ran her finger over his.

"It's a little red," she said, "but I don't think it's burned. An ant or something probably bit you while you were dreaming."

"No, it was the dragon," he said. "The one in the book."

"I think I'm going to send you home. You should get some rest. Is anyone home right now?"

"Yes," he said. "My mom should be there, but I didn't imagine it."

"I'm sure, but let's be on the safe side and send you home. Get some rest and a good night's sleep. If you still think it's real tomorrow, then we'll do something about it."

He hated how she patronized him, but what did he expect? He said a dragon in a book burned him. It even sounded crazy to him. Maybe it had been a dream. At least it had gotten him out of Art History, though by tomorrow, he'd be the laughing stock of the school.

FOUR

is mom showed up ten minutes after the nurse called
her. She fussed over him and felt his forehead, but the
nurse assured her he didn't have a fever. They went
home, and though he tried to argue with his mom, she insisted he
get into bed when they arrived. That never made sense to him. She
was a petite woman, and Henry stood almost a foot taller than her,
but she could always make him feel so small if she tried.

He lay in bed for a long time, trying to decide if it had been a
dream. He pulled the art history book out of his backpack and
flipped through it, touching most of the pictures, but they all felt
normal, and his hands never sunk in. One picture was of a forest
fire, but he rubbed his fingers together and decided to skip over it.
He shoved the book into his backpack and reached out to his
bookshelf for his remote. He flipped through channels, but
nothing good was on. His mind drifted back to the picture of the
painting, and for a moment, he imagined getting pulled into the
TV. He tried to tell himself he was being stupid, but he couldn't

bring himself to accept that, so he shut it off and stared at the ceiling.

His dad came in a few hours later. His hair stuck out in three different directions. No matter how he worked at it, it never stayed neat for more than half an hour. Henry was still lying on the bed and didn't get up.

"You want to tell me what happened, Henry?"

"I don't know," Henry said. "I must have fallen asleep."

"You shouldn't fall asleep in class, son."

"I know that, Dad." Henry drew out the last word.

"Don't take that tone with me."

"Look, I'm sorry," Henry yelled as he sat up. "I'm not perfect. Maybe your next kid will be better."

"Is that what this is about?" His voice had lost some of its edge, and Henry felt part of his anger drain away.

"No, Dad. It's not about anything. I just fell asleep and had a bad dream. I'm sorry. I'll apologize to Mrs. Cornell too."

"Just because we're having a baby doesn't mean we'll love you any less."

"I already know that," Henry said. "Look, there's nothing going on."

His dad sat on the edge of his bed, staring at him. Henry rolled over and tried to ignore him. After a few minutes, Henry felt his dad stand up and open the door. When Henry turned around, he saw his dad still in the doorway.

"We're ordering pizza tonight. Do you want me to bring you a few slices in here, or do you feel up to eating with us?"

Henry almost rolled his eyes but thought better of it. "I told you, Dad, there's nothing wrong with me. I just fell asleep in class and had a bad dream. I'll eat with you."

"If you're tired, you can stay here. That's fine too."

"Dad, I said I'm fine."

His dad stared at him for a few more seconds before smiling.

"We'll see you at dinner then, son."

Henry groaned as he walked out. He hoped they'd forget about the whole thing by the time the pizza got there, but he doubted it. He wondered how long they would keep on badgering him. He thought about telling them about the letter, but that would probably make things worse. He rubbed his finger. It still ached from the dragon's fire. He wasn't sure what he would do if it blistered.

Half an hour later, someone knocked at the front door. Assuming it was the pizza, Henry got up and went to the living room just as his dad opened the door. Their neighbor, Mrs. Thornberry, stood in the doorway. The old woman's strawberry blond hair fell down to her shoulders, and she wore glasses so thick they made her brown eyes look like saucers.

"Claire, hi," his dad said. "This is a surprise."

"Good evening, Jacob. I heard the news about Sarah," she said. "I just had to come by and offer my congratulations."

"Why thank you," he said as he turned over his shoulder. "Sarah! It's Claire. Come in. Have a seat."

His mother came out of their room and greeted Mrs. Thornberry with a hug. The first thing the old lady did was hold a hand to his mom's stomach. Henry didn't get what the big deal was. She wasn't even far enough along to be showing. He knew enough biology to know there wouldn't be anything to feel. They talked about how the baby would look. His mom kept insisting it would be a boy and he would look just like Henry, but she kept changing her mind about what color his eyes would be. First, she said they would be blue, then gray, green, brown, and then back to blue. Henry let out a sigh and was about to head back to his room when his mother caught sight of him.

"Henry, come out here and say hello to Mrs. Thornberry."

Henry tried to hide his sigh, but the look on his dad's face told him he hadn't succeeded. He put on a fake smile and walked into the living room.

"Hello Mrs. Thornberry," he said in an even voice.

"Oh, you must be so excited about having a new little brother or sister," she said. "Goodness knows some of the best times I ever had were with my little sister."

"There probably wasn't fourteen years between you," Henry mumbled.

"Sorry, I didn't catch that," Mrs. Thornberry said as she turned her ear to him. Her hearing aid always made him a little uncomfortable, and though he tried to resist the impulse, he looked away.

"I'm really excited," he said loud enough for her to hear. "Everyone is excited. It'll be so great when mom has the new kid."

The old woman turned back to him. She put her hand on his shoulder and gave him a patronizing smile. She obviously didn't catch the sarcasm in his voice. He only hoped his parents missed it too. He tried to think of something else to say, but the doorbell saved him. This time, it was the pizza guy.

"Claire, would you like to join us for dinner?" his dad asked said as he paid.

"Thank you for the offer, Jacob, but I'll pass. Congratulations again."

His mom walked her out. Henry went for a slice of pizza, but his dad stopped him with a glare. His mom and Mrs. Thornberry proceeded to talk for five more minutes. The smell made Henry's stomach growl. He could almost feel the pizza getting cold. When his mother finally came back in, she had a wide grin on her face.

"That was sweet of her, don't you think?"

"Yes, dear," Henry's dad said. "Why don't we sit down before Henry starves to death right in front of us?"

"You didn't have to wait for me," she said.

Henry shot his dad a glare, but he didn't seem to notice. The pizza hadn't gotten too cold. Henry could almost feel his parents wanting to ask about his day, just like they did every day at dinner. He could almost thank them for the awkward silence. Even that was better than talking about what had happened at school. He reached out to take a third slice when the phone rang. His dad picked it up.

"Hello?" he said. "This is Jacob Gideon."

Whatever the person on the other end said must've been bad news because his dad's jaw dropped. He didn't say anything for several seconds.

"Honey, are you okay?" his mom asked.

His dad stared at her with a blank expression. "Are you sure? How did this happen?"

The conversation went on for a few minutes before his dad hung up. Henry realized his hand was still reaching for the pizza slice. He pulled it back and waited for his dad to sit down. His mouth felt dry, and his mom's face had gone paler by several shades. A strand of dark brown hair hung in front of her eyes, but she focused on her husband and didn't seem to notice it.

"What is it, Jacob?" she asked.

"That was Dr. Thompson's office."

He spoke slowly as if he wasn't sure of his own words. He just stared off into space like he didn't see them. Henry saw tears well up in his mother's eyes. Dr. Thompson was their fertility doctor. Henry didn't know much about him except that his parents had used the same doctor the first time they wanted to have children.

"He said there's been a mistake. You're not pregnant." His mom took in an unsteady breath, and Henry thought he saw the exact second his mother's heart broke. In that moment, he regretted every unkind thing he'd ever said to her.

"Mom, I'm sorry," he said.

"Oh honey," she said through tears. "It's not so bad. It just hurts to raise our hopes and then have something like this happen. You're more than enough for us."

Henry smiled at her, but the smile was just as much of a lie as his mom's words. Try as he might, he'd never be able to compete with the child who would never be born.

FIVE

enry didn't sleep well that night. Every time he closed his eyes, he saw the crushed look on his mom's face. At four in the morning, he gave up any hope of sleep and flicked on the TV. He almost hoped it would suck him in, if only to get him away from everything. He turned the volume down and flipped through channels. He found mostly infomercials, which given the hour, didn't surprise him. He ended up on a news program about a war in some country he'd never heard of. Apparently, the US had agreed to grant sanctuary to some of the refugees. A list of various towns that had agreed to take in people scrolled across the screen. He was surprised when he saw Trenton on the list.

Once the story of the war ended the TV went back to advertising. After a few minutes of watching a guy try to convince him he needed a new juicer, Henry turned off the TV and pulled his laptop out from under his bed. He read through a bunch of messages in his spam folder. Those always made him chuckle, particularly those written in such broken English that he couldn't tell what they wanted him to do.

Reading through spam made Henry think of the letter. His gaze drifted to his pants which lay on top of his dirty clothes pile off in one corner of the room. He walked over and pulled the letter out of the pocket. He read over it a dozen times. At first, he'd thought the guy was just crazy, but if it really had been Hermes, what else could Henry do? How often did a person get a chance to talk to a flesh and blood god?

"Hermes," Henry whispered. "Are you there?"

He wasn't sure what he expected. He felt a little silly calling for a Greek god and almost jumped out of his skin when the god answered.

"I'm here, imaginary boy."

Hermes stood next to his bed. Henry's door and window were still closed. There hadn't even been a sound. One moment, the room had been empty, and the next Hermes was there. He no longer wore the plain street clothes from before. He'd abandoned all pretenses and wore a white toga and carried a staff with a golden bird on top. Henry couldn't help but look at Hermes's feet. He wore actual winged sandals. When Henry looked up, the messenger god had a mischievous grin on his face.

"Why do you keep calling me that?" Henry asked.

"It's who you are."

"But I'm not imaginary. I'm real."

"Incorrect, my boy," Hermes said. "You are real, but you're not only real. Your parents dreamed of you long before they conceived you. You see, Henry, you were imaginary before you were real. You being born did not negate the imaginary just like imagining something doesn't invalidate the reality. So, are you ready?"

"Ready for what?

"Ready to cross over, of course." Hermes spoke slowly as if explaining something simple to a child. "I thought that was why you called me."

"No, I called you because..." Henry paused. "I don't know why I called you. I guess it was as much to see if you would come as anything else. What do you mean cross over?"

"To Kurnugi," Hermes said. He must've seen the confused look on Henry's face because he continued. "The netherworld, the other side, or whatever you want to call it. The land of human imagination. Kurnugi is the setting of every story."

"And you want me to go there?"

"Whether you go or not is up to you," Hermes said. "Didn't you read the letter?"

"I did," Henry said. "I just wasn't sure which parts of it to believe."

"All of it," Hermes said.

"And you can take me into this Kurnugi?"

"It's part of my job, to usher souls to the other side."

"But I'm still alive."

"Semantics," Hermes said.

"I burned my finger this morning."

"Yes, I heard about it. You almost crossed over without me. That could've been very bad."

"Why is that?"

"Because you have no idea how to behave on the other side. There are dangers there you can't imagine." Hermes paused. "Actually, I guess you can imagine them. That's the whole point. Somebody imagined them anyway."

"How did it happen?" Henry asked. "Did I do some kind of spell?"

Hermes laughed. "No, of course not."

The god walked over to Henry's bookshelf and started thumbing through his collection. He stopped at one near the beginning and pulled it out. It was *Voyage of the Dawn Treader* by CS Lewis.

"Have you read this?" Hermes asked. Henry nodded. "Do you remember how they got into Narnia?"

Henry thought about it for a second. It was something about an old painting. Understanding dawned on him.

"You're saying Kurnugi is Narnia?" Henry smirked. "Who's the one who sent the message then? Aslan?"

"No, of course not. Narnia is only the smallest part of Kurnugi," Hermes said. "Besides, Aslan doesn't have the authority to send me."

"So what? Lewis went to Narnia?"

Hermes raised an eyebrow. "No, Lewis didn't tell the story of a place that already existed. The place exists because Lewis told the story."

"I don't understand."

"It's not that complicated," Hermes said. "Kurnugi is every story ever told. It is the imagination of mankind."

"Then who sent the message?"

Hermes looked at him, and the god's eyes twinkled.

He gave Henry a thin smile that showed no teeth.

"I can't give you all the answers, can I?" he asked.

"I'm not going with you if you won't tell me who you want me to see."

"Me?" Hermes asked. "I don't want you to do anything. I'm just a messenger."

"I'm not going with you."

"That's up to you," Hermes said. "I won't be here for long. Come after me if you want."

Hermes stood up. Movement caught Henry's eye and he looked toward the ground. The golden wings of Hermes's sandals reached outward. They were no bigger than Henry's hand, but their size didn't seem to matter. The messenger lifted an inch off the ground. For the first time, Henry really believed he was who he said he was.

"If I decide to follow you, how do I get there?" Henry asked.

Hermes raised an eyebrow. He looked at Henry's backpack, and Henry remembered the picture of Saint George that he had almost reached into. He rubbed his finger. The spot the dragon had burned felt rough. A chill ran down Henry's spine.

"You want me to jump into a picture of a dragon?"

"It had a knight too," Hermes said as if that made it better, "but there are other ways if you insist."

"Such as?"

"You take a red pill or you ride a tornado or you go down a rabbit hole. Every story that told how to cross from this world to the next tells you how to cross into Kurnugi. It does for imaginary people anyway."

Hermes smiled again. The wings at his heels raised themselves. In that instant, they grew large enough to obscure the god. The feathers glittered in the light. They lowered and Hermes was gone. Henry climbed into bed and stared at the ceiling until he fell asleep.

He awoke to his alarm beeping. He stumbled across his room and turned it off. It must've been a dream, just like the incident with the dragon. They had both been dreams. He'd almost convinced himself of that when the rising sun shone through the branches of the old ash tree in the backyard and glimmered off something on the ground. He bent down and picked up a golden feather. He held it between his fingers and noticed a blister had formed on one. He felt like he was going to be sick.

SIX

Henry showered and got dressed. He didn't know what his parents would do if they found the gold feather, so he stuck it in his pocket. He felt a little silly about doing it. He had tons of random junk in his room. Even if they did find it, they probably wouldn't think anything of it. Probably. He walked out of his room and found his dad seated at the dining room table with a steaming bowl in front of him.

"Feeling better?" his dad asked as Henry sat down.

"I think so," Henry said. He scowled at the oatmeal.

"Your mom didn't feel up to making breakfast today."

"How's she doing?" Henry asked.

"She'll be fine. She's stronger than you think. She just needs time to get over it. She was really looking forward to the baby. We both were."

Henry stared at his oatmeal and swirled it with his spoon. He took a bite and didn't look at his dad. Breakfast passed without another word. When he was done, Henry went back to his room to get his bag. His dad came in a few seconds later.

"Want a ride today?"

"I'm good," Henry said.

"Come on. I took the morning off to spend some time with your mom. She's still in bed though, and I have a few minutes. Let me take you."

Henry shrugged. "Fine."

The two of them got into the car. As they drove, Henry kept looking out the window half expecting to see the messenger god, but Hermes never appeared.

"Are you sure you're all right?" his dad asked. "You seem a little distracted."

"I'm fine, Dad. I kind of made a fool of myself yesterday. I'm just wondering how people are going to treat me."

"I remember being a teenager," his dad said. Henry groaned. "I know you think everything is so different. Right now, you feel like every problem is the end of the world. Believe me, after one or two days, no one will even remember it."

"Is that how long it will take mom to feel better?" he asked dryly. "Just one or two days?"

"It's a little different. What she's going through is a little more serious than you making a fool of yourself in front of your friends."

"Right," Henry glanced down a street as they passed it but didn't see anyone. They passed three more before he realized he was still looking for the wandering god.

They didn't talk throughout the rest of the trip. His dad dropped him off, and Henry went into the school. As he walked down the hall to history, people whispered at his back. He tried to ignore them. When he got to class, he saw that Daniel hadn't saved a seat for him, so Henry had to sit in the back right corner. He glared at his friend as he passed, but Daniel either didn't notice, or he pretended not to.

"Turn your books to page 134," Mr. Adams said after the bell rang.

"Watch out, Henry," David said. "It's a book."

Laughter rumbled through the class, but Mr. Adams silenced them with a glare. He went on to give a lesson on reconstruction. Henry only halfway listened to it. He could almost feel the class laughing at him. It would go on all day, and then he would go home where his parents would pretend to be all right while he felt guilty for not being enough for them. Forty-five minutes into the class, Henry raised his hand.

"Can I go to the restroom?" he asked.

"Can it wait? The bell rings in fifteen minutes."

"Please, Mr. Adams?"

"Fine," the teacher said.

He wrote a hall pass, and Henry walked out of the class. He went down the hall and into the bathroom. He didn't really need to go, so he just stared at himself in the mirror and wondered if there was anything he could do to stop being the loser everyone laughed at and who his parents wanted to replace. He splashed water on his face, but it didn't help. He just stood there, staring at his own reflection. What was it Hermes had said?

You take a red pill or you ride a tornado or you go down a rabbit hole. Every story that told how to cross from this world to the next tells you how to cross into Kurnugi.

"Through the Looking Glass," Henry said to himself.

He reached forward. When his fingers touched the mirror, the surface rippled as if a stone had been thrown into a still pool. Henry pulled back and, for a second, the mirror held on to him like he had dipped his hand into molasses. Once it came free, Henry looked at his finger. It seemed more or less intact. He hadn't felt excessive heat or cold. Whatever was on the other side of the mirror was probably safe. He hesitated for a second, but he knew the bell would ring any minute, and he doubted he'd have the courage once other people came into the bathroom.

"Goodbye, Mom," Henry said. "I hope you have better luck with your next kid."

He touched the mirror again, and his fingers sunk in. He pushed harder and after a second, his arm had gone halfway in. His reflection pulled at him as he climbed onto the counter and slowly crawled into the mirror.

SEVEN

Henry didn't know what he'd expected a trip through a mirror to feel like, but this wasn't it. At first, he felt like he was swimming through mud. Abruptly, the mud became frozen slush. The shock of the cold drove air from his lungs. He tried to take a breath, but there was no air. His lungs burned, and just when he thought he could bear it no longer, he was through.

The air smelled crisp and clean. He hadn't even realized how dirty the air of the city had smelled until that moment. He was standing in the middle of a frozen wasteland. The wind carried a biting cold, and snow came up to his knees. His teeth chattered, and he couldn't stop shaking. He wished he'd thought to bring a coat, but he'd left a world in the tail end of spring where it had been a month since he'd needed a jacket. Now, the arctic chill gripped him, and he could feel it draining the life out of him. He turned around and scanned the landscape for the way back. He expected to see a gateway or a mirror or some other sign, but snow blanketed the land as far as he could see. The sun reflected off the snow and almost blinded him. He could be in the middle of Alaska for all he knew. Henry cursed. He'd been so caught up in getting here he'd never stopped to consider how he would get back.

He looked around, desperately hoping to find shelter, but he just saw more of the same bleak and lifeless landscape. He didn't see so much as a shrub. He wouldn't last long if he stayed out here, so he picked a direction at random and took a shaky step. The snow resisted him, and he had to force his way through. He held his arms against his chest and tried rubbing them together to keep warm, but that was like a drop of hot water against a blizzard. He shook hard with every step. When flurries of snow began to fall Henry panicked, but there was nothing to do but keep moving forward.

Slowly, feeling left his body. He thought he'd heard somewhere that this was a bad sign, but it was so hard to think straight. By the time the weather gave way to a heavy snowfall, the cold had numbed him to the core. Before long, he could barely see two feet in front of him. Every step had to be forced through the slush, and Henry knew if he fell, he wouldn't get back up. A small part of him clung to the possibility that this was all a dream. Any moment now, he would wake up in class. The students would have a good laugh at his expense, just like last time. It would be embarrassing, but he'd be in class, warm and with others instead of out here, dying, frozen and alone.

He took another step forward, but the cold had sapped him of his strength, and he fell to the ground. He tried to get up, but he may as well have tried to lift a mountain. He had nothing left. Henry just lay there, waiting to die. A shadow passed over him. He tried to focus on it, but his eyes didn't work the way they should, and he just saw a big blob of color.

"I don't know how you got here," the blob said. "I doubt you'll make it out again. You want help?"

Henry tried to nod, but his head wouldn't respond. He mumbled something, but even if the stranger heard it over the wind, Henry doubted he'd spoken anything intelligible. The stranger apparently understood him, though. Henry felt something close around his shoulder. For a second, he tried to shove it off, but his arms didn't respond the way they should. It was only after the stranger carried him for half an hour that Henry realized the thing around his shoulders was a blanket. Thinking became easier, and after a few minutes, he could move again. Henry tried to tell the man he was okay to walk. The man either didn't notice or didn't care. Still, it was probably a good thing. Without the man to hold him up, Henry doubted he'd make it more than a few steps.

He didn't know how long it was before they came to a building that was more shed than house. The sticks it was made of looked out of place in the ocean of white. Once inside, the man laid Henry down on a bed and started a fire in the fireplace.

Slowly, the warmth seeped into him, bringing with it a return of feeling. Once his strength had returned, he sat up and looked around. The single room building had a wooden table in the center with two chairs, one of which held a man wrapped in layers of clothing, presumably the one who had saved Henry. Even his face was obscured by a scarf wrapped around his head. The bed Henry lay in was along one wall, with the fire burning in the wall adjacent to it. The wall opposite the fire held a door and a small window. A large pile of wood sat in a corner. Given the bleak landscape, Henry could only imagine where it had come from.

"Who are you?" Henry asked. "Why are you doing this?"

"I'm doing it because it was within my power." The scarf

muffled the stranger's voice. "I do it because there is need. I wouldn't do it for either reason alone."

"That's why," Henry said. "But you still haven't told me who you are."

The man unwrapped the scarf from his head, and for a moment, Henry thought he was looking in a mirror. The man's face was an older, rougher face than Henry's. Dark circles had formed around blue eyes, and silver streaked his otherwise black hair.

"My name is Virgil," the man said as he stood and walked over to Henry. He had a voice like sandpaper.

Henry took the offered hand. Virgil's callused hand gripped Henry's tightly and it almost hurt, though Henry got the impression it was the man's natural grip rather than an attempt to bully him.

"I'm Henry. Where exactly am I?"

"Winter."

"That's more of a time than a place."

Virgil sighed. "We are in the realm of perpetual winter and the home of every inhabitant of the frozen lands you've ever heard of, as well as a number you haven't. You'd have been hard-pressed to pick a worse part of Kurnugi to cross over into."

"Kurnugi?"

"Specifically, you're in the Near Kurnugi."

"Near?"

Virgil rolled his eyes. "Did you really cross over without knowing anything? Near Kurnugi is the today of the mortal world. Every bedtime story told to a child at night, every book read in a quiet corner, and every story shown on a screen has its place here."

"You mean movies?" Henry asked.

"Movies, television shows, mini-series. They all exist here."

Henry looked out the window for several long heartbeats. The storm had worsened. The wind outside blew so fiercely the snow looked like it fell sideways. A white carpet extended as far as he could see, which wasn't far in this weather. The house groaned and creaked. Henry could hardly believe how effectively it kept the cold at bay.

"I guess you're going to tell me Santa Clause lives out there," Henry said, only half joking.

"Don't be ridiculous," Virgil said. "You almost died out there. Do you really think this is the home of someone who spends his time making toys for children? Santa's realm is a gentle land. It might be cold, but even if you went out without any clothes on, you'd never be in any real danger of dying."

Henry stared out the window again. He wondered if anything was alive out there. For a second, he thought he saw a figure moving around outside, but the blizzard was so thick, he couldn't be sure.

"I think there's something out there," Henry said.

"It wouldn't surprise me," Virgil said. "We're no more than a mile from the citadel of the ruler of Winter."

"The ruler of Winter?" he asked. "Who? Jack Frost? The White Witch?"

"Yes."

"That wasn't really a yes or no question."

Virgil shrugged. "Yes, was the proper answer."

"How could yes be the right answer? It's one or the other or someone else entirely."

"Yes."

"There you go again."

"Yes, it is Jack Frost," Virgil said. "Yes, it is the White Witch. Yes, it is someone else entirely."

"I don't understand."

Virgil glared at Henry for a second and then sighed. When he spoke, Henry could barely hear his voice over the crackling flames in the fireplace.

"Every time there has been a ruler of winter, that person has been the one who lives here. They are cruel and evil and unbelievably powerful, and you don't want to attract their attention, not if you want to live"

"Then why do you live so close?"

"Oh, I don't live here. I'm just staying here for now."

"Are we safe?"

"No, not especially," Virgil said. "We're not freezing to death, though, and that's something."

"So you're saying any moment now, a yeti could break through the door, and kill us."

"No, of course not. A yeti is too big to fit through the door. He could break through the wall, but he'd have to tear out a good bit of the roof in order to get to us."

Virgil spoke so calmly that Henry wondered if he was serious. The snow had piled up outside and completely covered the window. The fire made shadows dance across the room, and Henry suppressed a shiver at the thought of what could be out there.

"But that could happen?" Henry asked in a voice barely above a whisper.

"Yes, of course. We are in the heart of their realm, after all."

"Shouldn't we be going somewhere else then?"

"Probably." Virgil waved his hand at the blocked window. "The weather outside doesn't exactly lend itself to traveling, though."

"How long will the storm last?"

"It's hard to say. It could last a week or it could last an hour. It just depends on the ruler's mood."

Henry looked at the window again. The house continued to

groan, and he could imagine a mountain of snow piling up on top of the flimsy looking roof.

"It'll hold," Virgil said, guessing his thoughts.

"Are you sure?"

"It wouldn't do any good to think otherwise."

Henry tried to swallow down his fear, but it caught on a lump in his throat. At least all the snow would keep whatever was out there from finding them. Probably.

EIGHT

Hour after hour, the blizzard continued, though the only way they knew that was by a tunnel Virgil dug through the snow. Once, Henry went to sleep. The small house was empty when he awoke. The only sound was the crackling flame. Panic gripped him. He rolled out of bed on shaky legs and stumbled to the door. It took several minutes of straining to pull it open. The tunnel in the snow had an ominous feel to it. A howling reached him, and though Henry told himself it was only the wind, he couldn't help but think of the yetis Virgil had mentioned. He huddled by the fire for what felt like hours until the door swung open again. Virgil stepped inside, shaking the snow off his heavy coat.

"Sorry," Virgil said. "I didn't think you'd wake up so soon."

"Where were you?"

Virgil reached into his pack and pulled out a double handful of nuts and berries. Henry's stomach growled, and they devoured them eagerly. The food disappeared all too quickly, and they sat in near silence for several hours. Eventually, Virgil got up and moved to the door again. The thought of being left alone sent chills down Henry's spine.

"I'll go with you," Henry said.

Virgil smirked. "And what exactly do you think you could do to help? You don't even have the proper clothes to survive the storm."

"But..."

"You'd only slow me down."

Henry was about to argue, but Virgil didn't wait for him to say anything, and he disappeared into the tunnel. Henry scrambled after him, but he didn't even have gloves, and the snow burned his hands as he climbed through the tunnel. When he broke out onto the surface, freezing cold enveloped him. The wind had kicked up a thick mist of snow, and Virgil was nowhere to be seen.

Henry retreated back into the house. It groaned under the weight of the snow, and Henry could imagine it collapsing on him. This time, it wasn't long before Virgil came back carrying a rabbit. By then, so much snow had fallen that the fireplace had been clogged, so they had to cook the meat on a small fire in the tunnel Virgil had dug which allowed the smoke to escape. They drank melted snow and continued to wait. All too often, as the hours passed, Henry found himself glancing at the ever shrinking pile of wood. Even with the provisions Virgil had found, they were starving by the end of the storm. It didn't so much stop as it lessened into a light snow.

"We should go," Virgil said. "I doubt it will get much better."

"Where will we go?" Henry asked.

"Anywhere is better than this. We're in one of the more dangerous places of the Near Kurnugi."

"If it's so dangerous, what were you doing here?"

"If I were you, I wouldn't question your good fortune. My business is my own."

Henry raised his hand. "Look, I'm sorry. If you don't want to tell me, that's fine."

Virgil shrugged and pulled a heavy jacket out of his pack and handed it to Henry. Henry glared at him for not giving him the clothes before, but Virgil only shrugged again. They set off with the rising sun to their right, and travelled south, though Henry supposed that in this strange land, the sun didn't necessarily rise in the east. They travelled in silence. Every time Henry started to speak, Virgil gave him an icy glare. In spite of his companion, Henry felt very alone.

After a day, they came across a stream, and Virgil spent the next several minutes fishing. His catches were pitifully small, but they were enough to take the edge off Henry's hunger.

Once they were done, they crossed the stream into a forest of evergreens, the shortest of which had to be at least fifty feet tall. Henry was thankful that the trees sheltered him from the wind. At first, he thought there was nothing living in the woods, but he realized that wasn't the case. Every once in a while, a bird flitted from one branch to another. Once, a white fox darted in front of them. It still seemed devoid of larger animals, though. As the sun began to set, Virgil started to move faster.

"Shouldn't we make camp?" Henry asked. "I'm exhausted."

"We're still within the lands of the ruler of winter," Virgil said. "I'd prefer not to stop here if I can avoid it."

"Are the lands really so small that we can go from their center to their edge after only a day of walking."

"Spring is coming to an end," Virgil said. "Summer is just around the corner. Winter's lands are shrinking."

"But it's only spring in half the world," Henry said. "South of the equator, it's almost winter."

"And if you had crossed over from south of the equator, that would be an issue. Kurnugi is shaped by its observer. At least it is when that observer is from the mortal realm. Where you came from, it's almost summer, and so winter's lands are shrinking."

"But what if we meet someone who came from the South."

"Do all humans ask so many stupid questions?"

"You're human too, as far as I can see."

"Only on the surface," Virgil said.

"Who imagined you then?"

Virgil gave him a level look. His gray eyes looked into Henry's soul, but he didn't say anything.

"Were your eyes that color before?"

"We don't have time for this," Virgil said. "The agents of winter are strongest at night, and we should get out of their territory by then."

"Why are they stronger at night?"

Virgil rolled his eyes. "It's always questions with you, isn't it? They're stronger at night because night is longer in the winter. Let's go."

Henry wanted to ask more questions, but Virgil took off in a slow jog. Henry followed. He wasn't in bad shape, but neither was he used to running on uneven ground in freezing weather. After a few minutes, his lungs burned from the cold. The day's journey had tired him, and he didn't have the strength to keep this up. His legs felt like mush. He was about to collapse when something howled behind him. He looked back and saw a shadow drifting through the trees. It moved on two legs, and looked vaguely like a man, except for the fact that it was at least half as tall as the trees.

"Run!" Virgil yelled before vanishing into the forest.

Henry ran after him. He'd never imagined he could move so fast. Behind him, he heard the creature crashing through the underbrush. It let out a roar that sounded halfway between a dog and a man. Henry cried out in fear as the ground sloped downward. It was getting closer. He slipped on a wet patch of snow and screamed as he tumbled down. His face splashed into a puddle and Henry knew he was about to die. He looked up expecting to see a monster. The white dusting of snow on the trees disappeared, and it was only then that Henry realized he was hot. The creature was nowhere to be seen. Virgil appeared over him and rolled his eyes.

"Well, I was going to set up camp," Virgil said, "but you can just sleep there if you want."

NINE

Henry sat up and wiped the mud off his face. His heart beat so fast he thought it might break out of his chest. "Are we safe now?"

"Yes, the line of evergreens marks the border of winter's realm. Its minions can't follow us here."

"Virgil, that thing was huge. It's not going to stop just because there's no snow on the ground."

"You still don't get it, do you?" Virgil said. "Not everything can cross from one story to another."

"So what?" Henry asked. "You're saying it won't cross over because it's against the rules?"

Virgil sighed. "Yes, there are rules, but not the kind you're thinking of. The rules of Kurnugi are absolutely binding on its inhabitants. We can't choose to disobey them like you can."

Henry thought about that for a second. It sounded familiar, but his thoughts were racing, and it took him a while to realize why. His eyes went wide as he sat up and pulled his backpack off. He rifled through it and withdrew the crumpled letter Hermes had given him. He'd completely forgotten about it until Virgil reminded him. Henry took a moment to straighten it and ran his finger down it until he found the right line.

"There are certain rules we are bound by, and unlike you, we cannot choose to ignore them," Henry read aloud.

Virgil moved to stand behind him. Suddenly, his breathing stopped. Henry turned to look at him, and his eyes had gone wide. They'd also changed to green, and his face had gone several shades paler.

"What is it?" Henry asked as he stood up. "Where did you get that?"

"Hermes gave it to me," Henry said. Here, outside the boundary of winter, after being chased through the woods by a monster, that didn't seem like such a strange thing anymore.

"Hermes?"

"The messenger god," Henry said. "Don't tell me you don't know who he is."

"Of course I know who Hermes is. There are many who can pass through stories, but few can do it as effortlessly as he can. Few of those are his equal and none are greater."

"You did it easily enough."

Virgil looked at him. His brow wrinkled, and his mouth opened in surprise. He closed his mouth and brushed a pine needle off his shirt.

"What about that seemed easy to you?" he asked.

"Good point," Henry said. "So what's the big deal about Hermes?"

"I told you, he's the greatest of those who can pass between stories."

"Until someone invents someone greater, you mean."

"What do you mean?"

"Couldn't someone just make up a story about someone who can pass between worlds who's stronger than Hermes? That's the point of this place, isn't it?"

"It's not that easy. Hermes is of the Far Kurnugi." When he saw the look on Henry's face, Virgil let out a long breath. "Stories of Hermes have been told for countless generations. He is rooted in the imagination of mankind. No being from a single story could be greater than him. Yes, someone could invent a story like you said, but such a being would only be greater than a shadow of Hermes, and only within the scope of the story."

"I don't understand."

"I don't know how else to explain it."

"I don't guess it really matters," Henry said. "So, where are we now?"

Virgil looked around. He made a wide gesture as if the answer to Henry's question was obvious.

"We're in the forest."

"Well, I know that."

"Then, why did you ask?"

"I mean what story are we in?"

"You still don't understand, do you?"

"Then, explain it to me."

"A story is never just one story. They draw from each other. They are built on what came before, and elements from one bleed into the next. You go that way, and you'll find a sword destined to be used to stop an evil sorcerer from uniting Power, Wisdom, and Courage into an unbeatable force. Over there is a sleeping princess, and a little ways beyond that is a grove where walking trees meet. Just as the ruler of winter was every ruler of winter, so this forest is every forest."

"Doesn't that make this place dangerous?" Henry asked.

"Yes, but it's not nearly as dangerous as the area a dozen feet that way."

"What do we do now?"

"Let me see that letter."

Henry handed it to him. Virgil turned it over in his hand. He ran his fingers over the paper. When a finger touched the hourglass sticker, Virgil disappeared. He was back a heartbeat later. Then, he was a baby and then an old man. He dropped the letter, and his face twisted. The skin tightened, and his hair darkened. After a few seconds, he'd returned to his normal age.

"Moirai." Virgil's voice was barely above a whisper.

"What?"

"The Fates. The Norns. The weird sisters. Whatever you call them, they are the women who are privy to the secrets of time itself."

"Far Kurnugi?"

"So far there's almost no name for it," Virgil said. "I've never heard of something like this. Either a person makes the journey to see them or they come to the person. They've never sent for anyone, as far as I know."

"And they want me to come see them."

"So it would seem. What are you going to do?"

"What should I do?"

"I have no idea."

"Virgil, do you know how I get back home?"

"Hermes could take you," Virgil said. "There's probably a way in Winter's territory, if you can survive long enough to find it. Other than that, I don't know. In most stories, the hero doesn't go back."

"So you're saying I'm stuck here?"

"No," Virgil said. "Not necessarily. From time to time, they do return, but only after they've finished their journey and are no longer the hero."

"I guess it's to the Moirai then," Henry said. "Would you happen to know the way?"

"It's Far Kurnugi, Henry," Virgil said. "You don't understand what that means. Near Kurnugi is weak. You can pass through it as an observer without taking any great part in the story, but that won't work in the Far. It has to be your story, and you have no idea how to get there."

"Are you coming with me?" Henry asked, half afraid to hear the answer.

"You won't make it without me," Virgil said. "You've already almost died twice."

"How do we get there?"

"How else?" Virgil asked. "We need to go on a quest."

TEN

Virgil went out hunting while Henry set up camp, which is to say Henry stacked some firewood. He had never been camping, and he had no idea what else setting up camp meant. He spent a long time staring at winter's wood. Though snow covered the ground a few feet away, he didn't feel so much as a cold breeze. He walked up to it and held his hand an inch from where the woods changed, but all he felt was the warm air of a late spring evening.

"Be careful," Virgil's voice came from behind.

Henry jumped and his hand broke the plane of winter. It was so cold it burned his hand. He pulled back and gave Virgil a withering stare.

"You did that on purpose," Henry said.

"Me?" Virgil asked. "Never."

He set down the dead pig he was carrying and looked at the stacked wood.

"What is that?"

"That's our firewood," Henry said.

"You've got to be kidding me," Virgil said. "Half that stuff is still green."

"Well if you want it done better, then do it yourself."

"I'll have to. I'm fairly certain if this forest caught on fire, the only safe place would be that fire pit."

"Do you want me to prepare the pig while you handle the fire?"

"That depends. Can you do any better on that than you did on the fire?"

Henry thought about it for a second. "Maybe you should take care of dinner."

Virgil sighed. He kicked the stacked wood, and it crumbled. Virgil glared at Henry, but Henry shrugged. He didn't understand what the big deal was. Virgil spent several minutes building the fire. Before long, it was blazing. As warm as he was, the heat was almost unwelcome. Shadows danced in the trees, and it took a while for Henry to realize the light didn't cast shadows into winter's wood.

Virgil sliced up the pig. Before long, their dinner was roasting on the fire. Henry's mouth watered. The hunger from the previous day came crashing down on him. Virgil handed him a strip on a stick. He bit into it, and the juices burned his tongue. He downed it so quickly he barely even tasted it. It hardly made a dent in his hunger, but it still felt amazing to have something warm in his stomach. They finished half the pig before they lay down to sleep. He was unconscious before his head hit the ground.

Henry woke up to a low rumbling. He opened his eyes and saw twin yellow eyes floating in the darkness. He yelped and sat up. He shook Virgil awake.

"What?" the other man said, not quite awake.

"There's something out there," Henry said.

Virgil sat up and looked at the eyes. He uttered a stream of curses.

"What is it?" Henry asked.

"I think it's a leopard," Virgil's voice was pitched low.

"A leopard?" Henry asked. "I thought those lived in the jungle."

"A jungle is just a forest with certain types of animals."

"Is it going to attack?"

"Most likely," Virgil said. "We're probably in its territory."

"What do we do?" Henry asked.

"Do you have a weapon?" Virgil asked. When Henry shook his head, Virgil picked up a smoldering piece of wood from the fire pit. The glowing embers illuminated his face and gave him an evil look. "Pick up one of these. Guard your throat."

No sooner had Henry picked up the burning log than a shadow leaped out of the trees. It crashed into Henry. He fell on his back, trying to swing his stick, but he didn't have a good grip, and it flew from his hand. The beast's growl sent chills down his spine. Its footsteps crunched dried leaves nearby. Fear paralyzed him, and Henry closed his eyes. He heard a loud crack, and when he opened his eyes, the leopard had flopped down on him. The top of his head seemed collapsed inward.

A few feet away, Virgil was battling two more of the creatures. Henry had never seen anyone move so fast. One leaped at him, and Virgil hit it in in the side of the head. Before he could turn to face the other, it took a bite out of his shin. Virgil cried in pain. Henry rolled to his feet and lifted his own piece of wood. He swung it at the leopard's head as hard as he could. There was a loud crack as the animal fell to the ground.

The other leopard Virgil had hit had only been stunned, and it picked itself up. It growled at Henry who held his branch in front of him. The leopard he'd killed, he'd caught by surprise. He had no illusions about taking one head on. Out of the corner of his eye, he saw Virgil digging through his pack, but he didn't dare take his eyes off the leopard to see what he was doing. The leopard tensed its muscles and leaped. Henry screamed as something flew through the air. There was a thump just before the animal hit him. Henry fell to the ground again, but the animal didn't move. It was a struggle to push it off him, and when he did, he saw the knife embedded in its neck. He looked at Virgil in amazement. He was sitting on the ground and blood soaked his leg.

"Are you all right?" Henry asked. Virgil only glared at him. "What?"

"I told you to guard your throat. Help me up. We have to break camp and leave as soon as we can."

"Why?" Henry asked. "We killed the leopards."

"Don't be a fool," Virgil said. "There will be more, or something worse."

"What makes you so sure?"

Virgil sighed. "How many stories do you know where the heroes won a minor battle and had any time at all to rest?"

Henry thought about that. "None."

"Exactly," Virgil said. "There's more coming. Mark my words."

"But you're hurt," Henry said. "You can hardly walk."

"'Can hardly walk' is not the same as 'Can't walk'." Virgil said. "I'll make it because I have to."

"Which way?" Henry asked.

"I don't know," Virgil said. "Pick one, anything that doesn't go towards a frozen tower."

He limped over to the leopard and pulled out his knife. Henry heard him mumble something about it being his good cooking knife. He spent the next several minutes making a splint. When he was done, he looked at Henry with a raised eyebrow. Henry was going to ask more questions, but the look on Virgil's face told him it was a bad idea. He pointed in the direction opposite Winter's Wood, and they were off.

The full moon provided enough light to see by when it managed to break through the canopy, which wasn't often. The makeshift torch Henry carried provided a little light, but it wasn't much. That, combined with Virgil's hurt leg, slowed their progress to a crawl. Henry found himself jumping at every shadow.

"What's in these woods that are worse than those leopards?" Henry asked.

"Many things," Virgil said as his gaze darted from one shadow to the next. "Werewolves, for one thing. Giant spiders as well. There's even an occasional dragon."

"But you said the forest was safe."

"I said nothing of the sort," Virgil said. "I told you it was better to be here than winter's wood, but that's a far cry from being safe."

"Then when do we reach the boundary of the woods?" Henry asked.

"Why would we go to the boundary?" Virgil asked.

"You're hurt. We need to rest. Besides, you just said this place isn't safe."

"Of course not. We don't want safe."

"We don't?"

"Safe won't get you into Far Kurnugi," Virgil said.

"You're limping," Henry said, "and I don't know how far we can make it without you getting that taken care of. Isn't there a town somewhere? Some combination of every town?"

Virgil smiled weakly. "You're catching on. That might be the best place to start too. Let's go."

Virgil turned left and shuffled away. For a second, Henry stared after him, not quite believing how easy it had been to convince

Virgil. After a moment, the man disappeared into the trees, and Henry ran after him. It wasn't hard to keep pace with Virgil. His injured leg and the rough terrain slowed him to a pace a little faster than a quick walk. Henry tried to ignore the impromptu bandage on Virgil's leg, but it was hard to miss. The blood had already soaked through it, and he could see a rash developing around the wound. He didn't know what they would do if it got infected.

After an hour, the trees thinned, and Henry caught a glimpse of the sky more regularly. Birds flitted overhead, and for a moment, He could imagine the forest to be peaceful.

"How long until we get there?" Henry asked.

"We're almost there," Virgil said.

"We're not actually going to a town are we?" he asked as understanding dawned on him. "I mean, we're not going to any specific spot where a town is. We're going to a town because that's where we decided to go."

"Sort of," Virgil said. "We can do that because we're not going to a specific town. We're going to the generic town that exists in countless stories. It's called by a million names, but it's essentially the same. If we were going to Camelot, for instance, we'd have to be in England, or a reflection of England in any case."

"Could we really do that?" Henry asked. "Go to Camelot, I mean."

"There wouldn't be much point," Virgil said. "It's not in the direction we need to go. Camelot straddles the border between Near and Far Kurnugi."

"But we want to go to Far Kurnugi."

"It's complicated," Virgil said. "You can get to Far Kurnugi from Camelot, but only to those parts associated with Camelot, or at least with England. You can't get to where the Moirai are."

"But you said they're also the weird sisters."

"The Moirai sent for you, not the weird sisters."

"Aren't they the same?"

"Have you ever been to an amusement park?" Virgil asked.

"Yes, but what does that have to do..."

"How about a funeral?"

"Yes."

"Were you the same at the funeral as you were at the amusement park?"

"I was the same person," Henry said slowly.

"Just as the Moirai are the same as the weird sisters, but if you go them as the weird sisters, they can only be the weird sisters. For them to be the Moirai, you have to come to them in a place where the Moirai exist."

"You mean ancient Greece."

Virgil nodded. Henry was about to say something else when he saw a break in the tree line. He moved forward quickly. He came out of the trees expecting to see buildings, but instead, he saw a path of packed dirt surrounded by a plain of sickly looking grass. He caught the faint smell of rotting plants. He looked around in confusion as Virgil caught up.

"I don't understand."

"You can't travel through Kurnugi and not be part of a story," Virgil said. "We'll get where we're going, but Kurnugi itself will determine how. At least we don't have to travel through the woods anymore."

"Which way?" Henry asked.

"Pick one," Virgil said. "Roads go from one town to another."

They set off in one direction. In spite of the easier terrain, they traveled even slower than they had in the woods. Virgil grew paler by the hour. By the time the sun set, he was coughing constantly. He had to lean on Henry to walk. Virgil's skin felt clammy and it seemed like he stumbled every other step. The road curved and for a while, Henry thought it would take them back into the woods, but it turned again and they travelled parallel to the forest.

They stopped and set up camp near a brook. Virgil was in no condition to find food, and Henry had no idea what to look for. Virgil lay down by the brook and promptly fell asleep. Henry moved closer to examine him. His clothes were soaked in sweat, and when Henry put a hand on Virgil's forehead, he found it burning up. Henry tore a piece of his shirt off and immersed it in the water. He laid it across Virgil's head. He didn't sleep all night, and as he watched Virgil toss and turn, he wondered if the man would live until morning.

ELEVEN

The sky had just started to redden in the light of the rising sun when Virgil started mumbling. Henry moved closer to him.

"I want to be like him," Virgil said. "I want to be just like him."

"You want to be like who?" Henry asked. "Come on. Wake up. Tell me who you want to be like."

Henry didn't know what else to do. Virgil couldn't travel in this condition, and Henry wasn't about to leave him to die alone on the side of the road. Henry was only alive because of Virgil, and he didn't know if he could go on without him. Henry rewet the cloth and put it back on Virgil's head. He took a water skin out of the man's pack and tried to give him some water, but he started coughing after a few seconds.

"What do I do, Virgil?" Henry asked, practically in tears. "Tell me what to do."

"Town," Virgil said in a hoarse whisper.

"I can't leave you here."

"Town close," Virgil said. "Go get help."

"I can't." Henry was pleading.

Virgil went into another fit of coughing. When he stopped, he was unconscious again. Henry clung to Virgil's words. Maybe he could make it to town and come back with help. He hated to leave Virgil like this, but he didn't know what else to do. It probably wouldn't be too bad. They hadn't seen anything dangerous since the leopards, and that had been over a day ago. Besides, this was a road. People probably passed by all the time. Dangerous animals would avoid this place. They had to.

Henry kept telling himself that as he dragged Virgil into a nearby bush. He hid the sick man as best he could before setting off. As he walked down the path, Virgil's words kept running through his head. He hoped nothing worse than leopards would find his friend. Or him, for that matter.

The sun beat down on him, and the smell of rotting plants grew worse. The heat made the air before him shimmer, and there was no shade anywhere. He reached the top of a hill and jumped when a deer leaped into the road. Henry had no idea where it had come from. If Virgil had been there, he would've been able to take the animal down and provide them with a meal, but Henry could only watch. A heartbeat later, a yellow blur leaped from the trees and crashed into the dear. A massive paw struck just below the head. The crack as the deer's neck broke was so loud Henry could feel it. He backed away slowly.

"I guess a lion qualifies as worse than a leopard," he said under his breath.

The great cat tore at its prey, and blood ran into the road. The animal looked up at him, and Henry heard a low growl. He resisted the urge to run. What little he knew about such animals said running would only make it chase him.

"Of course, that's with dogs," Henry said to himself.

He took several steps back until the lion turned its attention back to its kill. Once it was no longer looking at him, Henry turned and ran. He didn't stop until he reached the spot he'd left Virgil. He found his friend sitting up against a large rock.

"What are you running from?" Virgil asked. His voice was weak and it looked like he struggled to speak.

"First leopards," Henry said, "and then a lion. What's next?"

"A wolf," Virgil said.

"What?"

"A wolf is next," Virgil said.

He started coughing again, and Henry went to his side. Virgil waved him off. "The bad news is we won't make it to town. The good news is we're on our way to Far Kurnugi."

"I don't understand," Henry said.

"A leopard, a lion, and a she-wolf," Virgil said.

"You're delirious," Henry said.

"No, there's a wolf. There is."

"No, there isn't."

"There." He lifted an arm. It was obviously difficult for him.

A growl came from behind Henry. He spun around and gaped.

"I guess there's your wolf," Henry said.

The wolf was bigger than the lion had been. It was as big as a car. Its coal-black fur bristled, and Henry could see blood on its teeth. Its eyes were bloodshot. Henry had seen wolves in zoos, and once, he'd been attacked by a dog. Neither of those experiences compared with this. They'd fought off the leopards, and he'd run from the lion, but neither one of those strategies would work here.

He didn't know how he knew, but he was certain that this wolf was evil. This thing hated everything that lived.

"Back away, Henry," Virgil wheezed.

Henry looked at him and saw Virgil holding his knife by the tip. He was prepared to throw, but he was rocking back and forth on his feet. Henry doubted he'd be able to get a straight shot. Virgil struggled to get to his feet, never taking his eyes off the wolf.

"Into the forest," he said.

"We can't get away from a wolf in the forest," Henry said. "Why don't you use that knife? She can't be any harder to take down than the leopards."

"The leopards were just leopards," Virgil said. "That wolf comes straight from hell."

Henry turned to him, but Virgil didn't take his eyes off the wolf.

"Are you serious?"

"Completely," he said. "Back into the forest. She won't follow us. She's just guarding the way forward. Fortunately, we need to go around."

"What?"

The growling grew louder. Henry turned back to the wolf as she took a step toward him. There wasn't time to argue. He grabbed Virgil and half dragged, half carried him back into the forest. He kept expecting it to jump on his back and tear out his throat, but the attack never came. After a few minutes, he stopped.

"What's going on here," Henry asked. "You know something you're not telling me."

"I'm not hiding anything," Virgil said. "We just didn't think of it. We thought we could fool Kurnugi."

"What do you mean?"

"We were never heading to town," Virgil said. "We pretended we were so we could get to one, but that was never our destination. Kurnugi is not a land easily fooled."

"So what? Kurnugi knew we were trying to trick it and decided to punish us? That doesn't make any sense."

"Not punish," Virgil said. "It's taking us where we want to go. Look."

He pointed at what Henry thought was a tree. When he approached it, he realized he was wrong. It was a pillar so old moss had overgrown it. Once he knew what to look for, he saw another a few yards away, forming a doorway. He and Virgil had been about to pass between them.

"What are these?" Henry asked.

Virgil leaned on one. He breathed heavily for a minute before he brushed the moss away. He spent a while doing that until he found the spot he was looking for. The letters carved into the stone were so faint, Henry almost couldn't see them. He had to get close, and when he made out the words, he felt the blood drain from his face.

"Are you sure you want to go in there?"

Virgil's laugh became a fit of coughing. "No one wants to go in there. Not if they're sane," Virgil said. "But it's the way we need to go if we're going to find the Moirai. It's either that or back to the wolf."

"You know, we can probably go around the wolf. It can't be everywhere."

"You can try that if you want," Virgil said, "but I think she wanted us to come this way. She's too strong to just ignore. She kills everyone who tries to get past her, and even if you managed it, you'd be going in the wrong direction. You'll never get home."

"Are you trying to depress me?"

"If it gets you to walk through that gate."

The two looked at each other. The wind had gone dead, the entire forest was silent. Henry nodded. As the two passed through the pillars, Henry couldn't help but look at the inscription.

Abandon hope, all you who enter here.

TWELVE

W here the forest had been silent only a moment ago, the air was now filled with the sound of buzzing insects. Henry couldn't take a step without swatting at least one. A crowd of people milled around with listless eyes. Their skin was devoid of color, and every one of them was wailing. Henry felt tears come to his eyes, though he couldn't say why. He felt the way he had at his grandfather's funeral when he was six years old. Though he hadn't known the man, Henry had been crushed by the sorrow of those around him. These were the people about whom the gate had spoken. These were those without hope.

"This isn't what I expected hell to be like," Henry said.

"This isn't hell," Virgil said between heavy breaths. "At least not the way you're thinking. Those suffering here couldn't get into hell."

"What kind of person can't get into hell?"

"These are those who, when presented with the choice between good and evil, decided not to choose. Heaven and hell have both been denied to them, and they're condemned to an eternity of this."

A little ways away, a wasp landed on a man's cheek. It stung him, tearing a gash in his skin. Blood dripped on the ground and was immediately consumed by worms that came out of the dirt. Henry moved to help him, but Virgil put a hand on his shoulder.

"There's nothing you can do to help him," he said between coughs. "Even if there was, he isn't capable of feeling mercy or gratitude anymore."

"So this is the price of not caring?"

Virgil nodded. They headed into the crowd, with Virgil leaning heavily on Henry. It was strange walking through them. Neither the two living nor the legion of dead had to work to avoid one another. They just never got in the other's way. Henry wanted to ask more questions, but even his breath was loud enough to feel like a sacrilege here. This was a place of sorrow. There was no room for curiosity.

"There," Virgil said as he pointed ahead to a crowd of people spread out in a line. As they neared, Henry saw they stood on the bank of a river. Fog blanketed the water, and Henry couldn't see across. The river was black. When they reached it, Henry bent down to dip his hand in the water, but Virgil stopped him.

"That's not water," he said. "That's liquid sorrow. The living were never meant to touch it. Even the dead fear it, or at least the smart ones do."

"What are we doing here?" Henry asked. "Did you come here to die?"

"Not if I can help it," Virgil said.

The people around them went silent. Henry's eyes were drawn to the fog. A figure was gliding through the water. A woman standing to Henry's left reached into her mouth and pulled out a coin. Henry was about to say something when he saw everyone doing the same thing.

The vessel, little more than a large canoe landed on the shore. Henry looked at its captain. The man, if it was a man, was covered in black robes. A hood obscured his face, but when he turned towards Henry, he had no doubt the man in the boat was looking at him. Strands of hair dangled down to the man's waist. For a second, he thought he saw twin points of fire in the hood. He extended a gnarled hand and pointed at Henry. The skin was so white it almost shone. The nails had been filed to points. The hairs on the back of Henry's neck stood up, and he took an involuntary step back.

"You are not among the dead."

The voice sounded like nails on a chalkboard. The crowd backed away from Henry, leaving him and Virgil isolated. Henry wanted nothing more in that moment than to turn invisible.

"Go. You have no place here." The ferryman pointed at Virgil. "You may remain. You are near enough to death. It will find you soon."

Virgil pushed Henry forward, and he stopped less than a foot in front of the ferryman. The smell made him think of tombstones. Henry looked back at his friend. He hadn't realized Virgil had that much strength left, but the effort had cost him and he had gone to one knee.

"Show him the letter," Virgil said.

Henry turned back to the robed man. He suppressed a shiver as he pulled the letter out of his bag and held it open between them. For the briefest instant, the fires in the ferryman's eyes blazed.

"He has been summoned by the Moirai, Charon," Virgil said. "You don't have the authority to bar his way."

At the sound of his name, Henry stared at the ferryman. Charon. Of course. Who else could this be but Charon, the one who ferried dead souls to the underworld?

"And what of you, half-dead man," Charon said. "Will you remain and wait for death?"

"I will not," Virgil said. "I go where he goes."

"And where does he go?"

"He is right here," Henry said, "and you can talk to him yourself." Henry thought for a second. If he needed to go to ancient Greece, then there was only one possible destination. "I go to the entrance to the underworld."

"That is where you are, living child."

Henry bit back a sharp retort at being called a child. Insulting Charon would not be the smartest thing to do.

"Not this entrance," Henry said. "I need to get to the Moirai, and I can't do that from here."

The ferryman nodded once and took a step back, leaving a space large enough for Henry and Virgil to stand in. Henry broke out in a cold sweat, and his heart raced. Speaking to Charon was one thing, but actually stepping in the boat that took the dead to the underworld was something else. Before he could think to object, Virgil walked passed him and practically collapsed into the boat. Henry looked around. The eyes of the dead were on him, and a chill ran down his spine. He swallowed his fear and stepped into the boat. Charon pushed off with a pole. A current caught them, and the waters of the river marking the boundary between life and death carried them towards ancient Greece.

THIRTEEN

They stayed near enough to the shore that Henry could see the faces of the dead; men and women, young and old, of every race. They went on for miles, and their faces were awash with sorrow. So many tears dripped into the river it was a wonder its bank didn't overflow. He had to turn away. He tried to see the other bank, but the fog was thick. If he squinted, he could almost make out movement through it.

"I wouldn't," Virgil said when he saw what Henry was doing.

"Wouldn't what?"

"Over there is death," Virgil said. "You can't look at it and come back unchanged."

"Heracles did," Henry said.

"If you feel up to wrestling a three-headed hound into submission, then go right ahead," Virgil said. "One hell beast a day is more than enough for me."

Just then, a howl pierced the fog. Henry jumped, and the hairs on the back of his neck stood on end. Virgil's eyes, now brown, went wide. Henry found himself inching to the side of the boat nearest the land of the living. He didn't try to look across the river again.

"There's so many of them," Henry said. "The dead waiting to cross, I mean. It's like they never end."

"It will end only when people stop dying, living child," Charon said.

"You can't possibly take them all across," Henry said. "There are too many."

"I would caution you against telling me what I can and cannot do on my own vessel."

"Sorry, I didn't mean anything by it," Henry said, but Charon made no move to accept his apology.

"Don't mind him," Virgil said. "It's pretty hard to get on Charon's bad side."

"If it's all the same to you," Henry said, "I'd prefer not to offend the ferryman of the dead while I'm on his boat in between the land of the living and the land of the dead."

"Fair enough," Virgil said.

"How are you feeling, by the way?" Henry asked.

He smiled but it was weak, and his face was pale. "I think I'm through the worst of it. I should be better any day now."

They both knew he was lying. Charon had said it. Death would not be long in finding Virgil if they didn't do something about it. Henry wondered how long it would be. After an hour, the fog thickened until Henry couldn't see from one side of the boat to the other. The living bank vanished. Slowly, the wailing faded and only the sound the boat cutting through the water could be heard. The next thing he knew, the fog had lifted, and the boat had run aground onto a grassy shore. Green hills rose in the distance, and a little ways away, the river emptied into the sea.

"I will go no further," Charon said.

"Where are we?" Henry asked.

"This is the land of the living," Charon said. "I do not belong. Leave my boat or return with me. I care not, but I will depart now."

Charon put his pole into the muddy ground and pushed off. Henry leaped onto the shore. Virgil tried to do the same, but he stumbled and fell into the water. Henry took in a sharp breath but calmed down when he noticed that the river was blue instead of black. He moved to help his friend onto the bank. When he looked up again, Charon was gone.

"I guess this is it," Henry said. "This is Far Kurnugi."

"Yes," Virgil said. "The ancient Greeks believed this river would lead to the underworld."

"So all we have to do is try to get to the Moirai, right?"

"If only it were that easy," Virgil said. "Near Kurnugi is mutable. The stories are always changing in the mortal world as people remember them differently or decide to add some detail that wasn't there before, but Far Kurnugi is deeply ingrained in the human subconscious. It's almost as solid as your world."

"Then how do we find them?"

"Short of scaling Olympus, you mean?"

Henry gulped. Charon had terrified him, and the ferryman had no power beyond his boat. He didn't relish the idea of going up against the Olympian gods.

"Yeah, let's try not to do that."

"Hermes could take you to them."

"Where's a messenger when you need one?" Henry thought for a second. "Hermes, are you there?" He waited for a second, but nothing happened.

"You didn't really expect that to work, did you?"

"It did before."

"That was because Hermes had been sent to you. Only the Olympians have the power to summon him."

"So what do we do?" Henry asked.

"Perhaps we should seek passage on that boat," a voice said from behind.

Henry whirled. He saw a tall man standing on the shore. His curly blond hair rustled slightly in the wind, and Henry caught the faint smell of grapes. The man's face was so smooth it could almost be marble, and his violet eyes saw everything before him. A rich purple robe flowed down around him.

"This is a strange place to find travelers," he said.

Henry blinked at him. "Where did you come from? Who are you?"

"Just a fellow wanderer," the man said. He held out a muscled arm and pointed out to sea. "The ship approaches."

Henry looked to where he pointed and saw a ship growing on the horizon. A wide sail spread out over a slim wooden frame.

"Maybe it's the Argo," he said, only half joking.

FOURTEEN

H o, travelers!" a voice cried out as the boat dropped anchor a short distance from the shore.

"Ho, the ship!" the stranger replied.

A few minutes later, a boat had been dropped, and a small crew began rowing toward them. As they neared, Henry could make out four men in the boat, though there seemed to be plenty of room. They landed on the beach. They were big men and didn't look like the kind of people Henry would want to offend. Each carried a sword or knife. One man stayed with the boat while the others approached the three people on the shore.

"These are evil shores to find strangers," a bearded man with a round belly said.

"And we eagerly desire to leave them," the stranger said. He waved a hand at Virgil. "As you can see, my friend has been wounded, and we would appreciate your help."

The stranger reached into his robe and pulled out two fat gold coins. Henry could almost see the crew's mouths water. The bearded man reached for the gold and the stranger deposited the coins in his hand. The man rolled them in his hand. The others with him gave the coins a hungry look before the man deposited them in a leather belt pouch.

"There's more if you can aid us," the stranger said.

"He sure has no problem speaking for us." Henry pitched low so only Virgil could hear, but the stranger looked over his shoulder at Henry with a raised eyebrow for a second before turning back to the boatmen.

"Don't complain," Virgil said. "We're caught up in a story, and there's no better way to attract the attention of the gods."

"That's for the captain to decide," the bearded man said.

"Don't be stupid, Thoas," one of the other men called out. "He's offering gold."

Thoas gave his crewman an evil glare and his hand went to a curved sword at his waist. The other man blanched and took a step back. Thoas cursed at him and turned back to address the stranger.

"Like I was saying, it's up to the captain, but if you show him the same gold you showed me, he won't turn you away."

The stranger nodded and moved next to Virgil. He draped the injured man's arm around his shoulder and helped him into the boat, seeming like he was having the time of his life. Henry followed them, and the small boat headed back to the ship.

The ship was about eighty feet long, and the sail rustled in the wind. The captain, a gruff looking man with a scar just under his left eye, scowled as they came aboard. Henry noticed his hand on the hilt of his sword, but he never drew it. The image of a squid decorated the scabbard.

The stranger leaped onto the deck and greeted the captain with an extravagant bow. The conversation the stranger had with Thoas was repeated almost verbatim with the captain, and the stranger lost two more gold coins. Henry noticed no one mentioned the coins the stranger had already given to Thoas. As the underling had predicted, the captain had no issues carrying passengers who could pay so well.

The ship smelled of beer and unwashed flesh. Henry tried to talk with the stranger a couple of times, but as soon as they started a conversation, the man would excuse himself and disappear below deck. Meanwhile, Virgil, robbed of the strength that urgency granted, grew weaker by the day. In spite of how well the stranger paid, they had no beds and had to sleep on the deck. Henry tried to talk to the crew to find out where they were heading, but each person he asked gave him a different answer, and he wondered if anyone knew their final destination.

The attack came in the middle of the night. Henry, finally accustomed to the moving ship, was asleep when a rough hand grabbed him. He tried to scream, but someone punched him in the stomach. He doubled over, and a sweaty rag was jammed into his mouth. The next thing he knew, his hands and feet were bound. Virgil was tied up near him as well as one of the crew. Nearby, Henry saw a group of men converging on the stranger. The tied up crewman managed to spit out his rag and yelled.

"No, you fools. That's no man. That's no man!"

The stranger stirred, and the men around him leaped. They forced his arms behind him and tied them together.

"Oh bother," the stranger said, not looking bothered at all.

He pulled his hands apart, and the rope just fell off.

The men stared in wide-eyed shock. One man was able to regain his composure before the others and pulled a sword on the stranger.

"On your knees," the pirate said.

"Of course," the stranger said as he got down, but he didn't stop.

He put his hands on the ground. The sleeves were tight on his arms. That was odd. Henry remembered the stranger's clothes fitting loose on him. They became tighter. At first, he thought they were shrinking, but then he realized the stranger was growing. Just as Henry thought the robes would tear, they disappeared into the stranger's growing form. His fingers came together and shortened. Dagger-like claws extended out from them. Henry caught a glimpse of the stranger's eyes. They were golden. Yellow fur sprouted all over his body, though it was longer at the head and neck. His muzzle extended and pointed teeth came from his jaw. In seconds, the young stranger was replaced by a lion at least twice as big as the one Henry had seen on the road.

It roared, and Henry felt the deck planks vibrate at the sound. He wanted to cover his ears, but his hands were still tied. He felt his eyes go wide when a vine crept in front of him. He was able to turn his head enough to see that they covered the entire ship. Meanwhile, the stranger attacked the sailors, and their only escape was to jump overboard.

The pirates splashed into the water, and the sound of dolphins rose from the sea. With the ship empty of all inhabitants, save those tied on the deck, the lion stopped in front of Henry. It might have been his imagination, but he thought the beast smiled. Its form melted away, and a few seconds later, a man stood before him. The vines snaked up his body. One wrapped around his head for a moment. When it receded it left a crown sprouting grapes. Another vine wrapped around his arm until it reached his hand. The stranger grabbed it, and the vine extended downward and upward until it formed a staff wrapped in vines and topped with a pinecone.

"Dionysus," Virgil said in a whisper.

"He tried to stop them," Dionysus said as he waved his hand to the bound crewman. "What did you do?"

"What?" Henry asked.

"That's what I thought. I've no use for someone who doesn't pull their own weight. I'm afraid I'll have to throw you overboard," the god of wine said. He waved his hand at the sailor and the ropes fell away. "See to it, Acoetes."

Acoetes stood up and walked over Henry. He gave an apologetic look.

"I would never presume to question your orders, milord," he said, "but while these men didn't try to help you, neither were they among those who tried to capture you. Perhaps you would consider some mercy."

Dionysus thought about that for a second. His face brightened, and he clapped Acoetes on the back.

"Good point. I think I like you. You're right. A compromise is in order. Untie them. Then, throw them overboard."

"Umm...of course, milord." He looked at Henry. "Sorry."

"Don't do anything stupid when he unties you," Virgil said. "That's still a god over there, and we don't have the ability to resist him."

Henry grumbled but nodded. Acoetes untied him and led him to the side of the boat. He apologized again before giving Henry a shove. Henry's scream was drowned out by him hitting the water, but the sea was calm, and he easily swam to the surface. A few seconds later Virgil was next to him. He was having a hard time staying afloat. Dionysus looked down at them and waved.

"Goodbye," the god shouted. "I'll give your regards to my brother."

"Is he insane?" Henry asked.

"Dionysus? Sometimes."

"Oh right," Henry said, realizing what he'd asked. "I forgot. The legends do say that about him, don't they? So what do we do now?"

"Dolphins sometimes help those lost at sea," Virgil said.

He motioned with his head. At first, Henry thought he was indicating the ship disappearing over the horizon, but then Henry realized they were surrounded. Strangely, some of the animals struggled to free themselves of clothes. One dolphin had cut itself on a sword that was tangled up with it. Henry pulled out the weapon. Its leather scabbard was decorated by a squid. Henry looked at the animal and saw a scar near its left eye. He felt his eyes go wide.

"These haven't been dolphins for very long, you know," he said. "Plus, they used to be pirates."

"We're treading water in the middle of the sea, who knows how far from the shore, and you're worried about the work history of the only ones who can save us?"

"I'm not saying we don't take their help," Henry said. "I'm just saying we should be careful."

"I think at this point being careful means going with the dolphins," Virgil said. "It's not as if we have any choice."

Henry nodded. He was about to toss the sword away but thought better of it. It was a struggle to belt it on while keeping his head above water, but he managed. Then they swam towards the animals. He kept an eye on Virgil in case he started floundering, but the other man seemed to have regained some of his strength. The dolphins allowed them to come close, but as soon as they were in arms reach, they swam away, laughing as they did.

"Henry, I can't keep this up," Virgil said as he struggled to keep his head above water.

"Keep trying," Henry said. "We've come too far to die like this."

Virgil tried to respond but he coughed as water rushed into his mouth. Henry reached out for him, but before he could grab on,

Virgil sank beneath the waves. Henry cried out and dove. He flailed and tried to find Virgil, but he couldn't find anything in the water. He stayed down until his lungs burned. He burst through the surface and took in a deep breath. A dolphin swam next to him and Henry grabbed on. He looked around and saw another dolphin in Virgil's grasp.

"They must've realized we weren't playing games," Virgil said.

He offered Henry a weak smile. Before Henry could say anything else, the dolphins carried him away, shooting through the water like a motor boat.

FIFTEEN

Henry laughed out loud at the sheer thrill of moving through the water so fast. Wind beat against his face, and he had to close his eyes against the ocean spray. He spared a quick glance for Virgil. The man had a death grip on one of the dolphins. Just as Henry worried Virgil would fall off, the dolphins slowed, and Virgil was able to regrip the animal. Then, they streaked through the water like a comet, and after an hour, they had reached calmer waters. Henry looked around. Red stone dotted the area. After a few minutes, the dolphins had taken them to waters shallow enough to stand, and they walked onto a rocky beach.

"Where are we?" Henry asked.

"I don't know," Virgil said. "You could always ask them."

Virgil pointed at the dolphins. As if understanding his joke, they laughed. One by one, the creatures disappeared into the ocean. Henry and Virgil looked at each other for a long time before walking further inland. No one living was in sight, so Henry laid their clothes on the ground and waited for the sun to dry them. He kept glancing at Virgil who had sat against a large rock. The area around his wound had grown purple. Virgil noticed him looking, but neither one said anything. There was nothing to do. Once their clothes had dried, they put them on again.

"I lost my pack," Virgil said. "How about you?"

Henry scanned the shore for his backpack but the beach was empty. He shook his head.

"The letter?" Virgil asked.

Henry checked his pockets, but he knew it was useless. He remembered putting the letter back in his bag after showing it to Charon, but even if he was wrong, there was no way the letter could've survived the trip through the water. As he expected, his pockets were empty.

"It's gone," Henry said.

"I was afraid of that," Virgil said, breathing heavily. "That letter was as good as a king's writ."

"So we don't know where we are. We have no supplies, and we lost the one thing that proves the Moirai actually summoned me," Henry said. "It sounds like we're worse than when we started."

"We attracted the attention of a god, at least," Virgil said.

"Yeah, and that turned out so well for us." Henry rolled his eyes.

"You're not helping," Virgil said. "Obviously, we need to find shelter. We should climb one of those hills. Maybe there's a settlement nearby."

"Are you sure you can make it?" Henry asked.

Virgil tried to stand up, but he fell back to the ground. He shook his head.

"Stay here then," Henry said.

The nearest hill had a sheer face towards the sea, but it had plenty of outcroppings around back. It didn't take him long to find a way up. His arms felt like lead. The events of the past several days were wearing him down. Once, he put his weight on a loose rock and he fell forward. He managed to twist so his shoulder hit the rocky ground instead of his head. He grasped for anything his hands could find and caught a rock. Heated by the sun, it seared his fingers, but he held on long enough to steady himself. His shoulder throbbed. The ground shook, and Henry realized he was standing on a loose boulder the size of a minivan. He scurried off of it and continued his climb.

He almost made it to the top, but he wasn't sure he could make it all the way. Henry squatted on the hot stone and looked around. The landscape was barren. There was nothing but rocks as far as he could see. He was about to head back down when he heard a soft weeping coming from the top. He listened just long enough to be sure he wasn't imagining before rushing to the top, his fatigue and pain forgotten.

As he reached the top, he gasped. A girl no older than he was, had been chained to the rock. Her skin looked like it had been white once, but exposure to the sun had turned it red. It had peeled in several places. Her red hair was tangled at her shoulders. The dirt in it made it look more like dying embers than a blazing fire. She wore black robes, but they had been torn in several places by her struggles. Her wrists bled where the manacles bit into her, and her bare feet had been cut by the rocks. She looked at him, her deep green eyes magnified by tears.

"Sir, please," the woman said. "You have to run. It'll be here soon."

"Calm down," Henry said. "I can help you."

Her eyes went wide and her jaw dropped. "No! You can't. The gods have decreed this."

"I don't care what the gods have decreed," Henry said. "I'm not about to leave you chained up here until you die of thirst."

"I should be so lucky as to die of thirst," she said. "Please, you have to go. There's no need for you to die here too."

"What are you talking about?" he asked. "Let's start at the beginning. What's your name?"

She looked at him again and started to calm down. Tears streamed down her eyes. He lifted his sword to try to break the chains, but she shook her head.

"No, I'll tell you, just don't free me. My name is Andromeda."

The name struck him like a ton of bricks. Andromeda. In Greek mythology, she was the princess of the kingdom of Aethiopia. Before he could say anything, a roar shook the earth. Lighter rocks were dislodged. Henry turned to the ocean. A massive sea serpent rose out of the water, no more than a hundred feet away. Seaweed green scales covered its body. Its teeth shimmered as if they were made of pearls. Though the top of the hill Andromeda had been chained to was at least two hundred feet above the surface of the water, the beast's head rose and looked down at them as he might look at a rabbit. Henry looked up at it and tried to swallow his fear.

"You have got to be kidding me."

Henry drew his sword, but he didn't know what such a small weapon could do against a creature that big. He stood between it and Andromeda holding the weapon in two hands. He tried to hold it steady, but it shook in his hands.

The monster dove at him. Henry shrieked and thrust the sword forward. It felt like his hand slammed into rocks. The monster roared and recoiled. A thin trickle of blood ran down its face from between its eyes. It glared at Henry as if not believing that such an insignificant creature would dare to hurt him. Henry backed up until he was standing next to Andromeda. The monster swayed back and forth. Doing the only thing that came to mind, Henry slashed at the chains holding the captive girl's right arm. They must've been rustier than they first appeared because they broke right away. The serpent roared as he cut the other one.

"What are you doing?"

"Unless you really want that thing to eat you, you should probably run," Henry said.

She looked like she was about to argue but nodded. The two moved around the hill and started down as quickly as they could, but the rough terrain stopped them from going too fast. For a moment, Henry thought the hill would shield them, but the monster wound around it and appeared under them. It snapped, forcing them to move back up.

"How do we stop this thing?" Henry asked.

"Sir, this creature has been plaguing our shores for months," Andromeda said. "My father petitioned the gods, and they told him the only way to stop this monster is to sacrifice me. I don't know of another way to stop it."

"Let's think of a different plan," Henry said.

The creature lunged at them. It came so close to Henry's foot that he tripped and fell. The ground rumbled under his weight and he realized he'd fallen on the same boulder he'd nearly dislodged on the way up. He jumped off of it, pulling Andromeda with him. The boulder came loose and crashed down the hill, smashing into the serpent's open jaw. Stunned, the sea serpent fell back and crashed to the ground. The bolder dislodged other rocks on its way down and buried the creature's head an instant later. The rest of its body went slack.

"I think it's dead," Henry said.

His voice was a whisper as if he was afraid the monster would awaken again if he spoke too loud.

"Cetus," Andromeda said, her voice just as soft as his had been. She looked at him. Her look of terror had been replaced by one of awe. "You killed Cetus."

"I guess I did," he said, still not quite able to believe it. He extended his hand to her and she took it, wincing as she did.

"We should get you out of the sun or you'll burn worse than you already have," he said.

"I was not expecting to have to worry about my skin burning." She looked at the dead monster. It smelled of salt and seaweed.

"I guess not," Henry said. "Come on. My friend is on the shore. We'll find him, and then we'll get to some shelter."

"There are many caves scattered throughout the hills," Andromeda said.

"That'll do for a start," Henry said as he walked down the hill hand in hand with someone who was, almost literally, a storybook princess.

"I guess she is," he said under his breath. "It just depends on how old the storybook is."

SIXTEEN

I see you've made a new friend," Virgil said once they came into view.

"Did you see that?" Henry asked.

"It was hard to miss. Cetus, if I don't miss my guess," Virgil said.

"I thought it was supposed to be the Kraken."

"Maybe in Near Kurnugi," Virgil said "in some world spawned by a movie. It was Cetus originally, and that would make this Andromeda. I would rise to meet you, milady, but I am somewhat indisposed at the moment."

"How did you know my name, sir? Are you an oracle?"

Virgil coughed. "Nothing so extravagant. You might call me a collector of stories, and your story, milady, has spread farther than you can imagine. The princess sacrificed for the good of her people."

"But sir, it just happened."

"Please, milady, let's drop the formalities. You may call me Virgil."

"And I am Andromeda, as you know. Are you unwell, sir...Virgil?"

Virgil pulled up his pant leg and showed her the leopard bite. The purple had given way to black in places, and it smelled of rot. Andromeda put her hand to her mouth. "I don't know much of medicine, but your wound is infected. You need to see a physician. You should've seen one long ago."

"We've had little opportunity before now," Virgil said.

"I will see to it," Andromeda stood up straight. "It is the least I can do for a friend of the one who saved my life."

"Is your city nearby?" Henry asked. "I couldn't see anything from the top of the hill."

"It's a few miles distant," Andromeda said. "We should find shelter for your friend. You can stay with him while I go get help."

"Didn't those people try to kill you?" Henry asked. "Are you sure it's safe for you to go there alone?"

"They may try to bring me back," Andromeda conceded, "but if they do, they have only to see Cetus's body. Regardless, I can get them to bring back a physician."

"No, he's right," Virgil said. "Take me to a cave if you want, but leave me there. The two of you will have a better chance to make it than one."

"That's not necessary," Andromeda said.

"How about we get Virgil to safety before we discuss this?"

Andromeda's face went pale. "Oh, of course. Forgive me. I wasn't thinking."

Virgil tried to object, but the two others ignored him. Though Henry didn't want her to go alone, he couldn't think of a better way so he remained with Virgil while Andromeda searched for a cave. It didn't take her long to find a suitable one, and the two of them carried Virgil to it. He was limp in their hands, and they had to carry all of his weight. Henry didn't know how Virgil had done such a good job of keeping his condition secret, but he was frightened at how weak his friend was.

"How long would it take you to reach your city?" Henry asked.

"Half a day," she said. "I can be back tomorrow."

"That's too long to leave him alone."

"No," Virgil said. "Go."

"I'll be back as soon as I can," Andromeda said.

Henry bent down and took off his shoes. He offered them to her. They were several sizes too big, and the last several days had left them in a sorry shape, but they were better than nothing. She looked at him and raised an eyebrow. He looked down at her feet. Most of the wounds had closed, but some had broken open in the struggle, and she'd left a bloody trail of footprints. That she hadn't said anything before now, told him she wasn't the standard princess.

"It's rough terrain," Henry said. "These should make it a little easier."

She nodded and put them on. Henry almost laughed out loud at the sight of a Greek princess in sneakers. She glared at him as if knowing what he was thinking, but she said nothing. They clasped hands, and she left.

"We're in ancient Greece, right?" Henry asked. "Or at least the mythological version of it."

"Yeah, more or less," Virgil said. His eyes had turned blue and he seemed to be having trouble keeping them open.

"Are they speaking English or are we speaking Greek?"

"This is your story," Virgil said. "You're the only one here who's not imaginary. The story is shaped by you, and we all speak the same language because it isn't one about finding a translation."

"You're saying they're speaking English."

"No."

"We're speaking Greek then."

"No."

"But we're both speaking the same language."

"Yes."

"How is that possible?"

"Honestly," Virgil said between strained breaths. "I haven't the slightest idea."

SEVENTEEN

A light rain that night provided them with drinking water, but with their supplies lost, they had no way to retain it. Henry went out looking for food. He found some berries he thought might be edible, but with help coming the next day, he decided to wait rather than risk it. A few hours after dawn, Henry heard horses outside their cave and went to look.

A band of eight riders with Andromeda at their head had stopped. There were two spare horses and one of the mounted ones had a wagon hitched to it. Most of the men carried spears and wore bronze armor. Andromeda looked amazing. She wore white robes and a thin crown of golden leaves adorned her head. Her red hair blazed in the morning light. Though her sunburned skin was peeling, she still looked regal. He didn't know how he'd mistaken her for anything other than a princess. She started to dismount, but one of the guards put a hand on her shoulder. She pushed it off.

"Captain please," she said. "This is the man who killed Cetus and saved my life. I am in no danger from him."

"I don't care about me," Henry said. "You have to help Virgil."

Andromeda nodded to a wiry man, the only one of the men who wasn't armed. Half a dozen pouches hung from his belt, and he looked uneasy among so many soldiers. He dismounted and went into the cave. Henry smiled at Andromeda before following him. When the man saw Virgil, he gasped.

"This isn't good," he said. "The rot has him. He may have to lose that leg."

"Let's avoid that if we can, Doc," Virgil said.

"What? Oh yes, of course."

The physician reached into one of his belt pouches and withdrew a small clay jar. He undid the stopper and turned it over above Virgil's wound. A clump of maggots plopped down. Both Henry and Virgil cried out. The physician looked at them quizzically.

"What are you doing?" Henry asked.

"I'm helping your friend. These creatures may look unpleasant, but if they don't eat away the rot, he won't survive more than a few more days. As it is, we may already be too late."

Henry felt like he was going to throw up, but Virgil shook his head. He suddenly noticed Andromeda standing beside him.

"Don't worry," she said. "Galen is the best physician in the kingdom. He'll save Virgil if he can be saved."

"But does he have to use those?" Henry asked. "He may as well use leeches."

"Don't be ridiculous," Galen said. "Leeches are for sicknesses of the blood. That's not what's wrong here."

"That makes me feel a lot better," Henry said.

"Good," Andromeda said, missing the sarcasm. "Why don't we leave him to his work? Captain Cyril would like to have a word with you."

Virgil nodded at him, and Henry followed Andromeda back

out of the cave. The guards had dismounted. When they saw him, one stepped forward. He had arms as thick as Henry's legs, and faint scars ran down them. He looked Henry up and down and sneered.

"You are the one who killed Cetus?"

His tone made it obvious he didn't believe it. Henry straightened his back and did his best to appear intimidating, though he didn't think he did a very good job of it. The man had to be a foot taller than Henry and weighed at least twice as much. Added to that, he wasn't just some bully from school. This was a man who'd been hardened by years of battle.

"I am," Henry said.

The guard snorted, but Andromeda wrinkled her brow, and the guard pretended he'd been coughing.

"The princess took us to the body," the guard said. "It looked more like a lucky accident than anything else. It's hardly the work of the great hero she made you out to be."

Andromeda scowled. "Tell me, Captain, what would you call a man who accomplished by accident what all of my father's armies could not do?"

The captain's face reddened, and he looked to the ground. Henry found himself hoping he was never on the receiving end of Andromeda's glare.

"I meant no disrespect, Princess," he said. He looked Henry in the eye. "The king has decided to throw a feast for you. I don't recognize your garb. Who are you and from what land do you come. Which gods do you serve?"

"My name is Henry," he said. The name sounded so plain next to theirs, and he felt like he had to add something. "Alexander. Henry Alexander. I'm from America, and I don't serve any of your gods."

His disgust of what the gods had demanded of Andromeda's parents came through his voice. The guards whispered among themselves. The captain visibly shivered before inclining his head. "I've never heard of your realm, Lord Alexander, but I would caution you against speaking such against the gods. It is for such careless words that Cetus was unleashed on our land in the first place."

It seemed almost silly for a man like the captain to be scared of mere words, but then Henry thought about the sea serpent. According to the legend, the creature had been set against the kingdom because Andromeda's mother claimed she was more beautiful than the daughters of a sea god. This man had good reason to fear blasphemy against his gods.

"I'll be careful."

The captain nodded. Just then Galen came out of the cave. Virgil was leaning on him and had a clean bandage around his leg. He was still pale, and his eyes looked like they had trouble focusing. The physician led Virgil to the cart and helped him up. Then, Galen came to where Henry was standing with the others.

"He's not out of danger," he said. "Not by a long way. We need to get him back to Joppa as soon as we can."

The captain nodded and mounted. The rest of the guards did as well.

"Will you ride in the cart with him?" Galen asked. "It's hardly the entrance to the city a hero such as yourself deserves, but your friend is having bouts of delirium. It would do him good to hear a familiar voice."

Henry looked at the horses. They were huge, at least seven feet tall, and their muscles rippled under gleaming fur. One of them looked at Henry as if it was considering eating him. He nodded at the physician, grateful he didn't have to think of a way to get out of riding one of these monsters. The physician handed him a pack of food and four water skins. Henry got in the cart and started eating bread and cheese.

The bumpy ride took several hours. Virgil came in and out of consciousness, and whenever he seemed strong enough, Henry offered him water and a few bites to eat. Occasionally, he spoke, but it was incoherent most of the time. Once, he sat up and seemed to have his wits about him.

"You're the hero, you know." Virgil's voice was dry, and Henry gave him a water skin.

"I don't think so."

"You killed the monster and saved the princess. You're the very definition of a hero."

"Not in Greece," Henry said, thinking back to Mr. Bulfinch's class.

"What do you mean?"

"In Greek myths, the heroes are always at least partially god."

"Don't you know why you're able to cross between worlds?"

"Hermes said it was because my parents were imagining me for a long time before I was born."

"Long enough to make you partially imaginary, yes. That makes you god enough."

"But everyone here is completely imaginary."

"You really don't understand, do you?"

"Understand what?"

"There was a Gilgamesh in your world. There was a Heracles and an Arthur Pendragon. At least there were real people on whom these heroes were based. They were as you were, partially imaginary, for one reason or another. The reason great legends sprung up around them is not that they were partially god. It's that they were partially man."

EIGHTEEN

They rounded a large hill and the city of Joppa came into view. Henry almost gasped. It sat atop a hill and gleamed in the sunlight. The whole city was made of marble. People made way for them as they rode through. Every house seemed a masterwork of architecture. Shining white pillars surrounded a city square, and gardens dotted the city. It was exactly what he would have imagined an ancient Greek city to be like. They even passed a statue of Zeus holding a golden lightning bolt.

They reached the large white staircase of the central palace. Pillars lined the walkway leading to a huge gold enameled door. A man and woman wearing so much jewelry they could only be Andromeda's parents stood in front of it. As Henry got up, they came down the stairs to greet him. Unsure of what else to do, Henry fell to one knee and bowed his head. He was stiff from sitting so long, and the gesture hurt, but he didn't want to offend the rulers of a kingdom while he was surrounded by their guards.

"No please," the man said. "You have saved our daughter and our kingdom. You never have need to bow before me."

"Thank you, Your Majesty," Henry said. "My friend is sick."

"Yes yes, of course," he said. "Galen, see to him. Use whatever resources you require. We owe this man a debt we cannot begin to repay."

"Of course, Your Majesty," the physician said with a low bow.

Galen stood up and shouted orders to servants, and in no time, they had carried Virgil away. The king ushered him through the doors. Once they were out of sight of the crowd, the two monarchs bowed before Henry. Henry tried to say something, but he was too shocked for words.

"My Lord Alexander," the king said. "I am Cepheus, and this is my wife, Cassiopeia. You cannot begin to imagine the depth of our gratitude. You have brought our daughter back from the dead."

Henry felt tears well up in his eyes as he remembered his own parents. How long had he been gone? A week? More? He wondered if time passed the same in the real world as it did in Kurnugi. Were his parents worried? On top of finding out they weren't having a new kid, did they think they'd lost the old one too?

"Please don't do that," Henry said. "I only did what anyone would."

The king and queen rose and Cepheus drew Henry into a hug. The man was strong, and the embrace hurt Henry's ribs.

"No, milord," he said. "You did what only the bravest of men would and what only the greatest heroes could. If there is anything we can do for you, you have but to ask."

"My friend..."

"Consider it done," Cepheus said, "but surely there must be something else."

"We've been through a lot, your Majesty," Henry said. "We

were shipwrecked and lost most of our supplies. Right now, I don't own anything but the clothes on my back."

The king looked him up and down. His t-shirt and jeans were little more than tatters, and he was still barefoot. He felt his face redden, but the king waved him off.

"A man who killed a beast sent by the gods and saved a kingdom shouldn't be embarrassed when standing before a king, no matter what he's wearing. We will see to it you have clothes befitting a man of your stature."

"I don't need anything fancy."

"Nonsense," the king said, "I owe you my daughter's life. It would be a poor repayment if I gave you nothing more than food and clothing."

Henry hesitated. "There is one thing."

"Name it," the king said. "You have but to ask."

"I was summoned by the Moirai," Henry said.

The king took a step back and the queen's jaw dropped. They both gasped.

"Are you certain?" Cassiopeia asked.

"Yes, milady," Henry said. "I had a letter, but we lost it at sea."

"If it were anyone else making that claim, I would not believe them," the king said. "What would you have me do?"

"I don't know how to get to them," Henry said, "and I don't know anything about this place."

"The Moirai go when and where they please," the queen said. "It is said even Zeus is subject to them. You can't find them unless they wish to be found."

"But they do wish to be found," Henry said. "That's why they summoned me."

"Hero you may be," the queen said, "but do not presume to

speak for the gods. I made that mistake once. I will not make it again."

"About that," Henry said, "you would have sacrificed your daughter?"

Cepheus let out a slow breath. He turned away for a second, and Cassiopeia put a hand on his shoulder. When Cepheus looked back, he'd regained his composure. "I am king," he said. "I must be king first and father second. It was not an easy choice."

"But you would've really done it?"

The king's eyes went wide. "Of course. I sent word to the Oracle at Delphi. She said I must chain my daughter and offer her to Cetus in order to find peace for my kingdom."

Henry snorted. "So much for the Oracle."

"But the Oracle was right, young hero."

"How do you figure?"

"Would you have fought Cetus had Andromeda not been chained?"

"Well, no."

"My kingdom is safe because I did as the Oracle instructed, though it did not end in the tragedy I was expecting. I will send word to the Oracle again. You will be our guest in the meantime. You should have your answer by the time your friend has recovered."

NINETEEN

Henry stayed by Virgil's side. Galen and two other physicians scurried around applying salves and giving Virgil medicine when he was strong enough, but he remained unconscious most of the day. It was as if he'd used up all of his strength in getting Henry this far, and now, he had none left.

The room smelled like a hospital. Even the marble walls reminded him of the sterile surroundings of a doctor's office. Virgil's breathing was unsteady, and Henry didn't realize how long he'd been in that room until the sunlight shining through the window began to dim. He looked up just as Andromeda came into the room carrying a covered silver platter.

"You didn't come to dinner," she said.

"Sorry, I just didn't feel right leaving him here alone."

"I understand," she said as she placed the tray down on a small table. "I brought you this."

She uncovered the tray, revealing a slice of beef and a small bowl of mixed fruit. Henry's stomach growled at the smell of it. He cut himself a piece of meat and popped it into his mouth. It was so tender it almost melted in his mouth. The spices were perfect, and it tasted faintly of cinnamon.

"Do you like it?" she asked. Her eyes looked like blue pools, and he stumbled a little before answering.

"Yes, it's delicious."

She smiled. "It's seasoned with moly. They say it's proof against enchantment, but that's only a story. It is very rare though. I love it, but even we can't have it more than about a dozen times a year."

Henry felt himself blush, but he didn't know why. It wasn't like giving someone a rare spice was the Greek equivalent of giving flowers, but then again, maybe it was. Before he had a chance to say anything, Virgil took in a sharp breath, and Henry focused his attention on his fallen friend. He muttered something about being real before going silent again. Andromeda stayed with Henry for a few more minutes, but neither said anything.

As the days passed, Virgil grew worse. Henry spent most of his waking hours in the room with him. On occasion, he ate at the king's table, but he always returned to Virgil. Every time Henry looked at him, Virgil looked paler. His bouts of consciousness were further and further apart, and each one was shorter than the one before. After a few days, Virgil didn't have the strength to lift his head when he was awake at all. The strange thing was the infection on his wound had receded. Galen discontinued the use of maggots after the first day. He said the rot was gone, but Virgil never got better.

"Henry, is that you?" Virgil said one day as Henry walked into his sick room. His voice was strained, and he sounded so weak.

"Of course it's me," Henry said. "Who else would it be?"

"Sorry, it's just so dark in here."

"Dark? Virgil, the windows are open, and it's a clear day outside. We'd need floodlight to make it any brighter."

"Really?" he said as he turned to look at Henry. "I can't see anything at all."

Henry gasped. Virgil's eyes had gone completely white. Even the pupils had vanished. Henry cried for the physician who came in after a few minutes. He examined Virgil before standing before Henry.

"I don't understand it, Lord Alexander," Galen said. "I've never heard of any illness robbing a man's sight so suddenly, and those eyes…I've never seen the like."

Henry stayed with Virgil all day and well into the night until his friend fell asleep. Then he went to the room set aside for him, though he made sure a servant would awaken him if Virgil woke up. Henry slept fitfully. The few times he managed to sleep, he dreamed. It wasn't like any dream he'd ever had before. He didn't actually see anything. It was just a sound, almost a hum, but that wasn't exactly right. The third time he heard it, he was able to identify it. It was the sound of his mother crying. At one point, Henry realized he was crying along with her.

At a time closer to sunrise than sunset, a soft knock came at the door. Henry woke up instantly. The light of the half-moon shining through the window was enough for him to see by, which was fortunate since he still hadn't mastered lighting a lamp without a lighter. When he opened the door, the servant went to one knee.

"Lord Alexander," he said, "Master Galen sends word for you to hurry. Your friend doesn't have much time." Henry stared at him, dumbfounded. Slowly, the weight of the servant's words descended on him. His heart pounded in his chest and the lamp the servant carried grew blurry as he blinked away the tears.

"No," Henry said. "You're wrong. He's not dying."

"I can only say what I've been told, milord," the servant said. "Master Galen says if you would come, it must be quick."

Henry nodded and stepped out of his room. The servant looked him up and down, obviously trying to decide if he should say something about the sleeping robe Henry wore. Before the servant could say anything, Henry scowled.

"I'm not going to waste time changing out of night clothes while my friend dies down the hall. Lead the way."

The servant paled at his tone. Henry knew he should feel bad, but he couldn't bring himself to. He fell in behind the servant. The stone floor felt cold on his bare feet, and the sandaled footsteps of his guide echoed through the hall. When he reached the sickroom, the royal family was waiting for him. Henry ignored them and went to Virgil's side. He rested a hand on the sick man's shoulder. Tears welled in Henry's eyes at the feeling of the clammy skin. Virgil kept his face toward the ceiling, and he was drenched in sweat.

"I'm sorry, Mother," Virgil said between breaths. His voice was raspy and barely recognizable, and when he spoke, Henry saw blood on his teeth. "I tried." He coughed several times. "I tried to get him home, but there just wasn't enough time. I tried. I swear I tried."

"It's ok, Virgil," Henry said, wishing he knew what his friend was talking about. "I'll get him home. Don't worry about that."

Virgil lifted his head for the first time in days and turned to Henry. His white eyes held Henry like a chain.

"I tried to take care of you. Maybe, one day, you can return the favor."

"I will, Virgil. I promise."

Virgil screamed and gripped Henry's hand like a vice. Then, his hand went slack. He took one more breath and stopped moving. Henry lowered his head and slumped his shoulders. He felt a hand on his shoulder and looked up. Andromeda stood over him. She knelt down and drew him into a hug and he cried on her shoulder. He knew he should be embarrassed. He was the great hero. He had saved the kingdom. He was supposed to be strong, but for that moment, he didn't care.

"He will have a grand funeral," Cepheus said. "Songs of his deeds will be sung as long as there are men to sing them."

Henry glared at the king. Did he really think that would make a difference? It took all Henry had to hold back a retort. He let go of Andromeda and started stalking out of the room. He froze when he heard the sound of wings flapping. He turned around and saw everyone had fallen to their knees. In the center of the room suspended a foot off the ground by his winged sandals, floated Hermes, messenger of the gods.

TWENTY

W hy didn't you come sooner?" Henry screamed. "You could have saved him!"

Cepheus twitched. He sounded like he couldn't decide whether to gasp or remain silent. Cassiopeia was pressing her face to the ground as was Andromeda. All three had gone pale.

"I'm sorry, Henry," Hermes said. "None of us expected you to come the way you did. We didn't even know it was possible to come here through the underworld."

"How could you not know? You're working for the Fates. They're supposed to know everything. If you had been doing your job, Virgil wouldn't be dead."

"Please forgive him, milord," Cepheus said, though his voice was muffled from his face being pressed so closely to the ground.

"Be at peace, Cepheus," Hermes said. "Neither you nor your house will be held accountable for what this man says. You were reconciled with the gods the moment you bound your daughter to that hill. We want nothing more of you."

Cepheus whimpered something that might have been a thanks.

"You and your family may rise," Hermes said. "I've no desire for your worship. I have matters to discuss with your guest. You may stay or go as it pleases you."

The king and queen got up and started backing out of the room, but Andromeda looked from Hermes to her parents. She set her jaw and took Henry's hand in hers. His anger and sorrow defused at her touch. It wasn't gone. Not by a longshot, but he could, at least, think clearly. For a second, her parents looked like they were going to say something, but Hermes smiled at them, and they scurried away.

"The Moirai's sight doesn't extend far beyond these lands," Hermes said. "They never knew of the entrance you took because they never thought to look for it. It wasn't until my brother told us where he found you that they were able to figure it out."

"Your brother? You mean Dionysus?"

"Of course."

"A lot of help he was," Henry grumbled. "He's as much to blame for Virgil as anyone."

"No, Henry, the blame is yours."

Henry's anger sputtered, and for a moment, he glanced at Virgil's body.

"What?" he asked.

"If you had come with me the first time, he wouldn't have been hurt protecting you. On the other hand, if you had stood by your decision to not come with me, he would have been safe as well."

"You're just twisting things around to get me to do what you want."

"The Moirai still want to see you, Henry," Hermes said.

"What if I say no? Will you take me home?"

"No, milord," Andromeda squeezed his hand. "You can't refuse the call of the gods."

"In fact, he can," Hermes said. "Henry is one of the rare few who can refuse whatever he wishes. It wouldn't be wise, especially not here. No, Henry, I can't take you home. You made that choice when you stepped into the mirror."

"Fine," Henry said. "Let's get this over with. Take me to the Moirai."

"I can't do that."

"But you said they want to see me."

"They do, but it's not the place of the messenger to take the hero."

Henry stared at him for a moment. The god looked back at him with impassive eyes. The only sound was the flapping of his sandals.

"Are you kidding me?" Henry asked after a second. "You're not going to take me because it's not your job?"

"It's a little more complicated than that," Hermes said. "The Moirai are thousands of miles away. I could've gotten you there from your world, but from this one? No, I'm afraid you have to take the long way."

Henry's jaw dropped. "Thousands of miles? I can't exactly hop on a plane. That would take...I don't even know. Weeks? Months?"

"Probably even longer," Hermes said, "that is if you went by foot."

"By ship?"

"That wouldn't do you any good," Hermes said. "It's completely landlocked. I was thinking you could fly."

"Didn't I just get done explaining that I can't hop on a plane?"

"You don't need a plane to fly," Hermes said. "You just need the proper footwear."

Henry looked down at Hermes's feet and his eyes went wide. "Are you going to give me your shoes?"

"What?" Hermes asked. "No, of course not." He reached into his robe and tossed Henry a pair of golden sandals.

"These were made for you. They can't do everything mine can do, and they can't take you between worlds, at least no more than any other shoes can. Go south. Even with these, it'll take you a few days. You'll come to a titan holding up the heavens."

"Great Atlas?" Andromeda asked, but she paled when she realized she'd spoken.

Hermes waved her off. "You'll find the Moirai in his shadow."

Henry looked at his friend's body and then at the window. He'd never seen so many stars and tried to imagine what kind of being could hold the sky, but it defied imagination.

"Your friend died to bring you to this point, Henry," Hermes said. "Don't let his death be for nothing."

"Are you going to take him to the underworld?"

"No," Hermes said. "He's not one of ours. Hades has no claim on him."

"What happens to him, then?" Henry asked.

"I don't know what land he came from," Hermes said, "and I don't know how the various powers of death cross between stories. He may be in his version of paradise."

"Or he could have ceased to exist altogether."

Hermes shrugged. "Some secrets even the gods don't know, or at least this one doesn't. Who knows? Maybe one day, you'll see him again."

Henry was about to say something when the wings at Hermes's sandals flapped once, engulfing him, and the god was gone.

"Then, you'll be going, Lord Alexander."

Not for the first time, Henry regretted not sticking with just his first name. "Please, stop with that," Henry said. "My name is Henry, and yes, I'll go. Tell your father to give Virgil a dignified funeral. That's all he would want."

"But milord," Andromeda said. She flushed as she realized what she'd said. "Henry, surely you're not going to leave before his funeral."

Henry held out the winged sandals. "Would the gods have given me these if they didn't want me to hurry?"

"But the Lord Hermes said you can refuse if you wish. Surely, you can manage a delay of a few days."

Henry spoke without taking his eyes off of Virgil. "From what I've seen, delay can be even worse than refusal. I'll go to my room and get some of the clothes your father has given me, but I intend to be gone before the sun rises."

Andromeda nodded. "I'll send word to the kitchens to prepare travelling food."

Less than an hour later, Henry was outside with the royal family. He'd changed into a plain woolen shirt and sturdy brown pants. He could see the barest hint of red on the eastern horizon. He'd stuffed a couple of sets of clothing in a pack as well as bread, cheese, and salted meat. Overall, he was much better prepared than he had been when he'd carried only his backpack. Idly, he wondered if he'd get in trouble for losing the textbooks he'd had in there, but he laughed at the thought. If the school wanted them, they could search the Aegean Sea, or wherever it was he'd been thrown overboard.

He looked back at the royal family. For a moment, he thought he saw Andromeda smile at him, but it was only his imagination. He waved and turned south. He took a few steps and leaped into the air. Exhilaration rushed through him for a second, but then gravity caught him, and he fell back to the earth. He threw his hands forward, but he had been moving too fast and tumbled on the ground. Henry uttered a silent thanks that the ground hadn't been rocky. He stood up and spit out dirt. Behind him, he thought he heard someone choke down a laugh. It was probably Andromeda. He felt his face redden as he looked to his feet. The sandals Hermes had given him gleamed in the moonlight, but the wings at their heels remained inert.

"At least Hermes could've told me how to use them," he said under his breath.

Acutely aware of Andromeda's eyes on his back, Henry concentrated on his sandals, willing them to fly. Nothing happened. He closed his eyes and imagined himself soaring through the sky. He could feel the wind rushing around him, and he pictured the earth far below. When he opened his eyes, his feet were still firmly on the ground. A fly buzzed around his head, and he swatted at it, but he hit only air and it disappeared into the distance.

"Show off," he murmured. Then, he spoke to the sandals. "Come on. Work. I have to get to Atlas. You know Atlas? Big guy. He holds up the sky. You can't miss him."

The sandals refused to respond. Henry closed his eyes and lowered his head. He could almost imagine Atlas himself laughing at him even while he held up the sky. He might as well talk to Cepheus about getting a horse. Maybe he could bring someone along to help him figure out how to ride the thing.

He heard gasps, and it took him a second to realize they came from below him. He opened his eyes and felt a surge of panic when he saw that he was floating six feet above the ground. The wings on his sandals were moving so fast he could see little other than a golden blur, though they didn't make a sound. He was so shocked he lost the image of Atlas in his mind. The wings went still, and Henry felt weightless for a second before he crashed to the ground.

The next thing he knew, Cassiopeia was helping him up and Andromeda was dusting off his clothes. Henry tried to stop them, but they wouldn't hear any of it.

"Are you well, Lord Alexander?" Cassiopeia asked.

"I'm fine," Henry said. "It's just that I've never used flying sandals before. I wasn't quite sure what to expect."

The king stifled back a laugh, and the queen raised a hand to cover her mouth. Andromeda smiled openly. Henry grinned at her and closed his eyes. He focused on being in front of her, three feet above the ground. Now that he expected it, he felt himself gliding through the air. He opened his eyes again and saw her emerald green eyes looking up at him. He felt a grin split his face. He focused on Atlas again and rose into the sky. His eyes went wide and his heart raced in his chest. He almost lost the image in his mind out of the sheer excitement. He rose so high he couldn't tell one person from another. Then, he shot through the air.

TWENTY-ONE

The rocky desert of the land passed beneath him in a blur. Henry kept his eyes open for harpies or furies or anything else ancient Greece would throw at him, but the skies ahead remained clear. He was high enough and moving fast enough that he should have trouble breathing, but he could've been sitting on the ground as far as his lungs were concerned. He was surprised at how warm he was. In fact, he was sweating. When he thought about it, he understood. While the skies of the real world might be cold, these were the lands where the wax of Icarus's wings had melted when he flew too close to the sun. If Virgil were here, he'd probably be chiding Henry about how he didn't understand sooner.

Henry flew until the sun hung directly overhead. The heat beat down at him, and he started feeling dizzy. He set down on a low hill. The sea of red sand around him shimmered in the sunlight. Henry rummaged through his pack until he found a water skin. He put it to his lips, and the cold water felt good going down his throat. He was surprised at how quickly it disappeared. He realized his hands were shaking, and he had to take several deep breaths. The only other time he'd felt this way was when he'd decided to get his chores done as soon as possible so he'd have his Saturday free. He'd spent most of the morning doing yard work. That had been a hot day, and by noon he'd been dehydrated.

Henry rubbed his fingers together and saw salt grains on his hands. He felt like an idiot. He'd been flying around, close to the sun. It had been so hot his sweat had evaporated before he'd noticed it was there.

"You're not a god, you idiot," he said to himself.

Kurnugi might be made of stories, but he was still flesh and blood. He had to remember that. He drank from another water skin, this time forcing himself to drink slowly. He ate a light lunch and decided to wait a few hours for the sun to lower. He kept on expecting some exotic creature to come over the horizon, but nothing came. He could've been in some desert in the real world for all he knew.

Once the sun had passed its zenith, Henry took to the air again. After a little while, the desert gave way to ocean. Even from his height, it stretched as far as he could see. Before long, the shore vanished behind him. The sun continued its relentless assault, and Henry lowered himself and flew in the ocean spray. The water was refreshing against his face. Once, a whale exploded out of the ocean a few yards to his right, and he stopped to gape at it before continuing on.

A few hours later, a small island appeared on the horizon. As it grew, he saw it was a barren place that looked like nothing more than a pile of rocks. Though he still had several hours of daylight left, he set down for a rest on the shore. He had just taken out a water skin when he heard a soft singing on the wind. Henry strained to hear, but then his eyes went wide, and he shot into the air faster than he'd known he could move. He'd heard stories of creatures who lured men to their deaths with their song. He didn't know if the singing was actually sirens, but he didn't dare take the chance.

When the sun set, there still wasn't land in sight. His eyes were getting heavy, and the next thing he knew, he was tumbling towards the water. In a surge of panic, he fixed the image of the titan in his mind. His body righted itself, and his descent slowed. His feet touched the water before he started to rise again. Thankfully, after a few minutes, he saw the shadow of a shoreline. The image in his mind shifted to the land before him. Though the sandals landed gracefully, Henry's legs didn't have the strength to hold him up anymore. He looked around just long enough to see that the sandy beach he'd landed on wasn't inhabited before collapsing to the ground.

Henry woke to the shining sun. The white sand of the beach gleamed in the morning light, the wind rustled palm trees nearby, and lush red fruit grew on a bush at the base of the trees. His stomach growled, and he dug into his pack. A piece of dried meat disappeared almost the instant he'd taken it out. He'd eaten it so fast he'd barely tasted it. All he was left with was the faint aftertaste of cinnamon. Andromeda had probably spiced his food with it. He smiled at the memory and took the next piece more slowly and ate a crust of bread as well. He emptied another water skin and realized he had only one left. He started packing everything away when he noticed he wasn't alone.

The bush rustled, and before Henry could react, a lion walked out of it. Henry froze in terror. It walked up to him and nuzzled his hand. His wits returned, and he screamed and leaped aside. The lion cocked its head. A low growl escaped its throat. Henry took a slow step forward and extended a shaky hand. It licked his fingers. He remembered hearing somewhere that lions had rough tongues that could scrape off skin, but it just tickled. He looked up and realized that an entire pride was looking at him from the bushes. Henry froze as they stepped onto the beach, but though he could see their dagger-like claws and teeth, they didn't look like predators. They moved with an easy stride that made them look like pets instead of wild beasts.

"Hello there," Henry said.

One of the cubs jumped back and forth at his voice. Henry felt himself start to calm down. After all he'd already seen, why couldn't there be friendly lions?

"Hi, Mr. Lion," Henry said to the one closest to him, speaking as he might speak to a dog. "You and your family live here, don't you? I need water. Do you know where water is?"

The lion rubbed its mane along Henry's fingers.

"Water," Henry said.

He pulled out his last full water skin and poured some in his cupped hand. He drank some and dropped the rest onto the ground. He pointed at it.

"Water," he said again. "You understand water?"

The cub walked up to the small puddle of water. He looked from Henry, to the big lion, and back again. Henry nodded, though he had no idea if the animal could understand. Amazingly, it did, and the lion cub lapped up the water. In no time, the small puddle was emptied. The animal looked up at him. Henry smiled. He wasn't sure if he was imagining it, but he could've sworn the its went wide. The cub disappeared into the wooded area around him. Henry didn't even bother to pick up his pack. He just took off after the cub, afraid he would lose it. Every time it did escape from sight, the animal would stop until Henry caught up to it. After a few minutes, they walked into a clearing with a stream running through it. The lion cub stopped at the shore and lapped up the water before looking back at Henry and making a roar that was, quite simply, the most adorable thing he had ever heard.

"Thank you for your help," Henry said as he bent down to fill his water skins.

"Don't you think you should at least ask for permission before taking what is mine?" a woman's voice asked from behind.

TWENTY-TWO

Henry spun around. Out of the shadows of a nearby tree stepped the most beautiful woman he'd ever seen. Her jet-black hair shimmered in the morning light. Her curls bounced as she moved her head. Her skin was like cream, and her eyes were twin sapphires. Her clothes seemed to shift between deep purple and dark blue. She didn't wear much jewelry, only a necklace and a pair of bracelets. Both were gold, and they practically shone with a light of their own. She looked at Henry and smiled. His heart started to race.

"Hello?" he said, feeling stupid as he did.

"Hello, my eagle," she said in a voice like honey.

Henry felt his cheeks heat up. He dropped to one knee, more because he didn't know what else to do than for any other reason. Surely this woman, whoever she was, warranted that kind of respect. She laughed at his gesture, and the sound was music to his ears. In that moment, he thought he would do anything just to hear that laugh.

"What would you have me do, milady?" His words tumbled over one another. "I am at your service."

"My, my," she said. "There's no need to be so formal, at least not yet. Why don't we start with you telling me your name?"

Henry almost smacked his head. How could he be so rude as to forget to introduce himself? He knew better than that.

"I'm sorry, milady," he said. "I don't know what came over me. I am Henry Alexander." He added his middle name without thinking. It still seemed woefully inadequate. "To the royal family of Aethiopia, I am Lord Alexander." That was better, but he didn't want her to think he was bragging. "You may call me Henry or whatever you wish. What do I call you?"

He felt stupid. Why would someone like her what to give him her name? Here he was, dirty and clumsy. He'd bumbled into her and now he asked her name as if he deserved to know it.

"Well, my eagle, I am glad you're here," she said. Her smile brightened the morning. "I think I enjoy the name you've already given me. You may call me, milady."

"Of course, milady," he said as his head bobbed up and down.

"Tell me, why are you here?"

"I was travelling, but I just saw ocean in every direction. I was tired and saw the shore, so I stopped here. I didn't mean to bother you."

"Oh, it's no bother," she said. She brushed a hand on his cheek, and his pulse raced. He was excited at the nearness of her. "I'm glad you're here. Did you come by boat?"

Henry shook his head. He'd been so stupid to allow her to think that. He should've known better than to imply something to her that wasn't true.

"No, milady," he said. "It was Hermes. He gave me these sandals."

He fell to the ground and started pulling them off so she could get a better look, but the laces were suddenly too complicated for his fingers. He just tugged at the knots until they came loose. He felt his face redden. They should've come off a lot easier. He didn't want her to think he was some kind of buffoon, but instead of deriding him, she just looked on with that same lovely smile. When he finally did get them off and handed them to her, his finger brushed her. Her skin felt like silk. He realized he was staring dumbly at her and drool was running down his cheek. His closed his mouth and wiped away the spit, hoping she hadn't noticed.

"These are a rare treasure, my eagle," she said. "It would give me great pleasure if I could keep them."

Henry's heart almost leaped into his throat at the thought of doing something that would please her. He nodded without even thinking about it. A voice inside told him he shouldn't, but it was a small, pitiful thing, and he squashed it with hardly any effort.

"Of course, milady," he said. "All I have is yours."

Her smile warmed him from the inside out. She held out her hand for him, and he took it in his. As he walked with her through the woods, the lions he'd seen before were joined by wolves. The animals almost looked like they bowed. He was struck by the strangeness of that only for a second. With a regal person such as her, what else should the animals do but bow?

Henry wasn't sure how long they walked. It was so hard to keep track of time when he was near her. Eventually, they came to a large clearing. He looked up and almost gasped. The grass was the purest green he'd ever seen. Throughout were scattered flowers of every color he could imagine. They almost seemed to sing in the wind. In the center was the very image of a fairytale castle. Its white stone walls gleamed, and the ruby topped towers rose high above the surrounding trees. A few hours ago, he would've said it was the most beautiful thing he'd ever seen, but now, the woman leading him by the hand held that honor.

"You live here, milady?" he asked.

"Yes, my eagle," she said, "but it's such a large and empty home. It's been too long since I've had visitors."

He gaped at her, unsure if he could believe it, but then he cursed at himself. Of course he could believe it. She had said it, hadn't she? That made it true.

"But milady," he said. "Surely a great woman such as yourself would have no shortage of visitors. I can't imagine you'd be alone for very long." His eyes went wide when he realized he'd contradicted her. "I meant no offense, milady."

"None was taken, my eagle," she said. "I suppose the remoteness of this island doesn't do much to attract visitors, which is why I'm so excited to have you here. We are going to have a grand time, you and I."

Henry could only nod at that. She led him into the castle. The halls they walked through were almost caverns. Crystals hanging from the ceiling glowed with their own inner light, and the walls were covered with tapestries depicting every animal he had ever imagined and a fair number he'd never even dreamed of.

She led him to large doors made of dark wood. Intricate scenes of men and animals were carved into it. As she neared them, the doors swung open, as if they would not dare bar her way. They walked into a room a hundred feet across with a large table in the middle. It was covered in food. There were at least three roast pigs and bread of every shape and size. Fruits and vegetables, steamed, boiled, and raw adorned plates made of solid gold. A large side of beef sat on one side along with several dishes Henry couldn't identify. He felt his stomach growl, and his mouth watered. At the same time, his cheeks heated in embarrassment. The woman gave him her musical laugh, and everything was fine.

"Please, indulge yourself, my eagle," she said. "This small meal is all that could be done on such short notice, but it has been prepared for you."

"Milady, I don't know what to say. I've eaten at a king's table that would be put to shame by this 'small' meal." Her smile showed her pearly white teeth, and he felt himself smile in return. She motioned him towards the table. He picked up a large plate and added pieces of every dish. She had gone through so much trouble to make this for him. The least he could do was try everything.

Henry sat at one end of the table, and she sat across from him. It felt strange to eat while she just watched, but it was clear that was what she wanted. He took a bite of buttered bread and suddenly, his hunger came to him in full force, and he devoured everything on his plate. Everything was so delicious. The meats were rich, soaked in their own juices, and the fruits tasted as if they were fresh from the tree. The next thing he knew, he was running his finger over his plate to pick up the last remnants of the meal. He looked at the woman who nodded, and he got up to refill his plate. It disappeared as quickly as the first. He was thirsty. No sooner had he had the thought than the woman placed a golden cup in front of him. A dark purple liquid that smelled like flowers filled it.

"Try this," she said. "It's my own special recipe."

The cup was almost to his lips before he thought to speak. "If you made it, I'm sure it will be wonderful."

She smiled and Henry felt his cheeks heat up. He took a sip. It tasted sweet. The way he could feel it running down his throat reminded him of drinking hot chocolate on a cold winter night. A tingling sensation ran from the top of his head to the bottom of his toes. He wanted more and took a gulp. Then a second. And a third.

After a few seconds, the cup was empty. He held it in front of him halfway expecting someone to fill it again.

Henry's eyes locked on movement on the far side of the room. A mouse scurried across the ground. He could see it in magnificent detail. Its eyes darted around, looking for danger, and its nose twitched constantly. He could've almost counted its hairs.

Henry lost his grip on the cup, and it clattered to the floor. He looked at his hands, surprised he'd dropped it, and his eyes went wide. His fingers had thinned and were even now sprouting brown hairs. After a few seconds, they'd been replaced by long feathers. He looked up and his eyes caught the mouse just as it escaped into a crack in the wall. It was only then that he realized it had been almost ninety feet away. He lifted his feathered hand to his nose and found it had hardened and curved to a point. He looked at the woman and his eyes went wide. He'd been so enthralled by her beauty he hadn't stopped to consider the strangeness of the situation. No, it hadn't been her beauty, or at least it hadn't been only that. There was magic at work. He remembered a story of a sorceress who turned men into animals. He tried to speak, but his voice came out as a squawk. He had to concentrate on his tongue to make anything even approaching the sounds of normal speech.

"Cur...key?" he asked.

The woman smiled, apparently having no difficulty understanding his broken speech.

"Yes, my eagle," she said. That voice which had sounded so alluring only a moment ago was now terrifying. "I am Circe, and you will make a fine addition to my menagerie."

She walked up to him and placed a finger on his head. A warm sensation spread throughout his body. His feathers ruffled and he leaped back, flapping his wings. He went a dozen feet into the air. He made a thousand tiny adjustments to muscles he didn't realize he had. It was pure instinct. He looked at her accusatorily. It was a stupid thought. What was he accusing her of? Turning him into a bird? It's not like she would deny that.

"Curious," she said. "The transformation should be fully on you by now, but you're still as much man as bird. How are you able to do that?"

Circe began to sing softly, and Henry felt himself calm down. He didn't know why he was so upset. He'd enjoyed flying with the sandals, but that couldn't compare with doing it as a creature who was born to it. He should just let her figure out what went wrong with the transformation so she could fix it. The witch extended a hand, and it began to emit a green glow. Tendrils of light extended outward. A few recoiled when they touched him, but most wrapped themselves around him. Circe raised an eyebrow at that. He felt one crawling down his throat and others going into his ears. Without warning, the tendrils whipped out of him, and he fell to the ground.

"You've consumed that blasted herb," Circe hissed. "Where did you get it?"

Henry backed away. He didn't understand why she was so angry. He just wanted to make her happy. He tried to tell her that, but he couldn't concentrate enough to speak.

"The moly!" She screeched. "Who gave it to you?"

Moly. He knew that word. Moly was rare and valuable. There was someone who liked it. She had seasoned his food with it. The name came to the quiet of his mind, like the memory of a dream. Andromeda.

Whatever spell of enticement Circe had laid on him shattered. Her eyes widened and Henry knew he had mere seconds. A glint of gold caught his eye. On the floor near the table sat the winged sandals he'd given Circe. A quick glance down at his bird-like feet told him he couldn't wear them anymore, but he didn't want Circe to have them either.

He leaped into the air, flapping his wings. He stayed low to the ground until he'd caught the sandals in his talons. Circe sang behind him, and for a second, he wanted to land. He drew on his memory of Andromeda and used it as a shield. He couldn't hold out for long, but he didn't have to. He just had to get out of the range of her voice. He flew towards the window near the ceiling. He braced himself for impact, but the window had no glass, and Henry sailed into the air. Below him, the forest erupted as the animals who had once been men shared in their mistress's rage.

TWENTY-THREE

Henry felt like he was clawing through the air as he made his way to the shore. His sharp eyes spotted the area where he'd first landed, and he swooped down to pick up his pack. He looked in the direction he'd originally been going, but that would take him over the center of the island, and he wasn't quite willing to risk that. He followed the coast until he reached the opposite side of the island before heading out over the sea again.

He flew for hours before he found another place to land. It was more a rock that poked out of the sea than it was an island. He fumbled with his pack, unsure of how to open it. His hands no longer had fingers, and his feet lacked the dexterity for fine manipulation. Finally, he was able to take the drawstring in his beak and the bag in his claws and tug it open.

He pulled out the wrapped bundle containing his food. He didn't bother to unwrap it. He just tore into it, gulping down the meat. His tongue no longer possessed the ability to taste it, but he ate all of it. Then he waited, but whatever power the spices held to block Circe's magic, they apparently were incapable of reversing it. Henry let his shoulders sag. There was nothing left to do but continue on and hope that the Moirai had the power to restore him.

His speed as a half bird was painfully slow next to what it had been when he wore winged sandals. Added to that was the fact that he was now carried by his own muscles rather than the power of the gods instilled in the sandals. He could be a thousand miles off course, and he wouldn't know it. He tried to put that thought out of his mind, but it kept nagging at him.

He flew all day. He found a small island once the sun was setting and set down to rest. The weight of the sandals in one talon and the pack in the other were starting to have an effect on him, but he didn't dare leave them behind. If he ever managed to turn back into a human, both would be invaluable.

Not if, when. He would return to his human form. He tried to keep that thought firmly in mind, but as far as he could remember from what he knew about Greek myth, the only one who had the power to reverse Circe's spell was Circe herself. He didn't think she would be too accommodating.

It was hard to sleep in this form. He lacked the innate balance needed to sleep perched on a tree, and if he tried to lie down, his bones creaked under his own weight, which made sense since birds had hollow bones. He almost laughed at the irony. He was too much a man to sleep as a bird and too much a bird to sleep as a man.

He slugged through the air the next day. It could've been his imagination, but he thought he saw a shore growing in the distance. By midday, he was sure. A vast forest stretched out before him. Henry flew higher to see if he could determine if this was another island or an actual continent. The land stretched out as far as he could see, and now that he was part eagle, he could see farther than he ever had as a man. He landed as soon as he reached the shore, though he still had several hours of daylight left. He left his pack and sandals hidden in a bush and rested against a tree.

A rabbit scurried across the beach. Before he knew what he was doing, he'd taken off into the air. He climbed a hundred feet and dove at the small animal. The rabbit, seeing his shadow, tried to dart to the underbrush, but it was too slow, and Henry caught it in his claws. It squealed as he squeezed the life out of it. He landed and tore into it. He felt its blood running down his beak.

His eyes went wide as he realized what he was doing. He threw it as far as he could, though with his new limbs, that wasn't very far.

"I am a human being," he said. It didn't sound remotely like human speech, but he didn't care. "I am human. I am not an eagle."

He repeated those words over and over again, trying to drive them into his subconscious. If he had been capable of tears, he would've been weeping. He was human. He had to hang on to that. Maybe when he reached the Moirai, they would know how to change him back. He clung to that hope as a drowning man might cling to a rope.

He went back to his pack and forced himself to eat bread and cheese. His stomach roiled at the food. He supposed that a creature designed to hunt was never meant to eat anything other than fresh meat, but if an upset stomach was the price for remaining human, it was one he was happy to pay.

He continued to fly in the same direction, though now that he was over land, he made many stops. Several times, he beat back his predatory instincts. So determined was he that as soon as he found a patch of berries, he ate them right off the bush. His stomach started to hurt after that, but he didn't know if it was because they were poisonous or if his digestive system just couldn't handle them. In the end, it didn't really matter.

He only covered a few miles that day. The lack of sleep combined with a diet never meant to be consumed by a bird of prey weighed down on him. He didn't know how long he could keep it up. The next day, he felt like he was clawing through the air. It was so hard. Every flap was like moving a mountain. He stayed close to the ground, partly because if he fell, he didn't want to hurt himself and partly because he didn't have the strength to go much farther. Even when he saw rodents darting below, his eagle half was too tired to go for them. As the sun set, he thought he saw a dark figure on the horizon, but his eyes, while excellent in the day, weren't much better than a man's at night.

When the sun rose the next morning, he knew he'd been right. In the distance was a man of almost unimaginable height, and hope welled up inside of him. He fought for every mile, for every yard, for every foot. Halfway through the day, he was sure. The figure he was nearing was man shaped, but too tall by far to be a man. It was almost too tall to be a mountain. Its arms were spread wide and its head was hunched as if it were carrying a great weight, as if it bore the weight of the heavens themselves.

Henry pushed. His heart felt like it would break out of his chest. He didn't take a break all day. He had to make it today, or there would be no point. He wouldn't have the strength to continue his journey the next day. If he didn't make it, he would die. There was no other possibility.

The sun neared the western horizon, and Atlas grew in the distance. He'd been farther than Henry had believed. The sheer size of the titan dwarfed anything Henry had ever imagined. He just kept getting bigger and bigger. Henry pressed on. As the blue sky turned to the red of twilight, he saw trees around the massive being.

He felt his heart drop. Those trees were so far that they looked like blades of grass. He was still hours away.

The sun passed beneath the horizon, but he kept on going. Though he couldn't see all that well, the massive form of Atlas blotted out the stars before him. Henry's mind reeled. Nothing living could be that big. It had to be near midnight before he reached the base of the giant. He landed near a sandal that looked like a slab of stone so large a castle could be carved out of it. With no strength left, Henry collapsed into unconsciousness.

TWENTY-FOUR

Is it a man?" a raspy voice asked.

"No, sister," another said. "It is a bird. See the wings and the feathers?"

"I think it is neither," a third said. "Or perhaps it is both."

Henry opened his eyes. He was on his side, lying on a bed of moss. He tried to sit up, but he couldn't move. The strength just wasn't in him. Three women stood in front of him dressed in dark robes. Their hoods cast shadows on their faces and he couldn't make out any details, but their hands were as wrinkled as anything he'd ever seen, and their fingers ended in long, pointed nails. He had the sense that they were weighing him with their eyes.

"I think it's dying," the one on the left said.

"Is it?" The one on the right asked as she pulled a string out of nowhere.

The string was taut and moved through her fingers. It appeared a few inches before her hand and disappeared a few inches after. She leaned in close and examined it. For some reason, it sent chills down Henry's spine.

"It's possible," she said. "This man bird thing was never meant to exist."

"And yet it does," the middle said. "How curious. What do you think we should do about it?"

"Are you the Moirai?" Henry asked, but his words were more squawk than voice.

"Did you hear that, sisters?" the middle one asked. "It knows who we are."

"I never knew any man bird thing," the one on the left said.

"It calls us by name," the middle said. "It obviously knows who we are."

"Please, help me," Henry squawked.

"It wants our help."

"What kind of help would one such as he want?"

"Maybe we should kill it," the middle one said. "It's obviously in pain and is just as obviously dying."

"I said it may die," the one on the right said. "Not that it will die. That part of its fate has not yet been determined."

"Please," Henry said again. "Circe."

"Ah the witch of the island," the middle said. "That explains it."

"Yes," the one on the left said. "She would do such a thing, but her workings are usually neater than this. This is so sloppy."

"But do we help him?"

"What can we do? We do not change fate. We only execute its weaving."

"There are others who could help," the center said. "Chiron is even now on his way to make a pilgrimage here."

"This man bird will be long dead by the time Chiron arrives, sister. Is there another?"

"Panacea?"

"I do not think she will come."

"What of the apples?"

"The apples have been corrupted."

"We don't wish them to grant eternal life. We only wish them to heal him. Surely that much is still in their power."

"Perhaps," the middle said. "Perhaps not."

"You," the one of the left said, "Man bird thing, would you like an apple? They were lovely to eat once, and they are still greater than most things that have ever passed through mortal lips." She raised an eyebrow. "But I suppose you lost your lips, didn't you?"

"Can't eat apples." Henry struggled for every word.

"You only need a piece," the middle one said. "At least that is what I think you need. It will either heal you or kill you, but you'll die without it anyway, so what do you have to lose?"

"No choice?" Henry asked.

"Oh, of course you have a choice," she said. "Didn't you hear what Atropos said? Your fate has not yet been determined. You die as a bird man thing or you can take your chance with an apple."

"Apple," Henry said.

"Well, let's get him an apple then."

All three walked away. Henry lay there waiting. It hurt him to breathe. He could hear himself wheezing. Even though he'd just woken up, his eyes already felt heavy. He knew that if he allowed himself to sleep he would never wake up.

Some time later, it might have been a minute or it might have been an hour, the trio came back. They all had a hand on an apple as if it were heavy enough to require all three. They put it down in front of him. The one on the left sliced into it with a long nail. The one on the right gave it another slice. The middle one pulled out the wedge and pried open Henry's beak. She put the apple slice in his mouth and pushed it closed. It wasn't a taste. Not exactly. He'd lost the ability to taste, but as it passed over his tongue, he was filled with the sensation of sweetness, and the image of dawn on a spring morning flashed through his mind. The woman backed up and all three stared at him.

"What are you waiting for?" the middle one asked. "It won't do you any good to just sit there with it in your mouth. You have to eat it."

Henry forced his tongue to push the apple into the back of his mouth. It was too big to go down. He felt it break in his throat. He coughed, and pain shot through him. He arched his back and screamed. He heard his bones cracking. His vision went blurry, and a tingling spread over his skin. There was a loud pop and an even worse pain shot through his legs. He twisted and writhed, screaming until his voice was gone. At some point, the pain became too much and he fell into darkness.

TWENTY-FIVE

Henry woke to sunlight stabbing his eyes. He shielded them with his hands and realized he had fingers again. He sat up and his head spun. It was a few seconds before he could look himself up and down. He was weak and so tired, but he was alive, and he was human. He stood up and stretched his arms. His clothes were in tatters, but he didn't care.

"I see you're awake," a woman's voice came from behind.

Henry whirled and saw the three crones standing there.

"I am, thanks to you," he said. "Was I right then? Are you the Moirai?"

"We are," they said in unison. "What would a boy want with us?"

"I could ask you the same question," Henry said. "You're the ones that summoned me."

"Did we?"

Henry stared at them, not believing what he'd heard. He'd come so far for this?

"Yes, you sent Hermes to me. Virgil said..."

"Ah yes, your brother," the one on the left said.

Henry's jaw dropped. "What?"

"Your brother," she said again. "The one who guided you until Aethiopia."

"He wasn't my brother," Henry said.

"You weren't a very good big brother, you know," she said. "You're supposed to watch out for him, not the other way around. It's the way of things."

"He wasn't my brother," Henry said again. "I hadn't met him until I crossed over into Kurnugi."

"What does that have to do with anything?"

"I'm from the real world," Henry said. "He was from here."

"You were from here long before you were from there," she said.

Henry opened his mouth to respond, but then he stopped and stared at them as the pieces fell into place. It all made sense. Hermes said he could only cross over because he was imaginary first. His parents had wanted a new kid for a long time now, and Virgil had looked like him, just like his parents had imagined. He'd fit the image they'd built up for themselves so well Henry didn't know why he hadn't realized it before. They'd pictured Virgil so completely, all except his eyes. He swallowed.

"Every time I looked at Virgil, he had different color eyes. Mom...our mom kept changing her mind about his eyes."

The three women nodded as one.

"But he died," Henry said. "I know my parents never imagined their child dying because of an infected leopard bite, so what does that mean? He'll never be born?"

"Your brother did not die of his wounds," the one on the left said. "He died because those who told his story forgot about him."

"What do you mean?" Henry asked.

The one in the center took a step forward. She put a gnarled finger on his forehead and everything else disappeared.

His mom was crying, and his dad had an arm around her. His own eyes were red from tears as well, but he held them in now. The phone rang, and he got up to answer it. His voice cracked as he spoke. Something was missing from his voice, though Henry couldn't identify it right away.

"Anything?" his mother asked once he'd returned.

"Nothing." His dad was angry, though obviously not at her. "They said they're expanding the search to other cities, but they still haven't found a trail."

"Do you think Henry is okay?"

"He's fine, Sarah," his dad said. He didn't sound too convinced, but his mom didn't contradict him. "The police will find whoever took him, and they'll bring him back to us."

"Whoever took me?" Henry asked, but his voice was hollow and empty. "No one took me, and I'm fine. I'm just a little stuck, but I'm doing my best to come home."

The vision swirled and colors blended into one another. When they resolved themselves, he was back in the forest looking at the three old women.

"Did that really happen?"

The center one touched the left one on the shoulder. "Only Clotho can show you what was."

"Lachesis showed you things as they are now," the one on the left, Clotho, said. "They grew so concerned about the child they'd lost that they've forgotten about the one they wished they had."

"They think I've been kidnapped," he said unable to keep the despair from his own voice.

"So they do," the middle one, Lachesis, said. "You've been gone a long time. What are they supposed to think?"

"Tell me how I get back home," Henry cried.

"It's not our place…"

"Don't give me that," Henry shouted. "You're the ones who sent Hermes with the letter. You knew this would happen. The letter said so. You have to know how I can get back."

"That answer belongs to Atropos," the one on the left said.

"Who is Atropos?" Henry asked.

The one on the right stepped forward. "I am."

"Tell me how to get home," Henry said. "Please, I'll do anything."

"We did not summon you here just to send you back," Atropos said.

"Then why did you summon me?"

"Our time is long past," Clotho said.

"This is your time now," Lachesis said.

"Fine," Henry said. "This is my time so let me go."

"You may go," Lachesis said.

"What?"

"You are not our prisoner, Henry Alexander Gideon," Lachesis said.

"You came of your own free will," Clotho said.

"If you wish to go, we will not stop you," Atropos said.

"But you won't help me."

"No," they said in unison.

"Why did you summon me?" He was screaming.

"War," Atropos said. "Terrible war."

"An attack on us has already failed," Clotho said.

"It will only skirt the edges of these lands in the future," Atropos said, "but there are others in which we exist that will be consumed entirely. Many will die. Near Kurnugi will fall."

A cool wind blew through the clearing and Henry suppressed a shiver. Birds went silent at her words.

"What does that have to do with me?" he asked.

"What do you imagine Kurnugi is?" Lachesis asked.

"Hermes and Virgil said it was every story ever told," Henry said.

"Anything else?"

Henry thought for a second. "Hermes called it the imagination of mankind."

"That was no exaggeration," Clotho said. "Neither was it a metaphor."

"Kurnugi is not a reflection of human imagination," Lachesis said, "nor is imagination a reflection of Kurnugi. The two are one and the same. War on Kurnugi is war on the imagination of mankind. If one is conquered so is the other."

"Never before," Clotho said, "not in all the history of your people, has one being held the whole of Kurnugi. Never before has one controlled the imagination of mankind."

"Who will wage this war?"

"We do not know," the three said. "This war comes from somewhere beyond our sight."

"But if it's only going to affect Near Kurnugi..."

"Far Kurnugi can only touch the mortal world through the lens of the Near."

"But I thought all Kurnugi was human imagination."

"When an old story is told, the hearers imagine it, but these imaginings belong to the Near. Without that, the old stories will wither and die."

"But why did you call me?"

"Because you can cross the boundaries between stories."

"But others can," Henry said. "Hermes can."

Lachesis shook her head. "Hermes is a messenger. It is not in him to do this."

"You're saying Hermes won't do it because it's against the rules?"

"Not will not. Cannot. Hermes is a part of the old stories. He cannot be other than what he is without giving up that which defines him."

"And he didn't want to do that?"

"Foolish boy," Lachesis said. "If he were to give up that, he would no longer be the messenger, and it is the messenger who has the ability to walk between worlds."

Henry sighed. A part of him had wished he could just pass this to Hermes, but he hadn't really expected it to work. He glanced upward at the mountain of a man standing over him. Even Atlas's toes were so big that Henry wouldn't have been able to tell what they were if he hadn't already known. Wouldn't the titan have been something else if he could have?

"What do you want me to do?" he asked.

"Though Kurnugi changes as human imagination changes, there are three things that do not change, three constants."

"And those are."

"Memory, action, and design," the three spoke as one. "Past, Present, and Future."

"But I thought that was you?"

"We can only see where we exist, but every place has a future, and the one who is an embodiment of that future can see all places."

"And who is that?"

"The Oracle of Delphi. She can tell you what is to come, and you, perhaps, can prevent this war before it ever happens."

"Why didn't you tell me in the letter?" Henry asked. "Cepheus had already sent word to the Oracle. I could've already learned what you want me to ask her."

"The Oracle will only answer questions you know to ask," they said, "and if you would've remained in the house of Cepheus you would even now be a prisoner."

"A prisoner? What are you talking about? They thought I was a lord."

"Cetus weakened the nation," said Clotho. "Seeing an opportunity, the enemies of Cepheus attacked."

"Even now, they hold his kingdom," Lachesis said.

"But that didn't happen in any of the old stories," Henry said.

"When a human comes to Kurnugi, new stories are born, even here," Lachesis said.

"I have to help them," Henry said.

"That is not for you to do."

"Forget about that," Henry said. "You said it yourself. I'm not of Kurnugi. I can choose to do something."

"So you can," Lachesis said.

"And what would you do?" Atropos asked. "Can you fight an army alone?"

"Perhaps he can, sister," Clotho said. "There have been heroes who have done such, and he did kill the monster."

"Oh, he can fight monsters," Atropos said, "but an army of men?"

Henry wracked his brain, looking for an answer. Atropos comment about fighting monsters brought another memory to the surface, and he almost recoiled from the idea.

"Medusa." Henry's voice was half whisper. "In the story, Perseus used Medusa's head to petrify an entire king's court."

"Yes," Atropos said. "You could do that. You might be able to kill her or she might kill you."

"Don't you know?" Henry asked. "You can't tell me Medusa doesn't fall in your sight."

"She does," Atropos said, "but you do not."

"Can't you see if she's going to die?"

"I can see that she may die," Atropos said. "You obscure everything."

Henry swallowed. He imagined Andromeda in chains and her parents in a cell. They had done so much for him. He couldn't let them be conquered.

"Where is she?" Henry asked.

"South," the middle said. "Far to the south. She is farther from us than we are from Aethiopia."

"I think I'll be fine as long as I avoid any witches," he said with a smirk.

"Go then," the middle said. "Save your friends if you can, but do not get so focused that you forget why you are here. Save us all."

Henry looked each in the eye and nodded. He put on the sandals and picked up his pack. He was surprised to find it was stuffed with food, bandages, and other assorted supplies.

"I thought I was outside of your sight," Henry said. "How did you know I would go?"

"I do not need to see the future to know how a hero will react when he is told the ones he loves are in danger. Remember, do not look into her eyes."

"Thank you," Henry said.

He put an image of Medusa in his mind and rose into the air. He went high enough to look Atlas in the eye. It was as big as an office building. His eyelashes were thicker than Henry's legs. The giant shuddered and thunder rumbled overhead. Atlas blinked, and the force of the gale it generated sent Henry flying backwards.

It was a while before he was able to right himself. Driven by curiosity, or perhaps insanity, Henry fixed the image of the titan's face in his mind, but he pictured it smaller, as if from a distance. The sandals took him a hundred feet away from the titan. Even at that distance, its massive face filled his vision. It opened its mouth, and the sky rumbled. Henry could feel it in his bones. His head felt like it was about to explode. He moved back another hundred feet. The sky rumbled again but this time, Henry could make out the barest hint of a word. He backed up still further, and this time, when the titan spoke, he understood.

"Mortal."

Henry knew the voice was halfway between a hurricane and an earthquake, though he had never experienced either. Henry nodded, though he couldn't imagine the titan could see someone as small as him. The titan's voice rumbled on.

"I am of the earth, and I would offer advice to one who has killed a beast of the sea. Earth and death are intertwined, and those who are of the earth can often stave off death."

"What do you mean?" Henry asked. "Who else is of the earth?"

The titan didn't speak again. Henry flew closer to him, but he was like a fly buzzing around a man determined to ignore him. He flew back down to ask the Moirai, but they were nowhere to be found. Atlas's warning unnerved him, but there was nothing he could do about that now. He fixed the image of Medusa in his mind and headed south. He kept looking over his shoulder until Atlas was out of sight.

TWENTY-SIX

Henry wasn't sure if the Moirai had done something or if the sandals sensed his urgency. Whatever the reason, he flew faster than he ever had. The forest beneath him was a blur. After a few minutes, it disappeared and was replaced by a sea of sand. The heat was oppressive. He was going to press on through the day, but he remembered too well the lessons he'd learned on his first trip, and before the sun was directly overhead, he landed in the desert to give himself a chance to recuperate.

It wasn't much of a rest. There was no shade in sight, and the sun sapped his strength. He gulped down one water skin almost the instant it was opened. He ate some dried meat as well and found that he missed the taste of moly. He hoped he wouldn't need its protection again.

He took off into the air once more. The sun's heat reflected off the desert sand and made the air ripple. This, combined with his own speed, made him think he imagined the figure in the air in front of him. He was flying so fast he actually passed it before his mind registered who it was. He turned around and flew back. A few seconds later, he floated before a man wearing winged sandals.

"Hermes," Henry said. "I wasn't expecting to find you here."

Hermes shrugged. "I go where I'm needed. It's a strategy you may want to consider."

"What's that supposed to mean?"

"You need to go to the Oracle," Hermes said, "not pursue some foolish quest to kill Medusa."

"I'm not going to leave my friends to rot in some prison."

Hermes smiled. "I know. I told Zeus you'd say that. Come with me."

He took off to the east, and Henry just stared after him. After a few seconds, Hermes returned and floated in front of him again.

"You can't just show up out of nowhere and expect me to follow you," Henry said. "I have to get to Medusa."

"And what do you plan to fight her with?" Hermes asked. "I know you've made yourself out to be a great hero, but you don't really think you can take her with your bare hands, do you? How do you intend to take care of her sisters?"

"Her sisters?"

Hermes sighed. "There are three gorgons. Two of them are immortal, and you want to kill the other one. Do you think they're just going to stand by and let you?"

"I guess I never thought of that."

"What is it with you humans?" Hermes asked. "First you ask too many questions. Now you don't ask any at all. If you go up against them now, you might kill Medusa, if you're extremely lucky. Of course, lucky people generally don't get turned to birdmen by Circe. Even if you did kill her, you'd be torn apart by her sisters. What's more likely is that you'd be just another statue for her garden."

"What am I supposed to do about that?" Henry asked.

"You're supposed to come with me so that I can give you what you need to come out of this alive."

"Why are you helping me?"

"What do you mean why?" Hermes asked. "Didn't you hear what the Moirai said? There's a war coming. They sent word to the gods, and the gods sent me to help you." Hermes focused his eyes behind Henry. "Cloud."

"What?" Henry asked, but when he turned around, he saw a cloud the size of a school bus heading towards him. Hermes had already flown lower and Henry followed him. "If they want me to succeed so badly, wouldn't it be easier for them to kill Medusa for me or to wipe out the enemy that attacked Aethiopia?"

"Again with the questions," Hermes said. "The gods can aid their champions, but the battle belongs to the hero."

"I guess it's up to me then," Henry said.

"That's what I've been trying to tell you. Now, are you going to come with me or not?"

Henry extended an arm towards the east. "Lead the way."

He'd thought he'd gone fast before, but that was like an Olympic runner comparing himself to a Formula 1 racecar. The wings on his sandals moved so fast they emitted a high-pitched hum. The land beneath shifted so quickly he couldn't tell if he was over desert, mountain, or forest. One moment, a landmark was on the horizon in front of him, and the next it was on the horizon behind him. They flew so fast he saw the sun falling in the sky. The stars traveled across the night too quickly to be able to identify them. The wind ripped against his face, and he didn't know how he was able to breathe. He only had a second to notice the glow in the distance before they came to a stop over it. The volcano glowed brightly in the night air. It rumbled, and he thought he caught the hint of a metallic smell in the air.

"How come there wasn't a sonic boom?" Henry asked between heavy breaths. Hermes raised an eyebrow. "With the stars moving like that, we had to be going faster than the speed of sound, right?"

Hermes rolled his eyes. "This is another one of those mortal world things, isn't it?"

"Forget I said anything. Why exactly did we come here?"

"You need weapons," Hermes said, "and some more specialized equipment."

Henry felt his eyes widen. He strained his ear until he heard an almost musical sound. The bang repeated over and over again at regular intervals. It was almost like a bell. Or a hammer.

"Are we where I think we are?" he asked, not quite ready to put words to it.

"That depends entirely on where you think we are," Hermes said.

Henry glared at him, his awe momentarily forgotten. "Are you really going to play those kinds of games after everything that's happened?"

"One must keep oneself entertained."

"Are we at Hephaestus's forge?"

"Where else would a hero like you get his weapons but from the god of blacksmithing? Come on. Let's go."

TWENTY-SEVEN

Hermes flew down into the heart of the volcano. Henry followed on his heels. The heat hit him with the force of a Mack Truck. It made the desert feel like an unusually warm winter day. He almost gagged at the smell of sulfur. He couldn't breathe, and the image of Hermes kept fading in his mind. Half of the time, Henry wasn't sure if he was flying or falling. The smoke was so thick he couldn't see. His eyes burned. He started to cough just as he slammed into a slab of rock.

He sprawled on his back and screamed, though he didn't know if it was from the pain of the impact or from the rock searing his skin. He'd never felt anything so hot. He tried to form an image in his mind of anyone, of anywhere, desperately hoping the sandals would take him away, but the heat and gases of the volcano clouded his mind. He still heard the metal sound, but he couldn't tell what direction it came from. If he just lay there, he knew he would die, so he did the first thing that came to mind. He started to roll. He half expected to pitch himself into the lava, but at least if he did, the pain would end.

Suddenly, the heat vanished, and Henry was lying on a cold stone floor. The air was clean, but he could barely breathe. His back screamed at him, and he wondered if he'd burned away all his skin. He felt even worse than he had when he'd been dying as a half bird.

"Hermes!" a deep voice bellowed through the room.

Henry tried to lift his head, but his neck wouldn't respond. He didn't even have the strength to roll on his side to see who was yelling. A shadow came to stand over him, but his vision couldn't focus enough to see who it was.

"Are you ok?" Hermes's voice asked softly. Then louder. "What?"

Heavy, irregular steps came into the room. Whoever it was shook the ground as they walked. There was a sharp gasp and the shadow over Henry vanished. He heard the scuttling of feet. He tried to focus on the sound, but his mind was swimming.

"You brought a *mortal* in through the *central corridor*?"

"Well, it's the fastest way in."

"Yes, if you require no air to breathe and can stand the heat coming from the heart of the earth. Foolish child. Fortunately for you, he still has the spark of life. Carry him to that table. I will do what I can."

Henry cringed when the arms came around him and touched his ruined flesh. Tears welled up in his eyes. It hurt so much he wasn't sure if he screamed. When his wits came back to him, another shadow stood over him, this one broader than the first. It lifted a large object over its head. Henry just had time to wonder what it was doing when the shadow brought the object down on his chest. Bones splintered. Henry would've screamed, but the impact forced the air out of his lungs. Again and again, the shadow smashed into Henry. He felt himself fading. The figure carried something red and glowing. It put the light down on Henry, and he felt awareness returning. He tried to take a breath, but his body wouldn't respond. The figure moved out of Henry's sight, and a second later, air rushed through him, though it wasn't he that drew the breath.

The shadow kept coming down on him, and each time brought a fresh wave of pain. Henry had no sense of himself other than that pain. Three or four times the shadowed figure hit him before disappearing to bring another light to place on Henry. Shortly afterward, he'd feel air moving through him. Then the pain would begin again. It happened so many times Henry lost count. After hours or days or years, the shadow came down on him again, and he screamed. It was only then that he realized he could breathe for himself again.

"Good," the deep voice said.

It was breathing heavily. Henry wanted to ask what was so good about this world of agony, but his tongue had stopped working. The shadow continued his work. Every time it hit him, Henry screamed. After a little while, it stopped and Henry heard the sound of metal scraping on stone followed by a long breath.

"What are you doing, Hephaestus?" Hermes's voice asked. "He's not finished yet."

"Even I can't work so long without ceasing, Hermes," the great smith said. "He will no longer die from the wounds you brought on him, but I need rest and so does he. I dislike working on living flesh. I've no ability to dull the pain, and his mind can't take much more. Once he's had a chance to recover, I'll finish."

Henry lay on that slab, unable to move or talk and barely able to breathe. His chest throbbed, and he couldn't feel his arms or legs at all. After a time that felt far too short, Hephaestus came back to him. The first couple of times the smith brought his hammer down again, Henry didn't feel anything. Abruptly, pain shot through his left leg. He tried to move it, but it was chained down. This time, it seemed there was no need to stop after a few hits, and Hephaestus kept on relentlessly. When Henry thought he could bear the pain no more, the work moved to his right leg. From there it went to one arm, and then the other. Finally, when his voice was too hoarse to scream anymore, the hammer came down on his head. Every time it hit, it cut a strained scream short.

"Stop," Henry cried out. "Please stop!"

"Almost," the shadow said.

The hammer came down once. Twice. Ten times. Twenty. Then it was done. Cool water poured in Henry's eyes and washed the blurriness away. There was a series of clicking sounds as the restraints at his arms and legs fell away. Henry sat up and examined himself. He was completely naked, but there wasn't a mark on him. Even the scrapes and bruises he'd accumulated over the past several days were gone. He looked around and saw he was in a room made of polished obsidian. He had been placed on a steel table, and a forge burned at one end of the room. Hermes huddled in a corner. Henry glared at him, and the messenger god tried to take a step back.

"How was I supposed to know mortals couldn't fly into a volcano?" he asked.

"It's called common sense, Hermes," Henry said. "I'm mortal. Why would you think I could fly into a volcano?"

"If it's so obvious, why did you follow me in?"

"I don't know. Maybe it's because you spent so much time convincing me the gods wanted to help me that I didn't expect one to lead me into a death trap!"

"I didn't lead you into a death trap!" Hermes said. "You're still alive, aren't you?"

The other person in the room cleared his throat. Henry turned and got his first clear look at the craftsman of the gods. He almost recoiled from the sight. He had the same olive as Hermes and Dionysus, but the resemblance ended there. His nose was twisted as if it had been broken several times. He had a mouth that looked too big for his face, and ears that seemed too small. His coarse black hair was tied behind him, but that did little other than keep it out of his eyes. Pockmarks littered his face. Though the god's arms were almost as thick as tree trunks, his left foot was shriveled and twisted to one side. It looked like he was avoiding putting weight on it.

"Hephaestus," Henry said in a whispered awe.

When he'd met Dionysus, he hadn't realized who he was. It'd been the same with Hermes, and since then, encounters with the messenger god had been so casual, he seemed almost mundane. This was the first time he'd met a god knowing full well who and what he was. Hephaestus had been born so ugly his mother had thrown him off Mount Olympus, but even as infants, the Greek gods did not easily die. Henry didn't know if he should bow his head or fall to one knee.

"And you are our hero," the maimed god said. If Henry's reply displeased him, he gave no sign.

"You healed me," Henry said.

Hephaestus let out a chuckle. "Healing is for Apollo and those who follow him. It's a gentler craft than what I do. I repaired you."

"I thought I was going to die," Henry said.

"It was a near thing. The spark of life was almost gone from you. I had to keep it lit using the fire from my forge, and I had to use my bellows to breathe for you."

"That's impossible."

"The fact that you're up and talking now suggests otherwise. It's not pleasant, though, as you've learned. It's much preferable to craft a body first then give it life as we did for Pandora."

"You repaired me by hitting me with a hammer?" Henry asked, still having trouble believing it.

"I can work with anything, be it metal, clay, or flesh. How are you feeling, young hero? My art may have restored you, but it is not easy for mortal flesh to undergo what yours has."

Henry opened and closed his hand. There was a slight tingling, a little like if his hand fell asleep and was only now waking up.

"I'm fine," he said.

"Perhaps you would like to get dressed." Henry looked down and felt his face heat up.

"Sorry," he said. "I forgot."

Hephaestus threw his head back and laughed. Hermes joined him a second later. Henry clenched his teeth and tried to keep from blushing.

"Young hero, you've nothing I haven't seen before. Come, let's see what we have for you."

TWENTY-EIGHT

Hephaestus led them down a long metal hall. The floor should've been cold on his bare feet, but it felt perfectly comfortable. They passed a passage that was glowing red. Henry stared down it and was surprised to see it open up into bare earth. Smoke billowed up from a surface of magma.

"That's where you brought me in from?"

"I said I was sorry," Hermes said.

"No, you didn't."

"Oh, right. Sorry."

Henry glanced down the hall once more. Ashes trailed down it, and there was a charred husk that Henry suspected was a piece of his own flesh. He thought he was going to be sick, and he hurried past it. The workshop was a maze of passages, and after a few minutes, Henry would've been hard-pressed to find his way back. In every room, there was something in the process of being built. Weapons and armor were prevalent, but there was also jewelry, furniture, and an entire room containing only horseshoes.

Eventually, they came to a room filled with clothing. Robes of every color hung from hooks on the wall. Shirts and pants stood stacked everywhere there was room, and he saw more than one pair of golden sandals, though whether they were like his and Hermes, he had no idea.

"Take your pick," Hephaestus said.

"You made all of these?"

"Of course."

"What do they all do?"

Hephaestus walked over to a blue cloak and passed his hand along it. It shimmered as he moved his fingers over it, and Henry realized points of light were dancing on the cloth. Henry tried to pull his eyes away but they were drawn to the cloak. It was as if it contained all the stars in the universe. The god's hand stopped. Henry took in a sharp breath and looked back up. The smith met his eyes and gave an ugly smile.

"It would take years to explain what every item in this workshop does. Pick whatever draws your eye."

Henry nodded and walked down the rows of clothes. He extended his hands and ran the various cloths through his fingers. He expected it to be soft, and for the most part, it was. Every once in a while, however, he felt something hard and unyielding. He pulled at one of those and found himself holding a shirt that looked like it was made from woven silver. If he let his hand rest, the cloth would envelop it and harden. To his surprise, he could still move his fingers. It was like they had a second skin, one made of metal. He was about to put it on when his eye caught a deep green shirt. He dropped the armored shirt to pick it up. The green one felt like cotton. Silver buttons ran down the middle and gold serpents were embroidered on the sleeve. He put it on. It fit perfectly.

"Good choice," Hephaestus said. "That shirt is proof against all poisons."

"How can a shirt protect me against poison?"

Hephaestus looked at him as if he didn't understand what Henry was asking. His eyes widened slightly as understanding dawned on him.

"You're still thinking too much like a mortal. Keep in mind I just finished repairing your flesh with a hammer."

"Good point," Henry said.

He continued to look and found a plain brown pair of pants. Like the shirt, they fit perfectly.

"With those, you can run for a night and a day without tiring," Hephaestus said. "All that remains is a cloak."

Henry nodded and kept walking. He almost picked up a purple one, but it didn't feel quite right, and he put it back. He rejected three more before he came to one that was midnight blue. He wrapped it around himself. He expected it to feel warm, but it didn't. He felt like he wasn't wearing anything around him at all. Hephaestus laughed.

"If you'd been wearing that, you would've had no problem coming in the way you did, or at least the flame wouldn't have bothered you. Neither heat nor cold will touch you while you wear that unless it's brought on by the strongest magic. Now that we've taken care of your basic needs, let's see about equipping you."

"You call those basic needs?" Henry asked.

"Those are fair examples of my work, but my specialty is weapons and armor. Come, I will arm you with items fit for the greatest hero. What is your weapon of choice, young mortal? A hammer? A mace? Wait, you're going to fight Medusa aren't you? A sword or axe would be best. Tell me, what's your preference?"

"I don't know," Henry said. "I've never actually used any of those."

Both the gods looked at him. Henry had never imagined a god could be surprised, but shock was evident on their faces.

"Never?" Hermes asked.

"You've never used a weapon? Why? You're of age, certainly."

"It's not something that's ever come up."

"And you want to face a creature powerful enough to defeat entire armies?" the smith asked.

"I don't have a choice," Henry said.

Hephaestus relaxed his muscles and gave him one of those ugly smiles. "The call of the hero. Come."

He led Henry back the way they'd come. They passed enough weapons to outfit an army. Hephaestus glanced into each room briefly before shaking his head and moving to the next.

"What are you looking for?" Henry asked.

"I can give you a sword that will allow you to win any duel or one that will let you fight on long after your wounds should have claimed you, but neither of those would do you any good against what you're going to face."

"Then what will?"

"Something simple, yet sharp. You don't have the training to handle a heavy blade. You also don't know the limitations of a light one, but we can turn that to your advantage."

"How?" Henry asked.

"Where was it?" Hephaestus mumbled to himself.

Occasionally, Henry caught a word or two about organizing his workshop better. They were passing a hall when Hephaestus's head snapped to one side. He grinned and shuffled down the hall, passing half a dozen rooms before he entered one. Henry went in after him.

At least fifty swords lined the wall opposite the door. Some were as big as Henry was, and he couldn't imagine the warrior that could carry them. Others were so small, they could almost be called knives. Some had two edges, and others had one. There were curved blades and straight ones. Most were made of steel, but one shone gold in the torchlight, and there was one blade that looked to be carved from a single piece of ruby. The hilts were of every style from jewel encrusted to plain leather. Hephaestus pulled out a long curved sword. Its three-foot blade had been so polished it almost looked like silver, and its hilt was made of some dark wood. Henry took the sword. It felt right in his hands. He swung it a few times and could almost hear it singing in the air.

"This blade will strike with the strength of ten men," Hephaestus said. "Even an offhand strike will have enough power to take an enemy's head. Though you've no experience with such things, you are formidable when so armed. With this, you might be able to kill Medusa."

"And armor?"

Hephaestus tugged at Henry's shirt. "This will provide greater protection than anything else I can give you. Medusa's hair is made of deadly snakes whose venom could kill in a heartbeat. In any case, you won't be trading blows with her, but perhaps there is something."

Again, they walked through the halls. Eventually, the contents of the rooms changed from weapons to armor. There was every type Henry had ever imagined, including several that weren't Greek. He even thought he saw samurai armor in one room, but Hephaestus moved too fast for him to stop to be sure. He turned into one room filled with shields. Some were along a wall, but most were stacked on top of each other. The smith moved from one pile to another until he came to the one he was looking for. He pulled a round shield about two feet wide from halfway down the stack, sending the rest clattering to the floor, and handed it to Henry.

Though the shield looked like steel, it was light. It felt like one of those plastic things kids played with. The metal was polished to a mirror-like shine. An image of a tree was embossed on the front. As the light danced across the image, Henry could almost see the leaves move in the wind.

"You know about Medusa?" Hephaestus asked.

"Yeah," Henry said. "Her hair is made of poisonous snakes, and she can turn people to stone by looking at them."

"No," Hephaestus said. "People who look at her turn to stone. At least they do if they look into her eyes directly. Look at her reflection through this shield, and you'll be safe."

"Can't I just make her look at her own reflection and turn her to stone?"

Hephaestus gaped. "Where would you get an idea like that? If you won't turn to stone by looking at her reflection, why would she? Besides, I thought you were going after her head. If all you want is a stone head, I can give that to you in a few minutes."

"No, you're right. So all this shield does is provide a reflection? Not that I'm ungrateful, but it seems a little ordinary after everything else you're giving me."

"Yes and no," Hephaestus said. "All it does is reflect, but it will reflect fire, lighting, and even magic as easily as light."

"But not a petrifying gaze."

"No, not that."

"I guess I should be going then," Henry said. "You said I can leave the same way I came in now that I have the cloak, right?"

"Yes, if you've suddenly developed the ability to breathe sulfur. You could always hold your breath, but that wouldn't stop the chemicals from damaging your eyes. Of course, you can come back here for me to fix them, but I get the feeling you didn't enjoy my care."

Henry winced at the memory. "Right, so there's another way out of here then?"

"Hermes can show you. You'll need his help to get back anyway if you don't want to spend weeks traveling."

"Can't you just tell me how to go that fast on my own? I think I've had enough of Hermes's help for a while."

"I heard that," Hermes said.

"What are you going to do about it? Lead me into a volcano?"

"You're just going to keep bringing that up, aren't you?" Hermes asked. "I said I was sorry. What more do you want?"

"Children," Hephaestus's voice thundered through the room, and they both fell silent. Henry felt his cheeks redden at being called a child, but he guessed someone who had existed for thousands of years could call anyone a child. "You can't go that fast on your own."

"Why not?"

"There are limits to what I can give any mortal, even you. I'm also afraid your supplies were burned, and I've little to give you in that regard." He handed Henry a pouch. Henry pulled it open to find herbs and bandages. "These are just the normal sort, I'm afraid." Hephaestus turned to Hermes. "He's lost a lot of time due to your mistake. Take him within sight of the gorgons' temple."

"Fine," Hermes said. "Are you ready, or do you want to spend more time complaining?"

"Let's go," Henry said.

"Hermes," Hephaestus said, a note of caution in his voice.

"What?"

"Unless he catches it on his shield, the equipment I've given

157

him won't help if he gets hit by lightning so be sure to go around any storms."

"I was planning on it," he said, though the defensive tone told Henry he'd planned nothing of the sort.

"There's one more thing I can do to help," Hephaestus said. "I'll call the south wind. Notus won't go near the gorgons' lair, but once you're far enough away, he'll speed your return."

"Come on, let's go," Hermes said.

Without waiting for a reply, the messenger god launched himself into the air. Surprised he would do that in such a confined space, Henry almost lost him. He gave Hephaestus a quick thanks before flying off.

Henry's heart felt like it was going to beat out of his chest. Hermes was flying like a madman. He navigated through the halls with the speed of the wind and a grace that could only be called god-like. Henry had no idea how he was able to keep up, but he screamed the whole time. It made the worst rollercoaster he'd even been on seem like a swing set. He was sure any moment he'd smash against a wall. At that speed, there probably wouldn't be enough left of him to fill a teacup. Between one breath and another, they rushed out of a cave and flew over the ocean. Henry barely had time to look back before Hephaestus's workshop disappeared into the distance.

TWENTY-NINE

L ike before, they moved fast enough to see the stars moving across the sky, though with them flying west, they moved more slowly. Henry had never really noticed the stars, but the sight of them moving from west to east struck him with a sense of profound wrongness. For a second, he thought he was going to be sick, but it passed.

The sun rose in the west and inched its way up until it was only slightly above the horizon. Hermes veered away to go around a storm cloud. After that, they flew on for a few seconds before stopping in front of a sheer cliff face.

The terrain reminded him of the desert he'd stopped on a few days before, but there were differences he couldn't place his finger on. The waves made a muted sound as they crashed against the shore, and the wind carried an eerie howl. Behind him, the clouds rumbled. This place felt dead. A structure perched on the edge of the cliff. Though it was made of yellow sandstone, the architecture was the very image of ancient Greece. Pillars held up a peaked stone roof, twice as long as it was wide. The building sat on a platform with stairs leading up on every side. Through the pillars on the side facing the cliff, Henry could just make out a door, though he couldn't see anything inside.

"Here we are," Hermes said.

Henry's heart pounded. He tried to swallow his fear, but his mouth had gone completely dry. For a second, he couldn't remember why fighting Medusa had sounded like such a good idea.

"Should I fight her now or should I wait until day?" he asked.

"It's up to you," Hermes said. "You're the one who was in a hurry. If you want my opinion, don't fight her at all. Just go to the Oracle and ask about the war."

"But then Andromeda," he let the statement hang.

"Oh come on, Henry. She may look human, but she's not. She's not even real."

"Neither is Medusa."

"For the record, this is stupider than when you followed me into the volcano."

"Wish me luck," Henry said.

He floated down, pulling the shield off of his back and strapped it onto his left arm. He drew the sword. His hands were sweaty, and he kept thinking he'd drop the weapon, but the hilt clung to him even more than he clung to it. He landed as lightly as he could near the entrance to the temple, but in the dead quiet of the night, it sounded like a thunderclap to his ears. He froze. The darkness played tricks on his eyes, and he kept imagining a monster leaping out at him.

Once he was sure no one had heard him, he stepped around the corner and into the temple. A dark hall spread out before him. He could only see up to a few feet away. His eyes adjusted slowly, and for several minutes, he saw monsters in every corner. He almost told himself to stop imagining things, but then he remembered that there really were monsters in this building.

He crept down the hall. Sand from outside had blown in and crunched under his feet. The faint hint of saltwater carried on the wind was overpowered by a smell somewhere between sweat and fresh cut grass. He came to an opening and peered into it, but while the hall was illuminated, if only dimly, by the starlight, the room was pitch black. He thought he heard the sound of breathing coming from inside, but it could just as easily have been the wind blowing through the building.

"This is pointless," he said.

"Yes, it is," a gravelly voice came from behind.

Henry yelped and turned around. A large shape was silhouetted against the stars. It looked almost human, but two large masses came out of its back. He could only guess those were wings. Henry closed his eyes and lifted the shield in front of his face. He thrust his sword forward, but there was a sound of metal on metal as it was hit aside. If not for the peculiar properties of the weapon, he was sure it would've flown from his grasp.

"Now, that's a rude way to treat your host."

The shadow in front of him chuckled. The sound made a chill run down his back. He took a step back and tripped over a rock. His eyes flew open as he fell. He threw his hands back to catch himself, but the shadow slashed against his stomach. Pain blossomed, and Henry screamed. He heard a scraping from deeper in the temple as something came closer.

"Don't worry about this one, sisters," the shadow in front of him said.

The shadow leaned in close. Henry tried to scurry away, but he felt something cold against his throat. He pictured outside in his mind and felt himself start to rise, but the shadow brought her weight down on him. He felt the sandals being torn from his feet, and the gorgon bent over him. He could see her hair writhing as she brought her face inches from his. The snakes lashed out at him, and he felt half a dozen stings on his face.

"Don't worry," the shadow said. "The venom won't kill you, not right away anyway. It would if we gave it time to do so, but I don't think that will be an issue. For now, it will just hold you immobile. We wouldn't want you to get away now, would we? It's been so long since we had live food."

The blood drained from Henry's face. He heard the sound of metal on stone as the other gorgons walked down the hall. He almost struggled, but some dim, coldly logical part of his mind told him that it wouldn't do any good. Without the sandals, he'd never be able to get away before they cut him down.

His captor dragged him by one leg further into the temple. The floor scraped across his back, and he heard his shirt tearing. He moved his arms as much as he dared, trying to find the sword, but all he felt was stone and sand. As he passed a doorway, his hand touched something hard. He closed his fingers around it and moved his wrist slightly to test it out. It was too light to be his sword, but it was better than nothing.

His captor dropped him on the floor, and a clicking sound came from the other side of the room. A few seconds later a fire lit. Henry almost gasped and dropped the object in his hand. He kept his eyes to the ground, but he managed to catch a glimpse of what he'd been holding. It was a foot-long bone. He wondered if it was human.

"Do we cook it?" the one who had captured him asked. "Or do we eat it raw?"

"It's been a long time since I tasted the lifeblood of a human,

Euryale," another said. "I think I would like to eat it raw. What of you, Medusa?"

"Take the lifeblood, Stheno," Medusa said. She spoke with a faint lisp and sounded sad. "Cook what remains when you are done."

"You always want your meat cooked," Euryale said. "Why is that? Do you still hunger for mortal ways?"

"You were born this way, sisters," Medusa said. "I was not."

"We have no place among mortals, Medusa," Stheno said. "We never did."

"It was not mortal kind that did this to me."

"The gods will fall in time," Euryale said.

"If she can really do what she claims," Medusa said. "Do not think they will just stand by and let her."

"We can discuss this later," Euryale said. "I don't like waiting too long to eat. The poison gives it a bitter taste. Take your lifeblood, Stheno. I think I will join Medusa in having cooked meat."

The shadow cast by the firelight moved towards him. It was now or never. Henry stretched out and grabbed the bone. The gorgons cried out in surprise, and he smashed it against the one nearest to him. Keeping his eyes to the ground, he ran towards the entrance. The sound of flapping wings came from above him. Henry didn't wait for it to land. He threw himself sideways into an adjoining room. Man-shaped figures decorated the area. Henry touched one and realized it was made of stone. They were Medusa's victims.

"I don't know how you're walking around with my poison in your veins," Euryale said as her shadow passed into the doorway. "It won't help you. You may as well give yourself up. My sister wants to drink your lifeblood, and I intend to give it to her even if I have to rip off your legs to keep you from running."

"Yeah, that'll make me give myself up," Henry said as he darted from one statue to another.

He couldn't tell if Euryale could see in the dark, but given how easily she'd snuck up on him, it was a safe bet. He only hoped that if he kept moving through the forest of statues, he could confuse her and eventually be able to get around her and through the door. He hoped the other two weren't guarding the way out of the room. His equipment was still in the hall. He needed his sword and shield if he was going to kill Medusa. More importantly, he needed the winged sandals if he had any hope of getting away.

Euryale stepped between two statues, forcing Henry to retreat further into the room. The light coming through the doorway was little more than a dim glow. The gorgon walked from statue to statue with a confident stride, heading right towards the statue he was hiding behind. He darted to one on his left, and she changed direction. There was nowhere left to go. He backed up and bumped into a statue. It fell to the ground with a crash, but there was something else, the sound of metal hitting stone.

"Medusa will be cross with you," Euryale said. "That was one of her favorites. He was a great hero once, but now no one even remembers his name. Do you think anyone will remember yours?"

Henry fell to his knees and pawed through the rubble of the statue. He heard scraping as the gorgon came closer. He picked up a stone and threw it at her, but she cackled. The sound made his blood run cold. He kept digging until his fingers brushed against a metal edge. He ran his fingers along the blade. The metal was rough, and Henry guessed it had been rusted. Finally, he wrapped his fingers around the hilt. Though Medusa had turned its previous owner to stone, his sword remained metal.

Even armed, Henry didn't feel very confident. The gorgon came closer, and Henry took an involuntary step back. He held the sword in front of him with two hands. He could feel it shaking in his grip.

"Don't be foolish, child," Euryale said. "You don't really think you can stop me with that, do you? The one you took it from was a greater warrior than you'll ever be, and he fell easily."

Henry's back was against the wall. The gorgon stopped right in front of him. It reached out a hand. Even in the dark, he could make out the claws. The wound on his stomach burned. Henry screeched and swung the sword as hard as he could. It hissed as it tore through the air. He half expected the gorgon to cry out in pain, but the sword struck her and shattered. She laughed again, and Henry knew he was going to die.

"I'm immortal, or didn't you know?" she asked. "No weapon, whether forged by god or man, can kill me. You, on the other hand..."

She extended a clawed hand and ran it down his cheek. It bit into his flesh, and he heard himself whimper. She moved it across his neck and then, moving faster than he could follow, she seized him by the throat and lifted him off the ground. Her claws felt like knives biting into his flesh.

"It's been a long time since I've had prey that gave me such a chase. It sets my blood aflame. I think I will join my sister in taking your lifeblood."

She carried him out the room and into the hall. At the room at the end of the corridor, the fire still burned. Two figures sat around it, and Henry squeezed his eyes shut.

"You know enough to fear Medusa's gaze, and yet you still came?" Euryale asked. "Come, tell me, human. Why are you here?"

"A puzzle?" Stheno asked with a wicked glee in her voice. "I enjoy puzzles! Let's try pulling out his entrails. He'll tell us then."

"Where's the fun in him telling us everything right away?" Medusa asked. "Let's start slow. Throw him in the cook pot for a few minutes. That should loosen his tongue a little."

"That's a good idea," Euryale said.

Henry felt himself being lifted up. A heartbeat later, he was flying through the air. He cried out as his shoulder slammed into something hard. There was a clank as a lid closed over the cook pot.

THIRTY

For a second, Henry was plunged into darkness, but after a few moments, the bottom glowed cherry red. Henry tried to lift the lid, but it wouldn't budge. He threw himself against the side of the pot. It rocked slightly but otherwise didn't move.

"Getting hot in there, isn't it?" a voice said, though from within the cook pot, it was impossible to tell which of the sisters had spoken.

The realization hit him like a ton of bricks. It wasn't hot. It wasn't even warm. He put his hand to the bottom of the pot. He was aware of its temperature, but it was a clinical sort of knowledge, like how he might know it was raining by looking out a window.

"Hermes?" he said quietly. "Are you here?"

He sat there, waiting for a reply, but none came. Then, he understood. It wasn't Hermes. It was Hephaestus. Specifically, it was the cloak he'd made. Henry had never imagined this when Hephaestus told him it would protect him from heat and cold. That was twice the smith's gifts had saved his life. Maybe if he could get his hands on the sword and shield they could save him a third time.

"Please, let me out," he cried out, trying to make his voice sound desperate. "Please, I'll tell you anything you want to know."

"Well that's disappointing," one of the sisters said.

"That was too easy," another said. "I wanted to pull out his entrails."

"We can still do that."

"It's not the same if we're not questioning him."

"At least you still get to eat the lifeblood of a human."

"I won't if we don't get him out of the pot."

The lid shifted a little, and Henry prepared himself to leap out.

"Are we sure we want to let him out? I've heard meat is best when it's cooked in its own juices."

"We don't all like our meat cooked, Medusa."

"Fine," Medusa said. "Let him out. We'll find out why he came and then we'll eat him."

"Look away, sister, we don't want you turning our dinner to stone."

The lid came off the pot, and Henry threw himself into the air. One of the gorgon's claws grazed his arm, and he wondered how damaged the shirt would have to be before it no longer protected him against poison. He couldn't stop to think about that now, however. He hit the ground and rolled. The gorgons let out a shriek of surprise. Henry got to his feet and ran, but he didn't go to the door. He ran back at the fire.

Two of the gorgons came at him, but the third had her eyes averted. Henry ducked under the attacks and grabbed a log from the fire. He shoved it at Medusa. The fire sizzled against her skin, and the smell almost made him gag. She screamed, and he ran back the way he'd come. Again, he heard the sound of flapping overhead, but this time, it was more than one. He looked around. The light of his improvised torch reflected off something shiny.

One of the gorgons dove at him, and Henry fell to the ground to avoid her. The claws missed him by a hair, and he scrambled toward the object he'd seen. It was the shield. He picked it up and rolled onto his back just in time to catch another gorgon's claw on it. The impact pressed him into the ground, and the torch fell from his hand. He didn't have time to pick it up again. He got to his feet just as one of the sisters landed in front of him. Henry threw himself to one side, afraid to meet the gaze of the one who might be Medusa. He slammed into another. Its claws raked across his chest, and he smashed her face with his shield. She screamed.

"So you're Medusa," he said under his breath.

He ran back towards the entrance and scanned the ground for either his sword or his sandals, but most of the temple was still shrouded in darkness. His impromptu torch sputtered out leaving the fire at the end of the hall as the only light source. He ran back to where the torch had been, sure that his sword must be nearby. He heard another scream and barely had time to drop to the ground before a gorgon sailed over him.

"You're toying with me," he said quietly.

"How perceptive," Euryale said from right beside him.

"Not this time," Henry said.

He held his shield before him and ran with full speed. He braced himself as he slammed into her. It was like crashing into a brick wall. He fell back, but he was ready for it and got to his feet, sidestepping the gorgon. He took a few steps and almost tripped. Something clattered a few feet away. He took in a sharp breath. The sword.

A scraping came from behind, and Henry threw himself forward. He reached blindly, and his hand closed around the blade.

He bit back the pain as he landed on his side. Moving his hand to the hilt, he grimaced. Pain shot through his hand as he gripped the weapon.

"So the hero has his sword," Stheno said from beside him.

Henry swung. Though he couldn't put much power behind the blow, it slammed into the beast. The sword rang against the immortal creature, but even a blade forged by Hephaestus himself couldn't pierce her skin. The slash was only a distraction, and he kept moving.

He moved towards the entrance, dodging and attacking the gorgons as he did. He needed more light than the fire would provide. A shriek came from behind, and he turned to catch the attack on his shield. The momentum sent him tumbling out the door. He came to stop just before he fell off the stairs, but another gorgon crashed into him. Pain shot through his injured shoulder as he fell down the stairs. The cliff edge rushed at him. In a panic, he stabbed into the sandstone half expecting the sword to break, but whether it was due to the strength of the steel or the weakness of the stone, the sword held.

Henry felt his feet dangling over the edge. One of the gorgons landed on the stairs in front of him. The moonlight glinted off her brass talons. Her skin, if it could be called skin, was covered in dark scales. Bat-like wings protruded from her back. His eyes were drawn up to her face before he could stop himself. Tusks like those of a boar jutted out of a mouth too big for that face. Her hair writhed around her head, and several of the snakes lashed out at him, but he was still too far. Then, he looked into her eyes. Black spheres with no white in them at all stared back at him. His breath caught in his throat, and too late he remembered to avert his eyes.

Nothing happened.

"Not Medusa, then," he said.

"I want your lifeblood, human," Stheno said. "I'll not be denied it."

"You will if I fall," Henry said.

He knew it was a desperate gamble. Stheno apparently did as well. She laughed. Quicker than he could follow, her hand lashed out and clamped around his wrist. She lifted him up, and it was like a thousand needles stabbing into his arm. He slammed the shield into her face as hard as he could, but if she noticed, she gave no sign.

"You've led us on a fine little chase, but it's time we brought it to an end."

She brought a clawed hand up to his chest and pressed it in. A trickle of blood ran down his chest and was absorbed by the fabric of his shirt. The two other gorgons landed nearby. Henry flailed wildly with his shield, hitting both. One gave no more reaction than Stheno had, but the other recoiled, though only slightly.

"He's a feisty one, isn't he?"

"No more games," Stheno said. "I mean to have his blood right now."

She slammed him against the ground, and one of the stairs jabbed into his back. Henry cried out in pain. He knew this was his only chance. He reached out to pick up his sword. Stheno jabbed a claw deeper into his chest, but he ignored it. The sword came free easier than he would've believed. He swung it at Medusa. Though the arm that held it was injured and he swung while on his back, Hephaestus blade stuck true.

Medusa screamed in pain as a clawed foot fell off her body. The other gorgons froze, staring at the foot as it tumbled down the stairs and off the cliff. Henry took advantage of the reprieve and got to his feet. He turned away from Medusa and gazed into his shield. He swung the sword behind him, trusting the smith's power to overcome the awkward angle. Stheno and Euryale screamed. In his shield, he saw the sword cleave into Medusa's neck with far more strength than he'd put in it. It sheared through the monster's throat as if it was made of paper. Her head fell to the ground and rolled down the stairs. Panic filled Henry, and he leaped for it, catching it by the serpentine hair. The body stood erect for a second before it fell. Blood poured from the neck and ran down the stairs before dripping into the ocean below.

THIRTY-ONE

The gorgons wailed at the death of their sister. Euryale jumped at him. Henry held the severed head in front of him expecting her to turn to stone, but she only cried louder. At the last second, he ducked under her attack. If she'd been lucid, he never would've avoided it, but she was mad with grief. So was Stheno.

The gorgons attacked, one after the other, never giving him a moment's rest. After the first few, he abandoned attacking with the sword. It wasn't doing any good, and he concentrated on the shield. His arm throbbed from the constant impacts. He had to use both arms to hold it up. The constant crashing of brass claws against his shield sent pangs of pain down his body. The sound and pains reminded him of Hephaestus's forge. Again and again, it came. The power of the blows made his legs scream. He couldn't bear the weight anymore. He fell onto his back and tucked in his legs, trying to cover his body with the shield.

Next to him, the blood flow out of Medusa's body had ceased.

It had drained of color. One of the gorgons came down on him and brushed her body. It twitched. Another attack came, but instead of crashing against the shield, she raked against his feet. Henry cried out. The force of the blow spun him around, and he scraped his back on the stone.

He was pressed against the dead gorgon. Her skin shuddered as the sisters landed next to him. They each put a talon on the edge of the shield and launched themselves into the air. He tried to hold on, but his arms were a bruised mess, and he didn't have the strength anymore. Held by the strap, he lifted into the air for a few feet before slipping away. He fell onto Medusa's body, and she cried out. Henry rolled off her and stared at it. Even the gorgons landed and gaped as his shield clattered down the stairs.

Medusa's body began to shake. It squealed as a red lump came out of the stump of her neck. The hole stretched and a lump became a snout, followed by a long head. It opened its mouth and let out a whinny. Blood flaked off, and he realized it wasn't red. It was white. For a second, Henry thought she would get up again with a horse's head, but the animal kept forcing its way out.

The hole grew bigger, and hooved legs emerged. Henry's jaw dropped, and it fell even further as the horse's body came out. Feathered wings extended from its back. It flapped as it pulled the rest of its body out, and the blood rolled off of him leaving a coat so white it shone even in the light of the crescent moon. The stallion danced back and forth, oblivious to both the uneven ground and the monsters around it. Henry gaped. He had forgotten that according to the myth, this was how this creature had been born.

"Pegasus."

Pegasus cocked his head at his name. One of the gorgons neared him, and the horse reared and slammed his hooves on the gorgon's face. She pulled back. Pegasus turned so his flank was to Henry and looked at him. Henry's eyes went wide. He nodded and threw his leg over the horse. Pegasus reared again and galloped down the stairs. Henry half expected him to trip, but he made it to the cliff and kept running. He extended his wings. Spread out, they were wider than he was tall. They glided through the air. Henry heard screaming behind them. He looked behind and saw the gorgons flying after them. He leaned in close.

"I hope you can fly faster than they can," he said into the horse's ear. "My sword isn't much good against them, and I don't have my shield anymore."

It might have been his imagination, but he could've sworn the horse nodded. Pegasus flapped his wings and started climbing at an alarming speed. He spread his wings and made a wide turn until they were facing the gorgons. Pegasus tucked his wings in and dove. Henry screamed, sure that at any moment, he'd feel their claws on him, but Pegasus was too fast. The wind tore at Henry. They flew so close he could make out individual snakes in their hair. Just before they crashed into the temple stairs, Pegasus spread his wings. Suddenly, they weren't going down but forward. The change of direction was so abrupt Henry expected to hear wings breaking. They landed on the ground a few feet from the shield. Henry stared at the horse, not sure if he believed the animal had understood him. Pegasus snorted and tossed his head. Henry looked up. The gorgons were heading towards him again. He jumped off the horse just long enough to pick up the shield. He didn't even have time to get a good grip before Pegasus launched himself into the air again. There was the sound of metal on stone as the gorgons landed behind them. By the time Henry turned to look at them, they were in the air again.

Pegasus's speed was nowhere near what Henry had done when wearing the sandals. The gorgons remained right behind him, neither gaining nor falling back. Henry started to worry. As impressive an animal as he might be, Pegasus was mortal, and Henry didn't know how long he could keep ahead of the gorgons.

In the distance, lightning flashed in the clouds. Thunder rumbled. Henry remembered Hephaestus's warning, and the hairs on the back of his neck stood on end. Pegasus turned to avoid it, but Henry leaned in.

"No, let's go through it." Pegasus whinnied, and Henry could almost hear the question in it. "Even other gods fear Zeus's power. We just might be able to lose them in the storm."

Pegasus nodded, though Henry had no idea how he could identify it as such. The dark clouds grew as they neared. He clenched his teeth as they flew into the storm.

THIRTY-TWO

As soon as he passed into the clouds, his face was drenched. He felt ice forming on the tip of his nose. Lightning flashed in the same instance thunder crashed. Henry covered his ears with his hands, but he felt as much as heard it. It reverberated through his flesh, and his bones felt like they were melting. Lightning arced between clouds. The air smelled of ozone. He forced himself to hold his shield in front of him. According to the smith, that would be his only defense against lightning. He took the sword off his back and strapped it to the inside of the shield. It wouldn't do to have a lightning rod on his back.

He glanced over his shoulder, but the clouds were too thick for him to see through. Lightning smashed into his shield. The force of the impact almost threw him off of Pegasus. The shield crackled and glowed bright blue. A heartbeat later, lightning streaked off the shield into the sky. He barely had time to steady himself before a gorgon shot out of the darkness. He didn't get a chance to react.

Pegasus spread his wings, and they flew backward, caught on the air currents of the storm.

Pegasus shot back with Henry pressed against the stallion's neck, and the gorgon flew past. Henry pushed himself up. It was sheer chance that he heard flapping overhead. He looked up just as a gorgon dove for him. He brought his shield to bear. In the same instant that bronze talons struck god-forged steel, lightning flashed again. Henry didn't know if it was attracted to the shield, the talons, or if the strike happened by chance. The gorgon screamed as electricity ran through her to the shield, and again as it was reflected away. She fell, and her body tumbled into the clouds below.

"One down," Henry said.

Pegasus screamed. Henry looked down and saw a wide gash along the horse's side just as another gorgon disappeared into the clouds. Blood mixed with water streaming down the flank. An instant later, the gorgon rose up and struck at the horse again. Henry tried to get to her, but she kept out of reach.

"Dive, Pegasus," Henry strained to be heard over the storm. "I have an idea."

The winged horse tucked in its wings and swooped downward. A second later, they were beneath the storm and heading for the icy sea below. Henry looked up and the gorgon came out of the clouds.

"Pull up!"

Pegasus spread his wings as Henry drew his sword. The gorgon, caught off guard by the maneuver, closed the distance faster than expected. She pulled up no more than a foot above them. Henry slashed, not at the body, but at the brass claws. He knew he wouldn't be able to pierce the immortal's skin, but as he'd hoped, her talons closed around the blade. Henry released it and leaned into Pegasus. The horse understood and dove again. An instant later, the storm rumbled. Lightning shot at the gorgon and struck the blade. She screamed and released the sword, and both fell towards the water. Without needing to be told, Pegasus matched the sword's speed. Henry grabbed it and hid it behind the shield again. Pegasus climbed back into the storm and over it. Only when they were far above the storm did Henry sheath his sword, and the two flew north. Henry just hoped they'd make it in time.

THIRTY-THREE

The storm dissipated after a few hours. Pegasus's flaps became slow and labored. Their flight was erratic, and Henry worried they wouldn't make it much farther. He scanned the surface of the ocean for somewhere to land, but there was water as far as the eye could see. He tried to lean over to examine the mount's wound. He could see that it was bad, but he didn't know enough of either horses or first aid to say anything else. It took several hours to be sure, but they were definitely descending.

"Hermes, we could really use some help right now," he called to the air, but there was no response.

As the sun was setting, they finally found a chain of rocky islands where they set down. His feet were covered with blood from cuts the gorgons had given him, and the rocks hurt to walk on. His stomach growled but he pushed back his hunger to examine Pegasus's wound. It didn't look as bad as it had from the air. In fact, it didn't look like a serious wound at all. He pulled out a pack of bandages and herbs Hephaestus had given him. He washed the wound and did what he could to bandage it, but what he had was meant for humans, and the bandages weren't big enough. He bent down and wrapped his feet as well before eating. He spent the night getting what sleep he could lying on a rock. He woke the next morning and looked under the bandages. His feet still looked like ground beef, but when he examined Pegasus, the wound had completely healed.

"The work of the gods?" Henry asked the horse. "Or is that just how you heal naturally?"

Pegasus stamped his feet and looked at Henry. He threw his head up in the air and extended his wings.

"All right," Henry said. "We need to go higher. Let's see if Hephaestus was able to make do on his promise."

Pegasus nodded. Henry got on, and they flew into the sky. Even at the speed Pegasus could climb, it took almost half an hour for them to get high enough to catch the south wind. Henry knew right away when they had reached the wind's territory. The nearness of the sun already had him sweating, but suddenly, there was a new source of heat, one carried by the wind itself. Pegasus sensed it too and the flying horse spread his wings. The ground became a blur of color. It wasn't fast enough to see the sun move as he'd done with Hermes, but it was still faster than he'd traveled with the sandals alone. At midday, he saw a figure in the distance. It grew slowly until he was able to identify the form of Atlas. He leaned down against the horse's neck.

"Let's put down," he yelled over the wind. "We could both use a rest."

Pegasus tucked in his wings, and they descended, touching down near the titan's feet, where the Moirai were waiting for him. He'd given their previous conversation a lot of thought, and now he believed he understood how they worked.

"Are Andromeda and her parents okay?" he asked Lachesis. He couldn't actually tell them apart, but he suspected she always stood in the center.

"Yes."

He turned to the Clotho with his question about the past. "Have they been hurt?"

"They have," she said. "Their physical wounds faded days ago."

"Their hearts still ache," the middle one said. "Andromeda most of all."

"Why Andromeda?"

"She will be forced to marry her conqueror," Atropos said.

"When?"

"You need rest," the middle one said.

"When?" He almost yelled. "Sorry," he said, a bit sheepishly. "Please, just tell me when."

"Tonight," Atropos said.

Henry leaped back on Pegasus. "I have to go."

"Even carried by the south wind, your steed needs rest, else he will not make it."

"But Andromeda..."

"There are still a few hours," she said. "Rest your mount. The south wind can carry you there with time to spare."

"Will Medusa's head be enough to stop them?"

"If you charge in like a warrior, you will face their army. Even Medusa's head won't protect you from the rain of arrows they will send against you. You will destroy many, but it won't be enough. You will die before the vows are spoken, and your death will not protect her."

"I thought you couldn't see my future," Henry said.

Atropos bowed her head. "This is not sight but sense."

"How do I save her then?"

"How would you attend the wedding of a princess?"

"My clothes are ruined," he said. "I won't exactly make an ideal guest."

"Are they?" Lachesis asked.

Henry looked down. The shirt was seamless. The holes the gorgons had ripped in it were gone. Even the blood hadn't left a stain.

"How?" he asked.

"Items forged by Hephaestus are not so easily destroyed," she said. "Even when they are damaged, they tend to repair themselves. Garbed as you are, you could go before a king without giving offense."

Henry remembered his first encounter with Cepheus where he'd been wearing little more than rags.

"Not all kings demand that people appear before them like this."

"No, they don't," Atropos said. "A few permit a man to appear as they are, but if you fail, their number will decrease by one."

"What do you mean?"

"What need has a conqueror of old kings?" she asked. "He will be killed, as will his wife. Their heads will be presented to Andromeda as a wedding gift. The act will break her spirit beyond any hope of healing."

"How do I save her?"

"We have already told you all you need," they said in unison. "We can say no more."

"Forget your rules for once!" Henry yelled.

"We will say no more," they said.

Henry turned to Pegasus. The horse had wandered to a nearby stream. When he saw Henry looking at him, he raised his head and shook his mane.

"Rest," Henry said, "but don't rest too long. We don't have time."

The horse nodded once and closed his eyes. Henry stared at he for a second before he realized he was asleep on his feet. Henry sat down and pulled out a light lunch from his pack. Occasionally, he glared at the Moirai, but they didn't seem to care. Instead, they were occupied by weaving. Clotho spun thread from around a ridged tube before passing it to Lachesis who measured the thread and handed it to Atropos. The last Moirai snipped the string with a pair of bronze scissors. The sound made Henry's mouth go dry. The Moirai spun lives and cut them when their time was up. He wondered who had just died. By the time he finished eating and refilled his water skins at the stream, Pegasus stirred. He walked over to Henry and nuzzled his shoulder.

"Are you ready?"

The horse nodded. Henry got on, and once again, they climbed to catch the south wind. Once they were high enough, Pegasus spread his wings wide, and Atlas disappeared behind them.

THIRTY-FOUR

The sun was still high in the sky when the buildings of
Aethiopia appeared beneath them. They circled the city,
descending slowly. If the Moirai were right, and from
what he understood, they always were, he needed to be seen by
everyone. He needed to be someone the conquerors couldn't ignore.
Once they were ten feet off the ground, Henry guided Pegasus to
the main street through the city. They glided down it and landed
before the steps of the palace. A circle of guards dressed in armor he
didn't recognize surrounded him. Most had dark hair, a thing he
hadn't often seen in Joppa. They leveled their spears. Henry
dismounted and tried to maintain the appearance of calm. One of
them stepped forward.

"Lord Alexander?"

Henry stared at him, then his eyes went wide. Though he didn't
remember the man's name, he was one of Cepheus's personal
guards.

"I see you've gone over to serve your enemies," Henry said.

"At the instructions of her father, milord," he said. "I would've fought to my last breath, but once the city was lost, he ordered me to surrender so that I might protect the princess."

"This man is an ally of Cepheus?" One of the other guards scowled.

"No captain. He is an ally of the princess and is the man who slew Cetus. He is a great hero, as you can see with your own eyes."

"What do you want, Alexander?" the captain said.

"I want to pay my respects to the princess and her husband-to-be."

"You were not invited."

"Didn't you hear me?" the other guard said. "He killed Cetus. You can try to bar his way, but you won't succeed. In any case, do you think King Polydectes would want a man such as this to leave without seeing him?"

The captain looked from Henry to the guard. Henry made a point of stroking Pegasus's mane. The gesture was not lost on the captain who gaped at the horse. As if on cue, Pegasus spread his wings wide and reared. As one, the circle of guards took a step back, but the winged horse just nuzzled at Henry's shoulder. Sweat sheened on the captain's brow. He looked at the sword sheathed at Henry's back.

"You cannot enter the palace so armed, Lord Alexander."

Henry drew the sword and held it before him. He smirked as if daring the guard to try to take it. The blade gleamed in the sunlight, brighter than any weapon of iron or bronze ever could. The captained shoved his spear at Henry, and Henry swung the sword without bothering to put much strength into the blow. The god forged steel sheared through the shaft as if it were made of paper. The guard's eyes bulged, and some of the other guards pressed in closer. For a moment, Henry thought he'd made a mistake.

"I told you," Cepheus's former guard said. "He killed by accident the thing that devastated Aethiopia's entire army. If he meant the king harm, we wouldn't be able to stop him."

The captain's face reddened. His hand went up to draw the sword at his back, but another guard stepped forward and put a hand on the captain's shoulder. The voice was too soft for Henry to hear. The captain scowled at him, but his hand dropped. He gave Henry a curt gesture and walked through the doors to the palace. Henry followed. As he passed Cepheus's guard, he saw sweat on the man's brow. Henry smiled at him. The guard shook his head, but Henry saw the smirk on his face.

The halls were stark. The conquerors had stripped it of all decorations. Their footsteps echoed through the corridor. Twice, they passed men patrolling, and in both cases, the patrols had the dark hair of the invaders. It heartened Henry. The fact that this Polydectes needed guards inside the palace said the people of Aethiopia were not entirely defeated.

As they neared the throne room, the sound of music wafted down the hall. The captain's steps quickened. He exchanged a few words with the men guarding the door. One went in and brought a beady-eyed, rat-faced man. He was dressed in fine clothes, but that just made him look like a well-dressed rat.

"How would you like me to announce you, lord?" he asked.

Henry answered, and for a moment, he thought the little man's eyes would pop out of his sockets. Henry nodded and gave him a dismissive gesture. The guard captain's hands clenched into fists, and his knuckles went white. Henry grinned at him. Inside, he heard the chamberlain announce him.

"Lord Henry Alexander Gideon, traverser of the Inferno,

destroyer of Cetus, survivor of Circe, slayer of Medusa, ally of the Princess Andromeda, of Hermes the Messenger, and Hephaestus the Smith."

The room went silent as Henry stepped into the room.

He felt every eye on him. He kept his back stiff and held his head high. Almost every head bore dark hair. The crowd parted, and a way opened to a man wearing gold-plated armor and a purple robe. A ruby encrusted crown rested on his head. Anger pulsed in his gray eyes. Andromeda stood next to him. When their eyes met, her face lit up in a smile. Henry walked towards them, but as he neared, two guards crossed their spears before him. Henry considered repeating the performance he'd done for the captain, but in this situation, it probably wouldn't do much good. Instead, he fell to his knees.

"King Polydectes," he said without raising his head. "I wanted to wish you congratulations on your wedding day."

"Thank you. Lord Alexander is it?" He spoke slowly and his words were careful. "You may rise. I must say we did not expect the presence of so great a hero such as you."

"The honor is mine," Henry said. "With your permission, I would like to speak to your bride."

The crowd took a collective gasp. Polydectes clenched his teeth, but Henry didn't give him a chance to respond. He extended his hand. Andromeda took it, and he pulled her into the crowd.

"What are you doing?" she asked. "I was half expecting him to call the guards on you."

"There's no time," he said, his voice pitched low. "That little stunt bought me a few minutes if I'm lucky. Where is your father?"

"Over there," she said, pointing to the side of the room where the thrones sat. "Polydectes said there will be a formal transfer of power once we're married."

"I need to speak to them. Are they guarded?"

Andromeda shook her head. "Polydectes said if they even stand up from the throne before he gives permission, he'll have me executed after the wedding. That's all the incentive they need."

"Good," he said. "I'm going to present a wedding gift in a little while. When I do, shield your eyes."

"You're not going to save me?" she asked.

Her voice squeaked, and Henry noticed several people staring at them.

"I will," he said softly, "but not quite the way you expect. Excuse me."

He left her and made his way through the crowd. He thanked whatever gods might be listening that she didn't know what the Fates had said Polydectes would do to her parents after the wedding. As he walked, he heard scattered whispers of "Lord Alexander." He smirked as he reached the end of the room. Seated on golden thrones were Cepheus and Cassiopeia.

"King Cepheus," Henry said, quiet, but still loud enough for those around to hear. "I hope you will forgive me for not bowing."

"I'm hardly a king anymore, Lord Alexander," he said, "I don't deserve your honor."

"You are king for a little while longer," Henry said. He took a step closer and leaned in, speaking so only the king and queen could hear. "With my help, you can be that king again."

Cepheus's eyes went wide. He looked at Henry, not daring to believe what he'd heard.

"Our mistakes almost killed our daughter once," Cepheus said. "I will not allow them to do so again. Andromeda may not be happy, but at least she's safe. Please don't do anything to jeopardize that."

"Is anyone here loyal to you?" Henry asked.

"Lord Alexander, Henry, please don't do this," Cassiopeia said. "Our daughter..."

"I can save your kingdom and your daughter," he said. "Just like I did before. I just need you to trust me."

Tears welled in her eyes, but she nodded.

Cepheus shook his head. "Those loyal to me who were not killed were either imprisoned or regulated to menial positions. A bare handful of my personal guards have gone over to the other side with the intention of protecting my daughter, for all the good that will do. Most of them aren't allowed anywhere important."

"Good," Henry said without thinking.

"What do you mean 'good'?"

"I meant good that none of your people are here. I'm going to present a gift to Polydectes. When I do, don't look at it."

He backed up without saying another word. A bearded man in the crowd called Henry over and begged him to tell the story of how he'd killed Cetus. Henry told a story, though the only relation it had to the truth was that Cetus was dead at the end of it. He told nothing about the sheer terror he'd felt, and every action was deliberate. He even gave Virgil a heroic role. When he was done, the crowd cheered. Henry went on to tell of his encounter with Circe and his conversation with Atlas. He explained each of the titles he'd given to the chamberlain. When he told them about his battle with Medusa and her sisters, and his subsequent escape into the storm, several expressed doubts.

"I will prove it to you," Henry called out at the top of his lungs.

He charged up to Polydectes again.

"My king," he said, deliberately slurring his words as if he'd had too much to drink. He hoped that would throw everyone else off guard. "Your people have accused me of being a liar. I demand to prove them wrong."

"A duel, Lord Alexander? On my wedding day?"

"No sire, not a duel. I merely wish to present you with a trophy of my travels. Consider it a wedding gift."

"A trophy? Really?" the usurper asked. "By all means, show me what you have."

Henry smiled and made his way to the king, deliberately stumbling every few steps. The crowd laughed, but his stories had made him the center of attention, and everyone was staring at him. Once he stood next to the king, he reached into his pack. He could feel the dead snakes in Medusa's hair squishing between his fingers. He pulled it out and held it inches from Polydectes's face. The king recoiled. His gray eyes went wide. Henry's breath caught in his throat, afraid it hadn't worked, but then the gray of Polydectes's eyes started to expand. After a second, his eyes had no white in them at all. He cried, but the color spread to his mouth and cut him off. It traveled down his body, leaving only his robe and crown unchanged. Before anyone could say anything, the conquering king had turned to stone.

THIRTY-FIVE

The room went dead quiet. Henry couldn't tell if anyone was even breathing. He wasn't sure he was. He'd heard the stories. He'd known what Medusa's head could do, but that knowledge hadn't prepared him for the reality of the situation. Nearby, he saw Andromeda's face in her hands. She was shaking, obviously terrified. The sight brought him back to reality. He swung the head at the guards. They moved to attack but froze where they stood. Then, he held the monster above his head, desperately hoping Cepheus and Cassiopeia weren't watching.

Those nearest tried to turn away, but it was too late. The statues spread out like a wave. A few had time to let out the beginnings of a scream, but they were cut short. A few seconds later, the entire room stood still, and statues stared at him with expressions of sheer terror. Henry stuffed the head in his pack. He walked over to Andromeda and put an arm around her. She looked up and gasped.

"My parents?" Her voice was almost too soft to hear.

He strained to see across the room, but the statues blocked his sight.

"I gave them the same warning I gave you," he said. "Let's go see."

It felt eerie walking through the statues that had been human only moments ago. They were so realistic that he kept on expecting one to jump out at him. They hadn't even made it halfway through the mass of statues when Cassiopeia's voice shattered the silence.

"Mother?" Andromeda said.

A second later, she was off. She ran so recklessly that she knocked down a number of statues which fell to the ground and shattered. Henry winced at each one, still barely able to believe they really were all stone. The king and queen came through the statues, and Andromeda threw herself at them. Henry saw tears streaming down every face. He felt them well up in his eyes as well, as he remembered the images of his home that the Moirai had shown him. He wiped away his tears before he went to join the royal family.

"Lord Alexander," Cassiopeia said. "You have saved our kingdom twice over. You have saved our daughter."

"Don't you still have their army to deal with?"

Cepheus shook his head. "Nearly every general and most of the high-ranking nobles were here. The army remains, but there is no one to lead them. What is it you want, Lord Alexander? Anything within my power to give is yours."

"I just want to go home," Henry said, "but that's not something you can give me. Aside from that, I need to see the Oracle of Delphi."

"Of course," Cepheus said. "I'll send a messenger right away. Just tell me your question."

"No," Henry said. "I need to go in person."

Cepheus nodded. "Very well. I'll arrange an escort."

Henry shook his head. "I can go faster on my own."

"But Lord Alexander…"

"I've gone a long way since the last time we spoke, Your Majesty," Henry said. "Trust me. I only need to know the way."

Cepheus looked around at the room full of statues and nodded. "I suppose you have proven that you can deal with great challenges. At least let me prepare a banquet, something fitting a man such as you."

"Prepare the banquet then," Henry said, "but I won't wait to see the Oracle. By the time it's ready, I'll be back."

"Hermes's winged sandals?"

"I'm afraid I lost those in the fight with Medusa," Henry said, "but I've found another way to travel."

The king looked at him in confusion, but Henry motioned for him to follow. They had to move carefully to avoid the guards in the hall, but that was no great challenge. They left the palace through a side entrance and made their way around to the front. There, still surrounded by the circle of guards, stood Pegasus.

"Amazing," Cepheus said.

Just then, a horn sounded. Most of the guards rushed inside the palace. Only two remained outside.

"That's Captain Cyril," Cepheus said. "He's loyal. Together, you should be able to take the other one without difficulty."

Henry nodded and drew his sword. He stepped out into the open, and both the guards leveled their spears. Cyril flinched when he saw who it was, but when Cepheus stepped beside him, the guard nodded and turned his spear on his companion.

"Traitor," the foreigner said, but he threw down his weapon.

"Not now," Cyril said. "Not ever." He turned to Cepheus and inclined his head. "My king. Is it time to take our kingdom back?"

"Yes," Cepheus said. "Their entire leadership has been destroyed."

Cyril looked at Henry. "Lord Alexander?"

"As great a hero as ever walked the streets of Joppa," the king said. "Do you know where to find those who still support me?"

"I do, my king," Cyril said.

"Very well then. We take back our land." Cepheus turned to Henry. "Go to the west. A man on a fast horse can make it to the mountains in a week. With that horse, I don't know. On the southwest slope of the tallest mountain in the area, you will find the temple where the Oracle resides."

"Thank you," Henry said.

"Sire, should we not enlist his aid?" the captain asked.

"No, I think not. He's done enough for us," he said. "This is our land, and we will take it back. Make haste my friend. We will take this land before long, and I have promised you a great feast."

Henry laughed and clasped the king's arm and then the captain's. They had already disappeared into a building when Henry took to the air.

THIRTY-SIX

Henry flew high to avoid attracting attention. After everything that had happened, he kept expecting to see harpies or furies on his way, but the skies between Joppa and the Oracle were blissfully silent. It took less than a day to reach the mountains. Though clouds hid the tallest peaks, he had no trouble determining which towered over the others. While most looked like they had only their tops obscured, one was so massive that Henry guessed that half of it rose above the clouds.

He flew to the southwest face. A town sprawled out on a flat outcropping. Like Joppa, most were squat buildings made of white marble. A large building with a gold roof dominated the area. It looked like every street ended at the temple. Henry landed a little ways away from it and walked Pegasus to the entrance. The flying horse attracted the eyes of onlookers, but not as many as he would've expected.

Gold decorated many of the buildings. Some had crude figurines in the windows while others had intricate scenes depicting battles or celebrations carved into a wall. Images of the sun were common as were engravings of a young man with a smooth face and short curly hair. Henry was surprised that so much of it was out in the open where anyone could take it, but then this city, possibly more than any other city in the whole of Kurnugi, was protected by the power of a god as well as an Oracle who could see the future.

He reached the base of the stairs leading up to the temple. A statue of the man he'd seen in the carvings sat in a chariot. The entire thing was made of gold. Henry circled it to get a better look. The man wore a robe and carried a drawn bow. His muscles were tense. The horses of the chariot shone in the sunlight. Each of the horses were at least twice as tall as Henry was. Their muscles bulged, and they looked like they were in a full gallop. The wheels of the chariot blazed in golden flame. Carvings on the chariot depicted the story of the rider. First, there were two babies on an island. Next to it was the image of the rider over a dead serpent. Then, the rider holding his bow, and another with him strumming a lyre. Finally, there was the rider, in his chariot, flying through the sky with shafts of light coming from the wheels. The statue of Apollo looked so real, Henry almost expected it to ride off the platform and leap into the sky.

He walked up the stairs. Two guards wearing red robes and armed with bows moved to stand before him. They were both young men, no older than he was. In fact, the one on the left looked a few years younger. Their short blond hair almost gleamed, and their skin was bronzed from the sun. The only word he could think of to describe them was pretty. It was like they had been selected for how similar they looked to their patron god. Their muscles were lean and they carried their bows as if knowing how to use them. Henry wondered if they were really capable of killing an intruder, but when he saw the hard gaze in their eyes, he suspected they wouldn't balk at it. In spite of their youth, he knew he wouldn't be able to bluff his way past them the way he'd done with the guards at Joppa.

"I'm here to see the Oracle," he said.

He considered adding an introduction similar to the one he'd given to the chamberlain at the wedding, but given the types of people who came here, he doubted a few titles would impress them.

"The Oracle is not seeing petitioners today," the one on the left said. He had a child's voice, and it was obvious he hadn't gone through puberty.

"Look," Henry said as he took a step forward.

The children raised their bows and drew arrows back. Henry froze. Their muscles were tense, and their aim was level. They looked at him the way any adult might look at a child. He almost pulled out his shield, but if he tried that, he doubted he'd survive the attempt, not with their arrows already trained on him. He took a step back, and they lowered their weapons.

"I've been sent by the gods," Henry said. "The Moirai themselves told me to speak to the Oracle. You have to let me through."

"The Oracle is not seeing petitioners today," he said again. "You may come back tomorrow."

One day. He could wait one more day. It was almost sunset anyway, and even on Pegasus, he didn't want to leave at night.

"If I come back tomorrow, I'll be able to see her?" he asked.

"No one can see the future, save the Oracle."

"When was the last time someone actually saw her?" he asked.

Before they had a chance to answer a tall man carrying a spear appeared out of the temple. He too had curly blond hair and bronze skin. He couldn't have been more than twenty-five. He looked so similar to the guards that Henry wondered if he'd ever held the position. When he saw Henry, he froze. His face went pale.

"Henry Alexander Gideon?"

"Yes, that's me."

"The Oracle wishes to speak to you."

The guard who had spoken turned to him. "But sir, you told us..."

"I told you what the priestesses told me to tell you," he said. "Now I'm giving you new instructions. Let him through."

His voice was hard, and Henry thought he saw tears in the eyes of one of the child guards, but he bit his lip. He nodded and he and his companion moved aside. The man at the entrance motioned to Henry.

He wasn't sure if the doors they passed through were solid gold or if they were only plated. Either way, there had to be enough wealth there to buy a city. Once they passed the doorway, they were in a large room with a domed roof. A bronze brazier dominated the room. Henry could feel the heat from the bonfire. Off to one side, wood had been stacked nearly to the ceiling, and a woman in a robe carried a few pieces to the fire. Sweat glistened on her forehead, but other than that, she seemed oblivious to the heat.

"You'll have to forgive the guards," his guide said. "They only do as they're trained."

"Would they really have killed me if I hadn't stepped back?"

"Only by accident," he said in a voice that unnerved Henry with its casualness. "If you had actually tried to a pass through the door, though, they wouldn't have hesitated."

"They're so young."

"It's what is required," he said. "Those who guard the entrance must do so with the visage of our lord Apollo. We are trained from birth to defend this temple, and are door guards until the first time we shave."

"Then they become like you," Henry said.

"Most live in the city." He smiled. "A thousand men would rise to defend this place, if the need arose."

Henry thought about what the Moirai had said. He imagined soldiers looting this place and tearing down the statue at its entrance. He saw the child guards fighting and dying. The thought almost made him sick.

"I sincerely hope you never have to," he said.

"We've had to once," the guard said. "The Oracle alone knows if we'll ever have to do it again. You should consider yourself fortunate. The Oracle normally speaks to the priestesses alone and has them relay her prophecies. I've never heard of her summoning anyone. I'll leave you here. I can go no further."

They stopped before a large double door. A golden sunburst had been embossed on them. A pair of red-robed priestesses stood with curved knives. The guide bowed to them and walked away. The priestesses glared at him. He was about to ask what was wrong when they turned around. Each pushed at a door until they swung open. Once the doors had opened all the way, they returned to their positions. Smoke filled the room beyond. It smelled a little like roses. He squinted his eyes and thought he saw a figure moving inside.

"Am I supposed to go in there?"

The priestesses nodded. "The Oracle awaits."

Henry's eyes went from one woman to the other. They didn't meet his eyes. Instead, they just stared forward as if he didn't exist. Henry took in a breath and stepped into the chamber of the Oracle of Delphi.

THIRTY-SEVEN

Henry's head swam as he passed through the cloud of smoke. On either side, fires burned giving off more smoke than they should. Shadows danced on the edge of his vision. He took another step, and the smoke was behind him. He'd been wrong. It didn't fill the room. Instead, it formed a wall at the entrance, preventing anyone from getting a clear view inside.

Before him was a woman seated on a golden throne. Deep scarlet robes draped over her, covering her from head to toe. He could just barely make out the outlines of a face through her hood. The eyes reflected the firelight, though he couldn't tell their color. Wisps of gray hair dangled from her face, and he could just see the tip of her nose. She walked to the fire with slow, deliberate steps and tossed in a green plant. It hissed and smoke billowed from the flame.

"So that's it?" Henry asked. "That's how you see the future? You burn some kind of drug and you see visions?"

The woman looked at him, and he felt his blood go cold. Though he couldn't see her face, he could've sworn she smiled.

"Would that put your mind at ease, Henry Alexander Gideon?" she asked. "Would you like to believe that my visions are nothing more than hallucinations?"

Henry took a step back. "It's just Henry."

"After all you have seen," she said as if he hadn't spoken, "do you still have so much trouble believing I can see the future?"

"Sorry," Henry said. "I guess I just wasn't thinking."

"You have questions for me."

He knew what he should ask. Everything he'd experienced in Kurnugi had been leading up to it. The lives of Andromeda and her family depended on it. As far as he knew, so did that of Hermes and Hephaestus, but another question burned in his mind, one that, to him, was greater than the others.

"How do I get home?"

Twin points of blue light appeared where the Oracle's eyes should be. He thought he heard the sound of hammer on rocks and the sound of rushing wind. The fires dimmed and he let out a breath he hadn't realized he was holding.

"You walk the path of the hero." Her voice came from everywhere at once and echoed off the walls until he could barely understand it. "The hero cannot return home before the task is done."

"Stop the war you mean?"

"If that is your task."

"How do I stop the war?"

"The corruption must be undone."

"What corruption?"

"I do not know," she said.

"How can you not know?" Henry asked. "I thought you were the Oracle of the Future."

"I am," she said. "I can see all that will be, and all that may be."

"But you don't know what corruption?"

"The corruption happened in the distant past. It is a thing that was, and what was is hidden from me."

"Fine," Henry said. "Can you tell me how I undo the corruption?"

"Defeat a general. Turn back an army. Revive the dead and cross a circle of fire."

"I don't suppose you can be more specific."

"I am bound."

"Again with the rules."

"No, not the rules. At least not as you think of them. Anything I say, I say in the now, and shortly after, it becomes the then. What will be becomes what is, and then what was."

"The other Oracles, you mean."

She nodded. "They are in the hands of the enemy. They watch my present and my past even as I watch their future. Everything is in flux."

"Who is the enemy?"

"One who holds life in her hands, and who uses that life to command an army. One who would take the mountain and the forest."

"The mountain and the forest?" Henry asked. "You're not being very helpful. Do you mean someone who lives in the mountains and the forest?"

"In the mountains?" she asked. "Yes, though not in the way you mean. They live deep beneath the surface, digging for metal and stone to fuel the forges of their master's flames. Though he is greater than they, Hephaestus would do much to secure the aid of such a people."

"Dwarves?" Henry asked. "This enemy is going to attack with an army of dwarves?"

"They have not fallen yet, though they will without aid."

"I guess the forest would be elves, then?"

"Such are among the enemy's army, though even the men are among the fiercest warriors to walk the surface of Kurnugi."

"You're telling me there's an army of elves and dwarves led by some kind of dark lord. What do I have to do? Throw a ring into a volcano?"

"Foolish human," she said. "Dark Lords are always defeated. This enemy is so fearsome because she is not a Dark Lord."

"So I'm supposed to fight this army of elves and dwarves?"

"Stop yes. Fight no."

"How do I stop an army without fighting it?"

The Oracle raised an eyebrow. "How do you stop an army by fighting it?"

"Good point," Henry said.

"Battles are often won or lost before they are fought with the gathering of the proper information."

"You're the Oracle of the Future," Henry said. "How much more information could I get?"

"I've told you, the help I can give is mitigated by the other Oracles."

"So I need to rescue the other Oracles?"

"Yes."

"Where are they?"

She smiled. "Are?"

Henry let out a breath in frustration. "Fine. Where will they be?"

"You will find the Oracle of the Present in a castle in a deep forest. It has long been held by a queen blinded by her vanity. She holds the armies of two lands and would kill her own daughter for the sake of her ambitions. There are traitors in her land as well, deep in the mountains. They can preserve life when all else fails."

"Ok, I think I know what you mean. How about the Oracle of the Past?"

"The Oracle of the Past lies in the very heart of enemy territory. It is at the center of all things. All roads come from the past, and you can follow all roads back to the past. Be warned. You can ask of any Oracle, though the Oracle of the Past gives the most, it demands the most in return."

"It?"

"Did you truly think the personifications of time all appear as human?"

"I guess I didn't think of it," Henry said. "What exactly are the other Oracles?"

"They are whatever they choose to be."

"You're not helping."

"I have told you what I can."

"So all I have to do is rescue two Oracles, stop an army, and undo some corruption I don't understand?"

"If it was an easy task, it would not require the efforts of a hero."

"I guess I'll go for the Oracle of the Present before I go up against all the armies of the enemy. If I'm understanding you, it's in one of the places between Near Kurnugi and Far, like the place I met Charon."

"Yes."

"How do I get there?"

"You will find the gateway in the shadow of Atlas."

"That makes sense. I guess the apples are the link. Is there anything else you can tell me?"

"Is there anything else you'd like to ask of me?"

"The rules?"

"The rules."

Henry wracked his brain for anything else to ask, but he just didn't have enough information to know the right questions.

"Is there anything I can do to help Cepheus take back his kingdom?"

"The battle is even now underway. By the time you return, it will already be decided. The Aethiopians will retake their land."

"Good," Henry said. "I'll find someplace to stay tonight and leave in the morning. I have a celebration to get to."

The Oracle nodded and turned away from him. The utter silence of the room was unnerving to him. He held his breath before walking through the curtain of smoke.

The priestess scowled as he passed them. They went into the Oracle's room. Stone grated on stone as they dragged the doors closed. He was surprised that they had been able to carry the weight. He wasn't sure he'd be able to. He waited for them to give him more instructions, but they didn't say a word. He walked back into the main chamber. The fire blazed, and when he came to the main doors he found they'd been closed. The guard waited for him there.

"You made it," he said. "Good."

"I made it?" Henry asked. "You mean there was a question?"

"It's the last test a priestess faces," he said. "They go in to speak to the Oracle. Not everyone has the strength of will to know the future. Some come out of that meeting insane."

Henry's jaw dropped. "And you didn't think that was important enough to tell me?"

"The Oracle wanted to see you," he said. "I am sworn to obey."

"You still might have given me a warning," he said.

"If I had, would it have changed anything?"

Henry thought about it. "No, I guess not."

"Then, nothing was harmed by my omission."

"You still could've told me."

The guard bowed his head. "If it will make you feel better, I apologize. Would you like me to take you to your room?"

"My room?"

"You don't intend to leave now, do you? It's almost midnight."

"What?" Henry asked. "How can that be?"

"You spent nearly three hours speaking with the Oracle."

"No, I didn't," Henry said. "It was only a few minutes."

The guard laughed. "I've heard priestesses talk about this. Apparently, it's easy to lose track of time when you're with her. Once I left you, I was instructed to prepare rooms."

"I guess the Oracle knew I'd be staying," Henry said. "Fine, take me to my room."

The guard nodded once. He walked through one of the side doors into a long hall. Unlike the rest of the temple, the walls here were plain stone, devoid of decorations. The guard walked to a door and opened it. He lit a candle. The room was as plain as the hall had been. It was barely large enough to hold the bed and the single stool inside. Henry thanked his guide. Once the door was closed, he took off his clothes. He laid on the bed and blew out the candle. The bed was lumpy and the pillow was hard. Before he'd come to Kurnugi, he would've thought it was impossible to sleep on it, but a lot had changed since then, and he had no trouble getting to sleep.

THIRTY-EIGHT

A soft knock woke him. He rolled out of bed and put on his clothes. He opened the door and a boy no older than ten was waiting for him. He carried a steaming bowl of soup and a gold chalice. He looked at Henry and smiled.

"Sir, once you eat, I'm to take you to the stables for your horse."

"The stables?" Henry asked. "You have Pegasus?"

"Yes sir," the boy said. "Servants stabled him just after you went in to see the Oracle."

"And he let you?"

"They didn't have any trouble so far as I know, but they don't really talk to me."

Henry nodded and took the food. The soup had some kind of meat that might have been chicken. It felt good going down his throat. The chalice held icy water, and he emptied it before he realized. The boy just stared at him while he ate.

"All right," Henry said once he'd emptied the bowl. "Let's go."

The boy led him down the hall and through a door. The horses stabled there were the most impressive he'd ever seen, though admittedly, he'd seen horses only once in his life. Even in this wondrous place, the horses still smelled like horses, and Henry wrinkled his nose. They were all taller than he was, and their coats almost shined. Pegasus moved back and forth in the last stable. His snow white fur put the rest of the animals to shame. When he saw Henry, he threw his head backed and neighed.

"Sorry I forgot about you." Henry felt the guilt in the pit of his stomach.

Pegasus moved forward and nuzzled his shoulder, and Henry ran his fingers through the mane.

"Sir, would you like him saddled?" the boy asked.

"Saddled?" Henry asked.

"Yes, sir. Leatherworkers have been working through the night to make one specially for your mount."

Pegasus snorted, and Henry could've sworn the horse raised an eyebrow as if daring Henry to try saddling him.

"Thanks for the offer," Henry said, "but Pegasus has never needed a saddle before. I don't see a reason to start now."

"As you say, sir. You may depart whenever you're ready."

He walked through the stable and unhooked the latch holding the door closed, though given the height of the ceiling, it hardly seemed necessary. Pegasus pushed open the stable door as the boy ran to a large door on one side. He threw it open, and the light of the rising sun shone in. Henry climbed on to Pegasus, and the winged horse took off in a gallop. People pointed as he passed. Henry felt himself smirking.

"You're showing off, aren't you?" he asked.

Pegasus reared and spread his wings. Henry rolled his eyes as he gripped the horse's neck. The crowd gasped. He thought he recognized one of the priestesses who'd been so intent on scowling at him the day before. She was as wide-eyed as some of the children. Pegasus let out a snort, and Henry wondered if he was laughing, but before he could say anything else, Pegasus leaped into the air and headed toward Joppa.

THIRTY-NINE

I t was early afternoon when they made it to the city. A mist had rolled in overnight, and the sun hadn't had time to burn it away. He saw a building with a collapsed wall and another whose ceiling had caved in. A few others were damaged, but there didn't seem to be any fighting in the streets. There wasn't much of anything going on. The few people outside were the only indication that Joppa wasn't a dead city.

He brought Pegasus down slowly in a flat area just outside the city. From what he'd seen of the animal, he doubted something as trivial as fog would stop him from landing safely, but it was better to be sure. The hooves on the stone streets were almost like thunderclaps. The shadow of the palace materialized through the fog. A pair of guards he didn't recognize stood at the entrance. When they saw him, they fell to one knee.

"Lord Alexander," one said. "The king will be pleased to see you on this dark day."

"Get up," Henry said. "What's wrong? You took back the kingdom, didn't you?"

"Yes, milord," the guard said, "but it was at a high price."

"What price? Is Andromeda hurt?"

"The princess is fine, physically. Her mother..."

"Queen Cassiopeia?"

"Killed in the fighting," the guard said.

Henry felt his stomach drop. "What?"

"The king and his daughter are in mourning. Most of the city mourns with them."

"I'll go see them," Henry said. "Can you make sure someone takes care of my horse?"

"Of course, Lord Alexander," he said as he put a hand on the horse's neck.

Pegasus looked from Henry to the guard. For a moment, Henry thought the horse would resist, but then he nodded and walked into the fog with the guard. Henry walked down the hall to the throne room. It wasn't supposed to be this way. Stories were supposed to have happy endings.

The hall stretched out before him. The tapestries hadn't been rehung, and the walls looked as dead as the rest of the city. They swallowed up the sound of his footsteps. At the end of the hall, a pair of guards stood vigilantly. They bowed their heads as he approached. One opened the door for him, and he stepped into the throne room.

Torches hung along the walls cast shadows throughout the room. Half of them had gone out, and no one had bothered to relight them. At the end of the room, seated just as he had been when he'd been a prisoner in his own home, sat Cepheus. Andromeda stood next to him. They leaned against each other, their heads held low.

At the sound of Henry's footsteps, the king looked up. His face was twisted in anger.

"I said I wasn't to be disturbed!" he screamed.

Henry froze. "King Cepheus, I'm so sorry." The king's face softened.

"Lord Alexander?" he said as he stood up. Andromeda's head popped up as well. "Forgive me. It's so dark in here. I didn't recognize you. What are you doing here?"

"You don't need to apologize to me," Henry said. "What do you mean what am I doing here? I told you I'd come back after I spoke to the Oracle."

"You made all the way there and back since yesterday afternoon?" the king asked. "That Pegasus of yours must be a remarkable animal."

"He is," Henry said. "I only wish he could've been faster. Maybe if I had been here, I could've done something."

"There was nothing to be done," Cepheus said. "The enemy never got close to us. She was hit by a stray arrow. The soldier who shot it wasn't even aiming for her. It's a cruel irony."

Henry nodded and moved to put a hand on the king's shoulder, but as soon as he'd stepped onto the first stair, Andromeda threw herself at him. She buried her face in his shoulder and cried softly. It was the kind of weeping someone did when they no longer had the strength for louder sobs, but the emotion remained strong. He held her close, and whispered into her ear, though he didn't know what he said. When he looked up, Cepheus nodded at him.

"I'm so sorry," he said again. "I wish there was something I could do."

"Your presence is enough," Cepheus said. He brushed at his robes. "I don't know what I'm doing. My kingdom is still recovering. Cassiopeia wouldn't want me to sit here in the dark with our home crumbling around us. There is still work to be done."

Andromeda pulled away from him. She looked him in the eye and gave him a forced smile. He bowed his head slightly, and she returned to her father's side.

"You can still take time to mourn," Henry said. "You're still human."

"I am a king first," Cepheus said. "Cassiopeia was my queen. She will be committed to the earth with all the honor and ceremony befitting a great woman such as she. I should see to the preparations. You will come, I hope."

"Of course," Henry said.

The king clasped his hand before leaving the room, with Andromeda following on his heels.

FORTY

The guards stood at attention to bid farewell to their queen. The armor of many had been polished until it shone almost as brightly as his own equipment. Others wore battered shields and broken mail. Joppa had been the site of two battles, and there wasn't enough undamaged equipment to go around, but no one who had fought chose to be seen without it today.

The queen's body, covered by a cloth of woven gold, was carried through the city by a group of servants. By tradition, Cepheus and Andromeda followed her on foot. They had asked Henry to walk with them. The request caught him off guard, and he tried to refuse, but they'd pleaded with him until he agreed. They walked through the city for two hours. Henry didn't think he saw a dry eye all day.

As evening approached, they took an isolated road out of town. They were circled by guards as they went into a nearby cave. Stone slabs lined the cavern and the servants took her to one near the back of the cave. Her name had been engraved on it. Next to it was one for Cepheus. Andromeda's was on the other side. Near them, he saw one with Virgil carved on it. He looked to the king, but he was focused on the body of his wife and didn't notice Henry's questioning gaze.

Once the servants had laid her down, Cepheus dismissed them. He reached into his robe and pulled out a small gold coin. He pried open Cassiopeia's mouth and put the coin under her tongue, her payment to Charon for passage to the afterlife. Andromeda stood next to him and took his hand in hers. He squeezed her hand. Her eyes looked like deep green pools, and after a few seconds, he put his arm around her. The three stood in silence for a long time. By the time they left, the sun had fallen beneath the horizon. There was no moon out that night, and they walked back to town by the light of the torches carried by the guards.

FORTY-ONE

W e buried your friend in much the same way," the king said as he took a sip of wine.

"I saw his grave," Henry said. "You are very generous."

They were seated at a small table in the castle. The king had ordered a simple dinner prepared and had told the servants not to disturb them. Henry ate alone with what remained of the royal family.

"How could I do any less for the men who saved my daughter? I would offer you a place in my house if I thought you'd take it."

"Yes, Lord Alexander," Andromeda said. He glared at her, and she blushed. "Henry, I mean. This could be your home."

The king looked from Henry to his daughter before taking another drink. Henry was fairly certain the goblet hid a smile.

"Thank you," Henry said, "but I'm afraid I can't accept. I already have a home, and I want to get back there."

Andromeda's face fell, but the king spoke up before she could say anything. "With a steed like yours, I don't imagine you'll be long in reaching it."

"It'll be longer than you think."

"How long can you stay?"

"Pegasus can't travel as fast as the sandals could," Henry said. "I should leave as soon as possible. Tomorrow morning, I think."

"So soon?"

"It'll be a long trip."

"Surely, you can spare one more day. My daughter would appreciate it, and I owe you a feast."

"That's really not necessary."

"Please," the king said. "Aethiopia has endured so much in recent days. It would do us good to celebrate, even if only for one night, and I'm sure you could do with another day of rest."

Henry's shoulder sagged. The king was right. It had been a hard couple of weeks, and he was exhausted. Pegasus probably was too. He nodded.

"One more day," he said.

FORTY-TWO

It was like the entire city had jammed into the throne room. Men and women from all walks of life sat at the tables and feasted on roast pig and duck. Several large fish were arrayed on every table. The smells mixed in the air until it was impossible to tell one from another. Everything made Henry's mouth water. People were happy, though there was a subdued mood in the air. The chair beside the king was empty, and though he smiled throughout the evening, more than once Henry caught him staring at the chair. Andromeda did as well. He didn't know where they got the strength to face the evening. Reminded of his own mother, he almost left the room several times.

Henry retold his story half a dozen times. Andromeda glared at him every time he mentioned Circe, and Henry realized he was blushing. By the end of the evening, at least ten other people were repeating the story for him. It was nearly midnight when the king stood up, and the room went silent.

"We've endured much. The beast Cetus ravaged our land, and the tyrant Polydectes thought he could claim our home. Either of these could have destroyed us if not for the efforts of one man, the great hero Lord Henry Alexander Gideon!"

The crowd erupted in a cheer. Henry felt his face heat up. He realized Andromeda stood next to him. The king raised his hand and waited for silence.

"We've all lost loved ones in the struggle. Lord Alexander had only just stepped into our walls when his dear friend passed. My own wife was interred only yesterday. Most of you can tell a similar story. Let us pause now and remember them."

In the stillness that followed, the sound of sobbing wafted to Henry's ear. Tears ran down his own cheeks as he thought of his parents. He looked at Andromeda, and she smiled at him. After a few minutes, the celebrations resumed, but by then, people had begun to trickle out. After another hour, all that remained were those who lived in the palace.

"Lord Alexander," Cepheus said. "I wonder if I might have a word before you retire."

"Of course, Your Majesty," Henry said.

"My kingdom is weak. It will be a long time before it is strong again, if it ever is."

"I'm sure it will be."

"Perhaps. Perhaps not. Until then, I would ask a favor of you."

"Your Majesty," Henry said, "I'm still going to leave in the morning."

"I know," Cepheus said. "I want you to take Andromeda with you."

"What?" Henry and Andromeda cried out in unison.

"I do not have the strength to protect her."

"Sire, where I'm going can hardly be called safe."

"Better the heart of danger with a hero than to be in the house of a weak king."

"Father, you're not weak."

"Yes, I am, dear one. I don't intend to stay that way, but for now, I am. Will you take her, Lord Alexander?"

This was insane. She was a princess. A princess who had faced a sea monster and survived two battles.

"I will take her if she will go," Henry said, not entirely sure he wasn't crazy.

The king looked at his daughter. For a second, she looked like she carried the weight of the world on her shoulders. The struggle going on in her heart was reflected on her face. Her eyes were pools of unshed tears.

"I leave in the morning," Henry said. "Come to say goodbye or come to join me. It's up to you."

Henry bowed to them and went to his room. In spite of everything, he had no trouble falling asleep.

"I have to go, Your Majesty," Henry said. "It's a long journey, and there are few safe places between there and here. I need to be able to reach one by nightfall."

The king nodded, and they clasped hands. Henry mounted on Pegasus and was about to fly off when Andromeda came running to them. There was a pack on her shoulder. Henry made a show of checking his own supplies while she and her father embraced. She got on the horse behind him.

"Guard her well," the king said.

"I will. You have my word."

Then, they were off. It took over a week to reach Atlas. Pegasus had an uncanny ability to find land in the ocean, though more than once, they had to reject their spot when the sea churned and waves threatened to wash over them. They gave Circe's island a wide berth. Andromeda gasped when she saw the titan holding up the sky. Henry brought Pegasus in for a landing, half expecting to find the Moirai. Instead, a lone figure waited for them.

"Hermes," Henry said. "I didn't think I'd see you here."

"I go where ever I need to in order to deliver my messages."

"And do you have one for me?"

"Yes. Not everything can cross the boundaries between worlds."

Henry felt his blood run cold. He hadn't even considered that Andromeda may not be able to go with him.

"The princess? Pegasus?"

"Pegasus is the steed of the hero. He may go anywhere the hero goes, though probably not in the way you think. Andromeda has a role of her own in your story. Medusa's head, on the other hand, belongs here."

"That's fine with me," Henry said as he pulled out the wrapped bundle. "I kept on worrying it would roll out of my pack and I'd wake up staring at it." He handed it over to Hermes. "Will I see you again?"

"If I have another message to deliver. Be careful. Not every land is as safe as this one."

"You call this safe?" Henry asked as he led Pegasus under a tree bearing golden apples.

"Just wait and see."

"Henry," Andromeda said once Hermes had vanished. "Where exactly are we going?"

"We're going to find allies. The Oracle told me the enemy has an army of dwarves, but not all of them are loyal to her."

"You know where to find one of these traitor dwarves?"

"Actually, I know where to find seven," he said as they walked over the hills and headed into the greenwood shade.

Stepmother's Mirror

ONE

The golden apples shone so brightly in the morning sun that Henry had to look away as he led Pegasus under the tree. Instead, he glanced over his shoulder at the huge being in the distance, and his eyes went wide.

Atlas, the titan cursed to carry the heavens on his shoulders until the end of time, shimmered. His body widened at the base, and for a moment, Henry worried the giant had fallen. The image of the sky crashing down rushed through his mind. Atlas didn't fall though. He just changed. His skin shifted from an earthen brown to a deep gray. His legs fused together and continued to widen even as the titan's other features blurred. A second later, a mountain towered over the surrounding peaks where Atlas had stood. The whole transformation had taken mere seconds and had been curiously silent. Songbirds chirped in the trees as if nothing had happened. It took several seconds for Henry to understand what he'd just seen. Atlas hadn't actually changed. Henry and Andromeda had passed out of the realm of Greek mythology. In the land they were in now, Atlas didn't exist, but the mountain did.

"Mount Himmnel is an amazing sight, isn't it?" Andromeda said.

Before Henry could answer, a glimmer of red caught his eye, and he pointed into the branches.

"The apples," he said. "They've changed."

She glanced up. "Have they?"

"Andromeda, they're red."

The princess rolled her eyes. "They're apples, Henry. They're always red."

"They were gold a second ago."

"Don't be ridiculous." Andromeda's eyes glazed over for a second, and she brought her hand to her forehead. When she spoke, her voice had grown quiet. "No, you're right. I'm sorry. I don't know how I could've forgotten that."

Henry looked over his shoulder. "I guess you don't remember that being different either."

"The mountain? Mount Himmnel has been there...but it hasn't has it? I remember a man holding up the sky, but that doesn't make sense. A man couldn't do that."

"A titan could," Henry said.

Andromeda didn't respond to that, and when Henry looked back at her, she was staring unblinking into the branches of the apple tree. Her hand inched toward one of the fruits. They were so big, at least as big as his hands clasped together, and their rosy color was so vibrant. A breeze rustled some of the apple blossoms and carried a faint smell of honey. The apples looked delicious. They were obviously ready to eat, and for a moment, he considered reaching out to take a bite of one, but he shook his head free from the compulsion. He grabbed Andromeda's wrist as she reached for one. She struggled against him momentarily but then blinked and looked at him.

"Let's go," Henry said. "I have a bad feeling about those apples. The sooner we get away from them, the better."

Andromeda nodded, and they pressed on down a path so overgrown with shrubbery that Henry had to cut their way through. A few minutes later, they broke out of the tree line and into a clearing. A verdant garden stretched out before them encircled by trees. Flowers lay in ordered rows, and the air was filled with the scent of fresh cut grass.

As soon as Pegasus took a step into the clearing, he reared. Henry and Andromeda scurried back, and the horse screeched in pain. Before they could do anything, Pegasus's great wings convulsed and fell to the ground. Henry gaped at them as their bones seemed to evaporate. The wings shriveled into a pile of dust. Feathers fell loose. The wind caught some of them, but most remained on the ground. A second later, even those collapsed to dust and vanished.

Pegasus, who now looked like a normal white stallion, started grazing as if nothing had happened.

"What happened to his wings?" Henry asked.

"I don't know," Andromeda said. "Lord Hermes said Pegasus was your horse, but I've never heard of such a thing as a winged horse until just now."

Henry stared at her. "Andromeda, what are you talking about? You've known about Pegasus since I got back from the Moirai."

Andromeda blinked at him. Her brow furled, and she looked confused for a second, but then she nodded.

"You're right, of course," she said. "I don't know what I was thinking."

Henry considered for a second. "You may be on to something.

Hermes said Pegasus is the hero's horse, but a winged horse doesn't exist in this world, so I guess he had to change, or maybe the land changed him. I don't really know, but it would explain what happened to the apples and Atlas too."

She nodded as Pegasus nuzzled his shoulder. Henry ran his fingers through the horse's hair but didn't find a mark on him. Even the spots where the wings had been were covered in white hair. Pegasus looked at him as if trying to discern what he was doing. As near as Henry could tell, the horse wasn't injured at all. He suppressed a shiver, and they made their way to the edge of the garden but stopped when they got near.

A wide swath of vegetation had been trampled. Trees had been cut and plant life had been crushed underfoot. Looking back, Henry could see signs of many people moving through the garden, though in the tended ground, they were so sparse, he couldn't tell where exactly they came from. Had more people traveled from Greece or was the garden the link to some other land as well?

"I guess we follow that," Henry said, indicating the trail.

"Are you sure?" Andromeda asked.

"No, but I don't really have any better ideas. The Oracle of the Future said we need the help of the dwarves in this land, and we should find the Oracle of the Present if we can. This is as good a place as any to start."

They traveled south along the path of destruction for the rest of the day. Dried leaves blanketing the ground crunched underfoot. Everywhere were signs of human passage. Branches were cracked and the remnants of fire pits littered the trail. Once, he even found a broken knife, but he still had no idea who they were following. He constantly checked Pegasus, but the animal never showed any sign that losing his wings had hurt him. Periodically, Andromeda would stop and put a hand to her head, but she always waved off Henry's concerns.

A full moon rose in the sky and lit their way, allowing them to continue a little while after the sun had set. As midnight approached, they found a small clearing near a brook and set up camp. Henry found plenty of firewood, and before long, he'd constructed a fire. They had a meal of dried meat and cheese.

"Do you know where we're going," Andromeda asked.

Henry shrugged. "I haven't really thought much past following this trail. Last time I did this, everything happened so fast that I didn't really have a chance to think about it. I guess I was just hoping it would be that easy again."

Andromeda raised an eyebrow. "Last time, you fought off a sea monster that had been plaguing my kingdom, were cursed by Circe and almost died as a half bird, were nearly incinerated in Hephaestus's workshop, battled one of the most fearsome monsters ever to walk the earth, and turned an army of your enemies to stone. Were I you, I would not wish to have such an easy journey ever again."

"Good point," Henry conceded. "Do you have any ideas?"

Andromeda thought for a second. "I'm not sure where we are exactly, but Daste is only two weeks travel from Mount Himmnel."

"Daste?"

Andromeda looked at him. "Daste, the capital of Argath." Henry shrugged, and she spoke slowly. "It's where my father's castle is. It's as good a place as any to start."

He stared at her, but she didn't seem to be joking. Andromeda was a princess, but Aethiopia was a kingdom in Greek myth. She was as much a product of that world as Pegasus. Her father wouldn't even exist in this world.

"Andromeda, your father's kingdom has to be a thousand miles from here, and most of that is over ocean. With Pegasus, we might be able to make it in a few days, but on foot? We'd be travelling for months. Even then, we'd be going backwards."

"No," She said, "I'm not talking about Aethiopia. I'm talking about Argath."

"I've never heard of Argath. Why would your father be there?"

"Why wouldn't he be there?" she asked. "It's my home. Where else would he be? He is the king after all."

"But he rules Aethiopia."

"Yes, I know."

"He rules two kingdoms?" It didn't make sense, especially considering the two kingdoms were in entirely different worlds, but he'd seen things that made even less sense since he'd been drawn into this place where every story ever told existed. It had been weeks, and he was just starting to understand the rules that governed Kurnugi.

"No, of course not," Andromeda said.

"I don't understand."

"What is it you don't understand?" she asked, a tone of puzzlement in her voice. "My father is the king of Argath."

"But your father is also the king of Aethiopia."

"I don't know what you mean by 'also'," she said, brushing at a fly buzzing in front of her face. "My father rules Aethiopia. That's all he rules."

"But you just said he rules Argath."

Her eyes glossed over for a second. Sweat beaded on her brow, and her breathing quickened. She closed her eyes and brought a hand to her head again. Henry moved to her side, but she steadied a moment later.

"I don't know," she said. "I don't understand it. I know my father is King Cepheus of Aethiopia, but I also know my father is

King Frederick of Argath. I know they can't both be true, but somehow, they are."

Henry gave a slow nod. "I think I understand. Hermes said you have your own role to play. I guess you were Andromeda in Greece, but here you're..."

"I am still Andromeda," she said with none of the uncertainty that had characterized her voice recently.

Henry looked at her, not sure what to think. The whole situation was giving him a headache. Finally, he shrugged and pulled out a pair of bedrolls. Andromeda gave him a sheepish grin, and they lay down. She fell asleep almost instantly, but Henry twisted and turned. He always seemed to have a rock or root under his back. There were too many crickets and too many birds. It was an hour before he realized what was really bothering him. Andromeda was going home, and she'd just left a different one. His home, on the other hand, was somewhere on the other side of the mirror, he didn't know how long it would be before he could return, assuming he ever could. When he finally fell asleep, it was to memories of a house in the suburbs with his mother and father.

TWO

When Henry woke the next morning, he almost yelped in surprise. Andromeda was nowhere to be seen. A raven-haired girl about his age sat on a tree stump tending the fire. Her skin was pale, but she didn't look weak or sickly. In fact, she had a glow of life about her, and her heart-shaped lips were deep red. She smiled at him, and he realized she was the most beautiful girl he'd ever seen. He stared at her for several seconds before he recognized the shape of her face and the emerald eyes.

"Andromeda?" he said, halfway expecting her to correct him.

"Did you sleep well?" she asked.

"Um, yes. You?"

"Passable," she said. "What's wrong? You look like you've seen a ghost."

He waved off her concern. "It's nothing. I was just surprised by something I probably should've expected."

"What's that?"

"Never mind," he said. "How far did you say it was to Daste?"

She shrugged. "It's hard to say exactly, but if we keep heading south, we'll hit the Northern Caravan Route. From there, it shouldn't be more than three or four days to Daste. Maybe less if we can ride."

She gave Pegasus a pointed look. It might've been Henry's imagination, but it almost looked like the horse inclined his head.

"I'm not sure," Henry said. "With what happened yesterday..."

"What are you talking about?"

"Yesterday, when Pegasus's wings fell off."

"Henry, there's no such thing as a winged horse."

For a second, he was speechless. Hermes had warned him about this, though Henry hadn't really believed him. Though Andromeda might look human, she wasn't. Not really. She was a creature of Kurnugi. She was a storybook princess. In fact, now that he thought about it, she just might be *the* storybook princess, the one who existed in more stories than he could count. From the looks of it, she didn't even realize who she was.

"Forget it," he said before turning to the horse.

Pegasus had possessed heightened intelligence in Greece, but Henry wasn't sure if that was still the case. "How about it? Do you feel up to carrying riders today?"

Pegasus cocked his head, and Henry found himself wondering if the horse remembered he'd been able to fly less than a day ago. He stepped closer, and Pegasus bent down to let him on. He offered a hand up to Andromeda, and they took off in a slow trot. A few seconds into the ride, Henry had a death grip on Pegasus's neck as he bounced up and down on the horse's bare back. Before, he'd always ridden Pegasus in the air, and while the ride hadn't always been smooth, it had never been this bumpy. He kept expecting to be knocked off by a tree branch, but Pegasus moved around them by a wide margin. Henry had heard stories about how it wasn't safe for a horse to go very fast in the woods, but Pegasus apparently disagreed with those and trotted through the forest with ease. Before long, Henry relaxed and actually found himself laughing as the trees blurred by. A few hours later, they came to a broad road made of gray stone.

"That's odd," Andromeda said. "I thought we were at least a week from the road."

"Maybe we're running into good luck for a change. Which way?"

The sun still hung low in the sky. Andromeda pointed away from it, and they set off to the west. Henry didn't find any more signs of the trail they'd been following. Once on smooth ground, Pegasus galloped for short bursts, but Henry always slowed him after a few minutes. He was still uneasy about the loss of the horse's wings and didn't want to push him too hard. Every once in a while, they passed a wagon or a group of people on foot. Almost every time, the people gave way and allowed them to pass without comment. A few stared at them, and more than once, Henry thought he heard them whispering.

"I wonder what they find so interesting," he said.

"I suspect it's me," Andromeda said. "I've traveled extensively through the kingdom, and many people know my face. They aren't used to seeing me garbed in travelling clothes with so little an escort. I expect they're trying to figure out if it's really me."

"They don't all look happy," he said as a passing wagoner glared at them.

"I know," she said, "and that worries me."

A few hours later, Henry caught a glimpse of a distant hill through the trees. He could just make out towers rising over walls.

"Is that it?" he asked.

Andromeda took in a sharp breath. "That's not possible." She looked north and scanned the sky. "Where is Mount Himmnel? We haven't gone nearly far enough for it to be out of sight."

Henry strained to see through the branches, but all he saw was empty sky.

"We probably just can't see it through the trees."

"No, I know that hill. That's Daste. How have we come so far so fast?"

"I don't have the slightest idea," Henry said, "but I've seen stranger things. We're still several hours away though. Let's stop for lunch."

Andromeda nodded and they dismounted. They didn't bother to build a fire and ate quickly of their dried rations. Neither said a word, and Andromeda kept looking over her shoulder at the hill. When they remounted, he urged Pegasus to a trot.

"How long have you been away?" Henry asked

"A few weeks," she said.

Henry couldn't help but wonder who she thought he was. Was he supposed to be a friend travelling with her? A guard? Someone she'd met on the road? The last thing he needed was for the king to think Henry had kidnapped his daughter. At least, she still seemed to like him, but he couldn't shake the uneasy feeling that he was walking into a bad situation.

THREE

Distance through the trees was deceptive, and less than an hour later, they broke through the tree line to see Daste sitting on a hill. Bleak, gray walls surrounded it, though Henry could see through the gates that the city itself was all white stone. Red clay roofs sat atop squat houses, and he could just make out people moving atop the walls. It was another fifteen minutes to climb the hill and pass through the gates. Children and dogs played in the street, and street vendors hawked their wares.

As soon as Henry and Andromeda passed by, everyone went silent. Henry could feel the eyes of the town on him. Even the children stopped to stare at them. They walked down the main road toward an ominous gray castle that was a sharp contrast to the rest of the town. The walls surrounding it looked thick and strong, and guards had been stationed at regular intervals. Towers reached up to the sky, and he could imagine archers littering invading forces with arrows from those vantage points.

Unlike the rest of the town, the castle was meant for war. Four guards stood before a heavy door of dark wood. Their helmets gleamed in the sun, and they each carried a sword on one side and a dagger at the other. A snowflake crest decorated their armor. As Henry and Andromeda approached, they drew their swords, but Andromeda dismounted and walked up to one wearing a gold chain.

"Captain," she said in a voice like ice. "Do you intend to skewer me, or are you going to let me pass?"

The guard's eyes widened. In one fluid motion, he sheathed his sword and removed his helmet. A heartbeat later, the rest of the guards followed suit, and they fell to one knee.

"Forgive me, Princess," the leader stammered. "We weren't expecting you back for some time. If you'd sent word you were returning, we would've been prepared."

"Don't give it any mind, Uncle Sholtz," she said.

All traces of coldness had vanished from her voice. He looked at her. For a second, they just stared at each other. Then, she threw her arms around him. He gave a great belly laugh and spun her around. The other guards looked a little uneasy. When Sholtz put her down, she had to brush a stand of hair away from her face. "I didn't expect to return so soon either." She waved her hand at Henry. "This is Lord…"

"Henry," Henry said, hoping to stop the 'Lord' nonsense before it started here as well. "It's just Henry."

"This is Master Henry Alexander Gideon," Andromeda said with a wry smile. Henry rolled his eyes. "He is a great warrior and a great friend. Can you send some of your men to escort us to my father?"

Sholtz's eyes drifted down to Henry's waist, and it took a second to realize the guard was looking at his sword. He'd gotten so used to carrying it, he'd almost forgotten about the weapon. Sholtz scowled at him.

"I cannot let an armed man in to see the king," he said.

Before Henry could say anything, Andromeda laughed. "Uncle, I've seen him use that sword. I very much doubt you could take it away from him."

Henry didn't share her confidence and was keenly aware of how much he depended on the sword's magic and on surprise. He didn't know how well he could stand up against a trained soldier who expected trouble. He started to unbelt the weapon before anything got out of hand.

"It's fine," he said.

"No, it isn't," Andromeda said as she put a hand on his to stop him. "Uncle, you can't imagine the dangers Master Henry has saved me from. I won't have him disarmed, not even to go before my father."

Henry let out a breath of relief that she still seemed to remember what he'd done, but Sholtz gave him a hard look before nodding. He waved a hand at one of the other guards.

"We'll see you right in," he said. "It's good to see you again, Princess. We have been poorer for your absence."

Her laugh sounded like music. "It's good to be home, Uncle. I've been away too long."

Sholtz stepped out across the bridge and waved at a window over the doors. A few seconds later, the doors ground across the stone floor for almost a full minute before they opened wide enough for the two of them to pass into the castle grounds. In spite of being Andromeda's friend, he couldn't help but think the door closing behind him sounded like a prison gate slamming shut.

They walked across the courtyard, stopping only briefly to give Pegasus to a stable man before passing through another door and entering a long corridor. Where the castle in Aethiopia had been opulent and decorated with sculptures and tapestries, this castle was stark and utilitarian.

The smell of lamp oil hung heavy in the air. Shadows danced across the hall, and the sound of the guard's heavy boots seemed to echo forever. Light flickered from an open door at the end of the passage. For a second, Henry wondered why the corridor was so long, but then he saw small holes scattered across the wall.

"Arrow slits?"

"What?" Andromeda looked around and saw what he was staring at. "Oh yes. Sorry. I don't even notice them anymore."

Henry almost tripped over his own feet. In Greece, she'd been willing to sacrifice herself for the good of her people. Here, the idea of walking through a kill zone didn't even warrant a second thought. He began to realize his original idea was wrong. This girl was much more than a storybook princess.

"The guard at the gate is your uncle?" he asked.

"Not really," she said. "Sholtz is in charge of security at the castle. I grew up with him always watching over me. I just always thought of him as Uncle Sholtz."

"He's in charge, and he watches the gate?"

"He tries to spend at least one shift a month doing the jobs ordinary guardsmen do so he doesn't forget what it's like. He says it's too easy to forget the value of men's lives if you don't walk in their shoes from time to time."

They exited the long corridor, and the guard led them through so many twists and turns that Henry lost all sense of direction. Eventually, they came to a plain wooden door. Two more men guarded it. One stepped forward and brought a hand to stop them, but his eyes widened when he saw Andromeda.

"Princess," he said with a bow. "How may I be of service?"

"We would speak to my father," she said.

"He's in conference with his generals," he said.

Andromeda and Henry exchanged glances. "Then, the war has reached us."

The guard's eyes darted from Henry to Andromeda and back again. "I think that's a matter best discussed with your father," he said.

"I agree. Now, see us in."

The guard looked like he was going to argue but let out a sigh of resignation and opened the door. Three men sat around a long rectangular table with a large map and sheets of paper scattered on it. They all looked up when the door creaked. One, a bearded man with raven black hair streaked with gray and a hawk-like nose glared at them. The guard took a step back, but when the man laid eyes on Andromeda, his face softened. The right side of his lip twitched as if, for a moment, he couldn't remember her name, but then a smile split his face.

"Andromeda!" he rose and almost knocked the table over.

"Father!" she said, practically leaping across the room.

They embraced and the king lifted her like she didn't weigh anything. The other men rose respectfully, though their stoic faces looked out of place next to the jovial expressions on Andromeda and her father. The king put her down and laughed before waving away his generals. Both glared at Henry as they walked out of the room.

"And who is this?" the king asked, his eyes flickering to the sword on Henry's belt.

"Father, I would like to present Master Henry Alexander Gideon. He is a great hero who's faced monsters and armies. He's saved my life more than once."

The king inclined his head slightly. "High praise," he said.

"Henry, this is my father, King Frederick of Argath."

Henry knelt before the king, but an instant later, the large man's shadow fell over him, and the king offered him a hand up.

"There's no need for that," he said. "Not in private anyway. With this war, we feared the worst, but you saved my daughter, and I have great need of a man who can face an army and walk away victorious."

"Sir, I'll gladly do what I can," Henry said, "but there's a lot more to the story than Andromeda is saying. Those weren't exactly normal circumstances."

The king chuckled. "They never are. Every battle is different, boy. I've fought in many wars, and I've yet to encounter one in normal circumstances."

"Then, I am at your service, Your Majesty."

The king clapped him on the back. "Good. Once Queen Zuab arrives, we'll truly have a force to be reckoned with."

"Queen Zuab?" Andromeda asked. "Of Neustad? Father, don't tell me you've formed an alliance with her."

"Oh, that's right. I forgot. It happened while you were away. Queen Zuab and I wed two weeks ago. Our unified kingdoms will be stronger than ever."

Andromeda stared at him for a second before she finally found her words. "But father, you always said she was an evil witch who should've been deposed long ago."

"Well, I may have been a little too harsh. She really is a gentle person once you get to know her."

Andromeda gaped at him. "The last ambassador you sent to Neustad never came back."

"The roads are very dangerous, Andromeda. She said she never saw him."

"And you believe her?"

"Yes, I do," he said in a voice that allowed for no further discussion.

"Maybe, I should wait outside," Henry said.

"Oh, there's no need for that. You must forgive a spat between father and daughter, Master Henry. Andromeda loved her mother very much, and she's never been comfortable with the idea of me marrying again," the king said, ignoring the look of rage on Andromeda. "I'll have the steward assign quarters to you. If the two of you will join me for breakfast tomorrow morning, we can discuss the coming war."

FOUR

Henry's room in the castle was every bit as decadent as his room in Aethiopia had been, though for different reasons. Half a dozen shields hung on the wall, each decorated with a different crest. The one bearing the snowflake was the largest and hung over the large four-poster bed. Curious, he stood on the mattress to pick it up and found it to be steel. This was no mere decoration.

Crossed swords had been mounted on the wall over the door. One had a nick in the blade, an indication that it had seen battle. The window overlooked the city, and it was easy to forget that he was in such a bleak castle. The setting sun painted the buildings fiery red, and Henry couldn't help but wonder if the coming war would set all of Kurnugi aflame.

He hadn't realized how much the day had tired him until he lay down. He felt like he'd just closed his eyes when a gentle rapping at the door woke him. Starlight still twinkled outside, and a thick fog blanketed the town. He slipped on the clothes he'd gotten from

Hephaestus and opened the door. Andromeda stood outside wearing a long black dress that contrasted with her skin so sharply it almost looked like she glowed. A tear glimmered as it ran down her cheek.

"What's wrong?" Henry asked.

"I'm sorry," she said, turning away. "I shouldn't have woken you. I'll go."

"Andromeda, wait," he said as he grabbed her arm. "Tell me what's the matter."

She looked down to his hand and followed his arm to his face. Her eyes were red, and she shook her head.

"It's nothing."

"Come on," he said. "We've been through too much for that. Tell me."

"It's just that Father always stood for justice. So did Mother. They always said it was one of the things that drew them together, but Neustad is an evil place ruled by an evil queen. We always opposed her and everything she stood for. I can't imagine what would make father ally with her, much less marry her."

"People can change," Henry said.

"Not Zuab," Andromeda said in an icy voice. "Not that much."

I was talking about your father. Henry didn't give voice to his thought, though.

"I would like very much to see my mother," Andromeda said. "Would you accompany me? We'll be back in time for breakfast with my father."

"Of course," he said, stepping out of the room.

They walked down the empty hall, and Andromeda wrapped a dark cloak around herself, but Henry's clothes warded off the cold. He was moderately surprised at that. Being crafted by a Greek god, he'd half expected them to lose their power in this world. That meant his shield and sword likely retained their special properties as well, which was a relief. In a war-torn land like this, he would need them.

It took a while for them to make it down to the lower level of the castle. Every once in a while, they passed a guard patrolling the halls. Each one put a hand on his hilt when the pair approached but removed it and inclined his head at the sight of Andromeda. They walked to a door that would've been ordinary had it not been for the pair of guards standing there. They stiffened, but relaxed when they saw Andromeda's face. One wordlessly handed Andromeda a torch. She muttered something that could've been a thanks before leading him down a stone stairway into the catacombs beneath the castle.

They were greeted by the scent of dust, and Henry had to brush cobwebs out of his face as they descended. The place felt old. Without knowing how he knew, Henry was certain it had been here long before the castle above. The air practically hummed with power. He thought he heard a soft whisper, and the darkness played tricks on his eyes making him think he saw figures just beyond the reach of the torches. Something brushed his cheek, and for a second, he thought it was fingers, but it was only another cobweb.

"There are no such things as ghosts," he said under his breath, but the words sounded hollow and empty. In this place formed of human imagination, who could say whether or not ghosts actually existed?

They reached the bottom and came to a large hallway. Andromeda held up her torch, but the light seemed pitifully small next to the darkness pressing in on all sides. Through the shadows, Henry could just make out massive pillars reaching up to a ceiling he couldn't see. He thought they had shapes carved into them, but it was impossible to be sure. Andromeda stepped forward, and

Henry hurried after her. He told himself he was being ridiculous. He'd ridden in a boat captained by Charon, the ferryman of the dead. He'd faced Cetus, Medusa, and Circe. There was no reason he should be afraid of a place like this, but somehow, these catacombs held more fear for him than all those other things put together.

"A hundred generations of the rulers of Argath rest here." Andromeda's voice was only one step above a whisper. "Not all of them were good, but I don't think even the worst of them would approve of Zuab."

"Is she really that bad?"

"Most of what we hear is rumors," she said. "Zuab doesn't suffer visitors to her realm. The spies my father has sent almost never come back. Those that do, speak of a people little more than slaves. She uses them to test her dark magic, and there is no law save that the strong rule over the weak."

"Then, she really is a witch."

Andromeda nodded but didn't say anything. They walked for a long while with no sound but their echoing footsteps. Eventually, Andromeda turned and walked between two pillars. As she came near them, her torch illuminated carved scenes of battles. She passed below a low arch and came into a small chamber. At first, Henry thought there was someone inside, but as Andromeda's torch illuminated the figure, he realized it was a statue standing on a raised platform. It had been so expertly carved Henry half expected the regal woman to step down to greet them.

Individual strands of hair had been cut into the stone, and her dress looked like it would ripple in the wind that wasn't there. She shared Andromeda's heart-shaped lips and lean face. A stone crown lay atop her head with a purple jewel shining with a soft light embedded in it. This woman was every inch a queen. A tear ran down Henry's cheek. He was separated from his parents until he could find his way out of Kurnugi, but at least he still had them. Andromeda had lost one mother in Greece and another here. He wondered if there was any land where her mother still lived.

"This statue is amazing," Henry said after a few minutes of silence.

"Carved by dwarves," she said. "I'm sorry for bothering you with this. We should go discuss the war with my father."

"Take your time," Henry said. "After all we've been through, another hour or so won't make much of a difference."

Andromeda nodded and turned back to her mother. She pulled out a flower from her robe and laid it at her mother's feet. She whispered something too softly for him to hear and stared up at the statue. Henry felt like an intruder. He would've stepped back, but he didn't think he could without disturbing her.

"I'm sorry," she said without turning around. "I shouldn't have brought you down."

"Andromeda, I've been here for you since I found you chained to that rock. I'm not about to leave you now."

She looked over her shoulder and gave him a smile. Suddenly, the darkness didn't seem so oppressive. He still wouldn't want to go wandering down here alone, but it no longer felt like something was crawling under his skin.

FIVE

Henry didn't know how long they stayed down there. He moved as far back as he could to give Andromeda some privacy. After a long while, she turned around and led him out. They didn't say anything as they climbed back out, but the catacombs seemed quieter, more at peace. When they emerged into the hall, a squat balding man dressed in silks was waiting for them.

"Oh thank goodness," he said in a nasal voice. "The king is waiting for you. I would've come down, but these two," he said as he pointed at the guards, "wouldn't let me pass."

"It's good that they didn't, Stewart," Andromeda sneered. "Don't presume to interrupt my time with my mother."

"Yes, well," the stuffy little man said. "Your father is expecting you, and unlike your mother, he actually can get upset if you waste his time."

Andromeda gave him a look that could have shattered glass, but Stewart just shrugged it off and turned to walk down the hall.

"I hate that man," she said more than loud enough for him to hear. "He's an insufferable little bootlicker. He makes my skin crawl."

She glared after him for a long second before letting out a sigh and following. Henry walked at her side. After going through yet another series of twists and turns, Henry wondered if the castle had been deliberately built to confuse its residents. Stewart seemed to have no trouble, though, and led them to a large room with a vaulted ceiling. King Frederick sat at the head of a small table, which apart from the chairs, was the only piece of furniture in the room. A roast chicken sat on it surrounded by assorted fruits and vegetables. A tall man in a bright red shirt stood behind the king. Frederick looked up and nodded at the other two seats.

As soon as the pair sat, the man behind the king cut a slice of chicken and scooped some of the fruit onto a plate before placing it in front of Andromeda. He did the same for Henry. Henry took a bite. The chicken tasted faintly of lemon and was so tender it almost melted in his mouth. The food practically vanished from his plate, and the servant piled more on.

"Why are you dressed that way?" the king asked.

"I was visiting Mother," she said without looking up from her plate. "There wasn't a flower on her grave. Have you even been to see her since you married that witch?"

"Andromeda, don't call her that."

"You called her that long before I did."

"True," he said, "but I was just as wrong then as you are now."

"Do you love her?" Andromeda asked. "Zuab, I mean."

"Andromeda..."

"Because I think this has to be a strictly political marriage. She maintains a strong army, and we'll need that for the coming war. Realm before king. You always taught me that. Is that what this is?

They say she uses her army against her own people. Are you going to overlook that?"

"Now just a…"

"You always said we should value love over political advantage, but I can't imagine you loving her."

"Yes, Andromeda, I do love her," the king said.

Whatever argument Andromeda had been about to hurl at him died on her lips. Her voice came out as a squeak that was almost lost in the cavernous room. "What?"

"I love her," he said. "Every bit as much as I did your mother."

"She must have you under some sort of spell," she said, almost in tears.

"That's enough, young lady," he said as he slammed his fist on the table. "Zuab is not evil. She's not a witch, and she's not out to get me. I love her. Can't you just be happy?"

"No." Andromeda's voice cracked. "Not with her. There are a thousand other women who would gladly be your queen. Why her?"

"I love her," he said again. "I don't know what else you want me to say."

Andromeda sniffled and wiped away a tear. Her father put one hand on hers and squeezed. A lump formed in Henry's throat, but he didn't say anything until the king turned to look at him.

"Come now, let's leave this discussion for another time and talk about this war. I'm much interested in hearing what you have to say, young hero."

Henry felt himself blushing at the title. His throat had gone dry, and he took a sip from the jewel-encrusted chalice in front of him. The red liquid tasted faintly of strawberries.

"We need to discuss allies, Your Majesty," Henry said.

"Yes, of course," Frederick said. "The soldiers of Neustad should be here soon."

"That's not exactly who I meant," Henry said.

The king raised a finger. "Watch yourself. I may suffer my daughter to speak ill of my new wife, but I will not suffer you."

"I meant no offense," Henry said. "But I was told to gather specific allies. The queen was not among those."

"Told?" the king asked. "Told by whom?"

Henry bit his lower lip. "Would you believe an Oracle?"

The king's brow furled. He idly tapped his fork against his plate. For a second, Henry thought the man would laugh at him, but he only nodded.

"Yes, I have heard of such. It is even said my lady wife has such a being in her kingdom."

"I was afraid of that," Henry said under his breath.

"What?"

"Nothing," Henry said. "Then, you believe me?"

"Let's just say I'm willing to accept the possibility."

Henry let out a slow breath. "The allies I've been told of are dwarves."

The king's smile faded, and his breathing slowed. His face looked like it was made of stone.

"Dwarves," he said in a level voice, "and with whom do you think I'm fighting a war?"

Henry's mouth opened slightly in surprise, and it took him a few seconds to find his voice. "You're fighting against the dwarves?"

"Obviously."

"We came here to warn you about an upcoming war," Henry said. "I didn't realize you were already in the middle of another one."

"This one shouldn't last much longer," the king said. "Once my forces join with those from Neustad, we'll be as close to unstoppable as a human army can be."

Henry stared at him. Andromeda's jaw dropped. He could tell she wanted to say something, but she obviously couldn't find the words. The king waved to a servant who put a bundle of grapes on his plate. Frederick popped a couple of grapes in while Henry thought about what to say. He knew he was on dangerous ground.

"And what will you do with this army?" Henry asked.

"We'll go into the mountains and root out the traitorous dwarves." The king's voice was more snarl than words. "By the time we're done, there won't be a dwarf left within a thousand miles."

"Father, the dwarves have always been our greatest allies. What did they do to make you hate them so?"

"They steal our jewels and precious ore. They maintain their own army on the outskirts of my kingdom. They refuse to subject themselves to the law of the land. What more reason do I need?"

"But..." Andromeda started.

"What then?" Henry asked. "Once you've eliminated the dwarves, what will you do then?"

"That will be for my queen and I to decide," he said.

"Father," Andromeda began, but Henry met her eyes and shook his head slightly. She stuttered a little before continuing. "When will Zuab be arriving?"

"I received word just before you got here. Her entourage should be arriving in a few hours."

"Then, I should go prepare myself," Andromeda said, rising. "It wouldn't do to greet my stepmother in mourning clothes. Master Henry, would you walk with me?"

Henry looked to the king who nodded. Andromeda walked quickly, and he almost had to jog to keep up. She didn't say anything until they'd turned several corners. Even then, she spoke so softly that he had to strain to hear.

"The dwarves have always been their own sovereign people," she said. "The mountains are theirs. They mark the edge of our kingdom. No ruler of Argath has ever tried to lay claim to them."

"Do you really think Queen Zuab cast a spell on him?"

She nodded. "I've never known him to be so angry at anyone, much less our allies. I can't imagine any other reason he would be."

"The Oracle said the dwarves can preserve life. I think that means we need them on our side."

"You think Zuab is working for this enemy you're so worried about."

"After everything you've said about her, would that really surprise you?"

"No," she said. "Come, we should hurry to your quarters."

"My quarters?" Henry asked. "Why are we going to my quarters?"

"Because I'd like you to stand guard outside my door while I get ready. You'll need your sword and shield."

SIX

There were already three men standing at the princess's door when Henry and Andromeda arrived. They straightened when Andromeda approached. One ran in and came back out a few seconds later.

"Your room is secure, Milady," he said.

"Make sure no one comes in," she said to Henry, drawing dark looks from the guards that vanished when she turned to address them. "Summon my maids."

She went in without waiting for them to reply. One ran down the hall, and Henry could feel the weight of the glares the other two threw at him. The hostility hung so thick in the air he had to resist the urge to rest a hand on his hilt. A young girl of perhaps thirteen appeared a few minutes later. She took one look at the guards before disappearing into the room.

After an agonizing hour of waiting and trying not to antagonize the guards further, Andromeda came out wearing a deep blue dress that shimmered in the light. She didn't even acknowledge the guards as she walked over to Henry and took his arm to lead him down the hall. She held her head high as if she couldn't imagine someone who wasn't beneath her notice. A crown of silver wire adorned with diamonds rested on her head. Her hair hung in a single braid, but that simplicity only augmented her splendor. The statue of her mother was the very image of a queen, but Andromeda was that image given life and breath. Her demeanor was so unlike anything he'd seen in her that he didn't know how to react. He felt like a bumbling idiot. Though only a princess by title, she declared herself a queen with every step.

"Did you really have to treat the guards that way?" Henry asked.

"I don't know who I can trust, not if Zuab really does have my father under her spell."

Henry was about to answer when a messenger turned the corner and almost barreled into them. His eyes widened and he bowed deeply to Andromeda.

"Forgive me, Your Highness," he said. "Queen Zuab has arrived. Your father requires that you join them in the throne room."

"We were already on our way," she said, inclining her head.

"Very good," he said and turned around to lead them.

Henry looked at Andromeda, but she only shrugged and followed the messenger. A few minutes later, they reached a set of massive doors inlaid with gold. The guards were both big men wearing mail shirts and carrying an arsenal of bladed weapons. They crossed their spears as Henry and Andromeda approached. Andromeda didn't slow until her face was an inch from their weapons. She cleared her throat, and the guards exchanged glances.

"Well?" Andromeda said.

"Forgiveness, Milady," one said in a deep voice that Henry

could practically feel in his bones. "No one is permitted to go before the queen armed. If the young master will surrender his weapon, we'll be happy to let you through."

Andromeda kept her gaze forward. "Master Henry is a greater warrior than any you've ever imagined. His sword is worth more than you are. More importantly, he is my guest, and he has the freedom to go armed wherever he wishes."

"Our orders are..."

"You will either let us pass or you will go in there and tell the queen you turned away her stepdaughter."

The guards paled slightly. They looked at each other before the one who'd spoken lowered his spear. The older one followed his lead a heartbeat later.

"Go right in, Princess," he said, his words tripping over each other. "Please forgive us for any misunderstanding."

Andromeda didn't even look at them. They pushed open the doors and Andromeda stepped through. Henry followed right behind her. The guards reminded him of mountains as he passed between them. A small crowd of people had gathered in the throne room. Every woman there wore a gown that would've probably cost a fortune back home, but none held a candle to Andromeda. A servant in a bright red coat announced them, and the room went silent. A red carpet ran from the door to two golden chairs on the other side of the room. The king and queen sat on a raised platform under a stained glass window that cast colored lights on the floor. Andromeda followed the carpet, and the crowd parted for her. She came to a stop in front of the king and queen. She curtsied, and Henry bowed. The queen rose and stepped down. She was beautiful. There was no question of that, but she was beautiful the same way lightning was, a beauty that struck fast and left nothing but charred husks in its wake.

Her raven hair fell to just past her shoulders. She had pale skin and dark eyes, and she stood at least six feet tall. When she looked at Henry, a chill ran down his back, and he had to resist the urge to look away. He didn't realize his hand had gone to his hilt until he noticed her eyes had locked onto it. A whisper ran through the crowd.

"My Lord," she said without turning around. "Is it the custom of Argath to threaten their queen? Or is this man an agent of the traitorous dwarves?"

"Oh no, Beloved," the king said as he rose from his throne. Devotion infused his voice so completely, it left no room for thought. "Master Henry is a stranger here, and his lands have different customs. Andromeda has been indulging him. I'm sure no offense was meant. Master Henry will surrender his weapon if you wish."

"Father, he is my guest," Andromeda said.

"Hush now, child," Frederick said. "Don't make a scene."

"It's quite alright, my love," Zuab said. "Let the boy have his sword if it makes him feel safe. He's of no concern to me." She turned to look at Andromeda. For a moment, her brow creased in a scowl, but a second later, she wore a smile that didn't reach her eyes. "Now this one is of great interest. The king speaks of you with a father's heart, seeing only the good. Parents can so rarely see their children's faults."

Andromeda's face turned bright red. He'd thought the room had gone quiet before, but now it seemed like no one even breathed. Henry's heart sounded like a thunderclap in his ears, and he tightened his grip on his sword.

"One could say the same of how husbands see their wives, particularly those who are newly married."

"Andromeda!" the king cried out. He was about to say more,

but the queen raised her hand, and his words cut off. His eyes bulged for a second, but then he relaxed.

"I can see your father has been lax in your discipline," the queen said. "We'll have to remedy that at the first opportunity."

"If you think I'll submit to the whims of a witch…"

The sound of the queen's slap rang through the throne room. It was so hard, Henry was surprised Andromeda didn't fall, but she only took a few steps back. She made a fist and prepared to swing at the queen, but before she could do anything, guards had drawn swords and leveled them at the princess. Henry didn't think. He drew his sword and swung in a single motion. Though the attack came from a bad angle, the god-forged weapon struck hard and tore a guard's sword from his hand. Three other men surrounded Henry with drawn weapons. Everyone else in the room became as still as statues.

"Enough!"

The king's shout rumbled through the room. Several people paled or took a step back. The doors to the throne room opened again, and the two doormen ran in, looking for someone to fight. When they saw Henry surrounded, they moved to join the circle.

"Master Henry," the king said through clenched teeth, "you have abused my hospitality. If you hadn't saved my daughter's life, I would have you in chains. Leave this reception now. I expect you to be out of the castle by sunset."

"Father no!"

"As for you, Andromeda, though it pains me to admit it, my lady wife is right. You are in need of discipline."

"Father…"

"That's enough, Andromeda. See your friend out if you wish. I doubt very much you'll ever see him again."

SEVEN

I can't believe he would do that," Andromeda said as Henry packed his few belongings. He was being slow about it to extend these last moments with Andromeda.

"What will you do now?"

"Go into the mountains and look for the dwarves," Henry said. "We still need them. After that, I'll head for Neustad."

"Why there?"

"Your father said Zuab has an Oracle in her lands. I think it's the Oracle of the Present."

"How would she get such a thing?"

"I have no idea," Henry said, "but if she has it, that's where I need to go."

"But I told you what that realm is like. How do you intend to find this Oracle?"

"I wish I knew. Maybe the dwarves will have some idea."

"Let me go with you."

Henry paused, sorely tempted to take her up on the offer, but he shook his head as he stuffed in the last of the clothes King Cepheus had given him in Greece. You need to stay here. Maybe you can still convince your father to stop this war."

"After what I saw today, I'm not sure I could convince him to eat if he were starving."

"Still, you have to try."

She put a hand on his shoulder and he met her eyes. They looked like emerald pools, and he felt a smile spread across his face.

"I will," she said. "Fare thee well, Henry Alexander Gideon. You saved my father's kingdom twice over. I still have faith that you'll be able to do so again."

He opened his mouth to speak but closed it again. It wouldn't do any good to correct her. They embraced, and Andromeda walked with him toward the front gate of the castle. They walked through the arrow slit lined hallway in silence. Henry tried to find words to say, but nothing came.

They were halfway down the hall when orange light erupted from behind them. Henry turned to see flames filling the passage and roaring towards them. Without thinking, he put himself in front of Andromeda and drew his shield. He didn't have time to strap it on his arm before the fire struck, and though the flames were many times the size of the shield, as soon as they reached him, they stopped their advance. They stayed there for a moment, the cracking fire drowing out every other sound. Sweat dripped from his face. A second later, the flames shot back down the hall and impacted the wall on the far side. They sizzled and died on the stone, but not before burning part way through and leaving molten rock glowing on the wall.

"What was that?" Andromeda asked.

"I don't know," Henry said, still holding the shield in front of him. "I think it was magic. Hephaestus said this shield could turn almost anything back."

"My father has no wizard in his service," Andromeda said, "Nor is there one in all of Argath as far as we know. There's only one person in the kingdom who would have the power to call up flame like that."

"Zuab," Henry said. Andromeda nodded, and Henry ran back into the castle.

"Where are you going?" Andromeda called out as she took off after him.

"We're going to see your father. Now that Zuab has tried to kill you, he has to listen to reason."

"He threw you out of the castle once already," she said. "If you go before him without being summoned, you'd be lucky to escape with your skin."

"We need the dwarves" Henry said. "If this can stop the war with them, then it's worth the risk. We might just be able to break Zuab's hold on your father."

EIGHT

The king will not see you." Stewart stood in front of Frederick's war room, blocking their path. "You should be on your way out of town."

"My father gave him until the end of the day," Andromeda said, "and even if he won't see Master Henry, he will see me."

"Spoiled child," Stewart said.

"I'm going through that door, Stewart, unless you intend to physically restrain me. Personally, I don't think you're bold enough to try."

She took a step forward, and the man paled slightly. Almost unconsciously, he took a step back. It was all the opportunity Andromeda needed. She pushed open the door, and conversation in the room died.

The king sat with the same two men Henry had seen earlier. Additionally, there was a man with blond hair and a scar running down his left cheek. He was so heavily muscled Henry wouldn't have been surprised if he could crush stones to powder with his bare hands. Though none of the other men were armed, he wore a long-handled axe strapped to his back. In the instant Henry stepped into the room, the big man looked him up and down and dismissed him. It infuriated Henry, but he had to admit, the other man was probably right. Magic sword or no, Henry doubted he'd last more than a few seconds against him.

"What is the meaning of this?" the king asked. He scowled at Henry. "I'm surprised you're still here."

"I would've been gone already, Your Majesty," Henry said, "but when someone tried to kill your daughter, I thought I should step in and put a stop to it. It seemed like the polite thing to do."

Anger flashed across his face but faded as the importance of Henry's words dawned on him.

"What?"

"Someone tried to kill me, Father," she said. "There is an assassin in your own castle."

The king was up and across the room before Henry knew it. He stood right in front of Andromeda. A look of terror painted his face.

"Are you hurt? What happened? Why do you smell like smoke?"

"I'm fine, Father," she said. "I was walking Henry out when it happened, but he saved me. Again."

The king looked from Henry to Andromeda. Then, he looked over his shoulder.

"Leave us," he said.

The generals rose. One left, but the other stopped before Andromeda.

"We will find whoever is responsible for this, Princess. On my life, I swear it."

"Thank you, General Rainard," she said, inclining her head.

The snowy-haired man bowed and left the room. The absolute dedication in his voice left no doubt that he meant what he said. Henry hoped he'd never be on the receiving end of his anger. He suspected that in many ways, that man was more dangerous than the hulking beast of a man who still sat at the war room table.

"You too, Hjal," the king said.

"Sire, I'm sure the queen would want me to stay," he said.

The king blinked. His shoulders slumped, and he took a deep breath. For a second, Henry thought he would allow Hjal to stay, but then the king's fists closed, and he set his jaw.

"No, Hjal," he said. "I will share whatever is relevant with the queen, but for now, I would speak to my daughter and the boy who saved her."

Hjal looked surprised but recovered after a second. "As you wish, sire."

He left the room without another word, and the king turned back to them.

"Now, tell me what happened."

"It was sorcery, Father."

"Andromeda, assassins are insidious creatures. They can do evil without the need for mystical aid. Don't try to turn this situation against your stepmother."

"No, father," she said. "If you don't believe me, go to the corridor to the western gate. You'll find the stone melted at one end. It was sorcery. It couldn't have been anything else."

The king sat down and motioned for them to do the same.

"Tell me what happened. From the beginning."

"It was fire," Andromeda said. "It shot down the corridor and came close to reducing us to ash. I know of no natural force capable of propelling flames like that."

"We're both glad you survived, Daughter," a voice came from behind them. "I'm curious. How is it you managed it?"

Henry turned around to see Zuab standing in the doorway. She met his eyes, and her lips curled up in a half snarl. After a second, her eyes widened, and Henry had the feeling he'd missed something. He turned back to the king and felt his stomach drop. All sign of concern on his face had vanished, replaced with empty adoration.

"I am not your daughter," Andromeda said, though she spoke so softly, Henry doubted anyone but he could hear.

"It was my shield," Henry said. "It has enchantments of its own. The one who forged it said it can turn back anything." Henry looked over his shoulder at the queen. "Even magic."

"You've worked your way back into my good graces, Master Henry," the king said. "Do not ruin that by making baseless accusations."

"Baseless?" Andromeda practically shouted. "That was powerful sorcery, Father. Who but she would have the power to do it?"

His expression softened, but then Zuab let out a breath and a barely controlled rage twisted his features.

"Andromeda, that's enough," he said. "I've accepted the fact that you don't care for your stepmother, but you will respect her."

"Respect her?" Andromeda shrieked. "She tried to kill me."

"She tried to kill us both," Henry said.

The king's face was red with anger, and he clenched his fists so tight his knuckles went white. Zuab walked up next to him and laid a hand on his. Henry could practically hear the wood of the table groan under the pressure the king was putting on it.

"Master Henry," the king said. "You are hereby banished from the Kingdom of Argath. If you are seen anywhere within its borders after this day, your life will be forfeit."

"But Father," Andromeda began, but he cut her off with a wave of his hand.

"As for you, I've had enough of your childish games. Zuab herself has offered to take over your education."

"Sire," Henry said, but the glare the king gave him stole his voice.

"Guards!" he called out. A second later, three men wearing the snowflake crest came in the room. "See this man out of the castle. If he resists, take his head."

"Father, no," Andromeda cried out. "He can help."

The guards didn't listen, though, and they practically dragged Henry from the room. They carried him down the hall and turned a corner.

"Go," a sandy-haired guard said to the others. "I can take care of him."

"Are you sure?" one of the others asked.

"He's just a pup," the first said. "I could watch him in my sleep."

"Suit yourself, but don't blame us if he gets away."

"I won't," the guard said. "Go on."

The other two turned down a passage while the one dragging Henry continued down the hall. After a few minutes of walking, the guard ducked into a small alcove lit by a single oil lamp.

"Was the princess right?" the guard asked.

"Right about what?" Henry asked.

"She said you could help. Can you?"

"I don't know," Henry said. "I've faced stronger witches than Zuab before."

The guard nodded, and for a moment, Henry considered telling him that the only way he'd gotten away from Circe was to flee, but he doubted it would've done any good, so he kept his mouth shut.

"The queen has too many guards assigned to her, and she's found a way to get rid of most of us who are loyal. We barely have enough to guard the castle. Two hours after sunset there is no watch on the south wall for at least ten minutes. If you go that way, you might be able to sneak Andromeda out."

Henry stopped and stared at the guard, barely able to believe what he was hearing. "Why are you doing this?"

"Many of us have seen the changes Zuab has brought on the king. I've known the princess for years. She is the heir to the throne of Argath, and when she sits on it, she'll be the greatest ruler in five generations but not if the queen has anything to say about it. If she tried to kill Andromeda once, she may well try again. I'm freeing you so that you can stop that from happening."

"Thank you," Henry said as they passed out of the door. "I'll keep her safe."

"That is all I can ask," the guard said.

He shoved Henry out the door and closed it behind him. Henry turned back and gave the castle he'd just been evicted from one last look before retrieving Pegasus and heading into town.

NINE

Henry spent the rest of the day in the forest near Daste. Once, he saw a hunter enter the woods, but the leather-garbed man didn't see him, which was a relief. There was no telling when these people would get word of Henry's banishment, nor how many would report his presence once they did hear. For all he knew, the king would put a price on his head. As the sun neared the horizon, Henry crept into town and made his way to the southern side of the castle. Two men marched on the castle wall, and Henry hid in a nearby alley, hoping they wouldn't see him.

For what felt like an eternity, Henry sat in the bush and waited. Men came and went from atop the wall. Finally, one left and wasn't replaced. A few minutes later, the second did as well, and Henry knew his time had come. He charged the wall.

He'd known the castle was old. Anyone could see that just by walking through the halls, but he hadn't realized what that meant until this moment. Cracks ran all the way up the wall, and ivy grew out of some spots. Though climbing wasn't easy, neither was it difficult, and he made good time. Five minutes later, he reached the top of the wall.

He scrambled down the other side and made his way across the courtyard. One of the windows in an unguarded area stood open, though whether it had been done deliberately or not, Henry didn't know. He slipped in and found himself in a servant's quarters. Whoever it belonged to wasn't present, so he ducked into the hall.

Inside, sneaking around was much easier. Most of the light was carried by patrolling guards, and whenever one approached, Henry ducked out of sight until they passed. Henry still found the castle confusing, though, and it took half an hour of searching before he turned the corner and saw two guards wearing the crescent moon crest standing at Andromeda's door. He scurried back behind the corner before they could see him. Briefly, he considered drawing his sword but dismissed the idea. Even if, by some miracle, he managed to overcome them, it wouldn't be quiet, and he'd have the whole castle on him within minutes. Instead, he ran back down the passage he'd come from until he found the stairs up.

As Henry neared the top of the staircase, the light of a lantern approached. He held his breath and went down a few steps, but the light passed after a couple of seconds. He crept down the hall and made his way to a room that, as near as he could tell, rested just above Andromeda's room. It was small and lacked any furniture save a single bed. The dust carpeting the floor told him no one had used this room in a long time, though he imagined it had once been inhabited by a servant. The window creaked as he pushed it open, and he waited several seconds to make sure no one had heard. As Henry stepped out onto the ledge, he realized he was much higher than he'd originally thought, at least five or six stories up, and the ground looked very far away. He felt at the wall, and his fingers ran along the stone. Unlike the outer wall, this was smooth. He'd never be able to climb down, but his hand fell to the sword at his waist.

Normal steel could never cut through stone, but god-forged steel was hardly normal. He drew the sword and knelt down. He shoved the sword into the wall beneath the ledge. It slid into the stone with a shower of sparks. Gripping the hilt with both hands, he stepped off the ledge. He yelped as he fell and swung from the weapon. It groaned as his weight dragged it down another foot, but then it stopped. His feet still dangled well above the top of Andromeda's window. Though he knew he shouldn't, he looked down. The ground might as well be a mile away, and he became keenly aware of his hands sweating, making his grip slip.

"I really need to start thinking things all the way through," he said to himself.

He kicked at the wall several times, but it felt solid under his blows. After a few minutes, his arms began to burn, and the stone groaned as the sword shifted.

"Andromeda," he called out as loud as he dared. He felt his fingers losing their grasp on the hilt. "Andromeda," he called out louder and kicked the wall again.

Beneath him, the window swung open. Andromeda poked her head out.

"Henry? What are you doing?"

"I'm here to rescue you," he said. "Sort of."

She laughed. "You do a much better job of saving me from monsters," she said. "What exactly do you intend to do now?"

"I haven't really worked that part out yet," he said. "I'm open to suggestions."

"Can you land on my ledge?" Andromeda asked.

"Are you serious?"

"I'm a prisoner in my own room. I don't exactly have a rope you can use. Drop. It's not that far, and I'll pull you in so you don't fall."

"I think we should think of a different plan," he said.

"After all you've been through, you're afraid of a little fall?"

The hilt began slipping from his fingers. He tried to regrip it, but it was useless. He looked down and tried to aim at the ledge. He was about to let go when the sword came free of the wall. For a second, he felt like he was flying, but pain lanced through his legs as soon as he landed. Before he could fall back, Andromeda reached out and grabbed him. He fell forward, and the two of them tumbled to the ground. His sword slid to the other side of the room. They untangled themselves, and Henry stood on shaky legs. He walked over to the wall and retrieved his sword.

"Thanks," Henry said.

Andromeda grinned. "And what now, my hero?"

"You're enjoying this way too much," he said. "There wouldn't happen to be another way out of here, would there? A secret passage or something?"

"We could go through the window." She laughed at his scowl, but it only lasted a second. "No, there's just the door, and that's guarded."

Henry touched the hilt of his sword. "I didn't want to use this on the way in," Henry said. "I was afraid they'd sound the alarm before I even got close, but if we call them in here, I might be able to surprise them."

Andromeda's face went a little green, but she nodded. "You call them. They'll come in quicker if they hear you."

Henry nodded and drew his sword. He stood next to the door but hesitated. His weapon shook in his hands. He didn't know if he could do this. He'd used the sword against monsters, and on a few occasions, he'd disarmed enemies who attacked him, but he'd never deliberately set an ambush to attack human beings before.

"Except they're not humans," he said under his breath, but no matter how many times he repeated that, it still sounded hollow and empty. "Guards!"

For a second, nothing happened, but then the door swung inward, and a big man wearing the snowflake crest stepped into the room. He looked at Henry.

"How the devil did you get here?" he asked.

"Uncle!" Andromeda said as she threw her arms around him.

Henry relaxed his grip on the sword. Through the doorway, he saw two men sprawled on the ground. He looked back to Sholtz, then to the window and raised an eyebrow.

"You can't be serious," he said. "You climbed up the wall?"

"Actually, I climbed down," Henry said. "It's not something I'd like to repeat."

"Uncle, are you responsible for this?" she said indicating the downed guards.

Sholtz nodded. "I saw the corridor the witch melted. I can see what's happening even if your father doesn't, and I'm not about to leave you here to die. I'm just glad I wasn't the only one." He turned to Henry. Firelight danced in his eyes.

"Can you protect her?"

"Where I'm going isn't safe," Henry said.

"It's safer than here, I'd wager."

"I wouldn't be so sure, but I'll do what I can."

"I am standing right here," Andromeda said. "I can take care of myself."

Sholtz gave her a polite nod. "With respect, Princess, by your own admission, this young hero has battled sorceresses, monsters, and armies and come out alive. You'll forgive me if I ask one such as him to watch over you."

Andromeda's face reddened but she didn't say anything, and Sholtz turned back to Henry. "Make your way to the stables, and get fast horses. I'll see if I can misdirect your pursuers."

He and Henry clasped arms, and Sholtz disappeared without another word. Henry turned around while Andromeda changed into a plain shirt and pants. Then, she spent a few minutes stuffing a pack before leading them back down to the ground level and out onto the grounds. Whatever Sholtz did apparently worked, because they didn't see anyone as they walked to the stables.

Henry sneezed at the straw in the air, but Andromeda seemed not to notice. She walked to the end of a long wooden building and opened a stall door. She spoke softly for a moment and a chocolate brown horse almost as big as Pegasus walked out.

"Oakash is the best we have," Andromeda said. "I've known her since she was a pony. Now, let's see to your horse."

Henry shook his head. "I'll ride with you. I left Pegasus outside the city."

"Are you sure?" she asked. "I know you're fond of him, but I'm not sure he can compare against my father's herd."

"He can hold his own," Henry said.

She nodded and they both mounted up and headed for the exit to the grounds. The man at the western gate was a pudgy little man with a round face. He wore the snowflake crest, and apparently, no one had told him to keep the princess in, because he let them through without a word. It was all Henry could do not to take off at a gallop as soon as they passed the gate.

TEN

They moved slowly through the town. At this hour, any decent person had long since gone to bed, and the windows were completely dark. A light mist had rolled in while they'd been in the castle. It didn't do much to obscure his sight, but combined with the myriad of lightless buildings and too-recent memories of the catacombs beneath the castle, it made his surroundings feel more like a cemetery than a city. Once, he saw a shadow duck into an alley, and he could only imagine what someone would be up to at this hour.

By the time they'd reached the edge of town, the fog had thickened. Pegasus came out of the trees and knelt down for Henry to get up. Andromeda turned back toward the castle. She gazed into town for a long time.

"I've left before," she said. "Many times, but it's always been home. Now, I'm not so sure."

"Don't worry," Henry said. "We'll find a way to stop Zuab."

"Like you stopped Circe?" she said without looking at him.

That stung worse than he would've expected it to, but he could hardly blame her for the comment. He moved his horse closer to her and put a hand on her shoulder. She looked at him with unshed tears in her eyes.

"Zuab isn't Circe," he said.

"No, Circe never had a kingdom at her back. She never controlled one of the fiercest armies in the land."

"Circe never needed it," he said. "We'll stop her, Andromeda."

She nodded and looked at the town one more time. She cocked her head.

"Do you hear something?"

Henry listened. A pinprick of orange light appeared in the fog, and he heard a low rumble. A second light appeared. Then a third. They swayed through the fog, and it took Henry a second to realize they were coming closer.

"What is that?" he asked.

Andromeda's eyes went wide. "Horses!" she said. "They're coming after us. Ride, Henry!"

She turned Oakash and drove her heels into the horse, and the animal leaped forward. Henry urged Pegasus to follow. Andromeda was already several strides ahead of him, but it didn't take long for Pegasus to close the distance. The wind beat against Henry's face. Even without the fog, he doubted he'd be able to see anything more than a blur. Pegasus might have lost his wings, but that didn't seem to make a difference. The horse flew across the ground as quickly as he'd ever flown through the air.

It took several minutes to realize that he'd left Andromeda behind. He slowed Pegasus to a trot. Before long, he heard the clomp of hooves on stone, and Andromeda came out of the fog. She slowed her pace and fell into step beside him.

"I take it back," she said. "Oakash doesn't even come close to

Pegasus. Neither does any other of my father's animals. He doesn't even look winded. Do you think he could keep that up all day?"

"I don't have the slightest idea," Henry said.

"You should go," she said. "They'd never be able to catch you."

"I'm not leaving you."

"Listen to me, Henry," she said. "If they're chasing us, they would've brought spare horses to switch out. Oakash can keep ahead of them for a while, but he can't maintain a full gallop with a rider for long."

"Then, let's go into the woods," Henry said.

"You can't be serious," she said. "You can't do hard riding through the woods. Your horse would break a leg."

"Neither can they," Henry said.

"But there are bandits and wild animals," she said.

"And neither one of those are more dangerous than a witch with an army at her back."

She looked at him. Her lower lip quivered. For a second, he thought she would refuse, but eventually, she nodded, and they turned into the forest. They moved slower than he would've believed as they maneuvered through the trees. The full moon provided little light through the forest canopy. After a few minutes, the sound of galloping horses came from behind them. They froze until the sounds faded, but no one came after them.

"Are they gone?" Andromeda asked.

"I think so," Henry said. "Let's walk the horses for a bit."

She nodded and they both dismounted. With the immediate danger gone, exhaustion caught up with him. From the slump of Andromeda's shoulders, he guessed she felt the same way. Neither one said anything though. By the time they stopped to make camp an hour later, Henry was practically asleep on his feet. Andromeda didn't have a bedroll with her, so he gave his to her. As tired as he was, he fell asleep as soon as he lay down.

ELEVEN

You know, if there are people chasing you, you really should keep watch," a voice said.

Henry's eyes shot open. He rolled onto his feet and drew his sword, swinging it without looking. The weapon cut neatly into a tree, slicing through it as if it didn't exist. Amber sap gleamed on the blade, and more oozed out of the cut. A wiry man dressed in green and brown sat on a nearby rock. His lean face reminded Henry of a cat. A neat fire pit had been built, and a boar was roasting on a spit. The man raised an eyebrow at the tree but didn't say anything. Andromeda woke more slowly. When she saw their intruder, she sat up with her eyes wide. The edges of her mouth turned down in a frown.

"Roderick," she said in a level voice.

"I'm glad to see you too, Andromeda," he said.

"I would say the same if I knew whose side you were on."

"I'm surprised you have to ask," he said as he jumped off the rock.

He landed lightly on his feet and strolled over to Andromeda as if it were a normal day. He offered her a hand up, and she took it cautiously. Henry let out a breath and sheathed his sword.

"I've been surprised by a great many things over the past couple of days," she said.

"It's not as bad as you think," Roderick said.

"Not as bad?" Andromeda practically yelled.

"Please, keep it down," he said. "There are people looking for you all over these woods, and not all of them are friendly."

"Not as bad?" Andromeda asked again, though this time, she spoke in a loud whisper. "I was imprisoned in my own room after my stepmother tried to kill me. I was chased out of town by my own guards, and I'm hiding in the woods in my father's lands. Please, tell me Roderick, how is it not as bad as I think?"

"Why do you think you were able to get away?" he asked. "Do you think Captain Sholtz is the only one loyal to you? More than one person turned a blind eye to you tonight or you wouldn't have made it out of the castle grounds. Many of us suspect Queen Zuab of working dark magic on the king."

"Then, why don't you do anything?"

A squirrel chattered at them from a nearby branch as if scolding them for being so loud, but neither Andromeda nor Roderick seemed to notice.

"What would you have us do?" he asked. "He is devoted to her. Should we take up arms against him? Should we depose him?"

"Well...no," Andromeda said, sounding much less sure of herself.

"There are many who would follow you, if you gave the word," he said as if she hadn't spoken. "As entrenched as Zuab's forces are in Argath, I don't think we could actually take the kingdom back from her, especially with how strong her army has grown recently.

A lot of people would die in the attempt, but we'd be willing to try."

"That's not what I mean," she said. The fire had faded from her voice.

"Then tell me, Princess, what should we do that we're not already doing?"

She turned away. "I don't know."

"Nor do we," he said. "No one is entirely sure that the king is enspelled. Without that certainty, we have only one truth. He is the king."

"What about the queen?" Henry asked.

"The queen ordered soldiers to come after you, Master Henry. She doesn't particularly care about you, but the princess is another matter. We're under orders to bring back her heart. The castle is not safe for you." Andromeda met his gaze. Her lower lip quivered. After a few seconds, the hunter closed his eyes and shook his head. "I'm sorry."

"What does the king have to say about that?" Henry asked.

Roderick looked over his shoulder at Henry and took a step away from Andromeda. "I'd be very surprised if she told him, and he wouldn't believe anyone who spoke against her."

"And you don't see that as proof that she's controlling the king?" Henry asked.

"I do," Roderick said, "but many don't, and Zuab won't rest until she holds Andromeda's heart."

Henry's stomach churned at the thought, and Andromeda looked like she was going to be sick, but Roderick pointed to a bundle wrapped in blood-soaked cloth sitting on a nearby rock.

"I took this from our friend here," Roderick said, indicating the boar. "I'll give it to Zuab. With a little luck, she'll think you're dead and you can be on your way doing whatever it is you need to do to free us from her."

"Isn't that dangerous?" Andromeda asked. "What if you get caught?"

"If I get caught, I suspect I'm in for a very slow and painful death." Roderick spoke as if the idea didn't bother him at all. "I don't intend to get caught though, so it's not something I'm terribly worried about. Now, if you don't mind, this boar is just about ready."

Before either could say anything, Roderick brought out wooden plates from his pack. He sliced meat from the boar and passed each of them a plate before making one for himself and plopping down next to the fire. Henry looked to Andromeda who nodded, and they sat around the fire with him. The meat was tough and gamey, but at least it was warm, and it was more than he'd had since they fled the palace.

"Thank you," Andromeda said, though whether it was for the meal or the information, Henry couldn't say.

"I live to serve, Princess," Roderick said without a trace of mockery. It apparently surprised Andromeda too because she gaped at him.

"Frederick is king," Roderick said, "but you are my princess. I'll get back to the castle as soon as I can. I should be able to give you at least a temporary respite."

He threw dirt on their makeshift fire pit and began spreading leaves over it until it looked like no one had been there.

"Oh, before I forget," Roderick said as he rummaged through his bag, pulling out a bedroll and a wrapped bundle of food. He placed them on the ground near the fire.

"I suspect you'll need these a great deal more than I will."

"Thank you, Roderick," Andromeda said. "For everything."

"I am still a man of Argath, Princess." He bowed to Andromeda. "No matter what the queen does, that will not change. Be careful in these woods. I saw the markings of a bear, and livestock has been disappearing from nearby towns. There may be a wolf pack near. I'll do what I can to throw the others off your trail before returning to the castle."

Henry nodded. Roderick inclined his head, first to Andromeda and then to Henry before he disappeared into the forest.

"You know, I used to think I would marry him," Andromeda said.

Henry blinked in the direction Roderick had gone. "Really?"

She waved a hand. "It was a childish fancy. I think I grew out of it when I was twelve, but I've always had a fondness for him. I'm glad he's on our side."

"So where do we go now?" he asked. "If they're searching the woods for us, I doubt the road would be any safer, and it'll be days before they hear that your friend returned with your heart."

Andromeda shook her head. "There's nothing but forest between here and the Nordi Mountains. If we keep going west, we'll hit them eventually."

"But will we hit them anywhere near the dwarves?"

Andromeda shrugged. "It's that or the road."

"I don't suppose you know how to avoid the wolves and bears Roderick mentioned."

"There was just one bear," Andromeda said. Henry glared at her. "No, I don't know. For some reason, they never considered woodcraft an essential skill for a princess. We'll just have to trust to luck."

Henry laughed. He couldn't help himself. Andromeda scowled, and it took effort for Henry to regain his composure.

"I'm sorry," he said between chuckles, "it's just with the way my luck's been lately, I'm almost sure we're about to find a dragon."

The edges of Andromeda's lips tightened as she tried to hold in a laugh.

"There's no such thing as dragons," she managed.

"Or flying horses," he said as he ran his fingers through Pegasus's mane.

Andromeda's brow furled and she gave him a questioning look.

"Never mind."

They packed up their bedrolls. Heavy cloud cover had rolled in overnight, and they had to guess at what direction was west. The clouds kept the worst of the sun's heat off them, but the air was thick with humidity, and before long, their clothes were soaked with sweat. Even the horses seemed grumpy. Every time they slowed, Henry thought he could hear people moving through the woods.

They didn't stop at midday. Instead, they finished off most of the remaining boar meat as they walked. They didn't see any sign of pursuit all day, and by the time the sky began to darken, the shroud of fear that they'd worn since escaping the castle had unraveled, and Henry stopped seeing enemies in every shadow. His legs ached and his eyelids felt like they were made of lead. They made camp in a small clearing and ate bread and dried fruit from Roderick's packs. He told Andromeda to sleep first. She complained that she was just as capable as he was, but it wasn't heartfelt, and before long, she snored softly by the fire.

TWELVE

Without the constant threat of soldiers, the forest felt almost peaceful. The insects chirping made a peculiar song, and Henry found himself drawn into it. It was hard to believe that out there was a powerful witch who wanted them dead. He didn't realize he was falling asleep until something tugged at his pack. The horses whinnied, and Henry opened his eyes and looked over his shoulder. Golden eyes stared back at him from the darkness. He cried out and fell back. The animal tore at his pack until it had found the remaining boar meat. Henry looked around and saw half a dozen other pairs of eyes surrounding them.

"What's going on?" Andromeda asked groggily.

In the light of the dying embers, he could see her jaw drop as a great black wolf strode into the light.

"Don't let it know you're afraid." Henry tried to sound brave but didn't think he succeeded.

He drew his sword and rose slowly. His mind wandered back to a night that seemed a lifetime ago, when his friend Virgil had been mortally wounded by an animal attack just like this. His fist tightened around the hilt of his sword. He would *not* let it happen again.

The wolf walked up to Andromeda and sniffed. Henry crept closer and was about to strike when it licked her face. Andromeda gasped, but after a second, she began to laugh. Slowly, the other wolves came into the light, but they looked more curious than predatory. They sniffed Andromeda, and many of them wagged their tails.

"Do you have any more boar meat?" Henry asked.

"I think so," she said and pulled it out of her pack.

She unwrapped it and put it on the ground. There wasn't much, but the wolves devoured it eagerly. The black one barked a few times and licked Andromeda's hand before disappearing into the darkness. The others followed him. Henry and Andromeda stared after them for a long time.

"What do you think that was about?" Henry asked.

"I honestly don't know," she said. "I've never heard of anything like that, but I suppose it's about time something happened that wasn't a disaster."

"Maybe we should go looking for the bear," Henry said.

Andromeda laughed. "Let's not try our luck." She looked at the sky. "It'll be dawn soon," she said.

Henry felt his face redden. "I didn't realize I'd slept all night."

Andromeda shrugged. "Nothing came of it. Why don't we get an early start?"

"Good idea," Henry said. "I don't think I could sleep now if I tried."

"Neither could I."

They packed supplies as quickly as they could and departed. As the sky grew lighter, Henry tried to think of something to say, but no words came. It was Andromeda who finally broke the silence.

"I hope Uncle Sholtz is all right," she said.

The statement caught Henry off guard. To his shame, he hadn't even thought of the old soldier since they'd left the castle. "I'm sure he will be," Henry said. "He seemed like a resourceful man."

Andromeda gave him a weak smile. "He is," she said. "I'm just not sure it'll be enough."

"It will be," Henry said. "How long until we reach the mountains?"

"I'm not sure. With these clouds, I can't even be sure we're heading west, but it can't be more than three or four days."

Henry nodded. They pressed on for five more days before the clouds broke. Their packs were light, and they were running low on supplies when the sun finally peaked through.

"We've been heading southwest," Henry said, "and more south than west."

Andromeda didn't say anything, though Henry could see the bags under her eyes. She was as tired as he was. They turned west, and by the end of the day, they were catching glimpses of the mountains through the trees.

"Two days," she said. "Three at most, but getting there won't be the hard part."

"Then what will be?"

"It's no accident my father's been unable to drive them out. The dwarves are strong, and the mountains are theirs. They don't suffer intruders into their realm lightly."

"Well then, we'll just have to convince them we're on their side."

As the days passed, the mountains grew steadily larger in the distance. They had no more encounters with local wildlife. After two days, the trees began to thin, and the mountains dominated more of the sky.

Finally, they broke through the tree line and came upon a sheer rock face stretching into the sky. Henry's eyes sought out the top, but the angle made that impossible. He couldn't even begin to guess how tall this cliff was. High above, a large bird circled before landing in some hidden nest. His mind reeled at the scale of it, but Andromeda walked up to it as if it were the most ordinary thing in the world.

She hadn't taken more than a few steps when the shadows around her lengthened and became solid. Short, bearded men emerged from nooks and crannies in the rock that Henry could've sworn were too small to fit anyone. Their gray and brown faces could've been made of stone, and Henry doubted there was enough kindness in them to fill a thimble. They wore steel and each carried an axe as big as he was. A moment later, Henry and Andromeda were completely surrounded. Oakash began to dance back and forth, and Andromeda gripped her reins tight.

"We come in peace?" Henry spoke so meekly it sounded more like a question than a statement.

One dwarf with a long gray beard that fell to his knees walked up to them. Though the tallest, he couldn't be more than four feet tall, and the gray looked more like a natural color than something brought on by age.

"Off the horses," said the dwarf in a deep, rumbling voice. They complied, moving slowly so as not to appear threatening. "Who are you and what are you doing here?"

Andromeda held her chin high. "I am Princess Andromeda of Argath, and this is Master Henry Alexander Gideon."

Several of the dwarves lowered their weapons slightly at that, and their leader gave him a slight bow, but he scowled at Andromeda.

"Henry Alexander Gideon," he said. "Word of your exploits has reached us even beneath the mountains."

"You've heard of me?" Henry asked, somewhat taken aback.

"Well of course," a younger looking dwarf said. "We're not completely isolated."

"Since you all know me," Henry said, "maybe you should put down your weapons."

The leader shook his head. "I'm afraid that's not possible. Even the greatest stories tell of your alliance with the queen of Argath."

"What?" Henry said. "Zuab tried to kill us."

The dwarf rolled his eyes and nodded at Andromeda. "I said the queen of Argath boy, not the queen of Neustad."

"What are you talking about?" Andromeda said, but suddenly all color drained from her face. "No. My father? She killed my father?"

The dwarf shook his head. "Your father still lives, if you can call that sort of puppetry living."

"But that's why we're here," Andromeda said. "Zuab has some sort of control over him."

"Yes, we know," he said.

"If you know, then why do you have us under guard? You know she's our enemy."

"We are in the middle of a war. Your father may be under the witch's control, but you are not, and as queen, you bear responsibility for every dwarf that has died at the hands of your people."

"I'm not the queen," she said.

The dwarf snorted but didn't lower his weapon.

"Just take us prisoner, then," Henry said. Both the dwarf and Andromeda looked at him. "Look, we're no danger to you as prisoners, but I need to speak to your leader. If the fastest way I can do that is in chains, then so be it."

The dwarf considered for a second before nodding. He spoke in a low guttural language to a bald dwarf with one eye who grunted and took the reins from Henry and Andromeda. Pegasus struggled for a second, but Henry shook his head and the horse calmed down and followed the dwarf. The others began filing away, but the leader remained. After the rest had departed, he led them to a crack in the wall so narrow Henry would've missed it if the dwarf hadn't pointed it out to him. It was only about six feet tall and though the dwarf could fit through the wider bottom portion with ease, the top was too thin, and they had to slouch to follow. Their guide seemed to have no need for empty conversation and walked in near perfect silence.

Even his footsteps barely registered. Henry and Andromeda, on the other hand, continually scraped across the wall and kicked loose pebbles, and the cave amplified every sound they made. Once, when Henry stumbled, he thought he saw the dwarf snicker, but it was already too dark to be sure. As the light faded behind them, the dwarf pulled a stone out of his shirt and struck it against the wall. It began emitting a soft yellow light, and the dwarf held it in front of him.

"Will you at least tell us your name?" Henry asked.

"Valin," he said.

"You were waiting for us."

"Yes," Valin said. "We've been watching you for a day and a half."

"Why didn't you show yourselves?" Andromeda asked. "Did you know we were looking for you?"

"Begging your pardon, Queen Andromeda," he said, "but we still don't know if you are truly an enemy of Zuab or her ally. The fact that she let you escape without an enchantment on you is not a good sign."

"She wasn't enchanted because I broke her out," Henry said.

"That may be true," Valin said, "but that's not for me to decide."

"Why do you keep calling me a queen?" Andromeda asked.

Valin turned and looked at them. "A man with no will of his own cannot be king." He spoke slowly like he was explaining something to a child. "No matter if blood flows through his veins. As his heir, the crown falls to you."

Andromeda shook her head. "That's not how human kingdoms work."

Valin snorted. "It's how every kingdom works, girl. You humans just haven't realized it. Let's go. We've wasted enough time here. The king will want to see you."

After a while, Henry's back ached from crouching, and the constant scraping against the walls had left a series of scratches on his arms. The constant smell of mud and clay in the air started to give him a headache. He was about to ask how much longer when the passage opened to a massive cavern, and his jaw practically hit the floor. The city had been carved out of the mountain itself.

Half a dozen towers encircled a walled city on what could only be described as a hill, though Henry didn't know if you could call something inside of a mountain a hill. Each tower had a glowing crystal atop it much like the one Valin carried, though much larger. Together, they shone as bright as the sun. The buildings were mainly short and squat, but some of them could have been small palaces. The castle in the center was at least twice as big as the one in Daste. It towered even over the walls, and on its roof sat a massive diamond emitting white light that filled the cavern.

"This place is amazing." Andromeda's voice was barely above a whisper.

"You should see our great cities," Valin said, "the ones that lie deep beneath the earth. They make Kerat look like a trading post. If not for the need to coordinate the war effort, our king would be there instead of here."

"Let's not keep him waiting," Henry said.

Valin nodded, and they headed into the city.

THIRTEEN

I t felt like they drew every eye as they made their way through Kerat. It wasn't really surprising. Henry was at least a foot taller than anyone else in the city. Almost everyone walked around on bare feet, and most carried a weapon or two. Every building bore intricate carvings to the point that he didn't see an empty wall anywhere. Once, he saw a small child with a hammer and chisel chipping away at a flat piece of rock the way a human child might play with paper and crayons. Every once in a while, he'd see a cart drawn by a donkey, but most people went around on foot.

Two dwarves with huge double-bladed battle axes stood at the castle gate. They brought a fist to their heart when Valin approached, and one looked up and made a hand signal. A second later, the gate groaned and began to rise. Valin nodded at the guards and went in. Henry and Andromeda followed right behind. The guards watched him as he passed, but no one demanded he surrender his weapon. Inside, glowing stones of every color hung from a ceiling that looked to be made of obsidian. If Henry squinted, he could imagine those to be electric lights and the stone floor to be ordinary linoleum. The thought only brought painful memories of home, and he forced it out of his mind.

"When we reach King Fjalar, be respectful," Andromeda said softly. "Follow my lead. It's customary for the males of his line to join him when he gives audiences, though they probably won't speak. If you speak to him, the proper form of address for a dwarven king is Stonelord."

Henry nodded. It only took a few minutes before they reached a pair of doors decorated with red and yellow gemstones. A picture of an erupting volcano had been carved where the doors met. Again, the guards let them through without incident, and Henry found himself in the dwarven throne room.

It looked like half the room was made of gold and the other half of silver. Gems of every size and color littered the wall. Even the carpeted floor looked to be woven from gold fibers. An old dwarf sat on a jewel-encrusted throne in the center of the room. His crown glowed with the same yellow light as Valin's stone. A dagger hung at his belt, and a war hammer sat mounted on the wall above him, high enough to be out of the way but low enough to be within easy reach. Two dwarves stood at his left, and three at his right. All carried weapons.

The dwarf on the throne sat so still that, for a moment, Henry thought he was a statue dressed in red and purple, but his eyes followed the trio as they entered his hall. A thick black beard streaked with white hid his expression. Valin went to one knee. Henry and Andromeda followed his example.

"Rise." The deep voice echoed through the room.

"Grandfather," Valin said.

"Grandfather?" Henry asked.

Everyone in the room glared at him, and he took a step back. Valin, combined with the other dwarven nobles made seven dwarves. Henry had wondered when they would come into play.

Valin cleared his throat and continued. "Allow me to present Queen Andromeda of Argath and Master Henry Alexander Gideon, hero of a thousand battles." He turned to them.

"Hero of a thousand battles? Where did that come from?" Henry asked Andromeda, but the princess shushed him.

"Welcome to Kerat," the king said with a nod of his head.

"Forgive me, Stonelord," Andromeda said, "but I'm afraid your grandson is in error. My father lives. I am not the queen."

Fjalar let out a long breath. "I had this conversation with your father long ago. Must I explain this to every human ruler?"

Andromeda sputtered. Fjalar rose from his throne. His feet thunked solidly on the woven gold carpet. He stood before them and looked up at Andromeda. After a few seconds, Andromeda turned away from him.

"I'm sorry," she said in a soft voice. "My father never told me."

"What realm does your family rule?"

"Argath."

"Where is Argath?"

"From the Nordi Mountains on the north and west to the Ebra River in the south and the Yulher Forest in the east," she said without hesitation.

"Is Argath the land or the people?" he asked.

"Well...the people," she said.

"Then, if I decide that twenty miles of forest east of here belong to me, there would be no issue. No people live there, so it is not Argath."

Andromeda shook her head. "No, that's not right. My father would never stand for it."

"And well that he shouldn't," Fjalar said, "though it is not fear of your father that would stop me. Your family has a pact with Argath, with the land as well as with the people. I could no more claim the forest than I could claim the sky. The land would not accept me, and it will not accept a king whose will has been stolen from him. Whether you will admit it or not, you are the queen, and the land knows it."

Andromeda mumbled something Henry couldn't hear. The king cocked his head but said nothing. Instead, he shook his head and walked back to his throne. It brightened again as he sat down but not so bright that Henry had to look away.

"He may be right." Henry pitched his voice low so only she could hear. "Remember how the wolves reacted?"

Andromeda gave him a sidelong glance but didn't otherwise react. Instead, she spoke to the king. "Your grandson said you suspect I am in league with Zuab."

"These are perilous times," Fjalar said. "It's not wise to take chances with such things."

"She turned my father against me and tried to kill me and my friend. She chased us into the forest and told the hunters to bring back my heart as proof of my death. I am as far from being her ally as it is possible to be."

"Perhaps," Fjalar said. "For now, I will take you at your word that you're not our enemy."

"Just like that?" Henry asked.

The king's shoulders sagged, and for the first time, he looked like something weaker than an immovable mountain. Even the lights of the surrounding stones dimmed.

"King Frederick had a saying. Realm before king. As a king, I would throw you in prison to pay for what your people have done, if I didn't decide to execute you, but the war does not go well. This realm needs allies more than it needs vengeance, so yes, I choose to believe you. Don't make me regret it."

"Thank you," Andromeda said. "How did this happen? When I left Argath, you and my father were allies."

"And he and Zuab were enemies," the king said. "Her army has doubled in size recently, and your father spoke to me about joining our forces against her, but then a plague tore through Argath. We did what we could to help, but it was beyond our abilities. Then, she showed up with the cure. Your father went to Neustad to thank her in person. From there, I suspect it was a simple matter to bring him under her spell. She made some pretense about us refusing to supply her with emberstones." He tapped his glowing crown. "I don't believe it, though. She knows as well as anyone that emberstones kept away from our kind dim to a faint glow. I suspect she wants something else from us, maybe even the land itself. She couldn't get to me, so she's going through your father."

"She probably caused the plague," Andromeda said.

"No, I don't think so," he said. "We may not have been able to stop it, but we could tell it was a natural thing. Perhaps she had encountered it before or maybe she used her power to divine a cure."

"Or maybe an Oracle told her what it was," Henry said.

"What's that, Master Henry?"

"I spoke to an Oracle not long ago," he said. "She told me Zuab holds an Oracle that can see all that is."

The dwarf king snorted. "If she had something like that, I think she'd set her sights a little higher than claiming three kingdoms."

"Maybe you would," Andromeda said, "but Zuab is the most

arrogant person I've ever met. She might try to take your kingdom and my father's just because you told her she couldn't have them."

The king glanced at Valin who shrugged. "You always did call her a petty queen, Grandfather. It does seem like something she would do."

"And it would explain some things," he said, drumming his fingers on the arm of his throne.

"The Oracle said Zuab isn't the greatest threat," Henry said. "She's working for someone."

"That doesn't seem likely," the king said. "Someone like her wouldn't lightly submit to anyone else."

"Where did Zuab get the Oracle?" Henry asked. "How has her army become so strong? For that matter, if she had the power to take control of the king, why didn't she do this long ago?"

"She tried," Valin said, "years ago, when those human brothers came here."

"What human brothers?"

Valin ran his hand through his beard and closed his eyes as if trying to remember something. "Grimm", he said finally. Henry waited, but the dwarf didn't say anything else.

"They were grim?" Henry asked.

"No, that was their name. They had dealings with seven miners."

Henry's eyes went wide, and he took in a sharp breath. Seven dwarves. He looked at Andromeda who in another version of this story might have had a different name. "The Brothers Grimm? They came here?"

"I remember them," Andromeda said. "Do you know them?"

"I know of them," he said. "They were two of the most famous storytellers in history, but they died hundreds of years before I was born."

"It must've been a different pair then," Andromeda said. "This was only a few years ago."

Henry looked at her in disbelief, but then it dawned on him. A few days ago, he'd been thousands of miles away and thousands of years ago, in ancient Greece. Time didn't work the same way in Kurnugi. If the Brothers Grimm had gotten the story of Snow White from here, it would've had to have been in Andromeda's lifetime. Why shouldn't she remember them?

"What happened?" he asked.

"She failed."

"But how?"

"It's not important," Fjalar said.

"I think it might be," Henry said.

Andromeda pursed her lips, and the dwarves exchanged glances. No one answered his question. It had been too much to hope for. They remembered the Brothers Grimm because they were human, but the story the brothers had documented was the one Henry was experiencing now. They were stuck in a paradox. For all he knew, they had no way of remembering any details.

"Never mind," Henry said. "My point is someone is helping Zuab succeed where she failed before. She may be the most immediate threat, but she's not the biggest one, and we may need your help."

The king thought for a second, then nodded. "Take them to the surface."

"But Grandfather..."

"Take them, Valin," Fjalar said. "You know very well we need to take chances. What the boy says makes a lot of sense, and you don't come asking for help from people you intend to betray. If Queen Andromeda truly opposes Zuab, she could be a great boon to our cause."

"And if she doesn't?"

"It's not as if the situation could grow much worse," he said darkly.

Valin started to say something else, but the king waved his hand in dismissal. Valin clenched his teeth and bowed. Henry and Andromeda did the same and they followed Valin out of the palace.

FOURTEEN

W hat's on the surface?" Henry asked as they walked near one of the city gates.

"We don't just intend to sit here and wait for Zuab to come to us," he said. "My father's been gathering his forces for months."

"What?" Andromeda cried causing many people to look in their direction. "You intend to attack Argath?"

"We intend to fight back," Valin growled. "Three outposts and a hundred lives have already fallen to your army."

"But now, Zuab has two," Henry pointed out. "Can you stand against both of them?"

Valin shook his head. "No, I don't think so."

"Why are you preparing to attack if you don't think you can win?"

"You're right," Valin said, "I don't think we can win, but I've been wrong before, and it would greatly please me to be wrong again."

Valin led them through the city gates and to another crack much like the one they'd walked through to reach Kerat. This one, however, was much taller and thicker, and they could walk upright without any difficulty. They'd only walked for about fifteen minutes when Henry caught sight of the moon shining through the opening of the passage. A few minutes later, they were out and he found himself looking into a valley covered in soldiers.

"How many are there?" Andromeda asked.

"Not quite ten thousand," Valin said. "It's enough to defend these mountains against your father's men, but not against the combined forces of Argath and Neustad."

"What will you do?" Andromeda asked.

"I think the question is what will you do?" Valin asked. "If you want our help, what help do you offer in return?"

"You want her to fight against her own father?" Henry asked.

Valin shook his head. "There is no father anymore. As long as Zuab controls him, there won't be."

"I don't know," Andromeda said.

"You are the queen of Argath," Valin said.

"No, I'm not. I don't care what you say. As long as my father is alive, I am not the queen."

"The land..."

"Forget the land," Andromeda said. "I'm talking about my father. As long as he draws breath, do not dare call me the queen."

Her voice was as cold as ice, and though her gaze did not waver, a single tear ran down her cheek and fell into the rocky ground. Valin paused and gave her a small bow.

"As you wish, Princess," he said. "Though you will not take the title, I assume your father taught you of ruling."

"Of course," Andromeda said.

"The ruler has a responsibility to her people. Queen or princess, you are their protector, and you must do what is best for them."

"Yes," Andromeda said.

"Do you think what's best for them is to fall under the thumb of a woman like Zuab?"

"No."

"Your father does," Valin said, "at least he does as he is now. You can't convince him otherwise, not while he's under her spell."

"Then, we should break it."

"Gladly," Valin said. "Would you care to tell us how?" Andromeda looked at him blankly. "We have access to some magic." He patted the pouch containing the emberstone, "but the magic of the mind is beyond us."

"Then, we find a way." Andromeda had tears streaming down her cheeks, and Henry put a hand on her shoulder.

"Would you have us sacrifice our people for the sake of one man?"

"For the sake of my father."

"I knew him," Valin said. "He would not sacrifice all of us for his sake."

"No, he wouldn't," she said. "I should've listened to Roderick when he said others would follow me."

"Then, you'll help us?" Valin said.

"Yes," she said, though from the anguished look on her face, she could've easier moved a mountain than say that word.

Valin nodded. "Then, we have work to do."

FIFTEEN

Valin led them down into the army camp. They didn't draw nearly as much attention here as they had in the city, but a fair number still stared at them. Most, however, kept their attention on their work. Everywhere dwarves trained with hammer and axe, and they passed one grizzled old warrior teaching toddlers the proper way to hold a wooden dagger. The ever-present ringing of hammer striking metal came from countless weapon smiths scattered throughout the valley. The smell of their burning coal was a steady presence throughout the encampment. As far as Henry could tell, nothing was being done that wasn't a preparation for war.

"I hardly see any camp followers," Andromeda said.

"Camp followers?" Henry asked.

"Wherever there is an army, there are camp followers," she said. "Wash women, merchants selling food to soldiers who want something more than rations, any number of others. All I see is blacksmiths."

"And even they know how to use the weapons they make. No one is here who will not fight when the time comes."

"Even the children?" Andromeda's face was pale.

"As my grandfather said, we're desperate."

"Why have them on the surface?" Henry asked. "Aren't they more exposed?"

"Yes, but also more mobile," Valin said. "Our tunnels work fine for transferring individuals, but it would take at least a day to bring all these men through. Here, by utilizing the passes, they can be at the base of the mountain and on their way in a quarter of that time."

"You seem to be doing well," Andromeda said. "From what the Stonelord said, I would've expected something a little more run down."

"We have a fine army," Valin said, "and a dwarf is more than equal to a human in combat, but your armies have been directed by Zuab, and she seems to always know where we are and what we're doing."

"Because of the Oracle," Henry said.

"Personally, I don't put much stock in such things," Valin said. "I think a spy is far more likely, but as my grandfather said, it would explain some things. Add that to the fact that once Zuab combines her army with Argath's she'll have a force five times greater than ours, and you can understand why we're losing this war."

"I'm just not sure how much I can do to help," Andromeda said.

"Every man who will follow you is one less that will follow your father."

Valin nodded at a dwarf beating an anvil. The blacksmith bowed his head, but when his eyes fell on Henry, he gasped. His hammer fell to the ground, and his elbow bumped the half-finished blade he'd been working on. The cherry-red tip blackened the grass and filled the air with an acrid scent before fading to a dull gray. Valin paused at looked at him.

"What is that?" the smith asked, his silver eyes locked on Henry. Then, remembering himself, he bowed. "Forgive me, Lord Valin. I meant no offense, but I've never seen anything like that."

Valin waved off the apology. "What do you mean, Alviss?"

"That one," Alviss pointed at Henry. "He's no normal human. His flesh has been worked."

"You can see that?" Henry asked.

Valin looked from Alviss to Henry. "What do you mean worked?"

Henry nodded, shivering at the memory of Hermes leading him into a volcano. "I was hurt," he said. "My skin burned off, and my eyes melted."

Valin shook his head. "A human cannot survive that."

"Not for long," Henry said. "I was in Hephaestus's workshop. He couldn't heal me, but he could repair me."

"Hephaestus?" Alviss asked.

"I guess you wouldn't know about him. To the Greeks, he's the god of blacksmithing."

"Children's stories," Valin huffed.

"I can't speak to that, Lord Valin," Alviss said. "I know of no magic capable of working flesh as metal, yet the proof stands before me."

"You're certain of this?"

"Without a doubt."

"How are you able to see that?" Henry asked.

"Forgive me," Valin said. "This is Alviss, chief weapon smith and master of the powers of the forge. Alviss, this is Andromeda of Argath and Master Henry Alexander Gideon."

"I've heard of Master Henry," Alviss said. "I thought your exploits were only stories. Now, I'm not so sure." He looked Henry up and down. A few younger dwarves nearby were staring as well. "Your clothes bear the mark of the forge as well."

Henry nodded. "He said he could work with anything."

"A powerful forgemaster indeed, if that's true." He looked at Henry's face. "Though I suppose there's ample evidence of that. May I see your sword?"

Henry shrugged. He drew the sword and held it out to the dwarf. Alviss's jaw dropped. Henry shifted his weight from one foot to the other as he noticed Alviss's assistants gaping at him. The smith extended his right hand slowly, but then pulled back.

"May I?"

"Go ahead," Henry said.

Alviss took the sword. He ran his fingers along the edge of the blade, drawing blood, though he seemed not to notice. He held it up to his eye and looked down the blade.

"Amazing," he said as he wiped off the blade and handed it back to Henry. "It's greater than anything I've ever made."

"Can you duplicate it?" Valin asked. "We could always use stronger weapons."

Alviss shook his head. "I can use what I've seen to improve on my own technique, but duplicate it? No, never. Master Henry carries more magic in his equipment than in all the rest of the camp put together. There are principles of magic in use here that I've never even conceived of. If I studied it for a hundred years, I might then begin to grasp the concepts. I know nothing of the faith of these Greeks, but if their Hephaestus isn't a god, he's close."

"Very well," Valin said. "See to your work. Improve what you can. We'll give you what time we can to make new weapons, but that may not be much."

"As you wish, Lord Valin. I'll speak to the other forgemasters right away."

Valin inclined his head and the smith scurried off. He turned back to Henry and Andromeda and gave them a much deeper bow.

"We should go to my pavilion," he said. "I'll show you our strategy and see what you have to say."

"Just like that?" Henry said. "Now you trust us?"

"I trust Alviss," Valin said. "You've just taught him to make greater weapons than we've ever had. I don't trust you completely, but I trust you enough, and if the stories about you really are true, we may just have a chance to win this war."

SIXTEEN

Valin's pavilion was the size of a large house. Canvas walls divided it into three rooms. A large table in the main room held a map of the surrounding area. It didn't look like any area Henry had ever seen, and he found himself wondering if it were wholly imaginary or if it were based on some real place. A mountain valley, presumably the one they were currently in, had a large red dot on it. Other dots ran along the mountain range, and still others of different colors had been placed in the forest and surrounding countryside.

"This is our main camp," he said pointing to the valley, "and we have outposts here, here, and here." He pointed to the dots in the mountains.

"And these would be my father's forces," she said, resting a finger on the spots in the countryside. She looked up at him. "They've effectively boxed you in."

Valin nodded. "They wouldn't be able to do that with their

numbers without knowing exactly where we are. You begin to see our problem."

"Yes," Andromeda said, "but who are the ones in the forest?"

"Not everyone is happy living in the kingdom Argath has become. Those who could, fled the kingdom. Others hid in the woods."

"These are my people?"

"Zuab doesn't know about them?" Henry asked.

"We don't think so, but if Zuab has this Oracle..."

"If I understand this right, and I'm not sure I do, the Oracles are all seeing, but they're limited in what information they can give. The one I spoke to could see the future, but she couldn't tell me anything unless I asked the right questions. If Zuab doesn't know about them, it's probably because she never thought to ask."

"What are they doing?" Andromeda asked.

Valin shrugged. "Many of them have taken to banditry. They could be useful if we joined their forces to ours, especially if Zuab truly knows nothing about them. They won't follow a dwarf, though."

He left the question unspoken. Andromeda stared at the map for several seconds before sighing and looking up at Valin.

"You think they'd follow me."

"I've little doubt," Valin said. "I'm sure you could gather even more support from the surrounding towns and villages."

Andromeda looked at the ground and spoke softly. "These aren't soldiers. They're farmers and woodsmen. You're talking about open rebellion against the crown. Many of these people will die."

"You said you'd help."

"I know. I just didn't expect it to be so..."

Her words hung in the air, and suddenly the sound of weapons being made outside took on an ominous tone. Valin nodded.

"War is never nice, Princess." He barely stumbled over the title.

"I'll go," she said. She looked at Henry who nodded.

"When should we leave?"

"As soon as possible," Valin said. "Please, make haste. Without additional troops, we'll lose this war."

"So, no pressure, then?" Henry asked. When the dwarf cocked his head, Henry sighed. "Never mind." He pointed to the town nearest to the dwarf camp. It was labeled, but the dwarven script was incomprehensible to him. "We'll go here first. I take it we won't have to go through the tunnels again?"

Valin shook his head. "That was just to reach the city. It'll be faster if you take the passes down."

"Aren't the soldiers still searching for us?"

"No one ever came close to the mountains," Valin said, "and by the time you get to the main road, they should be gone. I'll send someone for your horses. We can have you on your way within the hour."

SEVENTEEN

The passes were only slightly wider than the tunnels, but it was enough for them to go mounted. Henry took the lead. The sheer walls on either side made him feel a little claustrophobic, but he did his best not to show it. They had to go slowly for the sake of Andromeda's horse. Pegasus, on the other hand, seemed to have no trouble making his way down the rocky path. Once, he almost made Henry's heart stop when he leaped over a narrow gap in the rock. Andromeda let out a laugh, but it sounded strained. She took a few minutes to go around the gap, and they started on their way again.

"Are you okay?" Henry asked after they'd been riding for a little while.

"Yes, why wouldn't I be?"

"Because you're about to start a rebellion against your father."

"You heard Valin." Her voice wavered as she spoke. "It has to be done."

"I know that," Henry said. "That doesn't make it easy, which is why I want to know if you're okay."

She didn't say anything, and he looked over his shoulder, trusting Pegasus to walk without his guidance. She was biting her lower lip and looking at the ground. Henry cleared his throat. She looked up and nodded once.

"I'll be fine," she said. "Realm before king. I won't turn away from that now."

Henry nodded. He wished he were close enough to put a hand on her shoulder, but he just turned around. It took another fifteen minutes for them to reach the base of the mountain. Once they were in the woods, she brought Oakash alongside him.

"We'll find a way to break Zuab's spell," he said.

"I wish I could believe that."

"Oh, you can," Henry said with a grin. "I promise, and a hero always keeps his promises."

She laughed. "I'll hold you to that." Her face grew serious. "Are you sure we should be doing this?"

"You said so yourself," Henry said. "It has to be done."

"That's not what I mean," Andromeda said. "You came here to find the Oracle of the Present. Shouldn't you be doing that instead of wasting your time trying to save a king who couldn't keep his kingdom?"

"Somehow, I doubt she would've left it unguarded."

"Still, you could easier sneak into Neustad than you could turn the tide in this war."

"Maybe," Henry conceded.

"Then why don't you do that?" she asked. "Find the Oracle and get what you want. Then, leave. Maybe if you can defeat whoever Zuab is working for, it'll weaken her enough so we can beat her."

"Or maybe without her master, Zuab will just take over. There's no way to be sure, and until there is, I'm going to do what I think is right." Henry brought Pegasus to a stop and took her hand in his. She felt cold, and her fingers trembled slightly. He looked her in the eye. "Right now, that's helping to save your kingdom."

She smiled, and he could almost see a weight lifting off her shoulder at the knowledge that she wouldn't have to do this alone. The next several days passed without incident. They didn't see any sign of the men who'd been pursuing them, and after three days they reached the road. A day later, they crested a hill, and the town of Maroque came into view.

EIGHTEEN

It was a dusty little town. Most of the houses were made from wood and clay, though several had collapsed. Only the large building in the center was made of stone. The wind carried a rancid smell as if no one had bathed in a month. The people shambled around with half-dead looks on their faces. There weren't many of them. Henry couldn't be sure, but there didn't seem to be enough to account for the size of the town. Most of those who were out were either old or very young.

"I didn't realize it had gotten this bad," Andromeda said.

They drew every eye when they entered the town. Henry could hardly blame them. His horse was probably worth more than their entire village. A man wearing clothes slightly less ragged than the others stepped forward. He knelt before them and brought his face so close to the ground he could've taken a bite of the dirt.

"You honor us with your presence, Milady," he said. "How may we be of service?"

"Rise, Goodman," she said. "I don't require people to abase

themselves before me. What happened here? Last time I was in Maroque, it was a thriving trade post."

The man's eyes darted about. They paused for an instant on Henry's sword before moving up to his face and then looking into the woods. For a moment, Henry thought he was going to run, but he just bowed his head again.

"We're all good king's men here, Your Grace." His words tumbled over each other. "Some of the men resented paying taxes to fund a war against the dwarves that they wanted no part of, but they're gone now, fled to the woods. Good riddance. They're all traitors as far as I'm concerned, but we're all good king's men. I swear it."

"Calm yourself, Goodman," she said. "We're not here to bring any sort of judgment on you. Just tell me what happened."

The man bobbed his head but then paused. "It's like I told you, Your Grace," he said. "They didn't want to pay to fight the dwarves, so most of the men went into the woods. Most of them took their families. When the soldiers came there was no one here to pay taxes, so they wrecked the town."

"My father's men did this?" she asked.

"Your father?" the man's eyes went wide. He bowed his head to the ground again. "Oh, forgive me, Milady. I didn't know it was you. I meant no offense."

"No offense was taken," she assured him. "Please, calm down. Answer my question. Did my father's men do this?"

"Well, no," he said, shifting his weight from one foot to another. "They were soldiers from Neustad, though I suppose we are Neustad now, aren't we? What with King Frederick marrying Queen Zuab."

Andromeda ground her teeth. When she finally spoke, it was a growl, and even Pegasus took a step back.

"We are not Neustad. We are Argath, and we will be Argath as long as I draw breath."

"Of course, Milady, of course," the man stammered. "Like I said we're all good king's men here."

"I'm sorry, Goodman," she said. "My anger wasn't directed at you. I'm mad at Zuab and her brood. She has to be stopped. The men who fled were right to avoid her war."

He looked up, and for the first time, hope flashed in his eyes. "Milady?"

"Tell me, Goodman," she said. "Will you serve my father, or will you serve me?"

"Your father is the king," he said.

"That's not what I asked. I mean to see Zuab off the throne of Argath."

The man shuffled his feet for a few seconds, and Henry noticed the large crowd gathering around them.

"The only reason I didn't go with them was that I'm too old," he said. "If this is a trap, then you've caught me, but if not, I would gladly follow you, Milady."

"So it begins." Andromeda spoke so softly, Henry doubted anyone else could hear it. "You said most went into the woods."

"Yes, that's right," he said.

"Gather those that didn't flee," Andromeda said. "I would like to speak to them."

"Of course, Milady," he said as he dashed back into town.

"If my father really did this, then he's failed these people."

"But he already told you your father's men didn't do this."

"If they didn't do it, then he allowed it to happen. In either case, my father has failed them. Realm before king. It's what he always taught me, and if he did this, he is no longer fit to be king."

Unshed tears welled in her eyes, and Henry doubted he'd ever understand how much those words cost her.

"I'm sorry," Henry said.

She shook her head. "This is what the spies told us Neustad is like. I won't allow it to happen to Argath."

A crowd had begun to gather. There were a few younger adults there, but most had to be at least fifty. Everyone had a tired look about them, and Henry found it hard not to feel sorry for them.

"My father is lost," she said. The crowd went silent at her words.

One elderly man spoke up. "He betrayed us." Murmurs of agreements rippled through the people, and she waited for them to die before continuing.

"No," she said. "Queen Zuab has laid dark enchantments on him. She is to blame for this, not him."

Some of the people shouted their disagreement, but they went silent when she raised her hand. "Even so, I cannot ignore what's been happening to my people. No one deserves to live like this, not when it can be prevented. We are the people of Argath, and I will not permit our glory to fade. My father is no longer fit to wear the crown." Her voice cracked as she said the last word, and confidence leeched out of her voice. She bit her lower lip and took in a deep breath. She said something else, but it was too soft for anyone to hear. She lifted her head and spoke again. Her voice came loud and clear. "I, therefore, declare myself the Queen of Argath."

The silence stretched on for an eternity. The man who'd first met them began to clap. One by one, the others joined him, and before long, the entire town was applauding. Their listless expressions were gone. A few people even smiled. One, a tall lean man stepped forward. Though dirt covered his face and a dark stain ran down his shirt, he carried himself with pride. He stopped before Andromeda and bowed. It had none of the debasing servility that the first man had shown, and Henry had no doubt that this man had nothing but respect for Andromeda.

"We are your men, my queen," he said.

Those closest came up and bowed next to him. Others went to their knees where they stood. It spread out like a ripple through a pond until the entire town of Maroque bowed before their queen.

NINETEEN

"Do you know how to find the men in the forest?" Andromeda asked as she took a sip from the wooden spoon.

Henry thought she did an admirable job of pretending she liked the vegetable soup they'd been given. To him, it tasted like dirty water, but he tried not to let that show.

"I do, Your Majesty," Hartwin, the first man to swear fealty to her, said. "They provide us with what food and protection they can."

"I'd like to see them."

His gaze flickered to Henry. "I'm not sure that's a good idea. They still blame your father for what happened, and they won't hold you in high regard."

"They have reason," she said, "but they are my people. I owe them an explanation at the very least."

"As you wish, Milady," he said, but then he glanced at Henry again. "Your friend...well, they won't be happy if I bring an armed guardsman."

Andromeda glared at him. "Master Henry is not a guardsman. He owes no loyalty to me save that of friendship. He goes where he will, and greater warriors than you have tried to stop him."

Hartwin stiffened and threw Henry a contemptuous look. "Were those warriors experts at hiding in the woods and killing from a distance?"

The man's smug attitude annoyed Henry, and he spoke without thinking. "Some might have been. It's hard to say. Andromeda, how many would you say there were? Fifty or so?"

Andromeda rolled her eyes. Hartwin smirked, but his expression faded when Andromeda met his eyes.

"He's not joking," she said, "and that wasn't even the most impressive. I once saw him kill a sea serpent big enough to wrap itself around a small mountain."

"Like a hero out of legend, you mean?" Hartwin asked.

"That's exactly what I mean," she said. "Master Hartwin, not a quarter hour ago, you knelt and swore fealty to me. If you really meant that oath, then you will believe me. Master Henry is not someone to be trifled with, and you'd be much better off having him as an ally than an enemy."

Hartwin nodded, though Henry could tell he didn't believe her. "As my queen commands," he said in an emotionless voice. "When do you want to depart?"

"There is one thing I'd like to do first," she said. "Zuab's men came here?"

"Yes."

"Did they kill?" Hartwin nodded. "Take me to your cemetery. I will pay my respects to those my family failed."

Hartwin bowed his head. "Thank you, Your Majesty. This way."

He rose and walked out of the building. The wind calmed as they passed through the simple wooden gate. The cemetery was a small thing, little more than a series of lumps in the ground with stone markers. A few had fresh flowers on them. The wind died as Andromeda stopped before one.

"How many did they kill?" she asked. Her voice was pitched low, as if she didn't want to disturb the sanctity of the place.

"Three," Hartwin said, pointing to the graves.

Andromeda knelt before each and put a hand on the earth. A gentle breeze blew, but strangely, it touched neither her hair nor her dress. Briefly, Henry was reminded of the catacombs under the castle in Daste. Andromeda whispered something Henry couldn't hear, and when she turned back, she wiped a tear from her cheek.

"Let's go," she said.

Hartwin nodded. They stopped in town to gather a few supplies. By the time they left, the story of what Andromeda had done in the cemetery had spread through Maroque, and everyone they passed looked at her with wide-eyed reverence. They might've followed her before. Now, they would die for her.

TWENTY

"Don't move."

Henry looked around, but the forest was too thick. He didn't see where the voice came from until a bush rustled. A short man with suntanned skin and a long face stepped out of the shrubbery. He had a bow aimed at Henry with an arrow drawn. Henry reached for his shield, but the man shook his head, and Henry froze.

"Hartwin," the stranger said.

"Richard, calm down. These are friends."

"The child of some noble, and a boy who I can only assume is a soldier in training? These may be your friends, but they are not mine."

Andromeda stiffened in her saddle. "I am your queen."

Richard laughed. "Girl, if you were the queen, I would've already shot you."

"Not that queen," Hartwin said. "Richard, this is Andromeda."

Richard's grin widened. "Well now, that changes everything. I assume the boy is important too. It seems Hartwin brought us a pair of valuable hostages."

Cheering erupted from the foliage around them. Henry jumped and looked around as men and women armed with bows came out of the shadows. Most had mud on their face and leaves in their hair to help them hide. Henry hadn't even realized they'd been surrounded.

"We most certainly are not prisoners," Andromeda said, holding her head high. "I'm here to bring you into the battle against Queen Zuab."

"Your stepmother?"

"A usurper of the throne," she said.

"She would probably pay well for you."

"I'm sure you're right," she said, "but unless I miss my guess, you'd avoid giving her something for no other reason than she wants it."

Richard gave her a wide smile that showed a few missing teeth and lowered his bow. "That I would, girl."

"I am your queen," Andromeda said. "You may address me as Milady or Your Majesty, but don't presume to call me girl."

"Queen, are you? What about your father? If you two are fighting, well, I have no desire to get in the middle of a civil war."

"This isn't a civil war. Whether or not a heart beats in his chest, my father is already gone," she said. "All that remains is to remove Zuab."

"Maybe we can discuss this in your camp instead of out here in the forest," Hartwin said.

Richard nodded and put away his bow in favor of a long staff. "Fair enough. Follow me."

He moved through the forest like a ghost. Though he often pushed branches aside with his staff, he left no trail. Henry's, on the other hand, could've been followed by a blind man. When Richard saw how inept he was at moving through the forest, he sighed and took a detour that avoided most of the rough terrain.

When they reached the camp an hour later, Henry's jaw almost hit the ground. It was a village made of tree houses. It could've come right out of a Robin Hood story. Then again, stories did have a tendency to overlap, so maybe it did. Richard looked over his shoulder, obviously expecting them to be awed. When they didn't give him the response he wanted, he shrugged and began climbing a rope ladder. He turned back once he was halfway and waved for them to follow. Henry and Andromeda gave their horses to a boy to stable them before starting up the ladder.

Andromeda scrambled up it as if she'd been doing it all her life, but Henry was only halfway up when he made the mistake of looking down. It was much higher than it had looked, and the ground looked so far away. A gust set the ladder swinging, and Henry froze with a death grip on the rope. Once the wind subsided, he scrambled up to the house on the top. He fell to his knees, breathing heavily, as soon as he stepped off the ladder. After a few seconds, he stood on shaky legs, and Andromeda helped him up into the house's single room. A wooden table with four chairs sat in the center, and in one corner, Henry saw a cot. Richard sat at one of the chairs and motioned for them to do the same.

"Why don't you tell me what's going on?" Richard said.

Andromeda nodded and related all that had happened in the past several days. Sometimes, Henry had to correct her or add in some vital detail that she skipped. By the time she was done, Richard wore a grim expression

"Us," he said, "against all that?"

"It's that or surrender," Andromeda said.

"What about your soldier friend?"

"I'll help however I can," Henry said, "but this kind of battle isn't exactly my strong suit."

"Understandable," Richard said, "but how exactly do you intend to help if you can't fight?"

"I'm not going to fight Zuab's army," Henry said, "but I do plan on sneaking into her kingdom and taking away the source of her power."

"You may as well try to fight her army by yourself as try to enter Neustad. No one comes back from that place unchanged."

"Well then I'll just have to make sure my change is for the better."

"That's your plan? Walk into one of the most heavily fortified kingdoms in the world and what? Destroy their supply lines? It wouldn't accomplish much even if you could do it, not when the king has already surrendered his realm to Zuab."

"You don't speak as a disgruntled woodsman," Andromeda said. "You were a soldier."

Richard nodded, and for the first time, Henry noticed the faded scars on his arms. A knife hanging on his belt bore a snowflake sigil on the hilt.

"A deserter?" Andromeda asked.

"No, Milady," he said. "I served my time. I came back home because I'd had enough killing."

"A curious occupation you've chosen."

"The Argath I fought for doesn't exist anymore," he said. "It died when the king married that witch. I may not be able to bring it back, but I won't submit to what it has become."

"I could use a man such as you."

Richard looked at her for a long time. Henry's stomach felt uneasy as the tree house swayed in the wind. Andromeda's face looked like it was made of steel. Finally, Richard shook his head.

"What do you have?" he asked. "A village of old men and someone young enough that he'd still be called 'boy' in most places. No, my queen, I will not fight for a cause I know to be doomed."

"We have much more than that. King Fjalar stands with us, and his army is at our back."

Richard looked up at her. His face held an unasked question. Andromeda nodded once, and the bandit let out a breath. "Well, that would change things, wouldn't it?"

"Then, you'll join us?",

Richard stood up and walked to the door. He parted the cloth and stared out over his makeshift village. Henry and Andromeda went to stand by his side. At least a dozen other houses sat in the branches. The sun had begun to set and someone had started a bonfire on the ground. Children ran and played around it. Though he couldn't see them clearly, Henry imagined some weren't too much younger than he was.

"Queen Zuab's men will find us eventually. When they do, they'll show no mercy. We'll give them a good fight but..."

"You can't win alone," Andromeda said softly.

"No. I'm not sure you can either." He paused. "I'll fight. I'm not sure how many will follow me, but I'll lead any who do."

Andromeda reached up and touched his shoulder. She seemed like a child next to him, but Richard went to one knee and bowed his head.

"I name you General Richard of the Queen's Guard," she said.

"I am honored," he said rising.

"How many men do you have?"

"Thirty-seven, including myself."

"That's not much of an army," Henry said.

Andromeda glared at him, and he took a step back. She grinned. "It's a start."

TWENTY-ONE

They went from village to bandit camp to village. One by one, the crowds bowed and swore themselves to Andromeda's cause. At every opportunity, she stopped at the local cemetery to pay homage to the fallen, and the people loved her all the more for it. She was like a flame going through dried grass. Some started off apathetic. Others were downright hostile. On two separate occasions, someone fired arrows at them, and once Henry and Andromeda were separated from their army and left tied up for an entire night. It was only Andromeda's fiery words to the captors that saved their lives. No matter what kind of reception they received, when they left, Andromeda had gathered more people to their cause. As their group grew, they had to move slower, but even that was hardly an impediment. After two weeks, they were up to two hundred. They were a ragtag group, and only the occasional old soldier wore a faded uniform. Most carried simple farming implements, and no more than a dozen had swords.

"If we keep up this pace, we won't need to fight," Henry said as they rested from the day's march in a command tent they'd commandeered from Richard's camp. "The entire kingdom will bow down before you."

"We'll have to fight," she said. "I'd be surprised if Zuab hasn't already dispatched a force against us."

"You think she knows you're alive?"

Andromeda shook her head. "It doesn't matter. By any legal meaning, we are an army in rebellion. She can't afford to leave us free."

"How many men will she send?" Richard asked.

"It's hard to say," she said. "It depends on what rumors she's heard. I don't know anything about her way of thinking. If it were my father and the stories are anything resembling the truth, he'd have sent at least a hundred and fifty armed men."

"We'd still outnumber them."

"Trained soldiers against townspeople and farmers," Richard said. "They'd butcher us, and that's assuming the rumors are accurate about our numbers. Even trained observers are likely to give a number twice as big as the truth, if not more. I'd wager the king will send at least a thousand."

Henry let out a low whistle. "Then, what do we do?"

"What else can we do? We gather more men until we have a force that can contend with them."

"How many is that?"

Richard rapped his fingers on a small wooden table someone had given Andromeda. "I wouldn't want to do battle with anything less than two to one. Even that would be an even fight, and no commander wants that."

Before anyone could say anything, a skinny little man burst into the tent panting. It took Henry a second to recognize Garth, one of the men they'd been using as a scout.

"Forgive me, Milady," he said between heavy breaths. "There's an army on the road."

"How many?" Richard asked, rising.

"I don't know," Garth said. "Thousands. I've never seen so many people in one place."

The bottom dropped out of Henry's stomach and his mouth went dry. Everyone stared at Garth who looked very much like he wanted to disappear.

"Thousands," Richard said.

"My father would never send so many," Andromeda said. "Not against us."

"Zuab?" Henry asked.

"Did they fly a banner?" Richard asked. "Was it snowflake or moon?"

"Neither, General," Garth said. "They carried a red bolt of lightning."

"Fjalar?" Andromeda asked, and relief washed over Henry. "How did they get ahead of us?"

"I don't know," Richard said, "but I'm just glad to have them here instead of someone else."

The three walked out of the tent and followed Garth to a hill just as a dwarf came over it. He stopped before Andromeda and bowed.

"You are Princess Andromeda?" he asked.

Andromeda almost nodded, but suddenly shook her head. "You may tell Lord Valin that I have accepted his claim. I am the queen."

The dwarf bowed again, this time deeper. "Lord Valin wishes to tell you that he will meet with you at your earliest convenience."

"Thank you," she said. "We will go now, if you'll lead the way."

The dwarf bobbed his head and took off down the hill, barely stopping to make sure they followed. The dwarven forces encamped in the valley had been impressive. On the move, they were something else entirely.

Everyone wore armor. Even children had on leather vests, and Henry didn't see anyone who didn't have at least a belt knife. His nostrils flared at the scent of coal from the forges. More than one smith pointed at Henry's sword as he passed, and he saw a couple that wore similar weapons, no doubt Alviss's creations. They found Valin standing outside his pavilion. He waved and opened the tent flap. They went inside, and he followed.

"Two hundred," he said once they'd all taken a seat. "Impressive for so short a time, though it's not much."

"You won't find a person in our wake who hasn't sworn fealty to me," Andromeda said stiffly.

Valin waved his hand. "I meant no offense. We'd intended to give you more time to gather what support you could, but we're out of time."

"What happened?" Andromeda asked.

"Zuab came here with a force twenty times larger than anyone expected. She left them scattered throughout the kingdom before she went to Daste. Two days ago, she sent out word. Any hope we had of turning the king against her before the bulk of her force arrived is gone. Even if the entire army would suddenly obey you, the forces of Neustad have entrenched themselves. Argath is under their control, and we need to move now if we intend to take it back."

TWENTY-TWO

"My father?" Andromeda asked.

"He's alive, so far as I know," Valin said, "though Queen Zuab has all but dispensed with the illusion they share power."

"What do you mean?"

"He's issued a proclamation that she has power equal to his in every way. He's hardly even a figurehead anymore."

"Will she keep him alive?"

"Most likely," he said. "The army follows her because of him. Positioned as she is, she could probably defeat the army of Argath, but it wouldn't be easy, and she might well cripple herself enough that we could topple her. Rest assured, Your Majesty, your father is safe for now."

"Thank goodness," Andromeda said. "What..."

A black-robed dwarf with pale skin and a thin wispy beard stepped into the tent, and the air went cold. Valin raised a hand to silence Andromeda. For a moment, her face reddened, but when she saw the shocked look on Valin's face, she calmed down.

The pale dwarf seemed to glide across the ground. Deep purple eyes scanned the room and sent a chill down Henry's spine when they fell on him. The newcomer whispered something into Valin's ear. The dwarven commander's eyes widened, and he turned to Andromeda.

"What have you done?"

"What do you mean?" she asked, clearly confused.

"You spoke to the dead," he said.

Andromeda's brow furled in confusion. "Lord Valin, my father's failure has cost a lot of people their lives. Yes, I spoke to them. Whenever I came across a graveyard, I paused to remember them. How did you know?"

"You did much more than remember," he said, turning to the pale dwarf. "Show her, Nali."

Nali nodded and lifted a hand. The sleeve of his robe fell away revealing a long white nail extended from his bony finger. He stabbed it into the air, and for a moment, it looked like the air bled silver. He dragged his finger down, drawing a line of bright light. When he reached the ground, the light parted, and a man appeared just as all the heat fled from the tent.

He had white skin, hair, and clothes. Wisps of fog drifted from his skin, and if Henry really tried, he could see through the man. A wide gash ran along his stomach, and drops of fog-like blood dripped out, vanishing just before they hit the ground. The man kept his eyes locked on Andromeda. If he noticed the rest of them, he gave no sign.

"By the light," Richard said as his chair tumbled backward. When he got to his feet again, he held a dagger in a shaky hand. His eyes had become as wide as saucers, and color had drained from his face. "That's Otmar. When the soldiers came to Maroque he was the first to die."

Otmar's ghost gave no sign of having heard Richard. It just stared at Andromeda with listless eyes. He didn't move a muscle.

"There are dozens more," Valin said. "They're all over the camp. It's no easy feat to call beings such as them. How did you do it?"

"I didn't," Andromeda said, pointing at Nali. "He did. You saw him."

Nali shook his head. When he spoke, it sounded like stone grinding on stone. "No, Milady. I can only see what's there. I can reveal them and give them substance, but I cannot summon them nor do I command them."

"But how can you do even that?" she asked. "I thought dwarven magic was all metal and stonework."

Nali cocked his head at her. "We are dwarves, Milady. Our magic is of the earth and of all that lies beneath its surface. It is the magic of stone and metal, of gem and crystal, and it is the magic of death."

"Can we use them?" Henry asked. "Will they fight for us?"

Both Andromeda and Valin turned to Nali. The pale dwarf shook his head.

"They will not fight for *us*." He pointed at Andromeda. "They will fight for her."

Andromeda took a step back and shook her head. "No. I didn't call them. I don't command the dead."

"You command the land."

"It's like the wolves that wouldn't attack us," Henry said.

Nali shook his head. "These are to wolves as what a mountain is to a pebble." He met Andromeda's eyes. "Milady, you have done what no ruler in the past thousand years has been able to do. You have called the spirits of your land to war. I've never seen such as they in battle, but accounts I've been told about make me wish I'd never lived to see this day. The stories say they can suck the life right out of a person. Enough of them can tear through an army like a scythe through wheat."

Valin stood up and clapped once, but Andromeda looked a little green.

"What is it?" Henry asked.

Though he'd spoken to Andromeda, Valin answered. "Don't you understand? We're facing an enemy who can shoot balls of fire and enslave others to her will. Who knows what else she can do. Do you really think we could've beaten her with no real way to counter that?" He looked the ghost up and down. "With these, we actually have a chance."

Andromeda rose and nodded at the ghost. Before he could respond, she darted out of the tent. Henry followed her just in time to see her double over and throw up.

TWENTY-THREE

I 'm sorry," Andromeda sat on the ground. "It's just that opposing men with other men is one thing, but opposing them with something like that...I don't know if I can do this."

Henry sat down next to her, and she laid her head on his shoulder. After everything she'd done, a part of him had begun to think of her as more than human, but even though she was still a character out of a story, he couldn't see her as anything other than a very frightened person right now.

"What do you want to do?" he asked.

"You saw what Zuab did," she said. "We don't know the limits of her power. Valin was right. We need them."

"Let's go tell them," he said.

Andromeda nodded. She took Henry's arm, and they walked back into the tent. Valin raised an eyebrow, and Henry shook his head. The ghost's eyes followed them, the grim expression on his face never changing.

"Master Nali, you say these are here because of me," Andromeda said, and Nali nodded. "How do I command them?"

"Simply speak," he said.

"Otmar," she said. For a second, a light flickered in the ghost's eyes. "Draw your knife."

Only the ghost's right arm moved. The rest of him remained as still as a statue in a way a human never could. He held the knife out before him. Though its blade was as transparent as the rest of him, Henry saw a faint reflection of the lantern that lit the tent. Andromeda held out a hand.

"Prick my finger with your dagger," she said.

"Andromeda, no," Henry said, instinctively putting his own hand between her and the weapon. The knife passed right through him. It touched Andromeda, but she didn't react.

"I didn't feel anything." She turned to Nali. "I thought you said they were terrible in battle."

"He is not in battle, Milady," Nali said. "They are creatures of purpose and cannot exist apart from that. You called him up to defend his kingdom. Apart from that purpose, he is severely limited."

"So I would have to command him to fight?"

"Yes."

"And you said there are dozens?"

"Yes."

"What can they do?"

"I've never seen them in battle," he said, "but if what I've heard is true, with dozens, you can go through an entire army."

"Do they need to be visible?"

"They are stronger when they are."

Andromeda nodded. She turned back to Valin. "With your

permission?" she asked. The dwarven commander nodded, and she looked back to Nali. "Reveal them all."

TWENTY-FOUR

The ghost legion numbered only forty-seven. They all stood in a relaxed posture but looked all the more deadly for it. The air around them seemed darker and several degrees colder. They stood frozen in place unless Andromeda was near. When she approached, their expressionless faces followed her as if unable to look anywhere else. Each wore fatal wounds. A few were missing an arm or leg, and one had both eyes gouged out, but whatever wounds had originally taken their lives no longer seemed to inconvenience them. The legless could move as fast as any other, the blind could see. Those who had lost their fighting arm could attack with ghostly weapons floating before them, held by the arm that no longer existed.

Both dwarves and men avoided the part of camp the ghosts resided in, though a few humans came to see their lost loved ones. Inevitably, they left in tears, as the dead refused to acknowledge them. Even the birds wouldn't land anywhere near them. The most eerie thing, though, was how they marched.

The ghosts didn't move their legs. They just floated along carrying with them their aura of darkness and cold. While the rest of the army slowed with fatigue or from the terrain, they moved on at a steady pace. Once, as the army climbed over a hill, the ghosts passed right through it, emerging on the other side in the middle of half a dozen mounted men. The horses reared, and two threw their riders and galloped away. Though the riders weren't hurt, half were too skittish to ride the rest of the day, and one had woke screaming from nightmares the next three nights.

"Good," Valin said when he heard about the situation.

"What do you mean 'good'?" Henry asked.

"Look what they do without even trying. Imagine what they'll do to our enemy."

The large army made much slower progress. With nothing else to do, Henry spent part of each day with Richard who began teaching him the basics of using his sword. The general said he learned quickly, but Henry suspected he was just being nice. As news of Andromeda's survival spread, their numbers swelled. Soldiers and townspeople alike flocked to their banner to swear loyalty to their queen. For the first time, Henry realized that when they were done with Zuab, Andromeda might actually choose to stay. The thought bothered him more than he would've expected. On the eighth day after meeting with Valin's army, they came upon their first destroyed village.

They didn't recognize it as a village at first. It just looked like a circle of torn up land. Pegasus took a step, and a loud crack interrupted a conversation Henry had been having with Andromeda. He looked down and thought he was about to lose his breakfast. Pegasus had stepped on a bone. Any illusions that it might not be human were dashed by the blackened skull a few feet away. Once he knew what to look for, he found dozens of bones scattered through the area. Scorched areas on the ground told him where homes had been reduced to ash.

Andromeda took several sharp breaths before sliding off her horse. "What happened here?"

"We have seen this before," Valin said coming alongside her. "This is what Zuab does when she wages war."

Andromeda fell to her knees. When she spoke, her voice was on the edge of weeping. "But these people were innocent. She had no reason. They couldn't do anything to harm her."

"They could've joined us," Valin said.

"She didn't have to kill them."

"No, she didn't," Valin said. "That's part of why we're going to stop her."

He sounded very calm and rational about the whole thing, but tears flowed freely down Andromeda's cheeks. She reached up with an ash-covered hand to wipe them away. One dripped from her finger and fell to the ground. It sizzled for a few seconds before sinking into the ground and leaving a bright white spot where it had landed. Slowly, it expanded until Henry realized it wasn't just a white spot. It grew and widened until it congealed into the shape of a sword point. Slowly, the weapon rose out of the ground, and Henry saw the thick, muscular man holding it. He rose out of the ground and stared at Andromeda. In the distance, someone cried out. Henry looked around to see other spirits emerging. Fifty others had risen from the earth and stood facing her.

"Incredible," Nali said, stepping out of the gathered crowd. "I've never heard of ghosts so new being able to show themselves without a necromancer to aid them. Your connection to the land must be great indeed for you to be able to do this."

"They don't deserve this," she said. "Their spirits should be allowed to rest."

Nali shrugged. "Perhaps. Perhaps not," he said. "I get the feeling that we'll be glad to have them before the end."

"That doesn't make it right," Andromeda said.

Once she composed herself, Andromeda joined the new ghosts to the ones with the army. The darkness around them became almost tangible, and the column of fallen soldiers left a trail of frost in their wake.

They passed three more destroyed villages in as many days, though none offered their dead as soldiers to their growing army. By the end of it, Andromeda was a wreck. Her appetite was gone, and she went from having alabaster skin to skin that looked pale and devoid of life. She barely ate, and her eyes were red from lack of sleep.

"Andromeda, you can't keep this up," Henry said one day after they had made camp.

"There's no one else."

"There's Valin," he said. "There's me."

"You don't understand," she said. "You may be a great hero, but you've never led men."

"When was the last time you slept?"

"I don't know," she said. "Every time I close my eyes, I see one of the ghosts. There are some that look like children. I don't know what's worse: that Zuab's men killed them, or that I'm using their shades."

"I think they would want to do this," Henry said. "I don't think they would've come back if they didn't."

"I'm still using them to fight," she said. "I don't know if I'll be able to live with myself when this is all over."

"Try to get some rest," he said. "If you like, I can ask around the camp to see if anyone has something to give you a dreamless sleep."

She glared at him, and for a second, he saw fire in her emerald eyes. "Don't you dare. These people have given their lives for Argath, and yet they still fight. I won't dishonor them by forcing away my feelings just so I can have a nap."

Before Henry could say anything else, a messenger came into the command tent.

"Queen Andromeda, Master Henry. Nali would like to speak to you, if you'll see him."

"Of course," Andromeda said. "Send him in."

The tent flap barely rustled as Nali came in. As always, the pale dwarf entered without ceremony, gliding across the floor and coming to a stop before Andromeda.

"I think it's time we took the next step," he said.

Andromeda's face looked a little green at that. "What do you mean?"

"These ghosts are formidable," he said, "but there are others, greater spirits a ruler can call up."

Andromeda shook her head. "Please no. These have to be enough."

"Against the combined armies of Argath and Neustad? Perhaps, but not enough to oppose Zuab's wizards."

Andromeda closed her eyes and took several deep breaths. When she finally nodded, the look of absolute sorrow on her face almost broke Henry's heart.

"Where?" Andromeda asked.

"The catacombs under the castle," Henry spoke before he realized what he was saying. Nali nodded, looking surprised. Henry rested a hand on Andromeda's shoulder. "I felt something when you took me down there. I told myself it was my imagination, but now, I'm not so sure."

Nali nodded. "The kings and queens of old rest there, and their shades are ancient and powerful."

"And out of reach," Andromeda said. "They're under the castle. There's no way I can get to them."

"We built the catacombs," Nali said. "There is a secret way."

"Will they really be that much more powerful than what we already have?"

Nali nodded. "I don't know how many you'll be able to raise, but three or four kings would be greater than all our ghosts put together."

"Why?" Andromeda asked.

"Because they are the product of a pact between the land and the people. In a way, they are the strength of Argath itself."

"No, I mean if my family has had this ability, why have we never used it? Argath has been through many wars. Why is there no mention of it in our histories?"

Nali looked at the ground and shook his head. When he looked up, his skin had grown even more pale than usual. "The dead are a terrible weapon, Milady," he said. "I suspect those who have used them would've preferred never to remember them."

"But to wipe it from our history?"

Nali shrugged. "Many kingdoms omit the darkest parts of their own past."

Andromeda considered that for a second before nodding. "Tell me how to get in."

"After you get some sleep," Henry said. Andromeda glared at him. "Don't give me that. I'm not your subject, Andromeda. I'm your friend, and I'm not going to let you go out there so tired you'll fall out of your saddle."

Her jaw tightened, but she calmed down and nodded.

"You're probably right. I'll see about getting something to help me sleep. We'll leave in the morning."

TWENTY-FIVE

Once they got away from the army, they could travel much faster. Nali rode a horse that could almost have been called a pony, though it had no trouble keeping up with the larger mounts. In spite of Andromeda's instructions, the ghosts followed them. It unnerved Henry to see them pass through the trees. Once they'd gone a few miles, one ghost entered a wide oak and didn't come out the other side. Henry glanced around and noticed that their undead contingent had shrunk to a handful, and those who remained were more transparent than they had been.

"They're still here," Nali said when Henry asked, "but the queen called them up for a specific purpose. They are soldiers before they are anything else. In fact, given how recently they died, they may not be anything else. Away from the army it would take tremendous energy to give them form."

"What if we need them?" Henry asked.

"If we need them, I can bring them back, but I don't think I'll have to."

"What do you mean?" Henry asked.

Nali gave Andromeda a pointed glance. "They are your soldiers, Milady. If you need them, they'll be there."

After three days of hard travel, only Pegasus seemed unaffected. The horse pranced back and forth whenever they made camp and always seemed to want to run. Henry had to hold him back so that the other horses could keep pace. On the morning of the fourth day, Daste came into view.

"There are no patrols," Andromeda said. "With an army on their doorstep, you think they'd be more concerned with intruders."

"Not necessarily," Nali said. "The woods are thick here, and an army would be mired down. Our forces could not come from this direction, so it's likely this area has only light patrols."

"They should still have scouts," Andromeda said.

"They have the Oracle," Henry said.

"I think you put a little too much faith in them. They're not infallible."

"Actually, I think they are," Henry said as he brushed a strand of moss out of his face, "providing you know the right questions."

"But it's arrogant to assume you'll always know the right questions."

"From what I understand," Henry said, "arrogance pretty much defines Zuab."

"True enough," Andromeda said.

"Come," Nali said as he stepped off the road. "The passage is this way."

"You could've come into our castle at any time?" Andromeda said.

Nali laughed. "The protection on this passage is far greater than those that stand at the front gate of the castle. I wouldn't dare attempt this without the ruler of Argath at my side."

"What is this protection?" Andromeda asked.

"The very ghosts we are going to recruit. Unlike the newly dead you've already raised, some of these are ancient even by dwarven standards, and such spirits grow more powerful with time."

"My father still lives, whatever I say. Are you sure they'll recognize my authority?"

"As Fjalar said, the land will not abide your father anymore, and the spirits are the spirits of the land. They wouldn't obey him. You are the queen. Your laws simply haven't recognized that yet."

He led them to a small hill overlooking the eastern edge of town. A brook cut through the ground at its base, and the charred remnant of a tree sat atop it. Flowers covered the hillside, and their sweet scent tinged the air. All in all, it was a very beautiful and serene place.

"I used to play here." Andromeda's voice sounded far away. "When I was a girl, Uncle Sholtz brought me here with some of the other children in the castle. Roderick loved climbing that tree, but once lightning struck it, Uncle Sholtz stopped bringing us. I guess he thought it was too dangerous. This is the entrance?"

Nali nodded. He reached into his shirt and pulled out a stone that shed a deep purple light. He ran his hand along the bark and found a round jagged hole. The emberstone clicked into place, and the ground rumbled. A charred piece of wood crumbled to the ground. Nali touched the dirt, and his hand sank in as if the soil were water. Then, everything went still. Henry opened his mouth to speak, but before he could say anything, a circle of earth at the base of the tree fell inward. Henry and Andromeda walked up the hill to peer inside. Stairs with the sharp edges of newly cut stone descended into the earth. A sphere of red light gleamed just beyond the entrance. Henry's hand fell to his hilt as he moved to take a step inside, but Nali held out a hand.

"I believe it would be wise to permit the queen to go first."

"No," Henry said. "We have no idea what's down there, and I'm not about to let her go into that blind."

"We know exactly what's down there: a hundred of the most powerful ghosts in existence. Be calm, Master Henry. Even your sword couldn't protect her from an army of them. The blood that once flowed through their veins is the only thing they respect."

"It's fine, Henry," Andromeda said.

The sound of her voice caught him off guard. It had lost the weariness and uncertainty that had accumulated over the past several days. She stood with her back straight and her head held high. The weight she'd taken to bearing on her shoulders melted away. Though her hair was tangled, and her clothes were covered in the dust of the road, Andromeda was every inch a queen. Henry bowed his head before he even realized he'd done it. Andromeda stepped down into the passage with Henry and Nali right behind her. Their footsteps seemed to echo forever. Andromeda picked up the red emberstone hanging on the wall, but the light it gave was dim. Nali took it and whispered a few words. The stone brightened, and he handed it back to Andromeda.

"That should keep it bright for a few days."

"How long has this been here?" Henry asked. The tunnel gave his voice an odd sort of echo, and ancient dust sent him into a fit of coughing.

"Some two thousand years," Nali said once Henry stopped.

"That's older than the castle," Andromeda said.

"Yes, it was built when the catacombs lay inside the grounds of the old palace, but not directly under it."

"But why?"

"It was a means of escape if all else failed. The ghosts were intended to guard a retreating king."

"But not to defend the castle?"

"They were used that way once. It left half the city dead and the old castle destroyed."

"And this is what you want me to unleash?"

"The ghosts we already have give us a fighting chance, but not a good one if Zuab unleashes her magic. We need another advantage, and this is the only one I can think of."

Andromeda nodded but didn't say anything else. Before long, the uneasy feeling Henry had felt the first time he'd come into these catacombs began crawling up his back, and he found himself doubting it had been his imagination before. Abruptly, the passage ended at a smooth wall. Andromeda ran a finger along it, leaving trails in the dust.

"What do I do now?" she asked.

As if in response to her voice, the wall began to sink to the sound of stone rubbing against stone. When the cloud of dust it had thrown up settled, Henry saw the wide cavern of the cata-combs. Wind swirled around Andromeda in a storm of earth and air. At first, Henry thought the dust was taking form, but then he noticed some of those figures moving against the wind. They became semi-solid and gave off a pale light. At the same moment Henry realized what they were, the ghosts noticed him and Nali. A few broke off their attack on Andromeda to focus their attention on Henry and the dwarf. Other figures materialized, and Henry recog-nized a few as the spirits they'd gathered up from the villages of Argath. They threw themselves at the ghosts in the wind, but rather than holding them back, the new ghosts were caught up in the storm.

"What's going on?" Henry cried out, but the wind swallowed his voice.

He tried to call out again, but the words caught in his throat.

The wind blew stronger, and the spirits howled. One passed through Henry, and it felt like a knife stabbed into his gut. He tried to cry out, but another passed into him, stealing his breath, and he fell to the ground. More spirits went through him, Henry's mind flashed back to the time he'd lay with ruined flesh upon Hephaestus's table, but though that had also been excruciatingly painful, he'd been alive throughout the whole thing. This was something completely different. Every time a spirit entered him, it took a little bit of his life with it. He actually felt himself dying.

"I am Queen Andromeda of Argath," Andromeda called out. "I am your queen!"

As quickly as it had started, the wind died. When the dust settled, Henry gasped. Andromeda stood as regal as ever. Her skin even shimmered. The ghosts settled before her, each one emitting a pale blue glow. The ghosts of the villagers lay at their feet, but they were moving. Not all of the conquering spirits looked entirely human. Some had misshapen heads or arms. Others had put away even the semblance of humanity. They stood as monsters with three heads and six arms. One looked more like a giant snake than a man. Andromeda stared at them dumbfounded.

"These were the kings and queens of my kingdom? These monsters?"

"Why do ghosts wear clothes?" Nali asked.

"What?"

"Why do ghost wear clothes? They have no need of it."

"I have no idea," she said, obviously confused.

"Do you think that what a ghost wore when he was alive matters at all when he's dead?"

"Well, no," she said.

"A ghost's appearance is shaped by his will, by his self-perception. Not every ruler of Argath has been kind or gentle. Some were little more than monsters with human flesh. The worst of them knew exactly what kind of person they were, and that is now reflected in death."

A tall lanky man with hair tied in a braid stepped forward. Unlike the new ghosts, his face twitched in a way that resembled life, and his chest expanded and contracted in the semblance of breath. His eyes scanned each of them before settling on Andromeda.

"Dear Andromeda," he said. "It's good to see you."

Andromeda's jaw quivered. She began to fall, but instantly Henry was there to support her.

"You can speak," Henry said, but the ghost ignored him so Henry turned back to Nali. "Well?"

"The older ones regain the power of speech along with their self-awareness," the dwarf said. "Is that really so surprising?"

Henry shook his head. "I don't even know what counts as surprising anymore."

"Grandfather?" Andromeda's voice came out as a squeak. "What are you doing here?"

"You called the rulers of Argath to your service, dear one," he said. "Though I am a little surprised your father isn't here."

Andromeda lowered her head. "Father's not dead," she said.

"You're a usurper?" he asked, but then shook his head. "No, of course not. A usurper could've never called us. How?"

She briefly related the story of how her father had fallen under Zuab's spell and driven her and Henry out of the city.

"A queen not of our blood thinks she can claim our throne?"

His voice vibrated against Henry's skin. The air grew cold and frost spread from the spirit's feet. One of the monster-like creatures roared in defiance and every ghost in the catacombs howled in response and rose into the air.

TWENTY-SIX

S top them, Your Majesty!" Nali yelled.

"Stop them from what?"

"They're going to attack the castle!"

"What? Why?"

"Because you told them Zuab claimed the kingdom. They're going to go after her."

"Let them," Henry said. "They could take care of all our problems right now."

"She may not even be in the castle," Nali said, "but even if she was, Milady, they won't leave anyone alive."

Andromeda went pale. "What?"

"Stop them!"

"Stop!"

Her voice rang loud and clear. The ghosts froze in the air and looked down at her. One stopped halfway in the ceiling. Illuminated by the lights of the ghosts, Henry saw the stone begin to crack, and small flakes drifted down.

"Come down," Andromeda said, and they did.

Nali bent down and ran his finger through the stone dust. "Remember what I said about the previous castle. These beings are dead. Death is all they know. They lack both human compassion and human discretion. If you unleash them, they'll leave nothing alive in their path."

"But my grandfather..."

"King Erhard is an intelligent spirit with the purpose of violently destroying enemies of the crown."

"Will this be my fate as well?" she asked. "Am I to be nothing more than a spirit set to defend my descendants?"

Nali shook his head. "Your ghost will defend this realm, but fear not. A ghost is created by a soul departing this world for whatever lies beyond. These are formed from your ancestors, but they are not them."

"Good," Andromeda said softly. "We should return to the army."

"Agreed," Nali said, "though they are a bit conspicuous."

She turned to look at the ghosts. "Can you hide?"

"As you command, Granddaughter," Erhard said, and they all vanished.

"Please don't call me that," she said so softly Henry could barely hear her.

"As you wish, my queen," the empty air said.

They made their way back through the passage. Andromeda replaced the red emberstone before they started up. The light stabbed into Henry's eyes as they climbed the stairs out of the hill. The sun shone brightly overhead. Nali removed the emberstone in the tree, and the passage rumbled shut. Henry knelt down and ran his fingers through the grass, but he couldn't find any sign of the opening.

"Are they really here?" Henry asked.

"Oh yes," Nali said. "They're all around us."

"Can they keep up with our horses?"

"As long as we don't ride at a full gallop," Nali said. "Given that we're trying to remain unseen in hostile territory, that wouldn't be wise in any case."

Henry nodded. They found the horses grazing nearby and mounted up. The three days it took to reach the army camp passed without incident. An hour before they arrived, the ghosts materialized again. The ghosts of the villagers stood as translucent as ever, but the kings and queens of Argath looked almost solid, and many of them left frozen footsteps behind them. When the frost melted a few seconds later, the grass beneath it had died.

No sooner had they passed the sentries than a messenger came to summon them to Valin's tent. The dwarven commander was seated at his table which was covered in sheets of paper instead of the customary map.

"You were right, Master Henry," Valin said as soon as they stepped inside.

"About what?"

He handed Henry a paper. "Zuab is in the service of someone else. We intercepted this message."

Henry ran his eyes over it. "She's trying to secure a passage through the mountains?"

"So it would seem," he said, "though to where, I have no idea. It does make more sense than this fiction of her wanting emberstones."

"The Oracle said this place was between Far Kurnugi and Near," Henry said, more to himself than anyone else.

The place he was in now was of Middle Kurnugi. This was an old story, but not an ancient one. As such, it could serve as a bridge between Far Kurnugi, the lands of mythologies stretching to the dawn of humanity, and Near Kurnugi, where the modern tales exist. All stories had to reach through Near Kurnugi to touch the mortal world. Whoever was waging war against the imagination of mankind would need to seize a passage through Middle Kurnugi to achieve their goals.

"What are you thinking, Master Henry?" Valin asked.

Henry shook his head. With a few exceptions, the residents of Kurnugi didn't know they were stories. Even Andromeda who had crossed between worlds and who he had seen inhabit two roles couldn't grasp the concept.

"It's nothing," he said. "We don't know where they're going, but do we know where they're coming from?"

"I saw something about that," Valin said, rifling through his papers. "Here. It says something about a garden."

"The apples," Henry said.

Valin scanned the paper. "It does mention apples. How did you know?"

"It's the same place we entered Argath," he said. "We saw signs of a lot of people moving through the area."

"Then, you know where it is?"

"Where's the map?" Henry asked.

Valin pointed to a large rolled parchment leaning against a canvas wall. Henry retrieved it and unrolled it on top of the letters Valin had been reading. He pointed at a peak near the top of the map.

"Mount Himmnel?"

"Yes," Valin said.

Henry moved his finger down a little. "Then, the garden is here."

"We should go there," Andromeda said. "We might be able to cut off Zuab's support entirely."

"I'll go," Henry said. "You should stay here."

"I'm just as capable as you."

"With an army of ghosts at your command, I'd say you're much more capable than I am, but the ghosts will be needed here."

"He has a point, Your Majesty," Nali said.

"Forgive me for saying so, Master Henry," Valin said, "but one man can't cut her off, not even a man such as you."

"I'm not sure she can be cut off," Henry said, "not without a major offensive. Hopefully, I can learn something, though."

"But what's the point?" Valin asked.

"Zuab's support is coming from somewhere, and I get the feeling I won't be able to avoid confronting her allies eventually. The best I can do is learn what I can about them and make sure they don't get stronger before I get there. To do the first, I need Zuab's Oracle. To do the second, I need to break her hold on Argath."

"And what does the garden have to do with either of those?"

"I need to find out where they're coming from."

"They're from beyond the garden," Valin said. "For that matter, they're probably from the lands you just came from. From what I've heard, that's full of evil and monsters."

"No, I don't think so," Henry said. "I'm not sure I understand this all myself, but I think the paths in the garden lead many places."

"Can't the Oracle tell you which path to take?"

"Probably," Henry admitted, "but getting answers from the last one was like playing a game of riddles. The more I can learn before I see this one, the better."

"I still think you should take a small force with you," Valin said.

"This isn't an attack," Henry said. "I'm just going to get more information. Besides, none of you could keep up with Pegasus."

"We have fast horses," Valin said.

"Not that fast, Lord Valin," Andromeda said. "I thought he was boasting too, but the finest horse in my father's stables couldn't keep up with him. Just as his sword and shield are not ordinary tools, his steed is no ordinary horse. He could've escaped from the queen's pursuers when we fled Daste if he hadn't waited for me."

"You're willing to let him go?" Valin asked. "I've hardly seen the two of you apart."

Andromeda blushed, and Henry felt his face heat up. Valin laughed. Even Nali chuckled. The sound sent chills down Henry's back, which was an odd contrast to the embarrassment he was feeling.

"You've heard stories of what Master Henry has done. I've seen it, and he's right. I'm needed here. I may want to go with him, but duty demands that I stay."

"I'm not much of a strategist anyway," Henry said. "I couldn't do a whole lot to help you right now."

Valin nodded. "Very well. Is there anything you need?"

"Just a good night's sleep."

TWENTY-SEVEN

Henry rose before the sun and found Andromeda waiting by the stables. Pegasus almost shimmered in the moonlight. Henry tried to ignore the feeling of someone watching him, but he had no idea if some invisible ghost was looking over Andromeda's shoulder. Though he didn't need it, she helped him mount the horse.

"Be safe, Henry."

Her voice was very soft. He hadn't realized how much he'd missed being addressed by his name alone until that moment. He nodded, not trusting himself to speak. He kicked his heels into Pegasus's side, and they were off.

Henry could feel Pegasus wanting to run. With no real reason to restrain him, Henry let him go. Pegasus moved like the wind. The forest on either side of the road was little more than a blur. Even the sound of galloping hooves became little more than a hum. It took only a few minutes for the camp to vanish behind him. Though Henry had only a vague idea where the garden was, he had the sense Pegasus knew, and he trusted the horse to get him where he needed to go.

After only an hour of riding, Pegasus turned off the road. To Henry's surprise, the horse didn't slow. Henry still knew very little about horses, but he knew enough to know galloping through the forest was dangerous. Pegasus, however, seemed to know exactly where to step. The forest may as well have been an open field for all that it slowed the formerly flying horse.

The sun had just begun to peak over the horizon when they entered a familiar clearing, and Pegasus came to a stop. Henry dismounted and looked at the horse in awe. Pegasus had covered days of travel in hours.

"Did you enjoy that more than flying?" Henry asked.

Pegasus nuzzled his shoulder, and Henry wasn't sure whether or not to take that as an answer. He left Pegasus to graze and walked deeper into the garden. It wasn't long before he spotted the tree.

It stood in the center of a small grove. Its apples were large and looked juicier than those around it. They swayed in the wind and almost seemed to draw his eyes to them. He found himself staring. His stomach rumbled, and the next thing he knew, he was reaching out to take one.

"I wouldn't," a familiar voice said.

Henry almost jumped out of his skin. He'd been so enthralled by the apples themselves, he hadn't even noticed the man standing at the tree's base, though "man" wasn't entirely accurate.

He stood almost a foot taller than Henry and had pale blue eyes. He had curly black hair and his skin was perfectly smooth. He looked almost like a statue, but then Henry had actually seen statues carved in this person's image. He couldn't resist the urge to glance down at his feet and see the golden sandals with wings on their heels.

"Hermes, what are you doing here?"

"What else? I'm delivering a message," the messenger of the gods said.

"To me?"

"Of course. I'm to tell you Greece is preparing for war."

"But didn't the Morai say the war wouldn't touch Greece?"

"The Morai can't see everything," Hermes said. "The Oracle says the war will be a siege on Zeus's realm. Though no enemy soldier will set foot in our lands, we will be completely cut off from the mortal world. Without that, we'll wither and die. We need to do something about it."

"Good," Henry said. "We could use the help."

"I'm afraid we can't help you here," Hermes said.

"Why?"

"Because this link to Greece lies thousands of miles away from anywhere. It would take weeks or months to get an army here. You don't have that much time."

"But you're a god," Henry said. "At least you are in Greece. Can't you just use your power to get them here quickly?"

"Maybe," Hermes said, "but we won't."

"Why?"

"Because this is not the final battle," Hermes said. "If we bring them here, we might not be able to get them to whatever world the enemy is in. Our powers don't always work the same across the boundaries of worlds."

"But the enemy is sending troops here," Henry said. "That means there's a way to get from this world to theirs, doesn't it? That's why they're trying to conquer it. They need a path through Middle Kurnugi to reach the Near. You can use that same path to get there from here."

Hermes shook his head and pointed. "Look."

The path he was pointing down wound between two trees. Henry stared at it for a while before he saw what Hermes meant. The shadows hanging over it were darker than the surrounding trees could've cast, and there seemed to be a faint mist flowing across the ground. Henry tried to focus, but his gaze kept sliding off the path.

"Try to go down it," Hermes said.

"But that's the way to another world, isn't it?" Hermes nodded. "If I go down that, will I be able to come back?"

"Most doors go both ways."

"That doesn't really answer the question."

Hermes grinned. "No, it doesn't, does it?"

"Can't you ever give me a straight answer?"

Hermes cocked his head. "You know, I don't believe I can. So are you going to go down that path?"

"The last time I did what you said, I ended up in a volcano with skin burned off and my eyes melted."

"Don't be ridiculous. That was two times ago. Besides, you got better."

"You're not really making me want to trust you."

Hermes sighed. "Fine. I swear by the River Styx that if you go down that path you will not be trapped in another world. Is that good enough?"

Henry thought through Hermes's statement trying to find a loophole. Finally, he nodded and started walking down the path. When he reached the two trees, he ran into a wall. Surprised, he reached his hand forward. The air thickened, and after about an inch, he couldn't push forward anymore. He tried harder, but the air itself pushed back at him. He looked over his shoulder and glared at Hermes.

"This is one of those one-way doors, isn't it?" Henry asked. "It only goes here, but we can't take it there."

"More or less," Hermes said.

"Couldn't you have just said that?"

"You would've tried it anyway."

"That's not the point," Henry said.

"No, it's not," Hermes agreed. "The point is whatever is blocking this path has been put there. It's not natural."

"What do you mean?"

"Someone is blocking access to their world."

"Who could do something like that?"

"Zeus could," Hermes said. "So could any other who rules a world."

"I don't suppose you know who rules that one?"

"Sorry," Hermes said. "I don't know what world that is. Even I haven't taken every path."

"Then, are you sure it hasn't always been one-way?"

Hermes shook his head. "If it were always one way, there would be no need to block the path. It wouldn't exist."

"Then, how do I get there?"

"If I knew where the path led, I could tell you another way," Hermes said. "Every path can't be blocked."

"You're not going to be much help, are you?"

"I didn't come here to help you," Hermes said. "I came here to find a way for you to help us."

"How am I supposed to do that?"

"The Oracle can tell you where the enemy is. Then, you can send a message here."

"Can't you go see the Oracle yourself?"

"Remember what the Moirai told you. I'm only a messenger. It's not possible for me to be anything else. This falls on the hero. It's your task."

Henry let out a breath. "I can do that. At least this trip won't be a total loss."

Hermes reached up and plucked an apple from the tree. He tossed it to Henry who caught it in the air. It almost seemed to shine, and Henry found himself staring into it. It was so polished that he could make out his reflection staring back.

"Don't eat it," Hermes said.

"I wasn't going to," Henry said, but he quickly put it into his pack.

"Good. One taste of that and you'd be dead. Oh, by the way, while I was waiting for you, a woman came here and took one. I don't know what she intended to do, but it can't hurt for you to have one too." Hermes pursed his lips. "Actually, it can hurt, so just don't eat it."

"Got it," Henry said as he walked back toward Pegasus. "Anything else?"

"I got a message to your parents," Hermes said.

Henry froze in his tracks. Tears welled up in his eyes, and a lump formed in his throat. He'd managed to put them out of his mind.

"Are they ok?"

"As well as can be expected," Hermes said. "You left too suddenly to be able to come up with a good reason."

"That's why they think I've been kidnapped."

"They know you're okay now, but they're expecting to get a ransom demand soon."

"What?"

"You disappeared from school in the middle of the day without word," Hermes said.

"I don't even know how long I've been gone."

"A few days."

"It's been longer than that."

"Here," Hermes said. "Time doesn't always pass the same in Kurnugi as it does in the mortal world."

"Does that mean it could work the other way?" Henry said. "Could I be gone for years?"

"No, it doesn't work that way. Not for the hero, anyway. You'll return close to the same time you left. It'll only be a few days no matter how much time you spend here."

"But my parents will still think I was kidnapped."

"You'd prefer they heard nothing?"

"No, I guess not."

"I'm sorry, Henry. It was the only thing I could do."

"I didn't mean to overreact," Henry said. "Thanks for what you did."

"Remember to send us a message. We'll need to end this if you're ever to return home."

Hermes bowed and rose into the air. The wings at his heels expanded until they were bigger than he was. They flapped once, the wings growing to obscure Hermes. When they moved out of the way, he was gone. Henry walked up to Pegasus and ran his fingers through his hair. The horse wasn't even damp. There wasn't a drop of sweat on him.

"Are you good to take me back to camp?"

The horse whinnied and nuzzled Henry's shoulder.

"I guess that means yes," he said and threw his leg over the horse. "Let's go."

TWENTY-EIGHT

Henry had only been riding for an hour and a half before he saw smoke rising through the trees. He reined in Pegasus, and they slowed to a walk. The smell of wood smoke grew stronger, and before long, he saw people moving in the trees.

"You guys made good time," Henry called out. "I need to speak with Valin."

"Valin?" a voice said. A man stepped out of the shadows, and the bottom fell out of Henry's stomach. The burly soldier wore a crescent moon crest on his shield.

"It's the traitor," he yelled and he pointed a spear.

Instantly, Henry's hand went to his sword. He drew it and struck with one fluid motioned. The spear shaft exploded in a shower of splinters. Pegasus reared and kicked the man in the chest, sending him flying backward. A burning pain sliced across Henry's arm just before an arrow thunked into a tree behind him. He looked down at the blood slowly soaking his sleeve from a shallow cut made when the arrow nicked him.

Two other men appeared in the trees beside him, and still another from behind. Henry tried to turn Pegasus, but a fourth soldier came out of the forest, completing the circle around him. Henry swung his sword wildly, taking off another spear point, but the man slammed the broken spear shaft into him, and Henry flew off his horse. He crashed into the ground, driving the breath out of him. Someone put a boot on his neck, but a heartbeat later, Pegasus was there. He struck with his hooves, and though the soldier tried to avoid it, he was only partly successful. The hooves crashed into his right shoulder and sent the man spinning through the air. Henry rolled to his feet and pulled out his shield.

By then, half a dozen other soldiers had come out of the woods. Two threw ropes around Pegasus's neck. The horse reared, briefly lifting one man off his feet. Another ran forward and grabbed hold of one of the ropes. The three remaining men surrounded Henry. He caught one of their spears on his shield and struck with his own weapon, neatly slicing off a piece of the other man's shield, but the attack distracted him from the other two. One slammed his shaft on Henry's sword arm, sending the weapon flying. He backed up against a tree and tried to keep his shield between them and himself, but one used a spear to sweep Henry's legs out from under him. Another three attacks struck at his shield. The fourth ripped it from his arm, and in the next instant three spear points pressed against his throat. Henry froze, but one pushed on his weapon, and Henry felt a thin trickle of blood on his neck.

"Don't move," a bearded soldier said.

Pegasus cried out, and Henry's muscles tensed, but there was nothing he could do. One of them pulled out another rope and tied Henry's hands.

"Well now, gentlemen," one said. "It looks like we have a prisoner. March, boy."

TWENTY-NINE

Zuab's camp looked little like the dwarven one. Tents clustered in groups of three with a fire pit in the middle. Instead of having soldiers walking around armed, swords and spears sat neatly on racks. Men walked in formation as if they were in a parade. Most were thickly muscled with pale skin and heavy beards. Henry thought he recognized one or two from the castle in Daste. Those looked almost like children next to Zuab's men. The soldiers guiding Pegasus turned and went off in a different direction, while the others led Henry to a tent near the middle of the camp. Once inside, one of the men shoved Henry forward and kicked him in the back, sending him sprawling to the ground. They tied his feet and left, closing the heavy tent flap and shutting Henry away from the light.

He didn't know how long he lay there in the dark. The fight had drained him, and the ropes bit into his wrists. As the day wore on and no one came to feed him, his stomach growled until it felt like an empty pit. After what had to be hours, someone came in and put a sack over his head. It smelled of rotten fruit, and it was an effort not to throw up.

"What's going on?" Henry asked, but a fist in the stomach drove the words out of him.

They picked him up off the ground and carried him. He could hear men and horses moving around. After a little while, they tossed him over a horse. The ride was bumpy, and before long, every jolt pained him. His breathing was labored, and he lost all sense of time. After an eternity, they stopped and tried to force him to walk, but his legs gave out. Someone picked him up and threw him into another tent without bothering to remove the bag. His shoulder slammed into the ground, and he cried out, but no one responded.

"I don't suppose you can hear me, Hermes," Henry said to the darkness. "If you can, this would be a really good time to lend a hand."

The silence stretched on for several minutes before Henry realized he was expecting an answer. Nothing came. The darkness obscured everything. He tried to keep from panicking. He told himself the dwarven army and Andromeda's ghosts would defeat Zuab and set him free. He'd almost managed to convince himself when the bag was torn off his face. Torchlight stabbed at Henry's eyes, and when his vision cleared, a soldier stood over him, scowling. He tossed Henry a loaf of moldy bread before walking out.

With the tent flap closed, Henry was plunged into darkness. He told himself he should ignore the bread, that he shouldn't give them the satisfaction, but hunger overwhelmed him, and he groped around for it. The effort robbed him of what little hope he had managed to build for himself. When his face finally touched it, he took a bite and tried to ignore the gritty taste. With his hands bound, every bite was a struggle. By the time he'd taken half a dozen, tears filled his eye. He was in the middle of eating when the tent flap opened again. Henry recoiled from the light as a well-trimmed man carrying a lantern and wearing a crescent moon uniform stepped inside.

"It's a shame to see you reduced to this, Master Henry," a familiar voice said. Henry squinted, and it was several seconds before he could make out the face.

"Sholtz?" he asked.

"I'm flattered you remember," he said as he put down a platter with a few slices of beef still steaming from being cooked.

"You're wearing the crescent moon," Henry said, trying to ignore the food. It hurt his voice to speak. "Are you a traitor?"

"Never." Sholtz practically spat the word. "I wear this uniform on the command of my king."

"The king is Zuab's puppet," he said. "If you were really loyal, you should follow Andromeda."

"Andromeda is just the princess. Frederick is my king."

"And who would the king want you to follow? Zuab or his own daughter?"

"Zuab is his wife. You'd do well to remember that."

"She probably manipulated him into doing that too."

Sholtz sighed. He helped Henry sit up before pulling a knife out of his belt. Henry flinched, but Sholtz flicked his wrist and the ropes around Henry's hands fell away.

"I hope I can trust you not to try to escape."

Henry didn't say anything, and Sholtz handed him a fork and pushed the plate of meat toward him. Briefly, Henry entertained the thought of using the utensil as a weapon but rejected the idea. Even if he did manage to overpower Sholtz, it would only leave him in the middle of an enemy camp armed with nothing more than a fork. Instead, he attacked the beef. After the bread, the meat tasted amazing.

"I'm truly sorry for the way you've been treated," Sholtz said. "You came here looking for the leader of an invading army. On top of that, the people here know how much regard Andromeda has for you, and she is not highly thought of in the king's court right now."

Henry finished the last of the food before looking up and scowling. "Doesn't that tell you something?"

"It tells me a person cannot follow the princess without being a traitor."

"I might say the same thing about someone wearing that crest."

Henry coughed, and Sholtz handed him a canteen of water. He relished the feeling when it went down his throat. Once he was done, he handed it back to Sholtz.

"Argath and Neustad are one realm now," the soldier said.

"Then, why does everyone wear Zuab's crest? If I didn't know better, I'd say Argath was a conquered kingdom."

Sholtz's muscles tensed, and for a moment, Henry thought he was going to hit him, but then, the man relaxed.

"You're not the only one to think that way," Sholtz said. He let out a long breath. "Tell me, Master Henry. Does the princess still live?"

The change of subject caught Henry off guard. "She's fine."

"Where is she?"

Henry raised an eyebrow. "You don't really expect me to answer that, do you?"

Sholtz smiled. "No, I suppose not. For what it's worth, I don't mean her any harm. I would do anything in my power to protect her." Henry looked pointedly at the crescent moon on the man's chest. Sholtz huffed. "From what the princess has told me, you don't have kings where you come from. You couldn't understand what it means to swear your life to one."

"I've never lived under a king," Henry admitted, "but most of those following Andromeda have. I wouldn't call her a princess in front of them. To them, she is queen. Even the dwarves recognize her."

"The dwarves do not rule Argath."

"Neither does Frederick."

Sholtz shook his head and stood up to leave. He looked over his shoulder. "Why were you out here, Master Henry? Were you a scout?"

"We didn't even know you were out here," Henry said. "I thought you were Valin's army."

"It's probably just as well we captured you," Sholtz said. "Our intelligence reports tell us exactly where the dwarves are. We'll be on them in a few days."

"Those reports come from Zuab, don't they?" Henry asked.

"I can't say."

"You don't really need to. They don't tell you where Andromeda is, do they?" Sholtz hesitated but then shook his head. "Zuab knows exactly where she is. Did you ever consider that she may not be telling you so that your army will do the work for her?"

"I hardly think so," Sholtz said. "The princess is in disfavor with the court, but even Zuab wouldn't dare kill her. King Frederick may have given in to her on everything else, but he's still adamant on what is and is not proper punishment for a disobedient princess."

Henry's eyes went wide. "He's resisting her?"

Sholtz nodded. "He's not going to let Zuab give lashes to his daughter, no matter what she's done."

"Is he resisting on anything else?"

"I could only wish," Sholtz said. "Where is the princess?"

Henry thought about it but eventually nodded. "She's at the head of the army you're about to attack."

"That's impossible," Sholtz said.

Henry looked at Sholtz's face. Even in the flicker of firelight, he could see sincerity in those features. Sholtz seemed to genuinely care. Maybe he could be turned to their side.

"She was trained in warfare," Henry said softly. "She told me you helped with that."

"Because she was to be queen, and she needed to know, but even Frederick never personally leads his army."

"But he could."

Sholtz stood up and walked to the flap. His body obscured the lantern he carried leaving only his silhouette.

"Yes."

"And if an enemy took over his kingdom and cut off his access to his generals, would he just stand by and let someone else lead?"

"No."

"Neither would Andromeda," Henry said.

"Even if you're right, she wouldn't be harmed," Sholtz said. "We'd capture her and take her back to the king."

"You're assuming you would win."

"We have three men for every two of theirs, and a detachment from Neustad is approaching from the south. They'll be crushed between us."

"And you think Zuab's men would honor the king's wishes to spare his daughter?"

Sholtz turned back to Henry. "They are his men too, now."

"Like you're Zuab's?"

"If you're so worried about her, tell me about their defenses. Give me something I can use to beat them before Zuab's forces get here."

"I can't do that."

"Please." The note of desperation in Sholtz's voice surprised Henry.

"I'm sorry."

Sholtz sighed. "Then, I have no choice but to go through with the attack as planned. When we capture the princess, we'll bring her to you. I'll do my best to ensure you're treated well in the meantime, but one of Zuab's generals is in charge of this force, and I have to defer to his orders." He started walking out of the tent but looked over his shoulder. "Your sword and shield are most interesting. One of our best weaponsmiths on the northern edge of the camp is examining them. He can't quite figure out what metal they're made of."

As Sholtz opened the flap, Henry noticed the light he'd recoiled from before was that of the moon. Then, Sholtz was gone. Henry stared after him before looking down. Though he couldn't see, his hand still held the fork. The knots tying his feet were tight, but with the fork, he was able to pry them loose. He pulled open the tent flap just enough to look out. The man seated there was snoring softly. Henry moved quietly. Once, when the guard stirred, he froze, but the other man didn't awaken, and Henry hurried out of the light. He could see the Nordi Mountains silhouetted against the starlight in the west and used them to get his bearings. The guards weren't difficult to avoid. They all carried torches and lanterns and he could see them from a long way off. It didn't take much effort to find the smithy.

The smell of coal hung heavy in the air, and it was one of the few structures contained in a wagon instead of a tent. He tugged at the door and was surprised to find it open. He stepped inside. The moonlight revealed several dented pieces of armor as well as a broken sword. One lump of metal that looked like it might eventually be an axe leaned against a wall. On a small table, separate from everything else, sat his sword and shield.

He picked up his weapon and was surprised at how much relief he felt at having it in his hand. The sheath he'd originally worn was nowhere to be seen, but he found another that fit well enough and belted it on. He strapped his shield to his back and crept out of the wagon.

He did his best to move silently as he circled around the army. Every time a twig snapped underfoot, it sounded like a thunderclap, and he kept expecting enemy soldiers to leap out of the shadows and seize him. He considered sneaking back into camp to look for Pegasus, but it was like a small city. There was no way he'd be able to find the horse. He hated to do it, but he had to leave him behind. As soon as Henry was south of the army camp, he set off into the woods.

Unmounted, Henry felt like he was moving at a snail's pace. He realized this was the first time he'd had to travel on foot since he and Virgil had washed up on the shores of Aethiopia. That felt like a lifetime ago.

Bruised, beaten, and starving, he didn't know where he found the strength to press on, but he forced himself forward. If Zuab knew where they were, it wasn't impossible that she knew about the ghosts as well. She might even be able to counter them. Henry didn't know nearly enough about them to know if it was possible, but he needed to tell Andromeda. He didn't know how many hours he walked. Eventually, he stopped and leaned against a tree to take a short break. The next thing he knew, he was awakened by birdsong in the trees and sunlight streaming through the branches. His eyes shot open, and he leaped to his feet. He drew his sword and looked around. A squirrel darted up a tree and a bird flitted from branch to branch, but other than that, he was alone. He sheathed his sword and started on his way.

By the time the sun hung overhead, hunger gnawed at Henry, and his throat burned with thirst. The past two days had been strenuous, and with nothing but moldy bread and a few slices of beef in his stomach, he struggled to move forward.

Henry thought back to every story he'd ever heard. The hero always went hunting or set snares or found some other way to feed himself, but he didn't know how to do any of those. He uttered a silent curse at Sholtz for not giving him any food, but then he cursed himself for not thinking to steal any. He found some berries, but he'd heard too many stories of them being poisonous, and in the land of stories, he didn't want to take that chance.

The next couple of days passed as a blur. Day and night didn't mean anything to him. Henry had vague memories of drinking from a stream and of finding a handful of nuts. Several times, he found himself waking up having no memory of going to sleep. Once he saw someone in the woods, but he started to run before they could get close. He tripped on a root and didn't have the strength to get up again.

THIRTY

"Master Henry?" a voice in the darkness said.

Henry's eyes felt like lead weights. The indistinct figure in front of him was huge, and it took him a moment to realize it was a mounted rider.

"Over here!" the rider called. "It's Master Henry. I think he's hurt."

The next thing he knew, Henry was surrounded. They picked him up, but their actions held none of the roughness that Zuab's men had shown. Someone sat him on a horse, and a strong hand helped keep him upright. One person put a water skin to his mouth. Henry had never tasted anything so sweet. Before he'd done little more than wet his tongue, they pulled it away.

"Not so fast," the voice said. They brought it back to his lips a few seconds later.

By the time they'd reached the camp, Henry's vision had begun to clear, and he realized two people were walking on either side of him, holding him on the horse. To his relief, the only uniforms he saw were the faded ones worn by men who had been soldiers long ago. Andromeda ran out of a nearby tent. When she saw him, her eyes went wide.

"Henry, what happened to you?"

He tried to smile but didn't know how successful he was. "I was captured," he said in a raspy voice. He took another sip of water. "Sholtz helped me escape."

"Are you hurt? Where is Pegasus?"

Henry shook his head, but the effort made his head spin. He started to topple off the horse, but the men at his side held him steady.

"Not here," he said. "I need to speak to Valin and Richard."

"You should get some rest."

"No," Henry started but was interrupted by a fit of coughing. Instantly, Andromeda was at his side. "Please, Andromeda. I need to see them."

She looked into his eyes for a second. He thought she was going to argue, and he didn't have the strength for that. Instead, she nodded and helped him off the horse. His legs were shaky at first, but he managed to get them steady after a few seconds. He leaned on Andromeda as he walked, but by the time he'd gone a dozen steps he didn't need to anymore. She walked with him into the familiar command tent, though it was empty. She lit a lantern and helped him into a chair.

"I'll go get them," she said and disappeared.

He drank the rest of the water skin. A few minutes later, a boy came in and handed him a loaf of bread and an earthen bowl of soup. He tore off a piece of the bread and dipped it in the soup. He tried to eat slowly, but it disappeared so fast he didn't even have time to taste it. By the time Andromeda came back with the generals, his strength had started to return.

"Master Henry," Richard said, bowing.

Valin inclined his head but didn't say anything. Andromeda pulled up a chair next to Henry and put a hand on his. He squeezed it and smiled at her before turning back to the other men.

"I was captured by Zuab's forces," he said.

"You were fortunate to escape," Valin said. "I've heard how prisoners are treated in her lands."

"I didn't escape," Henry said. "I was released. You were right, Valin. Zuab doesn't have total control over the Argath army. Captain Sholtz told me where to get my equipment and set me free. He might have even drugged the guards for all I know."

"Why would he do that?" Valin asked.

"I got the feeling it was to get Andromeda out of here."

"What?"

"They know where this army is," Henry said.

"That's hardly surprising," Valin said. "Even without a spy, an army is difficult to hide. No one's close enough to do anything about it. I doubt this strike force that captured you would even slow us down."

Henry shook his head. "You don't understand. The ones who captured me weren't just a strike force. They were a full-fledged army only a few days to the north. There's another one coming from the south. Sholtz is sure they're about to crush you, and he wanted Andromeda kept safe."

"Impossible," Valin said. "Our own scouts would've found them."

"Don't you understand?" Henry asked. "They have an Oracle. They know where your scouts are, and they know where to go to avoid them."

"It can't be," Valin said.

"I told you about Master Henry, Lord Valin," Andromeda said. "He has done what an army couldn't do before. If he says there's a force out there that your scouts haven't detected, I believe him."

"And you," Valin said to Richard, "what do you think?"

Richard looked from Henry to Andromeda to Valin. His eyes wandered back to Henry and then to his sword. He sighed.

"Lord Valin, I am standing in the command tent of a dwarven general. We have a contingent of ghosts on our eastern flank. Even now, your forgemasters are creating weapons based on what Master Alviss learned from a sword made by a god. After all that, if my queen says to believe a person when he says there's a large army a few days away, well, I see no reason to doubt her."

Valin huffed and drummed his fingers on the table. "It seems I'm outnumbered. Very well. We'll proceed on the assumption that Master Henry is right. A little more caution won't hurt us in any case. How far away are they?"

"How long have I been gone?"

"Five days."

"I was captured on the first day, and I got away the morning of the second, so it must've taken me three days to get back here. I wasn't moving very fast, though."

"Probably faster than an army," Valin said. "It's a shame you didn't make it to the garden. We could've used whatever advantage that would've gotten us."

"I'm afraid there wasn't much," Henry said. "I did make it, though. I was on my way back when I got caught."

Valin and Richard gaped at him. "From what the queen has told us, that garden is several days away."

"Pegasus was a very fast horse."

"Was?" Andromeda asked, the pain obvious in her voice.

"He was taken when I was captured. I had no way to get to him when I escaped."

"I wouldn't worry overly about that, Master Henry," Richard said. "Good horses are worth their weight in gold. They won't have harmed him. This two-pronged attack, on the other hand, is a matter of great concern."

"I'm afraid I can't help you there," Henry said. "I all but killed myself trying to get that information to you as soon as possible."

"Yes, of course," Valin said. "Things would've been a lot worse without your warning. You should get some rest and have your injuries seen to. I'm sure we'll need your sword before the end of this."

Henry stood and wavered on his feet for a second. He gave them both a shallow bow and he and Andromeda left the command tent. She took him to a medic. His wounds weren't severe. He had a few scrapes and shallow cuts. The worst of it was a large bruise across his stomach that hurt every time he moved too quickly. The medic applied a salve and prepared a dark tea with the instructions to drink it and sleep all night. Henry thanked him and left for his tent. Andromeda walked by his side.

"You really don't have to do this," Henry said. "I'm sure you have more important things to do than walk me around the camp."

"After all you've done for me, it's the least I can do," she said. "Tell me about Uncle Sholtz."

"He looked well enough," Henry said. "He wore the crescent moon, but I got the sense he didn't like it."

"I never thought we'd have to go up against him."

"I think he'd follow you," Henry said.

Andromeda shook her head. "He is the most loyal man I've ever met. He'll follow Zuab because she controls my father. He won't go against that."

They reached his tent, and she said goodbye. He stepped in and lay down on the heavy fur blanket. The tea tasted faintly of mint, and no sooner had he finished the cup than his eyelids became as heavy as steel. They closed, almost of their own accord, and he drifted off into sleep.

THIRTY-ONE

Henry woke to the sound of steel on steel.

Someone yelled a battle cry that was quickly cut off. He leaped to his feet and found his balance much improved. Quickly, he belted his sword and strapped his shield to his arm before rushing out. In the camp, he found utter chaos. Several of the surrounding tents had collapsed and villagers and dwarves alike ran around half dressed, though some had found their weapons and were engaged with the attackers.

Huge men fought dwarves a quarter of their size. He'd thought Valin had been exaggerating when he said a dwarf was more than equal to a man in combat, but now he saw the truth. The dwarves didn't move like other fighters Henry had seen. Instead of shifting back and forth to avoid the enemy attacks, they stood firm and caught the heavy blows on their axes and hammers. Though Henry was sure parrying even one of those attacks would've left his arms feeling like jelly, the dwarves withstood them with all the strength of the mountains they had come from.

Henry screamed a battle cry and charged three men fighting against a single dwarf. One of the men lifted a large two-handed sword, but Henry didn't hesitate. He swung with all he had, and the blade of the soldier's sword came neatly off. The man stared at his broken weapon, but before he could do anything else, Henry slammed his shield into the enemy's face. The man was as big as a house, but he crumbled to the ground. The dwarf quickly dispatched the other two and nodded at Henry before running off to engage more of the enemies.

It was only then that Henry realized the fighting wasn't everywhere. Small pockets of resistance had already begun to die down. His tent had apparently only been at the outskirts of it. The man he'd knocked out began to groan. Henry glanced around and found a rope nearby. He took away the broken weapon and tied the man's hands and feet. He set a dwarven warrior to watch over the prisoner and rushed to the command tent. The guards at the opening stiffened as he approached but made no effort to stop him. Valin and Richard were already there. Richard had a bandage on his arm, and a fresh bruise adorned the left side of Valin's face. They gave Henry a slight bow.

"You're well, Master Henry?"

"Much better," he said. "What happened? How did they get to the middle of the camp?"

"They were trying to sneak in," Valin said. "I suspect I was their target, but a guard saw them and raised the alarm. There were only about three dozen of them."

"Looks like they got close."

Valin's hand went to his face, and he grimaced. "This? It's nothing. The alarm startled me, and I'm ashamed to admit I fell out of bed."

Henry tried to hold in a chuckle. Richard didn't bother, and his laugh rang clear in the night. Valin's face was like stone for a second, but then he cracked a smile.

"Your tent is constantly surrounded by guards," Henry said. "Did they really think they could get to you?"

"Probably not," Valin said, "but lives are cheap to Zuab. She wouldn't have hesitated to send them if she thought there was even a chance they would succeed."

"It's a wonder her own people don't overthrow her," Richard said.

Valin shrugged. "She rules by fear and by granting her soldiers power over the common people. Those who could challenge her, she enthralls much like she did to King Frederick."

"Were any taken alive?" Richard asked. "It might be useful to question one of them. Maybe we could get information on her for a change."

"I knocked one out," Henry said. They both looked at him, and Henry felt his face redden. "I've never actually killed a person before."

Richard's lips parted slightly, and his eyes widened. "Remark-able," he said and bowed deeply to Henry.

Valin stuck his head out of the tent and spoke to one of the guards. A little while later, a burly dwarf brought in the prisoner at sword point. The man was as big as an ox. He had arms like tree trunks that looked like they should've been able to snap the ropes with ease. Henry's blow had broken his nose, and blood dripped into his beard. His pale blue eyes could've been made of ice.

"Well, what do we have here?" Valin asked. The man grunted and spat on the ground, blood mixing with his saliva.

"Now, why did you have to do that?" Valin asked as he glanced at the spot on the tent floor. "That will almost certainly stain. This tent is worth more than you are."

"Dwarven scum," he said through clenched teeth.

Valin laughed. "Yes, well it's not the first time I've been called that. I very much doubt it will be the last. It doesn't really address anything we want to know. Let's start off simple. Where are you from? The force to the north or the one to the south? Or are you from some group we haven't heard of?"

Valin spoke with a casualness that surprised Henry. It was like this was an everyday affair and he couldn't be bothered to get worked up about it. It apparently surprised the prisoner as well because he looked at Valin in wide-eyed shock.

"Nothing to say?" Valin asked. "Well, perhaps that question was too difficult. I know Zuab doesn't employ the brightest men. Let's start with something simpler. What is your name?"

"I won't talk."

"Why that's a very strange name, but who am I to judge the customs of other people? Here's something you need to understand, I Won't Talk." Valin's voice became grim. He grabbed the man's beard and brought his face to within an inch of his own. "You don't matter. You are irrelevant. As far as I'm concerned, you're just trash. Dwarves don't spoil the land with needless garbage. We burn what we can until there's nothing left but ash and give that to the earth to help her grow. If you wish to prove you're not worthless as anything other than fertilizer, you're free to do so. If not, well, we'll be moving camp in the morning, and I see no reason to bring dead weight."

"You think I'm afraid of you?" the man said.

"I don't care if you're afraid, I Won't Talk," Valin said. "It doesn't make the slightest bit of difference to me if you live or die."

"My name is Egil," the man said.

"It really doesn't matter to me," Valin said, sounding bored.

Egil paled slightly. "I come from the south. It won't make any difference. This pitiful excuse for an army won't survive the week."

"Interesting," Valin said, kneeling down next to him. "Tell me, how is it you were able to avoid our scouts?"

"I don't know."

"You're going back to being worthless, Egil." He rose and walked to the tent flap before looking over his shoulder. "The sun will be up in another hour or so, and given your attack, I think it might be best to get an early start today. We wouldn't want a second attack to catch us in the same place, now would we?" He looked at Henry and Richard. "If the two of you don't mind, I'll see to breaking camp. Why don't you dispose of that? I wouldn't kill him though. That would make an awful mess, and the flames will do the job anyway."

"Wait," Egil cried out. "It's the queen. She sends runners with instructions on where and how to move. She knows whenever you send out scouts. Those we can't avoid, we kill."

"From where?" Henry asked.

"What?"

"She has to be close if she can send you information quick enough for you to do something about it. She's not at Daste, so where is she?"

"I don't know," Egil said.

Valin let out a deep sigh and opened the tent flap to leave.

"I don't know," Egil cried out again, practically in tears. "The runners come from the west and speak directly to General Hjal. That's all I know. I swear."

Valin looked at Henry. "That doesn't help us much. There are hundreds of caves less than a day's ride to the west. She could be in any one of them."

Richard shook his head. "We're not talking about just anyone.

This is Zuab. She wouldn't settle for being holed up in some cave. She'll be in the most opulent place she can find."

Valin thought for a second. "Karel is less than a day to the west. As I recall, the baron's manor is almost a palace in its own right. It would put her in position to strike at us while we're busy with the armies."

Richard nodded. "Yes, it makes sense. I can't think of anywhere else that does."

"If she's there sending messages, then she's brought the Oracle with her," Henry said. "What are we waiting for? If I go with Andromeda we fight her with the entire force of ghosts and over-whelm..." His blood went cold and his words caught in his throat. "Why didn't the ghosts help during the attack, and why hasn't Andromeda come here?" He turned back to the prisoner. "What did you do?"

Egil glanced at Valin and shrank back. "The princess was our target."

Henry dashed out of the command tent and headed to the one Andromeda used. His heart nearly stopped when he saw no guards. He opened the tent and went in. He almost tripped on the bodies of the two guards. One had a knife protruding from his throat, and the other had a dart with bright red plumes on his shoulder. Henry's eyes glazed over them to the person lying on the cot in the middle of the tent. Two other darts were embedded in Andromeda's neck.

She lay perfectly still, and Henry couldn't tell if she was breathing. He took a few shaky steps and put a hand on her neck. Her skin felt cold, and he couldn't find a pulse. He shook her, but she didn't move. His hand came away from her and he fell to his knees. A second later, Valin and Richard burst into the tent with the prisoner in tow bound and gagged. Valin uttered a curse, and Richard walked up to Andromeda and examined her. He shook his head. Tears flowed freely down his cheek.

"The queen is dead."

Valin shook his head and opened the tent flap. "Bring Nali," he cried out. "I need him here now!"

"She's gone," Henry said. "Don't bring back her ghost. She wouldn't want to be one of those."

"Not her ghost," Valin said, but before he could finish, Nali stepped into the tent.

He walked to the princess without saying a word. He passed his hand over her face, and a chill infused the air. Henry half expected her to wake up, but she just lay there as unmoving as a statue.

"Well?" Valin asked.

Nali kept his hand on Andromeda and sweat beaded on his brow. "The guards outside are already gone, but it's not too late for her. It's a near thing, though."

"You can heal her?" Henry asked.

"No," Nali said. "She is dead."

"Then what?"

"A deadly magic infuses her body, but her soul has not yet left this world. I can keep it here for a time."

"What's the point?"

"Her body is cursed," Nali said. "If it can be lifted before her soul departs, it might return to her."

"Can you lift it?"

"No. I'm not sure anyone can. The power inside her is like nothing I've ever seen." He turned to Valin. "Send for Brokkr. I need to speak with him, and I dare not leave the queen's side until all is ready."

"What are you going to do?" Henry asked.

"Master Henry, please be silent."

"What?"

Nali growled. "Holding a soul takes almost all my concentration. If you distract me, she'll slip through my fingers and be well and truly gone, so please be silent."

Henry wanted to ask more but held his tongue. A few minutes later, a dwarf in plain brown robes wearing glasses came into the tent. He looked at Andromeda and paled.

"Brokkr," Nali said. "I need a preserver."

"But surely Alviss—" the dwarf stammered.

"Alviss works with metal and stone. I need one made of crystal that's large enough to fit the queen."

"I don't know if I have enough."

"I don't care where you get it," Nali said. "Take anything anyone has made of it. The entire war may depend on it."

THIRTY-TWO

Henry's sword, shield, and clothing had been forged by Hephaestus. His flesh had been reformed by the master smith. He'd flown on winged sandals and had turned a throne room full of enemies to stone. In spite of all this, he'd never actually seen anyone work magic. Even when Circe had changed him into a half bird, his mind had been so muddled by her enchantment that he hadn't realized it was happening until it was done. Now that it was being done before his eyes, he couldn't turn away.

Brokkr put half a dozen irregular shards of crystal on a large metal sheet as big as Andromeda's bed. A number of other pieces were already on it, everything from intricate figurines to jewelry to a crystal bladed dagger. Brokkr had taken some from the men in camp. Though none were happy about it, no one had refused. The dwarf lit a fire under the plate, and to Henry surprise, it burned green.

"Is that a special kind of wood?" he asked.

"What?" Brokkr asked. "Oh no, it's just oak."

"But..."

"Master Henry," Nali said as he reached up to wipe sweat from his brow, "what Brokkr is doing is very nearly as difficult as what I am, and I have to split my attention between helping him and preserving the queen. It would be best if you didn't distract us."

Henry looked at him for a second and nodded. Egil started to mumble something, but Valin kicked him in the stomach, and the prisoner went quiet. The crystal began to melt, but instead of spilling over the side of the sheet, it congealed into a sphere in the middle. It rose into the air and began to hum. It spread out to fill the metal sheet. Its movements were painfully slow, and it took several minutes before it had transformed into a large block of crystal. Brokkr uttered something in a language that didn't quite sound like the dwarven tongue, and the top of the crystal melted away, leaving an empty box.

"It is done," Brokkr said.

The dwarf's face was drenched in sweat, and he was breathing heavily. He almost collapsed into a nearby chair before turning to Henry and smiling.

"I've never made anything this big in one sitting." He looked at Nali. "Is it enough?"

"I think so," Nali said. "Get her into it."

Andromeda wasn't heavy, and Henry was able to get her into the box without any trouble. As soon as she was inside, her body stiffened. Then, she relaxed. Henry put a finger to her neck, but he still didn't find a pulse.

"It looks like she's in a glass coffin," he said.

"In a way, she is. A coffin is meant to keep the dead inside. This preserver will do the same for her soul."

"For how long?" Henry asked.

Nali shook his head. "A soul is not easily kept. A day, perhaps two."

"What happens then?"

"Her soul departs, and she's beyond any help we could give her."

"Can we help her now?"

Nali put his hand in the box and held it just above Andromeda's face. He closed his eyes and concentrated. After a few seconds, he opened them and shook his head.

"If I had a thousand years, maybe I could draw out the death in her body. I doubt it, but it's possible. In two days? I'm sorry, Master Henry. There's enough death in her to kill everyone in this army a hundred times over. We need the source."

"The source?"

"Of the poison," he said. "With that, I could draw out the death."

"You mean the darts?"

Nali shook his head. "The poison was magic, and the darts were only how it was delivered. The magic in them is spent."

Henry looked at her unmoving form. Anger and sorrow warred inside of him. He didn't realize he'd closed his fist around his hilt until his hand started aching. He released it and let out a long breath.

"We have to go to Zuab."

"You know this poison?"

Henry nodded. "It's from the garden. Hermes told me he'd seen a woman taking it. It has to be her."

"Hermes?"

"You wouldn't believe me if I told you," Henry said.

"I don't know how many men we can send with you," Valin said. "Without the queen, we don't have the ghosts, and there are two armies about to crush us between them. We'll need every hand to do battle."

"I'll go alone then," Henry said. "My shield will protect me more than a dozen men would anyway."

"We could use you here."

Henry shook his head. "Our best bet is to wake Andromeda up and get the ghosts back."

"You just returned from being their prisoner. Are you well enough to travel?"

"I have to be."

"Very well," Valin said. "We'll get you a horse. Return as fast as you can."

Henry nodded just as Egil screamed. They looked down. The man, who'd been bound and gagged had chewed through the cloth in his mouth. He was shrieking and writhing on the ground. They stared at him, none of them sure what to do. It started so slowly Henry didn't see it at first. Egil began to get thinner. His muscles shriveled, and his eyes sunk into his skull. Pieces of skin flaked away, and moments later, nothing was left but a withered corpse.

"What..."

A translucent blade rose through the body. A second later, a hand and arm followed it until a ghost stood over him. Henry recognized it as the dead king Erhard.

"He was one of those who attacked the queen?"

"He was," Nali said, "but what..."

"He is no longer a danger to her."

"We had him bound," Nali said. "He wasn't a danger to anyone."

"He attacked the queen," the ghost said.

"We need you to move against the armies marching on us."

"We will protect the queen."

"We?" Nali asked.

As if on cue, more ghosts, both the ancient ones that had come from the palace, and the newly dead that Andromeda had gathered from the surrounding villages, rose from the ground. Henry began to shiver as frost crept up the side of the box. They formed a wall of mist and cold around her. Henry and his companions were forced back as the circle of spirits grew.

"Nali, do something," Valin said.

"There's nothing I can do, Lord Valin," he said. "I think I could stop one of the ancient ones. Two would overwhelm me in a matter of seconds, but there are a hundred here, not to mention the lesser spirits."

"We will guard her until she departs," Erhard said, apparently indifferent to Valin's concerns. "She is no longer any concern to you."

"It's no use trying to reason with them," Nali said. "They don't actually exist. All they can think to do is protect Andromeda."

"But that's a dead body..."

"Dead or alive, it doesn't matter to them in the slightest."

"She's safe then," Henry said.

"She's dead," Nali said. "She's as safe as that can make her. I just wish we could've gotten at least some of them to fight without her direct command."

"That would mean getting lucky," Henry said. "That doesn't really happen to us. This doesn't really change anything does it?"

"No, I don't think so," Valin said. "If anything, it only confirms what you were saying. They'll keep Zuab's forces away from her, but it won't do much good if the rest of the army falls."

Henry nodded. Nali stayed to see if there was anything he could do with the ghosts. Brokkr practically bolted as soon as he'd left the tent. Henry and Valin made their way to the stables.

"It should take you about eight hours to reach Karel on a good horse," Valin said. Henry winced. "What is it?"

"Nothing," Henry said. "It's just that in that time, Pegasus could take me a thousand miles."

Valin grinned. "I'm sure he's fast, but you must be exaggerating."

Henry shrugged. "Not by much."

Valin stared at him as if he didn't know whether or not to believe Henry. Finally, he shook his head and muttered something about humans and their stories. A stable boy bowed and scurried out of the way when they approached. A tall, lanky man looked at them and inclined his head.

"What can I do for you, Milords?"

"I need a horse," Henry said, "as fast as you've got."

"Of course." The man bowed again. "Please, follow me."

He led them to a picket line with several horses. They were tied fairly close together except for one area where a wide space separated the two horses.

"Why are those so far apart, Master Rudsind?" Valin asked.

The man nodded. "It's the strangest thing I've ever seen. That's where your horse used to be tied, Master Henry. They're not usually territorial, but none of the others will permit themselves to be tied there."

"But the camp has moved since Pegasus was here," Henry said.

The stable master nodded. "Like I said, it's strange. He wasn't mean or anything, but if I didn't know better, I'd say they all respected him."

"That's not all that unusual for horses, is it?" Valin asked.

"Not exactly, Milord," he said, "but this is different. It's like they don't want to take a spot that belonged to him. Horses just don't do that, especially when the camp is moving each day."

"A mystery for another time," Valin said. "The horse?"

"That one," Henry said pointing to a chocolate brown mare.

"The queen's horse," Vain nodded. "It seems appropriate."

"Of course," Rudsind said, bobbing his head. "She's as fast as any other, except of course yours, Master Henry."

He untied the horse and led her to Henry. He took her reigns and held them for a second, dumbfounded. He'd always ridden Pegasus bareback, and he realized he had no idea how to ride a normal horse. Oakash tossed her head and pulled back, but Henry held on.

"Shall I saddle her for you?" Rudsind asked.

"If you don't mind," Henry said, embarrassed to admit he didn't know how.

The stable master smiled and went into a nearby tent. He came back with a saddle and put it on the horse. Then, he offered Henry help up. Henry nodded to him and pulled on the reigns. The horse danced backward, and Henry's face heated up.

Before anyone could say anything, shouting erupted in the camp. Henry tried to turn the horse, but it was pointless. He hopped off and turned around. He gaped as people scrambled out of the way of a large stallion trailed by a cloud of dust. In spite of that, it had a coat so bright it practically gleamed in the sunlight.

"Pegasus!"

The horse ran right toward him. Valin and Rudsind jumped out of the way, but Henry had seen too much out of Pegasus to be worried. The horse came to a stop a few feet away. Henry ran up to him and threw his arms around his neck. Pegasus snorted and rubbed his nose against Henry's head.

"It's good to see you," Henry laughed. "Did you escape, or did Sholtz free you too?"

"I suppose I'll tie Oakash," Rudsind said, obviously trying to hold in a laugh.

"What's this?" Henry asked as he noticed the leather strap over Pegasus's neck. His face practically ached from smiling. "You managed to steal my pack?" A chill washed over him. He gasped, and his eyes went wide. "You stole my pack!"

He pulled it off Pegasus neck so fast that a part of him worried he'd hurt the horse. Pegasus, however, just stared at him. Henry tore open the pack and turned it over to shake it.

"What is it?" Valin asked as clothes and wrapped bundles of food and other odds and ends spilled out.

Henry was about to respond when a bright red apple tumbled out of the pack and rolled to Valin's feet. The dwarf stared at it, and Henry felt his heart in his throat. He reached out and took the apple before throwing his leg over Pegasus and galloping back into the camp.

"What is it?" Valin cried after him, but Henry didn't answer. He had to get back to Andromeda.

THIRTY-THREE

Once again, people leaped out of the horse's path. Several yelled curses at Henry, but he barely heard them. He was too focused on reaching the tent. At most, he'd saved five minutes by riding Pegasus instead of going to Andromeda's tent on foot, but every second counted. He jumped off Pegasus before the horse had come to a stop, and the momentum sent him flying into the tent. He couldn't stop himself from passing into the ring of ghosts. It felt like running into a wall of pure cold. Icy chills lanced through him, and he fell to the ground gasping for breath as the life slowly leached out of him. The ghost stared down at him.

Most had impassive expressions on their faces, but a few looked at him in confusion. Henry knew with cold certainty that what they were doing to him, they were doing without even trying. It took all the strength he could muster to roll out, and when he passed through one, he would've screamed if he'd had any energy left. By the time he'd moved past the edge of the circle, his hands were shaking, but he'd managed to keep his fingers around the apple. Nali ran over to him and knelt down.

"Do you have any idea how stupid that was?" he asked. "Ghosts that powerful can drive a man mad with their touch."

"Th..they w..weren't even trying," Henry said stammering so badly he wasn't sure Nali could understand.

"I should say not," the pale dwarf said. "You can't imagine what these can do if they try. I'm not sure you would want to."

Henry struggled to sit up. He extended a shaky arm and offered the apple to Nali. The dwarf took it and turned it in his hand.

"Not even bruised," Nali said, "but I'm not hungry."

He stared intently at it as Henry took several deep breaths to calm himself. He almost didn't notice Nali bringing the apple to his mouth.

"No!"

The dwarf froze. He blinked several times and let his arms fall to his side before looking at Henry.

"What is it?"

"The apple is poisoned," Henry said.

Nali looked from the apple to the ghosts. They'd gathered so thickly, Henry could no longer see Andromeda in their center. The dwarf raised the apple.

"Is this..."

Henry nodded. "It's the source of the poison."

"I've never heard of an apple being such," Nali said as he closed his eyes and began rolling the fruit in his hand.

A few seconds later, he let out a sharp breath and dropped the apple as if it had suddenly gotten very hot. His reflexes were amazingly fast though, and he scooped it up before it hit the ground. He looked at it again, but this time he held it away from himself as one might hold a snake.

"By earth and stone," he said in a voice barely above a whisper. "I've never felt so much magic in one place, nor have I ever known anything so dark. This thing not only kills, it entices you to eat it."

"Can you use it to cure Andromeda?"

"Master Henry, you don't understand. This apple isn't just poison. It's practically death given form."

"It's what she was poisoned with," Henry said. "Are you saying you can't use it?"

Nali shook his head. "It's too much. I can't channel that much power."

"Then, find some way to make the power less. Can't you cut off a slice or something?"

"Maybe someone could, but it would require a greater skill than I have to do that without losing most of the magic within."

"Isn't there anything you can do?" Henry asked.

Nali tapped his finger on the apple. "Maybe," he said, drawing out the word. "I'd need to get through them though."

"You can save the queen's life?" Erhard asked.

The ghost had stepped out of the ring and stood in front of the shifting mass. He looked straight forward, as if he couldn't see them.

Nali looked at Henry. "I've hardly been able to get a word out of them." He turned back to the ghost. "I don't know, but there's no one else who stands a chance."

The former king nodded and raised a hand. The ghosts around Andromeda parted, forming a narrow path. Off to one side, Egil's body was little more than skin and bones. His hair had fallen out, and an expression of pure terror was frozen on his face. Henry thought he was going to be sick.

Nali stepped into the path, giving the ghosts on either side uneasy glances, but they didn't even acknowledge him. He walked up to the glass coffin and placed the apple inside. He drew a knife from his belt and looked over his shoulder at Andromeda's grandfather. Then, he turned back and sliced the apple in two.

"I thought you said you couldn't do that." Henry said.

Nali held his hand over Andromeda's face for several seconds. "It's working."

"What's working?" Henry asked.

"The preserver is holding almost all of the magic inside. The only thing escaping is a trickle."

"What good does that do?" Henry asked.

"I can use the magic that's escaping," Nali said without turning around. "It's not enough to cure her all at once, but it's enough to slowly leach out the power in her body."

"How long will that take?"

"One or two days."

Henry gulped. "Can you finish before her soul departs?"

"I don't know," Nali said. "Tell Valin. I'll need someone to bring me food and water. I dare not leave her side until this is done."

Henry nodded and went outside. Valin was already approaching. When he saw the look on Henry's face, he started a slow jog. Henry met him and explained what had happened.

"I wondered why you'd left so quickly," Valin said. "I'll see to Nali. I assume you'll be heading to Karel."

"I don't know," Henry said. "Pegasus gives me more options."

"Such as?"

"Captain Sholtz said King Frederick resisted Zuab when she tried to turn him against Andromeda."

"And?"

"And maybe if I convince him that Zuab tried to kill Andromeda, he'll turn against her. Half of Zuab's army would disappear."

"You already tried that," Valin reminded him. "It got you banished."

"I didn't have the Oracle then."

"You don't have the Oracle now."

"But I know where it is. Maybe if I can't convince Frederick, the Oracle can. I also know a secret way into his castle, one that's unguarded since the ghosts are here. I might just be able to get him out and take him to the Oracle."

Valin raised his eyebrows. "You want to break into an enemy castle, kidnap their king, and take him to the stronghold of another enemy and have him speak to an Oracle that may or may not be there? What if Zuab catches you?"

"Probably the same thing that'll happen to you if Nali can't heal Andromeda in time."

Valin opened his mouth to speak, but then closed it again. He looked Henry in the eyes for a second before taking an emberstone amulet from around his neck. "Fair enough. Take this. It'll let you into the passage."

"Thanks," Henry said.

"Thank me by succeeding."

Henry nodded. They clasped hands, and Henry mounted Pegasus and urged him forward toward the man who once was king.

THIRTY-FOUR

Henry slowed as Daste appeared in the distance. As before, Pegasus knew the way better than Henry, and he came to a stop at the base of the hill with the lightning struck tree. Henry dismounted and ran his fingers through the thick hair of Pegasus's mane before walking up to the tree. He put the emberstone in the notch, and the hole opened. His footsteps sounded empty on the stone steps, and he kept expecting the uneasy feeling that had always gripped him when he went into the catacombs, but it never came. He picked up the red emberstone at the base of the stairs, though it only retained a dim glow from Nali's renewal, and made his way inside.

The wide room housing the monuments felt empty. He would've said it felt dead if it hadn't been the absence of the dead that had caused the feeling. He moved through the catacombs quickly. In a way, the emptiness was almost as unnerving as the crypts had been when they were filled with ghosts. Almost.

His heart raced as he walked up the steps to the castle. The heavy wooden door at the top scraped across the ground when he pushed it open. In the quiet, it sounded like an earthquake, and he held his breath until he was sure no one was coming.

The halls of the castle were dark, illuminated only by the light of the emberstone. Henry tried to ignore the red light's eerie resemblance to blood. A wind blowing through the passages kicked up a cloud of dust that set him coughing. The draft surprised him until he glanced into a room and saw a broken window. As he passed others, he saw the same thing more often than not. The walls were bare of any tapestry or decorations save for cobwebs. Even the weapons had been taken down, and without them, the place felt like an empty shell.

Henry crept through the halls for half an hour before he decided stealth wasn't necessary. He hadn't seen a soul, and there wasn't so much as a footprint in the layer of dust caking the floor. He almost turned around and gave up, but he held on to the thin hope that the king was still in the castle. He wandered around the maze of passages for another fifteen minutes, silently cursing himself for never taking the time to learn the layout of the palace.

Once, he passed another trail of footprints. Excited to have finally found signs of life, he almost started to follow them, but then he realized the footprints were his own. He'd gotten so lost in the twist and turns that he'd crossed his own path. He threw his arms up and turned to follow his own tracks back to the catacombs when he caught a flicker of light out of the corner of his eye. He gazed down the hall but saw only darkness. He'd almost convinced himself he'd imagined it when the orange light flickered again. Henry sniffed at the air. Under the musty scent of the dust, he caught a faint hint of smoke.

He hurried down the hall and came to another corner. The light became more pronounced. Slowly, he poked his head around the corner and looked down the torchlit hall. Two huge guards stood at a door several yards away. They each carried wicked looking axes and wore knives on their belts. One had a scar running down his arm. Though Henry couldn't say for sure in the weak light, he'd bet his life the men wore the crescent moon. They had to be guarding the king. Nothing else could be so important as to warrant Zuab's guards in an empty castle. Henry's hand fell to his sword, and he tightened his fingers around the hilt but shook his head. It would be a mistake. They'd cut him down. In spite of the training he'd received from Richard, he was still no soldier.

"But I am a hero," Henry said.

It was a long shot, but it was the only chance he had. He drew his sword and held his shield before him. Then, he strode boldly down the hall. The guards saw him and pulled out their weapons.

"I sincerely hope you try something," Henry said, desperately hoping he sounded confident.

The guards hesitated, and Henry took a step forward. One raised his axe, and Henry swung with an offhand swing. The man caught the sword on his axe, but he wasn't prepared for how the god-forged steel enhanced the strength of the blow. The axe flew from his hand and hit the floor in a shower of sparks. An instant later, he'd drawn a curved knife. The other held his axe before him and started moving around Henry.

"Drop the weapon," the one holding the axe said.

"No, I don't think so," Henry said, trying to ignore the sweat dripping into his eyes.

"You can't win," the guard said.

Henry moved his sword from one guard to the other and smirked. "I've heard that before."

He took a step towards the one with the dagger and swung. The man sidestepped his attack easily. Henry almost lost his balance but managed to catch himself. The impact of his sword on the wall rang up his arm, and the blade cut a gash half an inch deep in the stone. He looked back at the guards and tried to look as if it were deliberate. Each took a step back. The one holding the knife lowered it.

"Don't be a coward, Kuni," his companion said.

"I've heard stories about this one, Olaf," Kuni said. "Look what it did to stone. What could that do to flesh?"

"Much less than the queen will do if she finds out we let someone in."

Kuni shook his head, and his dagger fell to the ground. "I'll fight an army, but I'm not standing between Master Henry and the Queen." He turned and started walking down the hall. "That's a good way to get dead."

"Don't you dare leave me," Olaf said, but Kuni had already vanished around a corner.

"Go," Henry said, waving his sword in front of him.

With neither surprise nor the advantage of reach that the sword had given him over the dagger, Henry doubted he'd last very long in a fight. Olaf's eyes went from the sword to Henry's face. Henry tried not to hold his breath.

Olaf took a step back. Then another. Then he turned and jogged down the hall after Kuni. Henry waited until he'd disappeared around a corner before he let out a breath. His arms were shaking, and it took three tries before he could sheathe his sword. He took several seconds to calm himself before pushing open the door into the king's chamber.

Frederick sat on a plain wooden chair, the only piece of furniture in the windowless room. Runes had been carved on the wall and gave off a faint purple light. The king stared at the wall next to the door with an empty expression. His skin had gone pale, and his hair looked thin and unkempt. When Henry stepped inside, the king's eyes darted to him. For a moment, his brow creased in a scowl, but the expression faded a second later.

"Where are the guards?" The king sounded confused.

Henry came up to him and bowed. "They're gone, Milord. Everyone is gone."

"You kidnapped my daughter." Frederick's voice came out in a wheeze.

"What?" Henry asked. "No."

"My queen told me you did."

"Sire, Zuab sent men out to kill her."

"No, it was to capture you."

"We met Roderick in the woods," Henry said. "He told us Zuab had given orders to bring back Andromeda's heart."

"Yes," the king said. "I threw him in the dungeon."

"What? Why?"

The king blinked several times. "I'm not really sure. When he brought news of Andromeda's death, my queen was happy with him, but next day she told me Andromeda was still alive. She was furious, but I don't know why. She told me to throw Roderick in the dungeon, so I did."

"But he didn't do anything wrong?"

The king cocked his head. Several seconds passed, and Henry began to wonder if the king had fallen asleep, but then, he stirred, and the chair groaned under his weight.

"You know, I don't think he did. What a curious thing. I wonder why the queen wanted him imprisoned."

"And you didn't ask?"

"No, I'm sure she had a good reason."

"Like how Roderick pretended to kill Andromeda so Zuab's men would stop looking for her?"

His eyes hardened and life returned to his face. "No, she wouldn't harm Andromeda. I wouldn't allow it."

"Why don't you go ask Roderick?" Henry asked.

"That won't do any good," the king said as he slumped back into his chair. "Someone left his cell open one day, and he escaped. I never found out who, but my queen was in a rage for days afterward. Zuab told me he's a liar, so I couldn't believe anything he said anyway. She said the same about you, you know."

"And Andromeda?"

"Her too," he said, but he didn't sound so sure of himself.

"Sire, you know her," Henry said. "You raised her. Forget about what Zuab says. Is Andromeda a liar?"

Frederick's face twisted as if he were in a great deal of pain. After a few seconds, he let out a breath and shook his head, though he looked even paler than before.

"I can take you to her," Henry said.

His face lit up. "You can? That's right, you can. You kidnapped her, so you know where she is."

Henry clenched his jaw but nodded. "Yes, I know where she is. If you come with me, I'll take you to her. Then, you can throw me in the dungeon if you want."

"Yes, that sounds like an excellent idea."

The king rose, but as soon as he took a step, he faltered, and Henry moved to catch him.

"Why thank you," the king said. "I don't think we need to torture you. I'll talk to Zuab and try to change her mind."

"Um, thank you, Milord," Henry said. "That's very kind of you."

They moved through the halls with agonizing slowness. If the castle hadn't been so empty they never would've made it. The king stumbled regularly, and several times, they had to stop and wait for him to catch his breath. Apparently, he'd been in that room for a week, while the life slowly drained out of him. Getting him down the stairs to the catacombs took almost half an hour.

"There's something missing here," Frederick said when they reached the bottom. His voice sounded far away. He looked around, but his eyes never focused on anything. "It doesn't feel right."

"It's a long story, Your Majesty," Henry said. "This way."

By the time they made it to the entrance on the hill, the sun had fallen beneath the horizon. Henry removed the emberstone and closed the passage as Pegasus walked up to them.

"I rarely ride a horse," Frederick said.

"That's all right. Pegasus is a rare horse."

The king thought about that, but eventually, he shook his head and brought a hand to his brow.

"I'm sorry," he said. "It just hurts."

"That's probably Zuab's magic," Henry said. "Hopefully it'll get better now that we've gotten you away from those symbols."

Frederick shook his head firmly. "No, it's not. She would never do something like that to me."

Henry nodded as he got on Pegasus. "Of course not, Your Majesty. It was my mistake."

The king shrugged and accepted Henry's hand. Henry was surprised at how light the other man was. Pegasus didn't move as quickly as he had with only a single rider, but it was still far faster than any ordinary horse could manage.

Once, when they came within a few inches of a low hanging branch, the king screamed, but most of the time, he was stuck in his stupor. After a while, they turned off the main road and headed down a smaller path that would take them a little west of the army, and to the place where he hoped he would find Zuab.

THIRTY-FIVE

Henry guessed it was nearing midnight before a light appeared in the distance. It grew steadily larger until he was close enough to see that it was a window.

"Where are we?" the king asked.

"This is Karel," Henry said.

"Impossible, Karel is over a day's ride from the palace."

"Let's just say this is where we can get some answers."

He stepped down and offered a hand to Frederick, but when the king touched the ground, he collapsed. Henry walked over and helped him up. Frederick had to lean on him to stay steady. The gates to the city were unguarded, and they passed without incident.

Though the city itself seemed to be better off, the few people out at this hour had the same dead expression on their face that those of Maroque had worn. Most tried to avoid meeting Henry's eyes, though a few glanced at Pegasus.

"What's wrong with these people?"

"Are you surprised?" Henry asked. "From what I'm told, this is exactly what the people of Neustad are like."

"This is not Neustad," the king said.

Henry shrugged. "I only know what I've been told, but I get the feeling most of the people here wouldn't agree."

"I didn't know things were like this."

"How could you not know?"

"Zuab told me Argath was prospering."

"I'd say she lied."

"Watch your tongue," Frederick snapped. "You are speaking of my queen. Her word is not subject to question."

"With respect, Your Majesty," Henry said, "this place suggests otherwise."

The king let out a slow breath and avoided meeting Henry's eyes. For the first time, Henry realized color had begun to return to Frederick's face, though dressed in rags as he was, Henry doubted anyone would recognize him.

At the end of the main road stood a large house made of white stone. It was three stories tall, and gargoyles stood on the roof. Marble pillars held up a slate roof, and half a dozen guards stood before a massive door made of red wood. Others patrolled the area around the manor. Henry glanced over his shoulder at the king.

"I don't suppose you know a secret way in?"

"Why?" the king asked. "Is that where Andromeda is?"

"Not exactly," Henry said, "but we need to get in here if we're going to save her."

"Save her? You never said she was in danger."

"I told you Zuab wanted to kill her."

"She would never..."

"Open your eyes, Frederick. She's oppressed your people and lied about it. You threw an ally into prison because he tried to preserve your daughter's life. Do you really think she wouldn't lie to you?"

"She is my queen," Frederick said, though his voice had lost most of the certainty.

"She was a queen before you married her. What did you think of her then?"

"I was wrong," he said quickly.

"The proof is in there," Henry said, nodding to the manor.

"I thought I recognized that horse," a passing man said.

Henry looked up. It was a man with white hair, though he walked with a vigor that had deserted most of those around him. He wore plain wool clothes, though much cleaner than any other Henry had seen in town. He also looked vaguely familiar.

"General Rainard," the king said. "You're out late."

"I'm patrolling," he said. "Old habits die hard."

At the sound of his name, Henry recognized him as the man who'd been so angry when he'd heard that Zuab had tried to incinerate Andromeda. Rainard looked at the king in confusion for a second. Then, gasped and fell to his knees.

"My king," he said. "You don't know how good it is to see you here away from...her."

"Her?"

The general's eyes went to Henry, who shook his head. "I take it she's here."

"Yes, Master Henry," he said. "Is it true what they say about the princess? Has she really gathered an army to oppose..." he looked at the king.

Henry nodded. "More or less."

The general's eyes brightened, and he glanced over his shoulder at the manor before looking back to Henry. "Are you here to overthrow the witch?"

"If I can," Henry said. "I'm not sure if it will break her hold on the king, though."

"I'm willing to try," Rainard said. "What do you need?"

"Can you get me into the manor?"

"Not quietly," the general said.

"I'd settle for loud."

Rainard smiled. "The queen stripped me of my rank and I came here to retire, but there are a few fighting men who would follow me. We could get you inside."

"Who is this 'she' that you're talking about?"

"There's magic muddling your mind, Your Majesty," Henry said. "Let's just say it's an enemy of your people. Can you accept that?"

The king looked from Henry to Rainard. The old general nodded. Frederick closed his eyes and brought a hand to his head. After a few seconds, he let out a breath.

"Yes," he said, "from the two of you, I can."

Rainard banged on the door of a nearby inn until a fat man with thin brown hair opened the door. He wore a scowl, but Rainard spoke curtly to him, and the innkeeper blanched and suddenly couldn't get out of their way quickly enough. Henry and the king waited in the common room while the general went back into the city. In a surprisingly short time, he'd gathered a dozen men. Though none wore uniforms, each carried a sword, and all lacked the sleepy expressions that most would wear at this hour. These were rough looking men; the kind Henry would have avoided back home. They smelled of beer and unwashed flesh. One wore a faded tabard bearing a snowflake. Another was a wiry man Henry had seen before.

"Roderick. What are you doing here?"

"Master Henry," the hunter said, bowing. "The general has been gathering forces here ever since Zuab dismissed him. Why are you in Karel? You were supposed to keep the princess safe not lead her into the middle of the war."

Henry rolled his eyes. "Have you ever tried to keep her from doing something she's decided to do?"

Roderick laughed. "As a matter of fact, I have. I suspect you found it as futile as I did."

"If you two are done," Rainard said, "we should get going. Even this late, I doubt a group like ours can gather without spawning a swarm of rumors."

"What's the plan, General?" a rough-faced man with one eye asked.

"No plan today Kuno," the general said. "We leave the inn and charge."

The men cheered, and Henry found himself caught up in their excitement. They knocked over several chairs as they shuffled out. As soon as they were through the door, they took off in a dead run. The streets were silent, and Henry caught the occasional glimpse of someone glancing out of their window. He couldn't shake the feeling that this attack had been building for a long time. They were only a few blocks from the manor and reached it in under a minute.

They crashed against the men at the doors like a storm.

Caught off guard, they fell quickly. Blood soaked into the ground, but Rainard's men didn't stop. Three went at the door with heavy axes and in a matter of seconds had reduced it to splinters. The rest of them rushed inside.

"That was easy," Henry said.

"We had the element of surprise," Rainard said. "Believe me, Master Henry, if I thought it would be like this the entire time, I would've done this long ago."

As if on cue, the sounds of battle erupted from beyond the door. Henry ran inside with the king in tow and came to a large reception hall. There was a door on either side and a grand staircase rose to the second level on the other side of the room. Pitched battles were being fought at every way in and out of the room save the door he'd just come through. Roderick stood aside and shot arrows whenever he got a clear shot. Rainard's men were outnumbered but had positioned themselves in the openings so that only one or two enemy soldiers could come at them at once. They were holding their own but couldn't last much longer.

"Do you know where you're going?" Rainard asked.

"No," Henry said, desperately looking around for some sign.

"There," Rainard said pointing to a door on the second level. Four of his men held off twice as many of Zuab's.

"That's where most of the guards are coming from. If she's anywhere, it has to be there."

Henry nodded and ran up the stairs with Rainard right behind.

"Clear a path!" the general bellowed.

Two of the men surged forward. Rainard dove into the hole and engaged an enemy soldier. Henry grabbed the king's arm, and they ran into the hall. A door stood open at the end of the passage, and they charged through it. The sounds of battle faded behind him. Zuab stood with her back to the door wearing a black gown that almost seemed to suck the light from the room. The same crown Frederick had worn when Henry had first seen him adorned her head.

Nearby, an apple sat on a small table with half a dozen darts sticking out of it. The sight made Henry's blood boil. Zuab was staring at a mirror hanging on the wall. It was as tall as she was and framed with gold. Smoke swirled where reflections should have been, and Henry could just make out human forms. It was what he'd been looking for. The magic mirror. The Oracle of the Present.

Henry took a step forward, and a loose stone groaned under his weight. Zuab turned with a hand raised. She murmured a word and green lightning shot out at Henry. He barely had time to raise his shield. The lightning bounced off, breaking through a nearby window and illuminating the night sky.

"Well, isn't that impressive," she said. "I had thought you were exaggerating about that."

"It's over, Zuab," Henry said.

"Is it now? I find that rather curious. Within a day, my armies will crush that pathetic force Valin has raised, and there will be nothing stopping me from claiming all of Argath. Don't you agree, my love? Wouldn't you like to make a gift of your kingdom to me?"

"Yes, of course, beloved." All sign of thought had gone from Frederick's voice.

"What about Andromeda?" Henry asked. "She is your heir."

Zuab's face grew pouty. "Oh, my love, I regret to have to tell you this, but your daughter is dead because of this boy."

"What?" Anger dripped from Frederick's voice.

"Take hold of him."

Henry didn't dare turn to the king. Right now, his shield was the only thing standing between him and Zuab's magic. He felt the king's hand on his shoulder, and Henry ran forward, for once grateful that the king's strength had diminished under Zuab's spell. The witch shrieked and threw her hands forward. A tongue of flame erupted from her fingers. Henry thought his skin would blister from the heat in the air, but as soon as the fire struck the shield, it turned back. It crashed against the wall holding the mirror and sputtered out, leaving a pile of ashes where the table with the apple had been. He didn't see any sign of Zuab until he noticed her dress and crown on the floor. Outside the window a large black raven flew away from the manor. He turned back to see Frederick huddled in a corner.

"Please, don't kill me," he cried.

"I'm not going to hurt you," Henry said.

He walked to the window and picked up the crown and what remained of the dress. Then, he went to Frederick and placed the crown on his head. He helped the king up and led him by the hand back into the hall. Rainard's men had managed to consolidate inside.

"Zuab is defeated," he cried out.

A few men looked at him, but most concentrated on their fighting. Henry held the charred remnants of the dress against the stone wall of the passage and drove his sword into it. The weapon sunk to the hilt, sending stone shards flying. The fighting in the hall stopped.

"Zuab is defeated," he said again, this time, more quietly.

The men looked from the burned dress to the crown on Frederick's head. He could actually see their nerves leave them. One by one, Zuab's men put down their weapons and surrendered. They all carried looks of awed terror.

"See to your men, General," Henry said.

Rainard nodded and shouted orders. Then, he followed Henry back into the room where he'd fought Zuab.

"Is she truly dead?" Rainard asked.

"No," Henry said, "but it's enough that they think she is, at least for now." He walked toward the mirror. The smoke had faded, and he saw the room reflected there. "This is why I came here."

"A mirror?" the general asked.

"An Oracle," Henry said.

He stood in front of the mirror and his reflection stared back at him. More because he didn't know anything else to do than for any other reason, he asked the one question he knew the Oracle would answer.

"Mirror mirror on the wall, who's the fairest one of all?"

THIRTY-SEVEN

Smoke swirled in the glass until Henry could no longer see the reflection of the room. When it cleared, he saw a large black raven flying through the sky. Of course. Andromeda had been poisoned by the apple. With her lying dead in the glass coffin, it would be Zuab, just like all the stories said.

"Can you speak?" Henry asked.

"Yes." The voice was low and quiet. It echoed through Henry's mind.

"Did the fire hurt you?"

"There is no fire."

Henry let out a breath. "This again. You can only see the present, right?"

"Yes."

"Are you hurt?"

"I am undamaged," it said.

Henry looked over his shoulder at Frederick. "Do you still believe Zuab isn't your enemy?"

"She is my queen," he said in an unsteady voice.

Henry turned back to the mirror. "Show me Andromeda."

The raven flew into a cloud which obscured the mirror's sight. Faces began to take form, and before long, the cloud had given way to the dead kings of Argath standing guard over Andromeda's coffin. Nali stood nearby, and Henry could just make out the apple. The halves had withered to red husks. Nali looked thin and was breathing heavily.

"Andromeda," Frederick said in a quiet voice. "What happened to her?"

"Zuab sent an attack against Valin's forces. Their whole purpose was to kill Andromeda."

"They didn't succeed," Rainard said grasping for any hope.

"Yes, they did," Henry said.

"No," the king said. "You're lying. This is a trick."

"How can I prove it to you?" Henry asked.

Though he wasn't talking to the Oracle, the image in the mirror blurred. When it cleareed itself, the entrance hall of this manor showed in the glass. The bodies of Rainard's men had been cleared out, but Zuab's had been left to rot. The image floated through the room until it came to rest on a soldier that had been killed at the top of the staircase. It moved closer still, focusing on his waist until Henry could see little more than his belt. A piece of paper had been tucked behind it. Blood was slowly soaking the shirt. It would reach the note in a few seconds, likely ruining any writing. Henry looked at Rainard. The general nodded and disappeared through the door. A few seconds later, his hand appeared in the mirror and took the note. Frederick's face went a little pale.

"It is a little odd, isn't it? It's kind of like a security camera." Henry paused. "I guess you wouldn't know anything about that though."

The general reappeared and handed the note to Henry. Henry unfolded it and scanned the message. It was addressed to a general, though the name had been smudged. The message was orders to send men to attack Valin's camp. They were to cause whatever damage they could, but regardless of anything else, they were to kill Andromeda, if possible with the poison Zuab had provided them. Henry's eyes focused on the signature and the crescent moon crest. Wordlessly, he handed Frederick the letter. The king read it over a couple of times before closing his eyes and shaking his head.

"Do you recognize the signature?" Henry asked.

"Signatures can be faked," the king said.

"Frederick, this is her house," Rainard said. "I got that off one of her men. What would it take to convince you if a signed confession won't do?"

Frederick began to shake, and he spoke through clenched teeth. "You will address me as 'Your Majesty'."

"I would address the king as 'Your Majesty'," Rainard said. "I don't see a king standing before me."

"I never knew you were a traitor, Rainard," Frederick said.

"I never knew you were," the general countered. "I don't know who you are anymore."

"He is Frederick, former king of Argath."

The voice came from the mirror, and all three of them turned to look at it. A face appeared in the glass against a background of red smoke. It was pure white and had holes where its eyes and mouth should be. Henry would've thought it a mask if it didn't move as it spoke.

"Former king?" Frederick asked in a rage.

"There are two who rule Argath. Neither one is you."

"Two?" Henry asked.

"The first even now flies to do battle to wrest control from the second whose soul lies entombed in a crystal coffin."

"You're talking about Zuab and Andromeda."

"Yes."

"What do you mean her soul? What happened?" Frederick asked.

"What happened is what was."

"What's that supposed to mean?"

"He doesn't know," Henry said. "The first Oracle I spoke to only knew the future. She couldn't see the past or the present."

"Fine, then you tell me. What happened to my daughter?"

"You have the note in your hands," Henry said. "They poisoned her, but the dwarves kept her soul from departing until they could heal her body and hopefully restore her to life."

"You mean she's a hostage."

"She was one of their leaders," Henry yelled.

"Impossible!"

"No, Frederick," Rainard said. "I've heard the rumors for weeks now about how Andromeda is raising an army against Zuab."

Frederick sniffed. "Rumors."

"How would you know? You've been a hermit in your own castle, all because Zuab told you to."

"She said it would be best for the kingdom," Frederick said.

"Best for the kingdom?" Rainard was yelling. "You are the king, or at least you were before you handed Argath to Zuab. It's only Andromeda's rebellion that kept the kingdom out of her hands entirely."

"No, I..."

Frederick swayed on his feet, and Henry had a sudden flash of insight. He turned to the mirror.

"Show me Argath's greatest enemy." The face vanished and was replaced by the raven. "That is Zuab?"

"Yes."

"Show me the greatest enemy aside from her."

The raven faded, and the mirror showed the face of Frederick himself. The king recoiled, both in person and in the mirror.

"No," he said. "No no no!"

He grabbed his head in his hands and rocked back and forth. He shrieked, and a sphere of green light appeared around him. Cracks spidered across it, and it flaked away. The image of the king faded from the mirror, replaced by a burly man that Henry recognized as the enemy general Hjal. Frederick fell to his knees.

"What have I done?" he cried.

"Is the spell broken?" Henry asked the mirror.

"Yes."

Rainard was already kneeling before Frederick.

"My king," he said. "I am your man."

"I don't deserve your loyalty, Rainard," he said. "If you would serve Argath, serve my daughter. She has been a greater ruler than I."

Henry left them to sort that out as he addressed the mirror again. "Show me who's responsible for all this. Who does Zuab work for? Who's waging war on Kurnugi?"

Smoke clouded the image. It looked somehow thicker than before, and when it finally cleared, it showed a woman sitting on a tree stump. She wore a flowing white gown. Her braided hair went down to her waist and shone like fire in the sunlight. She looked young, no older than Henry himself. A basket of apples sat next to her, and she was listening to a man playing a harp.

"Who is that?" Henry asked,

"This is Idun," the mirror's voice said. "She holds the apples that are the source of the gods' power."

"Which gods?"

"The gods of the north, of a warrior people, they who rule over Midgard, Asgard, and Valhalla."

"Valhalla?" Henry asked. "You mean she's one of the Norse gods?"

"Yes."

"Vikings? I have to fight Vikings?"

"I do not know. That deals with future, and that is beyond my sight."

"Fine," Henry said. "Why is she fighting this war?"

"The apples that are the source of her power are corrupt, so she is corrupt as well. All she desires now is power."

"How did that happen?"

"It was in the past."

"So you don't know?"

"No."

"How do I stop her?"

"You are a hero," the mirror said. "There are few things that are not within your power to destroy."

"You want me to kill a god?"

"Killing Idun will stop her."

"She's in Far Kurnugi, isn't she?"

"Yes."

"And she's blocking the passage that exists in the garden?"

"It is done at her command."

"Then how do I get there?"

The image of the goddess was replaced by Fjalar sitting in his throne. He was reading a letter written in a language Henry didn't understand. It was sealed in red wax with the image of an exploding volcano.

"Hreidmar is high king of the dwarves of all realms, and the only one to whom Fjalar bows. The high king rules the realm of Nidavellir, which lies beneath Midgard. Valin can show you the way to Jord, the capital and the center of Hreidmar's power."

"Idun holds the Oracle of the Past, doesn't she?"

"She does."

"So she knows everything you've said to me."

"If she considers the right questions."

"Where is the Oracle?"

The images in the mirror vanished, and the face returned.

"The past lies at the root of all things. To find it you must find that root."

"Yeah, I didn't think it would be that easy. You know these rules are really starting to get on my nerves. I don't suppose there's any information you'd like to volunteer?"

"The future has not happened," the mirror said, "so there is no price to gain it. The present is all around you, and to get the right answers, you need only ask the right questions. It is not so for the past, and you must pay a heavy price to drink of its waters."

"Well, that's ominous."

He turned back to Frederick and Rainard. The king's color had returned, and Henry wasn't sure if it was his imagination, but he thought Frederick's hair was thicker than it had been a few minutes ago.

"This mirror is truly a marvel," the king said.

"You have no idea," Henry said. "I assume you'll keep it safe."

"I will," Frederick said, "but first we need to see to this army."

Henry nodded and looked to Rainard. "Valin's army is a day

east of here. Gather as many men as you can and join him. Don't waste any time."

"You're not coming with us?" Rainard asked.

"I can get there a lot quicker than you can," Henry said before looking at Frederick. "Your Majesty, you can come with me if you want. It's where Andromeda is."

"I'll come, Master Henry," he said, "and thank you. If Argath can be saved, it is because of you."

Henry didn't know what to say to that, so he just inclined his head. As they walked through town, people stared at them. Some wore relieved expressions as if they had just woken up from some terrible dream. Henry and the king went to the inn where Pegasus had been stabled and mounted up. They didn't even wait to get out of town before taking off in a full gallop.

THIRTY-EIGHT

It took less than an hour for Pegasus to cover the distance, and Henry slowed as soon as he saw a banner bearing a red bolt of lightning that almost glowed in the rising sun. They dismounted, but they were still a hundred yards away when half a dozen dwarven warriors came out of the forest and leveled axes at them.

"That's a valuable prisoner," one of the dwarves said, indicating the king.

"He's not a prisoner," Henry said. "He's here to help and to see his daughter."

"He is an enemy leader," the dwarf said.

"Take us to Valin," Henry said. "Let him decide what to do."

The dwarf nodded and put away his axe. Whispers followed them as they made their way through the camp. Renewed strength filled Frederick, and he held his head high in the same way Andromeda had done sometimes. Though he still wore dirty rags, no one could mistake him for anything but nobility. The humans had a mix of rage and awe on their faces. A few bowed, but most just stared.

"Andromeda did this?" he asked.

One of the dwarves guiding them stiffened. "Zuab's rule left Argath as kindling. The queen was a spark that set it aflame and restored its life."

"The queen?"

"As far as the dwarves are concerned, you surrendered the crown when you fell under Zuab's spell."

For a second, Frederick looked like he would argue, but his shoulders slumped, and he shook his head.

"I don't suppose I can blame them."

Valin stood at the entrance to his tent. He had a scowl on his face, and three guards were clustered around him.

"Frederick," he said in a flat voice.

"Lord Valin," Frederick said, giving the dwarf a bow. "I understand you've formed an alliance with my daughter."

Valin nodded. "To save us all from your foolishness."

"May I see her?"

"That may not be wise," Valin said.

"Why not?"

"It would be dangerous. She's gathered the spirits of your ancestors around her. They know what you've done, and they don't hold you in high regard."

"I don't hold myself in high regard just now," Frederick said. "I would still like to see her."

"Very well," Valin said. He looked at Henry. "Can you take him? If he survives, bring him back to see me."

"I have heard of dwarven superstition regarding the dead," Frederick said once they were out of earshot. "I didn't expect anyone as high as Valin to believe it though."

"Superstition?" Henry asked.

"Yes," Frederick said. "I can't imagine any reasonable person believing in ghosts."

Henry stopped and stared at him for a second. "After everything you've been through, do you really find it so hard to believe that there could be such things as ghosts?"

"I know dwarves can work wonders with metal and stone, and certainly Zuab had some power, but the spirits of the dead? No, I don't believe in them."

"You saw them in the mirror."

"I'm not sure what I saw. Remember, my mind was still clouded by Zuab's magic."

"You're in for a surprise," Henry said under his breath.

They continued on, and Henry opened the door to the command tent. Frederick stepped inside and gasped. The ghosts gathered around Andromeda ceased their writhing and turned to stare at him, and for the first time, Henry saw something other than dead impassivity in their eyes. These spirits were angry, and cold fire burned in their gaze. In the center of the circle, Nali stood with his arms held high. The pale dwarf was drenched in sweat, and his breathing was weak. Henry met his eyes and saw that the dwarf was completely exhausted.

The spirits wailed and flew toward Frederick. The king screamed and threw his arms up in front of his face. One after another, they passed through him, each one drawing a cry that grew increasingly weak as the seconds passed. Frederick fell and curled into a fetal position. He took short erratic breaths, and he couldn't seem to focus on anything. A thin layer of frost shimmered on his clothes and ice chips had formed in his hair.

"Who are you?" Frederick's voice came out as a whimper.

"Who are we?" Erhard's voice rang clear over the other spirits.

The shout was so loud Henry had to cover his ears. "Who are we? We are who you were supposed to be. We are what your daughter is. We are the kings and queens of Argath."

Frederick blinked several times and tried to focus. Tears had frozen onto his cheeks, and his eyes looked sunken.

"Father?"

"My son was a king, not a weak-minded fool who handed over the kingdom to its greatest enemy."

The ghost lifted his arm and smoke congealed in his hand forming a translucent blade. He brought it down with deadly speed. Henry didn't think. His own blade snapped out and caught the ghost's sword on his own. Everyone froze. Even Henry was surprised it had worked, but apparently, Hephaestus's sword worked even against the dead. Henry gritted his teeth. The Oracle had said that as a hero, there were few things that were not in his power to destroy. It wouldn't be easy, and he might die trying, but it was possible for him to destroy this ghost.

"He failed," Henry said, "but he's not a traitor. I won't let you kill him."

Fire burned in the ghost's eyes. "You can't stop me," he hissed.

Henry flicked his sword up as Richard had shown him. The ghost's weapon flew from his hand and vanished in a puff of smoke. The other ghosts gathered around him, and Henry tried not to show fear.

"This isn't what the queen would want," he said.

"You would dare speak for the queen?"

As one, the ghosts surged forward. Magic sword or no, there were too many of them. The cough coming from the center of the room was faint, but the sound somehow overpowered everything else. Every eye, both living and dead turned to Nali and the crystal coffin. The dwarf was leaning on it, and Henry thought he might collapse at any second. Henry's heart began to race when Andromeda moved. She took in a deep breath and her eyes opened. They looked like the most perfectly cut emeralds he had ever seen. She rose and scanned the room, obviously at a loss for words. The entire host of ghosts fell to their knees, and Frederick staggered to his feet.

"Father?" she said.

"Andromeda," he cried and ran to her.

The few ghosts between them melted away, though whether it was on their own initiative or by some unspoken command of Andromeda, Henry had no idea. Andromeda embraced her father, and he lifted her out of the box. When he put her on the ground, they both had tears in their eyes.

"Oh dear one," Frederick said. "I'm so sorry. I should've never allowed myself to fall under her spell."

"You're here now," Andromeda said. "That's all that matters."

They stood there, crying in each other's arms for several minutes before Henry cleared his throat. They looked at him, and Andromeda smiled.

"I hate to interrupt this," Henry said, "but we still have two armies that are about to attack. We need to go see Valin."

"Yes, of course," Andromeda said as she wiped the tears from her face. "We'll come immediately." Her face paled and she looked at her father. "I'm sorry. I didn't mean to overstep myself."

Frederick shook his head. "No, Andromeda, the dwarves are right. I surrendered my right to the throne when I handed the kingdom to Zuab. You are the queen."

"No father..."

"Maybe this is one of those things we should decide later," Henry said. "I take it you both want to stop Zuab?" They nodded.

"Then it doesn't really make a difference just now." He looked at Nali. "Are you all right?"

"I'm well," he said between heavy breaths. "I'm just so tired."

"What happened?" Andromeda asked.

"You were dead," Henry said. "Nali has been at your side nonstop drawing the death out of your body so your soul could return."

"I was dead?"

"Zuab's men poisoned you."

Andromeda looked like she was going to be sick.

"How long was I...gone?"

"Two days," Henry said.

"Two days?"

"We weren't sure you'd make it at all."

"What's happened?"

"Later. Let Nali get some rest," Henry said. "The rest of us should go see Valin. We're running out of time."

Andromeda nodded, and the three of them walked out of the command tent. A hush fell over the camp as people saw Andromeda. A few seconds later, the entire army erupted in a cheer. News had rushed ahead of them, and Valin and Richard greeted them before they'd made it halfway there. Each gave Andromeda a deep bow.

"My queen," Richard said, though he avoided looking Frederick in the eyes.

"Come," Valin said. "We have much to discuss."

They followed Valin into his pavilion. Maps of the surrounding area had overflowed from the table and many lay open on the ground. A red mark in the middle of the one on the table represented their army while blue marks showed the approaching forces.

"Do we have a chance?" Henry asked.

"Ten minutes ago, I would've said no," Valin said. He looked at Andromeda. "I take it you have command of the ghosts?"

"I do, Lord Valin."

"Good. Have them meet the southern force." He turned to Frederick. "Are you truly here to help?"

"Yes, I'll do whatever I can."

"Good," Valin said. "We'll put you in front of our army when they meet the force to the north."

"What?" Andromeda said. "You can't put him on the front lines. He'll be killed." She paused, and Henry could see the accusation in her eyes. "Is that what you want? Revenge?"

"No, Your Majesty," Valin said. "The northern force is still composed mainly of the men of Argath. They follow Zuab only because they follow your father. If they see him at the head of our army, they may turn against her."

"That's a big risk," she said.

"It is no more than I owe Argath," Frederick said. "I will do as you ask."

"Father you don't have to."

"Remember what I taught you. Realm before king. I may no longer be king, but I can still serve the realm."

Valin walked over to the king and clasped his arm. "It's a pity you lost the kingship. The land would've been well served by a king such as you."

"What do you want me to do?" Henry asked.

Valin raised an eyebrow. "I've learned my lesson about trying to give you orders, Master Henry. Do what you think is best. I'll pass orders to the men to obey any command you give."

"I'm no commander," Henry said.

Valin waved him off. "I don't expect you to lead the men into battle, but I think what you do may be more important than anything else. If any of my men can help, I mean to see it done."

"I doubt we've seen the end of Zuab, Master Henry," Frederick said. "You're the only one she's ever fled from."

"I surprised her," Henry said. "I have a feeling it won't be so easy when she comes for me."

"Did you?" Frederick said. "Here I thought she had access to an Oracle that would tell her everything that is."

"Only if she asked the right questions."

"And you don't think the location of her greatest enemy is a question she would've asked? She's vain to a fault, but she's not stupid. I made that mistake once. You're the only one who can stand against her."

"All right," Henry said. "I'll wait for her to show herself, but if I think I'm needed somewhere else, I won't hold back."

Valin grinned. "I wouldn't expect you to."

THIRTY-NINE

The attack came in the night. Horns sounded through the camp, and Henry was instantly awake. He drew his sword and ran outside. People were running past him, and it took him a moment to gather his bearings. They were heading north. It must be the force that Sholtz fought in. Henry only waited for about thirty seconds before throwing the plan to the winds and running with the human soldiers. Before he'd gone a dozen steps, Pegasus seemed to materialize out of the night. The frayed rope around his neck told Henry that he had broken free. He mounted up, and they charged into the attack.

Henry had heard of battles in stories and myths for as long as he could remember. They were supposed to be a spectacular clash of armies. Even after everything he'd seen since he crossed into Kurnugi, a part him had thought it would all be decided by one grand charge. He hadn't expected it to be chaotic, but though he was in a story, apparently, he wasn't in that kind of story. They didn't fight in unison like he'd thought. Instead, there were a thousand tiny battles scattered throughout the valley. Henry didn't know where to start. Half the time, in the dark, he couldn't even tell who was who. It was only when he saw dwarves that he committed himself.

They never saw him coming. He wove in and out of battles, striking as quick as lightning, though it was his presence more than his ability that had the greatest effect. Men and dwarves saw him and fought on with renewed vigor just knowing that such a hero fought for them. A group of enemy soldiers charged a cluster of men but pulled back when they saw the snowflake banner flying over them. Frederick rode at the front of the soldiers. The two groups stared at each other. Then, a cry sounded from the enemy fighters.

"The king fights with Valin! Argath and Nordi!"

The two groups rode at each other, but rather than crashing together, they joined, and several men tore off crescent moon tabards and left Zuab's symbol trampled on the ground.

Henry withdrew from the battle but stayed close enough to watch for a few minutes. Frederick's group continued to grow as they ran into others who recognized their king. Every once in a while, they encountered a group of men who fought, but these were dispatched in short order. In spite of that, the larger battle still raged on. There were just so many of Zuab's men, and only the barest fraction turned against them, but before Henry could do anything else, another horn sounded.

From the south, an eerie blue light arose from the ground, and a chill ran down Henry's back. Andromeda would be there. He urged Pegasus forward, and in a matter of moments, they were on the northern edge. The battle was gruesome. Already, shriveled bodies littered the ground. Others lay screaming and clawing at their eyes. Still others had been frozen. The ghosts tore through

Zuab's army as if they didn't exist. Every once in a while, steel would clash against ethereal blade, though whether this was because of magic or for some other reason, Henry had no idea. A couple of times fire or lightning shot across the field and struck a spirit. Sometimes, the ghost would dissipate, while other times, the magic bounced off.

Henry scanned the enemy trying to find the source of the blasts. Once, he saw a black-robed man shoot fire from his hands, but he was overcome by a dozen ghosts an instant later. Henry cursed. He'd forgotten that Zuab had other sorcerers in her service. Slowly, the advance of the ghosts was being halted. Henry's blood ran cold when the corpses of the dead enemies began to glow blue.

One by one, human figures arose from the bodies. As the new ghosts saw the old ones, they charged. Andromeda's ghosts were forced to fight on two fronts. Henry urged Pegasus forward, and he waded into the enemy spirits. The first two fell to his sword without even realizing he was there. When they finally noticed him, they swarmed around him. The movements of these new ghosts were sluggish, and his sword and shield seemed just as effective against them as against flesh, but he couldn't defend against all sides at once. Icy blades sang across his flesh, and he began to slow. Pegasus reared as a pair of transparent spears pierced his side. Henry was thrown to the ground and the ghosts fell on him. A weapon cut into his arm. Though it left no mark, pain shot through him, and his hand spasmed, dropping his sword. They banged on his shield, and Henry knew he wouldn't last much longer.

Then, Andromeda was there. Erhard stood beside her. With one great swing of his sword, three of the newly dead screamed and evaporated. Andromeda knelt by his side and helped him to his feet.

"What are you doing here?" he asked, his voice strained.

"You've already saved my life twice. It's long past time I started repaying the favor."

Henry laughed. "You won't hear me arguing." It was only then that he noticed Nali standing with her. "What's happening?"

Nali scanned the enemy. Then, his eyes narrowed, and he pointed at three robed men. One of Andromeda's ghosts neared them, but it vanished in a flash of green light.

"There," he said. "They're pooling their power to unleash these ghosts."

"I thought you said you couldn't call up so many spirits."

Nali shook his head. "These weren't called up. They were unleashed."

It was only then that Henry saw one of the new ghosts leap onto one of Zuab's armored man. Though the spirit had no weight, the man fell to the ground. The ghost ripped at him with claw-like hands. The man opened his mouth to scream, but no sound came out. In a few seconds, he'd stopped moving.

"Why..." Henry began but the words caught in his throat. The sight of the ghost ripping into the man was so terrible, he didn't even know how to put words to his question.

"This was an act of desperation," Nali said. "They're completely uncontrolled."

"Can you do anything?" Henry asked.

"Not much," Nali said. "It's all I can do to keep them off us."

"Can you open a path for me to them?"

"No," Nali said.

"I can," Erhard said. The air around the spirit pulsed with power. "Follow me."

The ghost didn't wait for Henry to answer. He strode toward the three men swinging his sword with an almost casual indifference. Everywhere it touched a ghost, the spirit vanished. Once, a man got in his way. The ethereal weapon passed through him, and he crumpled without making a sound.

One of the robed figures noticed Erhard and pointed a finger. A nimbus of green light appeared around the spirit, but he didn't slow. The wizard's brow furled, and he said something Henry couldn't hear. His companions turned and also raised their hands. The light around the dead king intensified. He groaned through gritted teeth and came to a stop. Henry didn't. He held his sword in front of him and approached the trio of wizards. One pointed at him and pain shot through Henry's body, but whatever energy the sorcerer used to stop Henry was apparently taken from the working holding Erhard, leaving it too weak to hold him. The spirit took one step forward and swung his sword. It passed through all three, and they collapsed in a heap. Robbed of the will and purpose that animated them, the ghosts of the enemy soldiers flickered and vanished. Andromeda's ghosts didn't cheer. They didn't have any reaction at all. They just continued on with ruthless efficiency, although the rest of Zuab's wizards did what they could to slow them down. More men poured out of the woods, and for a second, Henry thought they were going to be surrounded, but then he saw the man riding at their head.

"Rainard!" Henry called out.

"Master Henry," he said, "what in the name of all that is good and holy is going on here?"

"It would take too long," Henry said. "Ignore the ghosts. They're on our side. Attack the men. Stop the robed ones if you can."

The general dipped his head and raised a hand. His men scattered, engaging the enemy wherever they could as they fought side by side with those who had been their kings and queens.

"I think we're winning," Henry said.

"I think you spoke too soon," Nali said, pointing to a figure cresting the hill.

Henry looked at where he was pointing. Though she was still far away, he had no trouble recognizing Zuab. She pointed her hand and a streak of purple lighting shot out, incinerating three of Rainard's men along with four of her own. Half a dozen ghosts had also been destroyed.

"I guess it's time for me," Henry said.

He leaped onto Pegasus and kicked his heels into the horse's side. The stallion thundered across the field. Zuab saw him before they'd made it halfway there. She launched fireball after fireball at him, but they bounced off his shield.

"Really Zuab," Henry said when reached her, "do you expect to take me down using the same old trick that failed before?"

"I have a few new ones," she said with a smile.

Zuab held up her hand and the sky rumbled. Lightning flashed and struck her hand. It was so bright, he had to turn away. When he looked back, a sword of electricity was coming right at him. He didn't have time to do anything but fall off Pegasus to avoid it. He got to his feet as she struck again, and he lifted his own sword to meet it. There was a clang and Henry's blade began to glow. Energy ran down it and into his hand. Pain ran from the top of his head to the tip of his toes. He couldn't move. Acrid smoke drifted to his nostrils. His sword and shield fell from his grip. He didn't even notice when he fell to his knees.

"You never should've gotten involved in this," she said as she lifted her lightning sword to strike again.

"I've had scarier people than you throw lighting at me," Henry said between labored breaths.

She raised her sword to attack again. He rolled away, and the sword exploded into the ground, sending up a cloud of dirt and rock, blurring Henry's vision. Zuab coughed, and Henry fumbled around the ground until he found his shield. The queen attacked again, but this time, Henry raised his shield. Zuab wore the faintest hint of a smile. The shield was metal, just like the sword, and ordinary metal provided no defense against a weapon made of electricity. Henry almost felt sorry for her. She brought the sword down. In the last instant, her eyes widened and she tried to turn away the blow, but she'd realized her mistake too late.

The lightning sword struck his shield, and the energy reflected back on her. She screamed, and her hair began to smoke. Her blade dissipated, and she fell to the ground. Patches of clothes crumbled to ash, and blisters covered her face. Henry struggled to his feet. His limbs were sluggish, but he managed to pick up his sword. He held it over her, and she met his eyes. Pure terror showed there, and his heart fell.

"No," he said. "You're already beaten. I won't kill you."

He looked around and realized that the only men left standing were Rainard's. Zuab's men had either been killed, captured, or were fleeing. Andromeda and Nali walked up next to him. Andromeda sneered at her.

"This is the one who nearly brought Argath to ruin?" she said.

"What do you want to do with her?" Henry asked.

"I'd like to lock her away in the deepest part of our dungeon, but I don't think we can contain her power."

"Give her to me, my queen," Erhard said. "I will see that she pays for her crimes."

Andromeda looked at the dead covering the field. Her face took on a sickly cast, and she shook her head.

"In battle, maybe, but I won't have a ghost execute a prisoner."

"A compromise, then," Henry said. Nali and Andromeda

looked at him. "How many ghosts can she hold at bay? The ones of the kings I mean?"

Nali shrugged. "She's far stronger than I am, but her powers are more broadly focused. She might be able to defeat one, though I doubt it. Two would be too much for her."

"And they never tire?" Henry said.

"Never."

"Then, throw her in the dungeon and put two of them guarding her."

Andromeda looked at Nali, and the dwarf nodded. "It could work. Their purpose is to defend the kingdom, and there's no question Zuab is an enemy of Argath. If they have orders to attack if she used her powers, she'd be far more secure than any other prisoner."

She turned to the spirit of her grandfather. "Get one other and guard her. Do not hurt her unless she tries to escape. If she does, or if she tries to hurt anyone, stop her any way you can."

The ghost inclined his head. "By your command, my queen."

Erhard let out a howl that pierced the night. The ghost of a woman stepped out of the shadows. At least Henry thought she had once been a woman. Its figure was vaguely feminine, but thick fur covered its body, and it had the head of a wolf. It looked at Zuab with hungry eyes and the witch scurried back. Andromeda looked like she might throw up.

"That thing ruled Argath?"

Erhard nodded. "Queen Heul ruled a hundred and fifty years ago."

"Read your history girl," Zuab said. "Heul was a monster."

"Then, I suppose it's fitting to have her guard you."

Andromeda looked at her grandfather. "Take her back to the camp. Don't let her speak to anyone save Valin, Richard, or my father."

Erhard bowed and drew his sword. Zuab yelped and got to her feet. She looked like she was going to say something, but the ghosts forced her to walk away just as Rainard approached them. The general went to one knee.

"Rise, General," Andromeda said. "Your arrival was timely."

"My life for Argath, Milady," he said. "We've received word from the northern forces. The battle is won."

At those words, the ghosts nearest to them disappeared. It spread out like a wave as the spirits vanished. Henry and Andromeda looked at Nali.

"The old ones are still there. They'll remain so long as there is an Argath. The new ones only had the purpose of defeating Zuab. They no longer exist."

Henry looked around. He didn't miss the ghosts, not exactly, but they had been a constant part of the army since he and Andromeda had first joined them. Now, the night felt very empty.

"Rest easy," he said to the darkness.

FORTY

Valin set up an impromptu feast to celebrate the end of the war. It was unlike the one Henry attended in Greece. That one had taken place in a palace instead of a valley that had so recently been a battlefield. Instead of expertly prepared food from all corners of the world, Roderick and other hunters went out and caught deer and boar. Runners went to Karel and bought everything they could carry, and nearby farms received a pile of gold for any cows and sheep they were willing to sell. Mismatched tables and chairs were salvaged from anywhere they could be gotten. Most people sat on their sleeping mats, if they didn't sit on the bare floor. All in all, it was more like a massive picnic than a royal feast.

Henry sat with Andromeda and her father at Valin's table, which had until a few hours ago, held maps of the surrounding region. Halfway through the meal, Nali stopped by to pay his respects and offer his congratulations. Alviss did the same a few minutes later, followed by Richard and Rainard. Even Brokkr came by, though his words tumbled over each other. One by one, others, both human and dwarf stopped at their table to congratulate them on their victory. Universally, they bowed to Andromeda. Most avoided looking at Frederick altogether.

"You should probably do something about that," Valin said.

"What is there to do?" Frederick said. "They didn't really turn against me. I turned against them. The only good thing I've done in months is admit how badly I messed everything up."

"Don't say that, father," Andromeda said.

Frederick shrugged. "It's true. You are the rightful queen."

"I took the crown because I had to," Andromeda said.

"Now that you're back in your right mind, you're..."

"A deposed king," Frederick said, "and rightfully so. The people would not follow me."

"Yes, they would," Richard said, startling them.

The bandit-turned-general stood before the table. When they looked up, he fell to one knee.

"Rise, General," Andromeda said. "You have no need to bow before us. What were you saying?"

"The people would not follow a king who had given the kingdom to someone like Zuab, but a king who would lead men into battle to take it back is a different story."

"Powerful words from a man who not so long ago considered taking me hostage because of what you had done, father."

Richard blushed and cleared his throat, but Frederick waved a hand. "Be that as it may, you are the queen."

"Not if I relinquish the crown."

"Andromeda, no!" His face went white.

"If I am the queen, it is my decision."

"Valin, tell her she can't do that. Tell her about the land."

"I thought you didn't believe in that."

"I'll believe it if it'll keep her from doing this."

The dwarf laughed. "I'm sorry, my friend, but it doesn't work that way. The land rejected you as king when Zuab stole your will, but now that you've reclaimed it, it will submit to you again as long as Andromeda willingly relinquishes her claim."

"Which I do," Andromeda said. Frederick started to refuse, but Andromeda raised her hand. "It's not entirely for the reasons you think, father. Master Henry still has much to do before his task is done."

"Andromeda, that's my quest," Henry said.

"I've been with you this long," she said. "I'm not about to abandon you now." She turned to Frederick.

"Father, I need to see this through with him, and I can't leave Argath without a ruler."

Frederick looked from Henry to Andromeda. He let out a breath and nodded once. Andromeda stood and spoke in a voice that carried over the noise of the assembled army.

"Many of you have called me queen," she said, "but Zuab's hold over my father has been broken. I will be queen one day but not today. All hail King Frederick, king over all Argath!"

For a second, the crowd stared at her. In the distance, someone coughed. Then, Richard echoed her words.

"All hail King Frederick!"

Before long, the entire crowd had taken up the call. Andromeda offered a hand to her father, and he stood next to her. The cheering grew louder. When it finally died, they sat back down.

"The throne will be waiting for you when you return," he said in a low-pitched voice.

Andromeda shook her head. "No, father. The throne of Argath is not some toy to be passed around whenever it is most convenient.

I took it because I had to, but now I have to leave. I won't take it back until you can't wear it anymore."

"Your daughter is wise, King Frederick," Valin said. "She will make a good queen, one day."

"So she will," Frederick said. He turned to Henry.

"You will watch over her?"

Henry nodded. "I will do everything in my power to keep her safe."

"And who kept who safe an hour ago?" Andromeda asked with a smile.

Henry coughed and turned to Frederick. "We need to talk, Your Majesty."

"About what?"

"Zuab's master."

He felt the eyes of Valin and Andromeda on him. Frederick put down his cup and nodded.

"Zuab's purpose was to secure Argath and the Nordi as a passage through which a much larger army could pass."

Frederick shook his head. "I know my neighbors. No one could field such an army."

"It's not from your neighbors exactly," Henry said.

"There's a garden in the shadow of Mount Himmnel."

"I know of it," Frederick said. "Zuab favored it. I'm considering burning it to the ground."

"Part of her army came through there from somewhere else."

"Some kind of sorcery?" Frederick asked.

"Something like that," Henry said. "As far as I know that's the only place they can use to get here, at least the only one under their control."

Frederick nodded. "I'll set men to guard it."

"While you're there, could you deliver a message?"

The king nodded.

"In the garden, you'll find a man with curly black hair wearing a robe and gold sandals. Tell him the name of the enemy is Idun. We're going after her in her own home."

"I'll tell him," Frederick said.

"Thank you." Henry looked at Valin. "Does the name Hreidmar mean anything to you?"

Valin nodded. "The high king of all dwarfkind."

"I need to see him."

"Are you sure?" Valin said. "The journey is long and difficult. Few humans ever truly have need to go there. I can send a guide if you really need it, but you'd be better off finding another way. Perhaps my father can help you."

Henry shook his head. "No guide. It has to be Hreidmar, and it has to be you that takes us there."

Valin sighed. "It has been a while since I've been at court. I supposed it's time I made another trip."

FORTY-ONE

Andromeda and Frederick had a tear-filled goodbye. A lump formed in Henry's throat as he thought about his own parents worried sick because they thought he'd been kidnapped.

It took a few hours to break camp. Henry and Andromeda went with the dwarves. Deprived of the need to stay together, small groups broke off every once in a while to go to different cities scattered throughout the Nordi Mountains. By the time they reached the entrance to Kerat, four days later, they had less than a third of their original number. Valin showed them a different cave than the one they'd taken before. This one was taller and they had no difficulty walking upright, though they had to lead the horses. It took everything Henry and Andromeda had to coax Pegasus and Oakash into the caves. Once they'd reached the city, a pair of guards escorted them to the palace, though as honored guests rather than prisoners. It might've been his imagination, but Henry thought the emberstones shone brighter as they were led into the throne room.

As soon as they entered, Fjalar rose to greet them, and they all gave him a deep bow.

"Well met, Valin, leader of the dwarven host. You have done your people much honor. Well met, Master Henry, hero of a thousand battles. You continue to prove that great victories need not be won by armies. Well met, Andromeda, princess of Argath." The corners of Andromeda's mouth turned up in a smile at the title. "Through courage and sacrifice, you have saved my realm as well as yours. To you, I give the greatest honor. Rise all and welcome. Enjoy the hospitality of my hall."

"Thank you, grandfather," Valin said. "You do us great honor, but I'm afraid we cannot accept. Master Henry has placed a new charge on me."

"Oh?"

"He bids me to accompany them to the court of Hreidmar."

The dwarf king looked them over. "It's not a good time to visit Nidavellir. Hreidmar is preparing for war, though I don't know with whom. Humans are not well liked in Jord just now."

"Hreidmar's war is the reason we're going, Stonelord," Henry said.

"You've done great deeds, Master Henry, but I doubt even you can turn the high king away from a course of action once his mind has been set. He can be as slow to come to a decision as a mountain, but he can be just as stubborn as one once his mind is made up."

"I don't intend to stop him. I intend to make sure he wins."

The king mulled that over and nodded. "Bold words. If it were anyone else, I'd doubt you. Very well, I'll send a letter of introduction with you. It should make things a little easier."

In a surprisingly short time, they had been given new supplies and elaborate gifts of stone and metal for the High King. Fjalar himself led them to edge of a cavern housing the city where a cave sloped downward. Henry and Andromeda bowed once more before the king, and Valin clasped his hand. Then, they were off toward Nidavellir and Midgard. Toward Asgard, Idun, and the end of this war.

Mimir's Well

ONE

Henry kept his eyes on the glowing emberstone in Valin's hand as the dwarf led them forward. Total darkness waited just beyond the stone's reach as if threatening to swallow them whole. Henry could practically feel the tons upon tons of earth bearing down on them as they made their way through the underground tunnel.

"I swear, I don't even remember what the sun looks like," he grumbled. The cavern echoed his words, distorting his voice slightly.

"Stop complaining," Andromeda said. "It hasn't been that long."

He glared at her. Almost involuntarily, his eyes wandered to her hair, which had changed from black to blond several days ago, the result of crossing the boundary between worlds. Neither she nor Valin seemed to notice, and Henry had learned long ago that pointing out such things did no good. If the details of different worlds were remembered at all, it was only in the vaguest terms.

"It's been close," he said under his breath.

Without the rising and falling of the sun, it was hard to tell how long they'd been underground. They'd stopped to sleep several times, but sometimes, it felt like they had walked for days, and others it was only a few hours.

Henry suspected it had been at least a week since they'd left the kingdom of Argath, a realm rooted in the story of Snow White. After helping to win a war against the evil witch queen Zuab, Henry had convinced the dwarven prince Valin to lead them deep underground, to the home of Hreidmar, High King over all dwarfkind. He'd thought it would be a relatively quick journey. No such luck. The earth was honeycombed with so many passages, it might as well have been a maze. Though it shouldn't have caught him by surprise, he hadn't expected the darkness to be so absolute. Valin's yellow emberstone, the only source of light they carried, seemed pitifully small when compared with the darkness pressing in on all sides.

"How deep would you say we are, Valin?" Henry asked.

The dwarf thought for a second. "Seven or eight miles, maybe as many as nine, but no more than that."

Henry wracked his brain, trying to remember just how thick the earth's crust was, but he'd never been the best science student. In the end, he guessed it didn't matter. Kurnugi, the land of human imagination, had a way of ignoring pesky little details like geology, gravity, and the laws of physics.

"How long until we reach Jord?"

"Another day or so, depending on the weather."

"The weather?"

Valin shrugged. "Earthquakes or dust showers caused by shifting masses of rocks. Giant worms burrowing through stone occasionally collapse passages. Sometimes volcanic activity melts underground deposits of ice, and water seeps through cracks, making it rain in some of the larger caverns. In the wrong place, that can cause mudslides that cut off entire passages."

"I had no idea conditions down here could be so complex," Andromeda said.

Valin smiled. "No less so than on the surface."

Henry glanced from the ever-thinning bags of oats to the horses he and Andromeda rode. Henry had never ridden a horse before coming to Kurnugi, and Andromeda was a princess who'd always had others to take care of her animals. The dwarves had little experience with horses, and no one had anticipated how the animals would eat when not supplemented by grazing. Both Pegasus and Andromeda's mare, Oakash, were huge creatures, and they needed plenty of food. Henry just hoped they wouldn't run out of supplies before making it to Jord.

They came upon a large lake and made camp on the shore. The surface of the water was a smooth as glass and stretched far beyond the light provided by the emberstone. If Henry listened, he could just make out the sound of drops of water falling into the lake. The horses kept giving the water sidelong glances, and Henry checked their water skins and found most of them empty.

"Is it safe to drink?" he asked.

Valin looked up from a map he was studying by the light of his emberstone. He wrinkled his brow and thought for a second before looking down at his map.

"This would be Lake Tungl," he said, though it sounded more like a question than a statement.

"You don't seem very sure," Henry said.

Valin waved off his concern. "There's a large deposit of silver on the other side. It'll give the water a strange taste, but it's not actually dangerous."

"Unless this isn't Lake Tungl," Henry said flatly.

He looked over the dwarf's shoulder, but the map was covered in dwarven runes, and the lines crisscrossed each other in strange ways to take into account the three-dimensional nature of traveling underground. Valin had tried to explain it to him a few times, but the explanations went over Henry's head.

"No, I'm sure it is," Valin said as he rolled up the map and put it in a round case of polished stone. Henry glared at him, but the dwarf only shrugged. "I did offer to send someone else to guide you."

Henry shook his head. "The mirror said it had to be you."

"Then, you may as well trust me."

Henry let out a breath and walked to the shore. His boot sunk into wet clay as he approached, and he took a second to pull it out before dipping his hand into the water and bringing it to his mouth. He stopped and looked up at Valin.

"You know, the mirror can't actually see the future. It might not have thought about you leading us to poison water."

Valin rolled his eyes. "Master Henry, there are no poison lakes this side of Jord. I'm almost positive about that."

Henry groaned, but Andromeda sighed and forced her way past him, heedless of the water soaking her dress.

"For someone with a magic shirt that makes him immune to poison, you're awfully squeamish."

She brought water up in her cupped hands and drank. As soon as she swallowed, Valin went pale. He tore open the map case and practically ripped the map out. He unrolled it and ran his fingers down the paper. Henry's blood went cold, but Valin let out a breath of relief.

"No, it's not poisonous."

"Valin!"

"I thought we were somewhere else for a second, but don't worry. This is definitely Lake Tungl."

Laughter erupted from the shadows. Henry spun around. His sword hissed as he drew it, and he pointed it in the direction of the sound. A second later, Valin hefted an axe as big as he was, but he lowered it when half a dozen armored dwarves came out of the darkness. Each had skin the color of earth or stone, and they wore armor of interlocking plates. Given what little Henry knew of dwarven magic, he doubted that the armor was ordinary steel. A three-foot-tall red-bearded dwarf walked over to Valin and clapped him on the back.

"Valin, you old goat," he said through a smile. "How many times have you made this trip? Don't tell me you still don't know how to read a map."

"Normally, I'm not the one plotting the route, Nabbi," Valin said between laughs.

"King Hreidmar heard your footsteps on the stone and sent us to guide you the rest of the way." Nabbi looked at Henry and Andromeda. When he spoke, his voice had lost all hint of laughter. "He said nothing of these, though."

"They are my friends and allies of King Fjalar."

"They are human." The way he said 'human' made it sound like a curse.

Valin picked up his axe again and moved to stand in front of Andromeda. Henry stood beside him. He held his sword low but didn't sheathe it.

"They are under my protection, and you will not harm them, not while I can prevent it."

His voice practically dripped with the threat, and his feet were spread wide in a stance used by dwarven warriors. The other dwarves scrambled to surround them, their armored boots clanking on the stone.

"Gentlemen." Andromeda's voice was soft but somehow carried over the commotion. "We shouldn't be hasty here. King Hreidmar wants to see Valin, and we are his companions. Surely, the king can decide what to do with us."

"And who are you, girl?" Nabbi almost spat the words.

"I am Princess Andromeda daughter of..." she hesitated for a second. "Daughter of Budli, King of Gothia."

Henry's shock only lasted a second. He'd been half-expecting something like this. Though she didn't realize it, Andromeda was the princess of every story. Who her father was and what land he ruled changed whenever they crossed the boundary between tales. When he'd met her, she was a Greek princess. In Argath, her step-mother had poisoned her with an apple. He'd hoped when she finally revealed her new identity in this world, it would tell him something about the story he was in, but the names were a complete mystery.

"And this is Master Henry Alexander Gideon," Valin said. "Surely, his exploits have reached even as far as Jord."

Murmurs rippled through the dwarves, but Nabbi raised his hand to silence them. Some of the edge had gone out of his voice. "Noble visitors, but they're still human."

"Noble enough that the king would want to know of them."

Nabbi scowled. "If it were anyone but you, Valin..." He looked at the other dwarves. "Take the human's weapon."

"I wouldn't," Valin said.

"I won't take him into Jord armed."

"That is a *forged* blade, Nabbi, freely given to him by a forge-master. It is his and may not be taken from him, save in battle."

"One of your forgemasters gave him a weapon? A human?"

For a second, Henry thought Nabbi would order his dwarves to attack, and he tightened his grip on his sword. Valin just shook his head.

"My forgemasters couldn't duplicate that weapon if they had a thousand years. Neither could Hreidmar's, I'd wager."

"Then, how do you know it was given to him? He could have stolen it."

"It doesn't matter how I know. All that matters is that you have the sworn word of a prince of the Nordi Mountains that it is so."

Nabbi clenched his teeth and nodded. The soldiers put down their weapons, though many threw Henry nervous glances.

"Very well, Valin. Come with us. The high king himself will decide your fate."

TWO

"What was that about my sword?" Henry pitched his voice low so their escorts couldn't hear.

"Forgemasters are highly respected among our people," Valin said. "If one gifts a warrior with a weapon, that weapon is his, and no one may take it from him."

"But Hephaestus isn't a dwarf."

"It doesn't make the slightest bit of difference. Alviss is the greatest forgemaster I've ever known, not that I'd expect anyone here to admit that about a dwarf of the surface kingdoms. Still, Alviss acknowledged Hephaestus. By our laws, he is a forgemaster."

"Are we prisoners, then?"

Valin shrugged. "It's no different than when I first brought you before Fjalar."

"Are all dwarves this stubborn?"

"As the mountain," Valin said, grinning.

The dwarves hadn't brought food for the horses, but they kept a hard pace. After a day, or what passed for a day this far underground, they came through a narrow tunnel that opened up near the top of a wide cavern. The dwarven city of Jord, capital of the kingdom of Nidavellir, stretched out before them.

The other cities Henry had seen in Kurnugi had been small, no more than a few miles across. Even in the largest, a man on foot could make it from one side to the other in a couple of hours. Jord made them look like toys. Stone towers scattered throughout the city spiraled up as high as any skyscraper Henry had ever seen. Each held a glowing white emberstone that, when combined with the rest, illuminated the town as brightly as the sun could have. The buildings stretched out for miles, everything from small houses to palace-like structures that would've covered a couple of city blocks. Some glittered with precious gems or metals, but most were gray stone. That wasn't to say that their color was uniform, though. It shifted and changed, making the city look like it was made from storm clouds.

Even from this distance, he could tell the city was a flurry of activity. People flowed through the streets like blood through veins, and it took Henry several seconds to see that the streets themselves formed a pattern that could only be seen from above, that of a battle-axe crossed with a war hammer.

"I've never seen a city so large," Andromeda said.

Valin nodded. "It would take three days to walk from one end to the other, and that's only if you didn't stop to eat or sleep."

Nabbi grunted and guided them down a narrow path. It took them two hours to reach the iron gates of the city. Henry gaped. Hundreds of armed dwarves stood in their way. It was a small army. Their guides never slowed, and as they neared the gates Henry saw some of the dwarves were only statues. Dwarven stonework was so intricate, and the dwarves themselves so resembled stone, that it was impossible to tell which was statue and which was warrior unless it actually moved. It looked like only a few dozen were real. After a short exchange, the guards let them into the city.

The streets were packed with dwarves. Some stopped what they were doing to look at the humans, but most jeered at them, and every once in a while, a child would throw a pebble at them. The crowd reacted even stronger toward the horses, shouting curses and throwing rotten fruit, though how they got fruit so far under-ground, Henry had no idea. Oakash, Andromeda's mare, had to be spoken softly to almost the entire time to keep from spooking. Pegasus, on the other hand, seemed curious.

"What do they have against the animals?" Henry asked.

"They are of the surface," Valin said. "Horses don't belong down here."

"You should have told me that before."

"Would you have left Pegasus behind if I had?"

Henry thought about that for a second. "No."

"I didn't think so."

"We'll be staying there tonight." Nabbi pointed to a building with a hammer and anvil painted on a sign over the door.

"Why don't we go directly to the palace?" Andromeda asked.

"Your friend wasn't exaggerating when he said it would take three days to walk across this city," Nabbi said. "We're still a day from the palace, and that's only if we travel hard."

"The horses," Henry said.

"They know how to take care of them," Nabbi said, "even if they rarely have to."

He motioned to a boy who ran up to Andromeda and then to Henry and took the reins. Pegasus looked at Henry before going with the boy. They disappeared around the corner, though the stable boy looked over his shoulder at Henry for several seconds. Valin let out a sigh and rolled his eyes.

"Do we really need to do this, Nabbi?"

"I won't let him before the king armed on your word alone," Nabbi said.

"What are you two talking about?" Henry asked.

"The Hammer and Anvil is run by an old forgemaster," Valin said. "Last time I was here, it catered almost exclusively to those who follow that path."

"It still does," Nabbi said.

Henry let out a breath. "Not this again."

"Do you have some objection to having your weapon examined?" Nabbi asked.

"Not really. I just don't like being the center of attention."

Nabbi chuckled. "Don't be so arrogant. These aren't the forgemasters of the surface. They won't be easily impressed, and I can assure you, they've seen more complicated things than your sword."

"I doubt it," Henry said, "but I wasn't really talking about the sword."

"Oh?"

"Never mind," Henry said. "Let's go."

He moved past the dwarves and pushed open the door before strolling into the common room of the inn.

THREE

Conversation filled the common room. The smell of roasting meat wafted from an open door opposite the entrance, underscored by the faint scent of burning coal. No one noticed him at first, but eventually, a beardless dwarf with skin the color of red clay glanced over his shoulder. He saw Henry, and his eyes went wide. The young dwarf said something, and the other two seated at his table, a dwarf with skin and hair the same color as the surrounding stones, and a ruby-eyed elder with a snowy beard, turned and gasped. The silence spread out from the table until the entire common room stared at Henry. A few, ones who Henry guessed had no talent in the magic of the forge, were asking the others what they were seeing.

"Well, this is unexpected," Nabbi said.

Henry shrugged. "Only to you. Can we get this over with? I'm hungry, and I'm sure you want to get an early start tomorrow."

Nabbi glared at him but nodded and led Valin, Henry, and Andromeda to a large stone table while the rest of his men scattered and found places to sit. He ordered food from a serving maid and instructed her to get the innkeeper. Henry tried to pretend the eyes on him didn't bother him, but they made his skin crawl. A few minutes later, the tallest dwarf Henry had ever seen, almost five feet, walked into the room. He scanned the area until his steel gray eyes locked onto Henry. For a moment, he stood with the same wide-eyed shock as the rest of the room, but he got over it after a few seconds and plodded across the room to sit at their table. His mail shirt scratched against the stone chair with a sound that made Henry's hair stand on end.

"Captain Nabbi," he said, inclining his head.

"Master Vollr."

The forgemaster glanced at Henry. "Quite a marvel you've brought me. I thought Gulla had lost her senses when she said the whole room went quiet at the sight of a human. Of course, she can't see...that." He gestured at Henry.

"It caught me by surprise too," Nabbi said. "What exactly do you see?"

"You don't know?"

Nabbi shook his head. "We found them on the shores of Lake Tungl and are to present them King Hreidmar tomorrow. I brought them here so you could examine his sword, but I take it there's something else you find interesting."

"I was hurt," Henry said. "The forgemaster didn't have the ability to heal me, but he can work with flesh as easily as metal."

"Impossible!" Vollr said. "Flesh can't be worked."

Henry gave him a level gaze and waved his hand in front of the dwarf's face. Then, he picked up the edge of his cloak and put it on the table. "He could also work in cloth."

Vollr looked at him in shock, but the rest of the inn erupted into whispers. Henry drew his sword and laid it on the table.

"You might as well look at this. It's why Nabbi brought us here."

Vollr's eyes lingered on Henry for a second before he shook his head and examined the sword. He closed his eyes and held the blade between two fingers while mumbling under his breath. A few seconds later, he opened his eyes and handed the blade back to Henry.

"Thirty seconds ago, I would've said it was the most amazing thing I've ever seen, but now..." He bowed his head to Henry.

"Then, it really is a forged blade," Nabbi said.

Vollr laughed. "It's the most complex and powerful forged weapon I have ever seen."

"I don't suppose you can tell if it really is his?"

"Not just by looking at it, but Captain, this is so far beyond me, I wouldn't know where to start in making it. I'm not even sure what it does, but I'd wager the same one who made it is the one who worked his flesh."

"Are you sure?"

"No, but I thought working flesh was impossible before I saw him, and it would take a greater master than any I know to make that weapon. If he says the one who worked his flesh gave him a forged weapon, I'm inclined to believe him."

"Splendid," Valin said. "Now, if you're done questioning my word, perhaps we can see to food and rooms."

"I had to be sure, Lord Valin." The confidence had drained out of Nabbi's voice.

Valin grunted. A few minutes later, the serving maid brought a bowl of soup with spongy bits floating inside, along with a dark meat that was tough and gamey. Henry almost asked what it was, but then he remembered Valin talking about giant worms, and he decided he'd really rather not know.

Throughout the meal, the innkeeper assaulted Henry with a barrage of questions before finally accepting the fact that Henry knew as little about how his flesh had been forged as a sword knew about how it was made. The constant attention of every forgemaster in the room made Henry's skin crawl, and as soon as he'd finished his meal, Vollr led him to his room.

The starkness of the room surprised Henry. Where the rest of the city was covered in intricate carvings, the walls of the room were bare. The "bed" was nothing more than a hard mat on the side of the room, opposite the large fireplace that Henry suspected could double as a forge. Still, the room was better accommodations than sleeping outside on his bedroll, and sleep came easily.

FOUR

When Nabbi woke them, Henry felt like he'd hardly slept. Outside the inn, he shielded his eyes. The sheer number of people out this early surprised him, but the light shining from the raised crystals remained constant, so he supposed there wasn't really any day or night down here. The city probably never slept.

"Right," Henry said under his breath. "It's just an underground New York."

The people weren't the most amazing part. He'd been so distracted on his way in that he'd missed the finer details of the buildings. Intricate carvings decorated every wall, depicting elaborate scenes. They were so detailed that Henry could make out individual threads on the clothes. They walked for hours, though without the sun, he couldn't say how many. The carvings kept on going. He never saw one repeat itself.

They'd gone a few miles before he realized the carvings told a story, one so complex it took the entire city to tell. He saw dwarves fighting in battles and working with stone or metal. People other than dwarves were depicted too. A man was catching a fish. Then, the same man approached a waterfall, and again he stood and spoke with two others, one of whom had a single eye. The next scene depicted the three men standing before an enraged dwarf with a dead otter on the ground. They passed a street, and Henry could see the story progressing on the buildings there.

"It's our history," Nabbi said when Henry asked. "Everything, from our creation to the modern day is written on these walls."

"What is that?" Andromeda said pointing at a cliff face rising up over the buildings.

"It's the palace," Nabbi said.

Henry gaped as they neared it. The wall was sheer and went up at least a hundred feet and was so long that he couldn't see the end of it. A single scene had been carved into it. A massive human figure lay dead and other, smaller figures seemed to be forming the dwarves from the dead one's flesh. Gold runes, forming a large arch, had been inlaid in the midst of the dwarves.

Nabbi approached the guards standing in front of it. One stepped forward with a hand raised. Nabbi pulled out a rolled parchment and handed it to the guard who skimmed over it. The guard grunted and made a vague gesture with his hand. Someone appeared to take their horses as the runes on the wall began to glow. A vertical seam appeared down the middle of the arch. The door swung inward, revealing a passage lined with dwarven warriors armed with spears, though Henry couldn't tell if they were real or only statues. They didn't move as Nabbi led them past, though Henry thought the eyes followed them. They walked by several branches in the hall before stopping before a large pair of double doors made of some dark stone. No sooner had they stopped than the doors rumbled open. Henry glanced at Valin, who shrugged.

"Did you think the title 'Stonelord' was ceremonial? All dwarven kings have dominion over the earth. Fjalar could barely do anything. None can do more than Hreidmar."

Henry nodded and stepped into the room. He'd thought he'd seen splendor before, but that was nothing compared to the throne room of the high king of dwarfkind. It wasn't just big. It was the size of a football stadium. The floor and walls were made from gold, and so many gems covered the ceiling that he wasn't sure what it was made of. Bright red emberstones formed a path down the center of the room, and their footsteps sounded like musical notes. They were halfway across the room before Henry could make out the shining light at the end of the path. After another few minutes, it grew so bright he had to look away. Nabbi forced him forward, though the dwarf too looked at the ground. Soon, even the reflected light grew bright enough to make him shield his eyes. Nabbi and Valin fell to their knees. Henry and Andromeda did the same a heartbeat later.

"Rise Valin," a deep voice that made Henry think of a rockslide said. "Introduce me to your guests."

As if on cue, the light dimmed. Henry looked up and realized that Hreidmar's throne had been carved out of single diamond-like emberstone. The blinding light was now a soft white glow. The king himself was a squat dwarf wearing a robe of woven gold. His skin was the deep gray of mountain stone, and pearl white hair tumbling from his head gave him the appearance of a snow-capped peak. His eyes shimmered silver and showed all the strength of the earth itself.

"Stonelord," Valin said respectfully. "I present Princess Andromeda of the surface kingdom of Gothia and Master Henry Alexander Gideon..."

"Of Master Gideon, I know," the king said. "You caused quite a stir at the Hammer and Anvil. A human with forged flesh carrying one of the most powerful swords ever seen in this city. They say you can turn men to stone and that rulers who get in your way have a habit of losing their thrones."

"That's a little bit exaggerated, Stonelord," Henry said, as he tried to avoid looking the dwarf in the eyes. "What I mean is, I could only do those things because of special circumstances."

"Really?" Hreidmar asked. "Tell me, young human, how many rulers have you actually dethroned?"

"Two. One in Greece when he conquered a friend's kingdom, and another who tried to invade Argath." Henry said quickly. He bit his lower lip and corrected himself. "Well, three rulers if you count Frederick, but he got his throne back."

Hreidmar stared at him for what felt like an eternity. Then, the dwarf king threw back his head and howled with laughter. The light of his throne pulsed with every breath, and Henry could almost feel the room shaking as Hreidmar laughed.

"Why don't you tell me why you're here, young human?" the king said between chuckles.

"Fjalar said you're in the middle of a war."

Hreidmar shrugged. "I have fought wars before." He glared at Henry. "Though rarely against humans."

Henry raised his hands. "I'm not here to fight you, but this war is a little different."

"So it is. These humans seem to know secret ways through the earth that even we have forgotten, and some of my own people have turned against us. The gods have been using magics hidden away so long ago that we knew of them only by legend. Never before has Odin himself made war on us."

"That's because it's not Odin," Henry said.

The dwarven king snorted. "Who else could lead the gods?"

"Idun."

Hreidmar's face became stony. He stepped off his throne, which dimmed to a faint glimmer. The red emberstones shone brightly under his feet. He walked up to Henry, and though Henry was taller by a head, he couldn't shake the feeling that he was the smaller person.

"What do you know, boy?"

Henry swallowed and took a step back. "Her apples were corrupted."

Hreidmar's face became several shades lighter until it was the color of gravel. "How do you know this?"

"An Oracle told me."

"Her apples are a source of life. How could they become corrupted?"

"I don't know," Henry said. "The Oracle could only see the present. I'm here to find the one who knows the past."

"And where is this past-seeing Oracle?" the king asked.

"I don't know," Henry said. "All I can say that Idun has it."

"You don't know anything about it?"

Henry shook his head. Neither the magic mirror, which was the Oracle of the Present, nor the Oracle of Delphi, which was the Oracle of the Future, had been able to give him much information on that, though the mirror had giving him an ominous warning.

"It sees everything that was, and apparently, it demands a price for its knowledge."

Hreidmar thought about that for a second. Then, his eyes widened, the stones around him brightening in response to his mood. "Mimir."

"What?"

"Legend says Odin plucked out his eye and hung upside down from the great tree, Yggdrasil, for nine days, with a spear in his side to gain the right to drink from the Well of Mimir, which granted him the wisdom of the ages."

"That could be it. I need to go to it. It might tell me how to stop Idun."

Once again, the dwarven king laughed. He climbed back on his throne, causing the light in it to flicker and causing the more mundane gems to sparkle.

"You don't do things by half measure, do you boy?"

"What's that supposed to mean?" Henry asked.

"Mimir's Well lies near the root of the world tree, a place where the gods meet daily to discuss their war."

"I've been to dangerous places before," Henry said.

"Spoken like someone who's never seen a god."

This time, Henry was the one who snorted. "Who do you think forged my flesh?"

Hreidmar looked to Valin. "Interesting friends you have here. Very well. I will take you at your word that you intend me no harm. Still, you can't just stroll across Bifrost to reach the well. I'd wager even you don't want to directly confront a god, especially one whose whole purpose for being is to guard that bridge."

Henry nodded. "I'd prefer to avoid fighting one. That's the way the gods use, then?"

"It connects Asgard to Midgard and to the great tree," the king said. "Only Thor doesn't use it for fear it would break under his weight. There's another way though. How would you feel about fighting a dragon?"

Henry gaped at him. "What?"

"A dragon. Do you think you can kill it?"

"Are you serious?"

Hreidmar shrugged. "Yggdrasil lies at the center of all creation. Those worlds its roots don't touch, its branches do. I know of a root touching this world. You could climb it if you think you could defeat the dragon guarding the way."

"So you're saying my only options are to fight a god or fight a dragon?"

"If there are others, I don't know them."

Henry glanced at his companions. Andromeda shrugged and shifted her weight. Absently, she ran her foot along an emberstone at her feet. Its light dimmed, as if it were shying away from a human touch. Valin grunted and stepped forward.

"Stonelord, you said all the gods, save Thor, use Bifrost. How does he get there?"

"You don't want to fight the Heimdall or the dragon at the base of the tree, but you want to brave a valley only the strongest of gods dare to cross?"

"I take it Lord Heimdall can't be avoided?" Valin asked.

"He's a bridge guardian," Hreidmar said, shaking his head.

"Neither can the dragon?" The king shook his head. "But it should be possible to pass through the valley unseen."

"Perhaps," Hreidmar said slowly, "but that valley isn't a part of any world. It's a thing of borders and boundaries. The things that exist there are...wrong."

"It still sounds like our best option," Henry said. "How do we get there?"

"That's another problem," Hreidmar said. "I haven't the slightest idea."

"Who would then?"

Hreidmar paused for a second. Nabbi brought his hand to his forehead and shook his head. Finally, the king sighed. "Andvari, the stoneless."

Valin cursed.

"What is it?" Henry asked.

"A stoneless is a dwarf who has turned his back on earth and stone. He is no longer a dwarf in any way, save in body."

"But he was one of us once," Hreidmar said. "He just might be willing to help us."

"Okay, fine," Henry huffed. "That still doesn't tell us where to find him."

Valin sighed and turned to Henry. "Do you remember the lake that I wasn't sure was poisonous?"

"You said you were sure it wasn't."

"Yes, well, I may have exaggerated my certainty a little. Anyway, Andvari lives on the shores of a lake that is poisonous. In fact, once Andromeda drank from Lake Tungl, I worried it might actually be Lake Eitr. That's where Andvari lives."

"Fine," Henry said. "Let's go."

FIVE

I didn't realize dwarves could turn away from earth and stone," Henry said as they neared the black waters of the lake.

"It happens from time to time," Valin said almost too quietly for Henry to hear. He was the only one who had accompanied them, though he'd gotten directions from others who knew the way. "Most don't survive a week, but Andvari has lived as stoneless for millennia."

A faint splash sounded through the open cavern, but it was beyond the sight of their emberstones. Instantly, Henry saw the difference between the two lakes. Where Tungl had bits of moss creeping down the stone shores into the water, the area near Eitr was bare. A constant murk swirled around through water, stirred by the waterfall on the other side of the lake. It might have been Henry's imagination, but he thought he saw a shadow as big as he was swimming beneath the surface.

They made their way around the lake to the waterfall where the dwarves had said Andvari made his home. It took another half an hour, and Henry constantly caught himself looking out over the water to figure out what swam there, but he didn't see anything. It made the hairs on the back of his neck stand up to turn his back to the lake, but he focused his attention on the cavity behind the waterfall.

It was little more than a shallow cave with a hard sleeping mat on the floor and a rock that might have been used for a chair. A few fish bones had been scattered on the ground, and a net lay bundled near the mat. A pile of fabric that was more rags than clothes had been stuffed into a corner.

"He left Jord for this?" Valin didn't bother to try to hide his disgust.

"It doesn't seem like much of a life, does it?" Henry agreed.

"Where do you suppose he gets these from?" Andromeda said, as she kicked over the pile of fish bones.

"From the lake, probably," Henry said.

Valin shook his head. "Eitr is poisonous. Nothing can live there, but some of the other lakes are fed by streams that flow from the surface. He must've gotten them from one of those."

"Valin, I saw something swimming out there."

"You're mistaken, Henry. Those waters will even melt flesh if exposed for more than a few minutes."

Just then, he thought he heard another splash, but it was impossible to tell over the noise of the waterfall. He walked out of the cave and stood by the shore. About twenty feet in, he saw a definite ripple and pointed to it.

"A loose stone probably fell in. Trust me, Henry. Nothing can live there."

"Get me that net."

"Why?"

"Look, if I'm wrong, all I've done is waste ten seconds. Just get me the net."

Valin sighed, but Andromeda ran back to the cave and came back with Andvari's net. She gave it to Henry who looked at it in bewilderment. He tried to spread it out, but it started to tangle. Before long, it had become a hopeless mess. He looked up at Andromeda and Valin.

"I have no idea how to use this," he admitted.

Valin rolled his eyes and took the net and spent a few minutes untangling it. He slung it over his shoulder. They watched the water for several long moments before Henry finally shook his head. No sooner had they turned around than splash sounded behind them. Valin didn't wait. He whirled and tossed the net over the lake. It spread out and landed right where the water was rippling. An instant later, a silver pike four feet long leaped out of the lake. It rose at least five feet up before disappearing under the surface of the water. Valin gasped, and Henry moved to help him pull it in. When they finally got it to shore, it was no longer a fish, but a dwarf, soaked to the bone.

"Andvari," Valin said in a level voice.

"Lord Valin," the dwarf said as he untangled himself. "Was there some reason you decided to trap me with my own net?"

"We were curious what could swim in waters that should've killed anything. How did you manage that anyway?"

Andvari huffed. He made a chopping motion with his right hand, and all the water on him abruptly splashed to the ground leaving him perfectly dry. Valin stared at the water, his mouth opened. Andvari sniffed.

"There are magics beyond that of the earth," he said.

"Not for us," Valin said.

Andvari began rolling up his net and didn't look at Valin when he spoke. "What do you want?"

"We need to get to Mimir's well," Henry said.

"Take Bifrost."

"Bifrost is closed," Valin said. "If you ever bothered to keep up with your people, you'd know that. The gods are waging a war on us."

"They're not my people," Andvari said. "They made that perfectly clear."

"You..."

"Valin," Henry interrupted. "Let me."

Andvari huffed. "And what makes you think you'll do any better, boy?"

"Because if Idun's forces take Jord, they'll come here next, unless you actually believe no one in town knows where to find you. We did it easily enough. I get the feeling you're too powerful for her to ignore."

Andvari considered that for a second and nodded. He turned to Valin.

"I just want to be left alone."

"I'll speak to the king."

"You'll have to leave the horses."

"What?" Henry asked.

"Why do you think I live here?" Andvari asked. "Eitr is a gateway into other worlds. There's a passage down there that can take you where you need to go."

"So you're guarding the gateway to here?" Valin asked.

"I'm making sure nothing that doesn't belong here comes out. I'll change you into a fish and lead you to the valley of the rivers. That's the best I can do."

"The one between worlds?" Henry asked.

Andvari nodded. "You should be warned. The mind of a fish is not like that of a man. It can take some getting used to. Thinking won't be easy."

"This doesn't sound like a good idea," Valin said.

"I'm not sure we have a choice," Henry said. "Not unless I want to fight either a god or a dragon."

"You shouldn't go anyway, Valin," Andromeda said.

"What?"

"You fulfilled your obligations when you got us here," she said, "but your high king is preparing for war. In all likelihood, he's going to call for reinforcements from Fjalar and the other kings under him. You're needed here for when that happens."

"My grandfather can send generals."

"You are his general."

Henry could see that Valin wanted to argue, but finally, he nodded. Wordlessly, Henry handed him the reins to Pegasus.

"Okay," he said, turning to Andvari. "What do we do?"

The dwarf stepped into the water and motioned for Henry and Andromeda to follow. They did. As soon as Henry stepped inside, he tripped and fell on his face. A momentary panic seized him as he inhaled the poisonous water, but then he realized he could breathe. It was easy. He tried to get to his feet only to discover he didn't have them anymore. A great fish swam in front of him, and Henry knew instantly he should follow. The fish circled him a few times before vanishing. They swam into the murky water and found a hole in the bottom of the lake. Light was scarce, and he saw little but the occasional shimmer off the fish's scales as they swam through a network of tunnels.

Andvari. That was the fish's name. His thoughts felt like mush, and he struggled to remember. There had been someone else with him, but the name escaped him. Andvari led him through a series of tunnels infinitely more complex than they ones they'd crossed on their way to Jord. Sometimes other fish swam by, and occasionally, Henry had to fight back the urge to go after them and have them as a snack.

Abruptly, Andvari turned and swam down, disappearing into a crack so small Henry would've sworn the fish couldn't have fit. He darted down and entered the crack as well. He just barely fit and would've made it through unscathed, but a minnow charged out of the water and bumped into him. The little thing was strong and knocked him into the rocks. A particularly sharp one cut a line across his stomach. The smell of the water changed as blood spread out from him. The little fish bumped into him again and again. It was like it couldn't tell where it was going. Henry found himself flopping end over end as the rocks scraped him again.

A few seconds later, the minnow swam out in front of him, and Henry noticed it only had one eye. It disappeared just as they came into a larger cavern. Something tickled his side, and Henry would've laughed if he'd been capable of it. At first, he thought it was the minnow, but it didn't feel quite the same. Soon the tickling became an itch and then a burn. He swung his tail wildly, churning the water. Finally, the great fish turned to investigate. Somehow, its eyes went wide. A red fish with green eyes swam up to Henry and began ramming into his side, but he didn't feel it. Flakes of green film drifted in the water, and it took him a second to realize they were coming from him. The big fish blinked. Henry only had time to wonder if fish actually could blink when a current rushed on him and slammed him into the rock, knocking him unconscious.

SIX

Henry opened his eyes to a gray sky. It wasn't cloudy. It was just gray. The sun shone dimly overhead as if seen through fog. A gentle breeze threw a spray of water into his face. He coughed and sat up on muddy ground. His stomach clenched in pain, and he lifted his shirt. Scrapes and cuts littered his abdomen. Andromeda was next to him, just beginning to wake up. Andvari stood over them.

"Sorry about that," the dwarf said. "Those parasites eat flesh and are attracted to blood. I had to call a current to get them off of you."

"You could have warned us about them." Andvari shrugged, and Henry offered Andromeda a hand up. "Are you all right?"

She stood up and closed her eyes for a second before nodding. "I'm fine. Where are we?"

Henry turned around and took in their surroundings. They were on the shore of a slow flowing river. A little ways off, the bank gave way to a sea of pale green grass that swayed in the wind. The air wasn't exactly odorless. It smelled like nothing, though he didn't understand how he knew the difference.

"We're just outside of Asgard," Andvari said. "This is the Kormt, one of the two rivers Thor crosses to reach Yggdrasil. The Ormt is two days that way, and the great tree lies beyond it."

"What's between here and there?"

"Whatever lies in the space between worlds."

"You're not being very helpful."

The dwarf shrugged and waded back in the water. "I was never stupid enough to try to cross it."

"We don't exactly have much choice."

"Personally, I'd go with the dragon, but that's just me."

"You're just going to leave us then?"

Andvari looked over his shoulder at Henry. "If you're asking if I'm coming with you, the answer is no, but I can take you back if you wish."

"I don't think so," Henry said.

"Suit yourself," Andvari said.

The dwarf leaped into the air and shimmered. As he started coming down, his body compressed, and his limbs shrank. By the time he hit the water, he'd taken on the form of the great fish, and he disappeared into the river.

"Well, shall we go?" Andromeda asked.

The wind never varied, and only the occasional low hill broke up the terrain. Henry kept a look out for whatever everyone had been afraid of, but it was just more of the same as far as the eye could see. Even the sky remained the same uniform gray.

"I don't like this place," Andromeda said. "It feels...dead."

A flapping sound cut off Henry's reply as the wind gusted into his face. In front of him, two massive wings appeared held together as if hiding something. They separated and rapidly shrank until they fit on the side of golden sandals. The Greek god smiled and inclined his head to each of them.

"Well, she's not wrong," he said. "Not entirely anyway."

"Hermes, what are you doing here?"

Hermes sighed. "Do we really have to go through that again?"

"A message?" Henry asked.

"Of course."

"Fine. What did you mean when you said she's not wrong?"

"She said it feels dead. It is, in a way."

"In what way?"

Hermes rolled his eyes. "When you passed to this side of the Kormt, you passed between worlds. That's not the only river that marks that kind of boundary."

"The Styx?"

Hermes nodded. "It's how you first crossed into Greece. I thought I should explore it to see where else it led. When I got your message that the enemy was Idun, I knew you'd show up here eventually."

"You did?"

"I was pretty sure." The god shrugged. "I thought it was at least a one in three chance."

Henry shook his head and let out a breath. He met Hermes's eyes. Though pale blue, those eyes seemed to possess more life than the washed-out colors of the land around them.

"What was the message you had?" Henry asked

"I'm to tell you fighting has broken out at some of the boundaries of Argath."

"Is King Frederick all right?"

"He's holding his own. His new alliance with Fjalar seems more than capable of defending the kingdom. In fact, he's sending men here."

"What?"

"He doesn't particularly want Idun to send him another Zuab. Fjalar agrees. Both of them are coming here to help you."

"Through the tunnels?" Hermes nodded. "But that took days."

Hermes scanned the empty horizon for several seconds. Henry followed his gaze, but there was only the same nothingness he'd seen since they'd come into this valley.

"It's much less if you actually know where you're going," Hermes said. "A dozen or so dwarven masters of the earth can also speed things up a great deal. I expect they'll be able to meet up with you soon."

"How about the army from Greece?"

"That's a little easier. Zeus closed off Greece so Idun's army couldn't get in if they tried, not that they have. Anyway, without a need to keep so many men at home, Greece is able to send a large force through another way that I know."

"How big?"

"Twenty thousand or so. It won't be enough to conquer this land, but we should be able to take enough of Idun's strength so that she won't be a threat anymore."

"I don't suppose you know what corrupted her?"

Hermes shook his head. "If this were Greece then maybe, but this is a strange land with strange gods. I don't entirely understand their limits."

"All right," Henry said. "We're on our way to see the Oracle right now. With a little luck, it'll be able to tell us how to stop Idun. How will I find you once you get here?"

Hermes's sandals buzzed as the wings began to flap, sending

ripples through the grass. He raised an eyebrow at Henry. "We'll be the army not made up of Norsemen."

"Right." Henry rolled his eyes and turned to go.

"Henry," Hermes said, all trace of mirth gone from his voice. "Be careful. I've heard some of the stories of this place. These are harsh lands, and harsh lands breed strong people. The legends they tell are equally strong. If even half of what I've heard is true, there are creatures here that would make Cetus look like an earthworm and Medusa like a child."

Hermes inclined his head and lifted into the air. The wings on his sandals expanded. They flapped once, obscuring him, and then, he was gone. Henry turned to take in the landscape. The grass swayed in the wind, and the odorless air made his skin crawl. He wondered what monsters could lay hidden there. When he looked back at Andromeda, she gaped at him.

"What?"

"That was a god."

"Yes, I know."

"You talked to him like he was a normal person."

Henry blinked. She'd met Hermes before, but of course that had been in another world. After a few seconds, he laughed. "We've known each other for a long time. I wouldn't exactly call him a friend, but I do trust him, more or less. Just don't follow him if he leads you into a volcano."

Andromeda looked surprised at that. "Of course not. What kind of fool would do that?"

Henry groaned. "Never mind."

SEVEN

As the sun lowered, the day darkened, though it never colored the sky the way a normal sunset would. It simply vanished as it dipped beneath the horizon. The perpetual fog that had obscured the sun didn't seem to affect the stars as they poked holes in the darkness. Henry saw what looked like a large hill silhouetted against the sky. It was the only feature of note they'd seen all day, and they headed for it and made camp at its base. The stars didn't provide enough light to make out any details, but he suspected it was covered with the same pale grass as the rest of the field.

A dim half-moon arose into a sky and settled among the stars. He realized there were fewer of them than he'd normally seen in the wilderness. It was still more than would be visible in the city, but not by much. The wind remained constant and carried a slight chill but nothing that would require a coat. It was as if this whole place were trying to be average.

They took turns keeping watch, but the night passed without

incident. When the sun shone in his face, Henry realized he'd fallen asleep on his watch. He opened his eyes and rolled over to face the hill. His reflection stared back. He yelped and got to his feet.

"What is it?" Andromeda asked, rubbing sleep from her eyes.

Henry pointed at the glassy bulge growing out the hill. It was as tall as he was and almost perfectly round. The reflections were dark and misty. Cracks ran through the earth around the reflection and crept up the hill. Henry's eyes followed them up, and his heart began to race. About twenty feet up, the dirt fell away revealing blood red scales and razor-sharp teeth that had to be as long as his arm. The reptilian snout went up a ways beyond that. He looked back down at his reflection.

"I think it's an eye." His mind reeled as he tried to imagine a creature big enough to belong to that eye. "It looks like something died trying to come out of the ground. I thought Hermes was exaggerating when he talked about things this big."

Andromeda shook her head as she looked up and down the snout they'd mistaken for a hill. "What killed it?"

"Old age?" Henry suggested. Andromeda glared at him. "I can't think of anything else that could kill something like that."

It didn't take them long to find an answer. A little ways off, they found a fist-sized hole in the hill. Flies buzzed in and out, and Henry had to hold his breath against the smell of rotten meat. He bent down to peer inside and felt like he was going to be sick. The hole slanted down and went farther than the morning sun could reveal. After a few inches of dirt, the walls of the hole gave way to a white substance that Henry suspected was bone, and just past that, it became flesh. Blood and gore ran down it, and maggots as big as his fingers feasted on the remains. He looked back toward the eye and realized this hole must go straight through the brain.

"I think this died recently," he said. "Within the past day."

Andromeda paled. "Henry, if this thing hadn't died, it might have come after us."

"I know. Maybe we have someone looking out for us."

"But who?"

"I don't know, but I don't think we should wait around here for them to reveal themselves." He kicked a loose pebble at the dead monster. "That thing might have friends."

Andromeda nodded, and they set off again. They constantly scanned the area for more of the huge creatures, but it remained totally flat and featureless. Halfway through the day, a shadow that stretched all the way across the horizon appeared in the distance. The pair stared at each other wordlessly for a long time, silently asking the question of whether or not they should move forward. Finally, Henry put his hand on his hilt and nodded. Without saying anything, Andromeda fell back behind Henry, and he drew his sword.

The shadow grew as they approached, and after another few hours, they could see a canopy of branches and leaves causing the shadow. Something unnerved him about it, and it took another half hour of walking before he recognized it.

"Where are the trees?"

"What?" Andromeda asked. "They're right there."

"I see branches, but nothing holding them up."

Andromeda squinted and nodded. "You're right." She paused. "Does this change anything?"

Henry shrugged. "I guess not. Let's go."

The sun was still high in the sky when they reached the canopy, but they didn't see a single trunk. The air carried the scent of fresh cut grass, and an occasional white flower sprouted from between the leaves. Though the sun only sporadically glanced through the branches, they had no trouble seeing. It was as if the air itself were infused with an ambient glow. Dead leaves crunched underfoot, and a peculiar peace welled up in Henry. The giant monster seemed like a distant memory, and even Idun's war became something far off that didn't bear thinking of.

"Do you hear that?" Andromeda asked.

"Hear what?"

Andromeda had already pushed ahead of him. Henry sheathed his sword and picked up the pace to keep up with her. Before long, he heard the sound of running water. A few minutes later, he came to a stop next to Andromeda. A river so wide he could barely see the other side lay before them. A mist hung over it, and a few large rocks poked out of the water. It flowed so gently it almost seemed to be standing still. The Ormt flowed by quietly, interrupted only by a few large stones. Henry longed to just sit on the shore and watch the water flow by as it swallowed all his concerns.

"What do you think?" he asked.

"It doesn't seem to be terribly deep," Andromeda said as she tested the waters. "I think we could cross right here. It's not as if we're likely to find a bridge in any case."

Henry shrugged. "I guess you're right."

He took her hand and they stepped into the river. The waters went to just past his heel. They flowed around his boots, but never went in them. It was as if the waters didn't want to inconvenience him with wet feet. He took another step and began crossing into another world.

EIGHT

The river was quiet and peaceful. The current lapped around his legs and washed away all his worries. A part of him knew that if he allowed himself to drift on those waters, he wouldn't even be able to remember what those worries were. He longed to do just that. The past several weeks had been so hard, and it would be so easy to forget, but no. He took a deep breath and forced himself to concentrate.

"The river of forgetfulness," he said half to himself.

"What?" Andromeda asked, shaking her head. "Sorry, did you say something?"

"It's a story from another world," Henry said. "The Lethe is one of the five rivers bordering the underworld. It could erase all of a person's memories. I was just wondering if these two were related. Come on. I don't think we should stay here any longer than we have to."

Once he knew to guard against it, the thrall of the river became nothing more than a gentle humming in the back of his mind. Even so, when they finally stepped out of the river, it almost hurt. His worries came on him like a flood, and tears welled in his eyes. He glanced back at the Ormt and for a moment considered leaping in and letting everything go, but when he saw Andromeda looking longingly at those waters, the feeling passed. He put a hand on her shoulder, and she blinked and looked at him.

"I don't know what came over me," she said.

"Probably the same thing that came over me. Is this it?"

"It looks just like the other side of the river," she said. "The ground is a little more uneven, though."

He looked down and realized his feet had sunk into a carpet of leaves. He bent down to brush them away but found the layer to be surprisingly thick. The leaves went down almost a foot before he reached the bottom. Beneath, he didn't find dirt, but instead a twisted knot of wood. He pushed the leaves away until he could trace the root all the way to the bank of the river.

"Hreidmar did say the tree touched all worlds," Henry said. "I guess it makes sense that it would reach all the way to the river."

"So we're walking on Yggdrasil now?" Andromeda asked as she brushed away some leaves with her foot.

"That's what it looks like," Henry said. "Hopefully, we just have to follow those branches back to the tree, and we'll be able to find the Oracle."

"That seems simple enough."

Henry sighed. "Nothing has been simple so far. I wouldn't bet on things changing now."

"We won't know until we try," Andromeda said as she began moving further away from the river and toward the tree that lies at the center of all things.

NINE

It would've been hard to describe the branches precisely. Rather than being one tree, Yggdrasil seemed to be a combination of every tree that ever existed. One moment, sap oozed from the branches, and the next, bright fruit that looked like a strange mix between apples and cherries sprouted. Pine needles, as well as leaves as big as Henry's head and shaped like a star, danced in the wind. Every once in a while, they came to a large hole in the ground with several roots snaking down it. He stopped to examine one and could just make out a faint wailing. He looked at Andromeda.

"The roots touch all worlds," Andromeda said.

"I wonder why Idun didn't just use the tree to get where she needed to go instead of trying to conquer Argath."

Andromeda pointed at one of the holes. "It's only wide enough for one or two people at a time. It might take a year to get her army through one of those. Supplies would be almost impossible, not to mention the fact that if anyone discovered the invading army before enough people came through, it'd be an easy thing to destroy a small force and hold the entrance against anyone else."

"That makes sense, I guess," Henry said with a sigh.

"What is it?"

"Nothing, I was just wondering if one of these roots could take me home. If they touch all worlds, they have to touch mine too, right?"

Andromeda looked him in the eye. "Would you go if you found the way? I mean you came here to stop Idun. Would you leave without doing that?"

Henry thought about that for a second. "In Greece, I would've said yes without a second thought, but now?" He let out a long breath and shook his head. "No. Idun has to be stopped. I don't know what would happen if she actually conquered Kurnugi, but it wouldn't be good, for my world or for yours."

"Is that the only reason?"

Her voice was very soft, and her eyes were deep green pools. He wanted to say it wasn't, but he knew he shouldn't. She wasn't real, no matter how much he might wish she was. Still, he felt his cheeks heat up, and he looked away, focusing on the leaves dancing in the wind.

"We should get going."

The next few hours passed in silence. Andromeda avoided meeting his eyes, and Henry berated himself for how he'd responded. He hadn't intended to hurt her, and he kept telling himself that as much as she may appear human, she was only a story. He searched for the right words, but he himself wasn't sure how he felt or what he wanted to say. A wide pillar in the distance saved him from having to address the issue.

"I think that's it," he said. "That's Yggdrasil."

He ran ahead, hoping she would follow. It took longer than he thought it would to reach it. Its size had made it seem closer than it was. The tree wasn't just big. Its size was almost too big to be believed. He'd seen skyscrapers that were smaller. For that matter, city blocks were smaller. Its smooth trunk was only occasionally marred with knots, and for a moment, Henry entertained the urge of climbing the great tree but hesitated. Hreidmar had said that both the roots and the branches touch other worlds, and the last thing he wanted was to end up in some other story by accident.

Andromeda touched his shoulder lightly, and he turned, but her eyes were locked on a nearby stag that was reaching up to eat the leaves off of a low hanging branch. It couldn't quite reach. Its fur was a shade of brown so deep it almost looked red, and it had antlers so big they could almost be bushes. Lean muscles beneath its fur spoke of a lifetime spent running. The animal stopped trying to get to the leaves and looked at him, and Henry had the sudden impression that this creature was one of the oldest things to ever live. Much like Yggdrasil was the epitome of a tree, so this animal was a perfect deer. Henry took a slow step forward and drew his sword.

"I wouldn't," a high squeaky voice said.

Henry paused and looked around but didn't see anyone but Andromeda.

"Up here," the voice said.

Henry scanned the canopy above him, but aside from a gray squirrel moving from branch to branch, he didn't see anyone. The squirrel leaped down and landed gracefully in front of him. It chittered for a second, and then it spoke.

"Duneyrr is a sacred animal."

Henry's jaw dropped, and it took him several seconds to find his voice.

"You're a talking squirrel."

"And you're a talking human."

"Well, yes," Henry said. "All humans talk though."

"Oh believe me, I know," the squirrel said. "Maybe that's why you're all such fools. If you would shut your mouths and listen, maybe you would finally find some wisdom."

"Umm, I'm sorry?"

"Take what you're about to do. I can't think of anything stupider than trying to kill Duneyrr."

"What?" Henry looked at his sword. "Oh."

He swung the sword in a wide arc. It cut into the branch Duneyrr had been eating from, though Henry couldn't reach high enough to completely sever the limb. It took a few seconds for it to crack under its own weight, and it crashed to the ground. The deer looked at Henry and inclined its head before moving to eat from the newly downed branch.

"Oh," the squirrel said. "Never mind then."

It scurried across the ground and disappeared down one of the larger holes. Henry peered down it and thought he saw a faint red-orange glow.

"Well that was...odd." Henry turned to Andromeda. "Do you have any idea what that was about?"

Andromeda pursed her lips for a few seconds then shook her head. "I think my father once told me a story of a squirrel that lives on Yggdrasil, but it was so long ago." She smiled. "Sorry."

"I guess it doesn't really matter. It's not like a squirrel will be a whole lot of use to us. I don't suppose you know where to find the Well of Mimir?"

Again, Andromeda shook her head. "Every story I've ever heard says it's at the base of the tree."

"Let's go around, then," he said. "There could be a city on the other side, and we wouldn't know it."

It took them over an hour to make it all the way around, but there was just more of the same on every side. Henry was about to suggest they explore the caves when Duneyrr walked up to them and inclined its head. Then, it took off in a slow trot and stopped a few yards away and looked over its shoulder.

"I think he wants us to follow him," Andromeda said.

"Why not?" Henry said, and they started after it.

It went halfway around the tree before disappearing down one of the holes. Henry and Andromeda exchanged glances, but only hesitated a second before following.

An icy blast greeted them as they passed through the tunnel mouth. Darkness stretched out before them. Henry drew his cloak around himself but felt guilty when Andromeda shivered. She had a cloak of her own, but hers hadn't been made by Hephaestus to ward off heat and cold. He started to take his off, but she met his gaze and her eyes narrowed.

"You're cold," he said.

"And you will be too, if you take that off. I can stand a little cold if I have to."

"Andromeda..."

"Look, Henry, if it comes down to it, I'd rather your arm not be numb from the cold if you have to use your sword. I'm just a little chilly. I'm not going to freeze to death."

Reluctantly, Henry nodded, but he resolved to force her to take the cloak if this got much colder. He stood in front of Andromeda, hoping to provide at least a little protection against the cold. She mumbled something, but he pretended not to hear. He followed Duneyrr around a corner and froze in his tracks.

In the middle of the tunnel stood a pile of loose rocks. A soft blue glow emanated from their center. He took several slow steps and realized the rocks had been stacked around a hole in the ground. The water inside glowed and began to bubble. White foam took the form of a mouth and eyes with two bubbles appearing as pupils. Henry wondered if he was imagining things, but then the face spoke.

"Henry Alexander Gideon, who crossed over from the mortal world into the lands of winter."

The voice made the hairs on the back of his neck stand on end. It made him think of his house back in the real world. Henry sputtered for a second before finding his words. "I take it you're the Well of Mimir."

"I have been called such."

"I have to say, you were a lot easier to find than the other Oracles."

"The other Oracles were ends. I am but a means."

"Okay." Henry drew out the word. "We came here to stop Idun."

"Yes, I know."

"I guess you would. How do I stop her?"

"In all of history, Idun has never been an adversary to life. No hero has ever had need to fight her."

Henry sighed. "So because it's never been done, you can't tell me how to do it."

"You have spoken correctly. I cannot imagine. I cannot suppose. I only remember."

"I didn't think it would be that easy. How was Idun corrupted?"

"That was in the past."

"And you're the Oracle of the Past. You're supposed to tell me about things that happened in the past."

"I have told no one of nothing."

"You've been helping Idun."

"Idun drank of my waters and so gained insight into the past."

"So all I have to do is drink?"

The face moved back and forth on the surface of the water giving the impression of shaking its head. "Odin gave his eye and hung from the branches of Yggdrasil for nine days with a spear in his side to gain the right to drink. Idun, once loved by all, surrendered the adoration of multitudes and exchanged it for fear and hatred. You must pay a heavy price to drink of the waters of the past."

"I couldn't survive hanging from a tree with a spear in my side for nine days," Henry said, "and I don't have the adoration of multitudes."

"No, you must pay a different price, one which you have the capacity to pay."

"What's that?"

"You."

"Me?"

"To drink of the past, you must surrender what you are, all but the core. You must cease to be half of this world and half of the mortal realm and become only the hero."

Henry blinked, not willing to believe he'd heard correctly. His mouth went dry, and when he finally found his words, his voice came out raspy. "But Hermes said the only reason I could cross between worlds was because I'm partially imaginary."

"Yes."

"But if I give that..."

"The hero is not of the mortal realm. You must surrender your mortality and become a creature only of Kurnugi."

Henry blinked. For a second, he forgot how to breathe. His heart tried to break out of his chest, and his vision swam. If he did as the Oracle asked, he would be nothing more than a story.

"Home?" His voice came out as a squeak.

"You must forsake it."

"My parents?"

"They have been mourning for their lost child since you first stepped into the mirror. If you drink, you may not return."

"And they'll just keep mourning."

"The future is beyond my sight."

He thought back to the conversation he'd had with Andromeda. He didn't want to abandon her and the rest of Kurnugi to Idun, but the whole point of finishing this quest was to find his way back home. A tear fell into the water, and the ripples erased the face. He took a step back and shook his head.

"I can't." He looked at Andromeda. Tears blurred her face. "I'm sorry. I can't."

TEN

———

Can't what?" Andromeda asked. "Henry, what's wrong?"

He wiped at his eyes until his vision cleared. Worry painted Andromeda's face. She took his right hand in both of hers and stared into his eyes.

"I can't give up who I am."

"What are you talking about?"

Henry pointed at the Oracle. "Didn't you hear it?"

"I didn't hear anything. You just looked into the well for a minute and then backed off like you'd seen a ghost."

Henry shook his head. "The Oracle in Argath said there would be a price to drink of the past. I just didn't think it was being literal or that the price would be so high."

"What did it ask for?"

Henry bit his lower lip. He glanced back at the well. The water had gone still. For a second, he thought he saw the face again, but he looked away. "Everything."

Before he could explain further, movement caught his eye.

Nearby, Duneyrr raised its head. Its eyes darted around for a second. Then, it dashed off toward the entrance.

"What..."

His voice was cut off by the sound of dozens of heavy footsteps. Men shouted in surprise, and Henry thought he heard someone call out "deer." Nervous laughter came into the tunnel. Before he could suggest they run farther in, half a dozen armored men carrying swords and axes rounded the corner. They froze, the light from Mimir's well painting their faces blue. Henry just had time to draw his sword when the lead man shouted a battle cry and charged. He closed the distance quickly and swung a black-handled axe that had a long curved blade.

Before, Henry had disarmed enemies by cutting through the shafts of their weapons, but this warrior was too fast. Henry's sword crashed against the axe, sending out a shower of sparks. His arm felt like jelly. The man struck again, sending Henry tumbling to the ground. Desperately, Henry tried to pull his shield off his back, but then, the other men were there.

One kicked him in the stomach, and Henry curled up. Meaty fists and hard leather boots rained down blows on him. Pain blurred his vision. He was dimly aware of the fact that he'd dropped his sword. He groped for it, but a heavy foot came down on his fingers and ground them into the earth. He screamed, and the tunnel filled with laughter. He forced his eyes opened and saw a bearded warrior standing over him, foaming at the mouth. The wild look in his eyes made him look more like a beast than a man.

Andromeda screamed, and Henry's attention was drawn away from his captor. A bald man with a scarred face and twisted nose had her in a bear hug. She tried to kick him, but her feet bounced harmlessly off his legs. Henry didn't know where the strength came from. The next thing he knew, he was throwing himself against the leg that held his hand down.

It was like running into a pillar of stone.

Pain shot through both arms, and the man rocked on his feet slightly. The pressure on Henry's hand lessened. It wasn't a lot, but it was enough. He ripped his hand out from under the foot, doing his best to ignore the pain from his bleeding fingers. The man holding Andromeda turned to look at him, and she brought her head back and slammed it against his nose. The bald man cried out and dropped her. She backed away from him, but there was nowhere to go.

Two others closed in on her, and she took another step back and almost tripped over the well. One reached for her, and she scurried around to the other side. The water's light pulsed, and she looked down. For a second, everything else stopped. Andromeda's eyes widened, and her mouth quivered. She looked up at Henry. He saw what she was going to do an instant before she did it. He tried to cry out, but the words wouldn't come. Andromeda cupped her hand and dipped it into the well. She was trembling as she brought it to her lips and drank.

ELEVEN

Andromeda's scream was like knives in Henry's ears. The enemy soldiers grabbed their heads. An azure glow crept up Andromeda's arms and spread out into her torso. She screamed again, but it abruptly cut off as she fell unconscious.

Henry managed to pick up his sword and hold it awkwardly in his left hand. He couldn't feel his right one, and one glance told him most of his fingers had been broken. The enemy soldiers slowly got to their feet. One picked up Andromeda's limp form. Henry tried to go after him, but two swordsmen engaged him and effortlessly fended off his attacks. The one holding Andromeda sneered and carried her out of the cave, followed by three others, leaving only the two fighting Henry.

The magic sword allowed him to deliver strong blows, but the men he was fighting were equally strong, and they had the advantage of not being beaten half to death. They hacked at him. Every stroke he caught on his sword sent a jolt of pain up his arm. He couldn't last much longer.

They came at him from two sides. He could catch one but not both. He turned his back on one to parry the other attack, not wanting to see the blow that would end his life. A figure leaped out of the shadows, moving impossibly fast, too fast for him to get a good look. As the enemy's sword clashed with his, the blurred figure crashed into the warrior at Henry's back. Henry's sword was torn from his grasp, and a loud crack sounded behind him.

Before he could react, Duneyrr dashed forward and slammed its front hooves into the man, knocking him off his feet. Again and again, the stag rained down blows on the soldier, its cloven hooves tearing holes in his flesh. After a few seconds, he stopped moving. Henry turned to the man behind him and saw him on the ground, unmoving with his neck twisted at an odd angle.

"Andromeda," Henry said.

He scooped up his sword and shambled out of the cave. Pain lanced through his chest and sweat burned as it mixed into his wounds. It was all he could do to remain standing. He saw no sign of Andromeda. He pushed through the pain and forced himself to take a step forward. Then another. By the time he reached the tree, all he felt was pain. He laid a hand against Yggdrasil, but blood slickened his grip, and he fell, banging his head against a knot of wood. The world spun around him and faded into darkness.

TWELVE

Henry woke to leaves tickling his face. He tried to sit up, but the pain brought tears to his eyes. He didn't know how long he lay there, unable to move. Eventually, Duneyrr came back with a leafy branch in its mouth. It looked into Henry's eyes and inclined its head before laying the branch on his head so that its leaves blocked most of his vision. Henry couldn't shake the feeling that he was being buried, but he lacked the strength to do anything about it.

The nearby leaves rustled, and the stag darted out of sight. It took him a second to recognize the sound of footsteps. He craned his neck and could just make out about two dozen human shapes coming to a stop a dozen feet away. There were too many leaves in his face for him to see any details, and he didn't dare move them out of his way for fear he'd reveal himself to a potential enemy.

"Why did you take the girl?" a woman with a voice like honey asked.

"She drank from the well, Idun," an elderly man said. "Few enough have done that to make every one valuable."

Idun sniffed. "I will send some of my people to guard her."

"There is no need," the man said.

"It was not a request, Old Man," she spat.

"I was only offering a suggestion."

"Do not presume to give me advice. You have no greater wisdom than I."

"You drank from the well, but you do not know the charms."

Laughter rang in the air, and half a dozen other voices murmured. "Oh yes, your precious charms. You've had those from nearly the beginning, and what have you done with them? Nothing. Under my rule, we'll conquer all the worlds."

"This war is not won yet, Idun."

"It's only a matter of time. What happened to the boy?"

"Can't you see?"

"Something's hiding him." Silence stretched on. "Or someone."

"Don't be ridiculous, Idun. How could I hide something from someone who's drank from the well?"

"Continue to find the paths to other realms. I want the dwarves conquered." Other voices spoke up, but they were cut off by Idun's shout. "I have spoken."

One of the figures moved away from the others and out of Henry's sight. The others grumbled for a while before following. The last one stopped a few feet from Henry and laid his hand on the tree.

"I hung from you with a spear in my side for nine days, old friend," the voice of the man who'd been arguing with Idun said. "Eighteen charms I learned during that time which are known by neither men nor gods." The figure shifted, and Henry had the sense that it was looking at him. "The first can give help in times of strife and anguish."

It waved its hand with a finger extended, leaving a trail of light that faded a second later. The figure began walking away. Henry almost tried to call after him, but warmth blossomed in his chest and spread throughout his body. Pain receded, and strength flowed into his limbs replacing the fatigue. He pushed the branches off of himself and stood up, but the strange figure was gone.

THIRTEEN

I t's the talking human."

The high-pitched voice of the squirrel trickled down from the branches. Henry looked up just as a gray ball of fur streaked to the ground and stopped in front of him.

"And it's the talking squirrel," Henry said.

"You did really good at not talking earlier. That wouldn't have turned out well."

"Were those the gods?"

"Of course. Who else holds their meetings in the shadow of Yggdrasil?"

"And the last one who left. Who was that?"

"Odin. Who else?"

"He healed me."

"Oh, he does those things sometimes."

"But why would he help me? Doesn't he work for Idun?"

The squirrel let out a series of squeaks, and it took Henry a second to realize the little animal was laughing. The sound tickled him, and he found himself joining in a moment later.

"Weren't you listening?" the squirrel asked as it picked a nut off the ground. Its teeth cracked the shell, and it shoved a piece into its mouth. "Odin submits to no one save Odin."

"It sure seemed like he was submitting to me."

"Idun thinks that too, but I've been watching their meetings as long as they've been having them. Trust me. Odin is working his own plan."

"You've been watching them?"

"Yes."

"Did you see the ones who took Andromeda?"

"Yes, I saw them. They passed me when I was coming back out of the cave."

"What cave?"

"I'll show you."

The squirrel darted across the ground, and Henry rushed to follow. Once, he tripped over a root, but the squirrel stopped, jumping around as if impatient for Henry to get up. He scrambled to his feet and chased the rodent. A minute later, they came to a tunnel in the ground. A thick root extended into it and followed it for as long as Henry could see, no doubt terminating in another world.

"You're sure they went down there?"

"Of course. I told you, they walked passed me, and I go down that tunnel every day. I know how to find it."

"Is there anything dangerous in there?"

"I told you, I go down it every day."

"I mean something more dangerous than you."

The squirrel laid its head against the ground and looked up at him. "I'm not really that dangerous. Besides, I wasn't talking about..." It raised its head, and its tiny eyes went wide. "You don't know who I am, do you?"

"No, should I?"

The squirrel stood on two legs and puffed out its chest. It managed to look slightly offended, and it was all Henry could do to hold in his laughter.

"I should say so. I'm Ratatoskr."

Henry stared at him and pursed his lips. Ratatoskr scurried up a low hanging branch and ran along the limbs until he stood right above Henry. He chittered angrily.

"Don't you talking humans know anything? Every day, I carry insults between the eagle that lives at the top of the tree and the dragon that lives at its roots."

Henry stared at the rodent for several seconds.

"The dragon," he said flatly. "You mean after everything, I still have to fight the dragon."

"You can't cross Bifrost. Even if you could, you'd have to go through Asgard to get to Midgard. I really don't think you want to go to the home of the gods, and I only know one other way to get to Midgard. That's where they took her."

"What about the valley? The one that Thor crosses?"

"The valley leads from here to Asgard and from Asgard to Midgard. You'll not find Asgard's borders unguarded in the middle of a war."

Henry considered for a second, but there wasn't really a choice. Andromeda had done it for him. She'd drunk from the Well of Mimir because he hadn't been able to. Whatever price the Oracle had demanded of her had to be at least as much as it had asked of him, but she'd drank, and now she'd been taken. If the only way to get her back was to fight a dragon, that's what he would do.

"All right," he said. "Let's go."

FOURTEEN

Unlike the tunnel containing Mimir's Well, the heat here pressed against Henry, and he was aware of it even through the protection of the cloak. Within a few seconds of crossing the cave entrance, he was drenched in sweat. He wrapped his cloak around himself, trusting its mystical origin to protect him, but if it did anything to help, he couldn't tell.

Yggdrasil's root wound around the tunnel which had transformed from dirt to smooth black glass. Every footstep sounded like it echoed forever, and Henry held his shield forward, ready to deflect any fire the dragon sent against him.

Ratatoskr danced around him like he was having the time of his life. He kept throwing ridiculous suggestions at Henry, everything from saying he should just try being nice, to throwing acorns at the dragon's head. To be fair, when Henry pointed out that there were no acorns in the tunnel, the squirrel concluded that it was probably a bad idea.

Once, the ground started to shake. Henry reached for the wall, but there was nothing to grip, and his feet flew out from under him. His sword cut a gash in the ground, and he cut his hand on the edge when he stood up.

"What was that?" Henry asked.

"The dragon. He was probably growling or something."

"Ratatoskr, just how big is this thing?"

"Bigger than you."

Henry rolled his eyes. "I figured that. How much bigger?"

The squirrel stopped its skittering and looked Henry up and down. Its tail flitted around sending up a thin cloud of dust and ash.

"You could probably fit in its mouth." It chittered for a second. "Maybe not, probably everything but your head. He doesn't like eating food whole anyway."

"Well, thanks. That's a nice thought. Is there any chance I can slip by him?"

"Not unless you can turn invisible." He paused and cocked his head. "Can you?"

"How many humans do you know who can turn invisible?"

"Well, I don't really know that many humans."

Henry sighed. "No, I can't turn invisible."

"Then, you're going to have to fight him. How sharp is your sword?"

Henry tapped it on the edge of the rent in the black glass. "Pretty sharp. Why?"

The squirrel looked away. "It's just that I forgot to tell you that the dragon's scales are stronger than steel."

Henry gave it a level look. "That's an important thing to forget."

"Sorry," the squirrel said. "I've never tried to kill him, so I forget all the things you need to know to do that."

"Anything else you're forgetting?"

Ratatoskr paused and looked at him. It scurried from one side of the tunnel to the other, making a clinking sound as it ran across the obsidian floor. It lost its footing and slid into the wall. Henry held down a laugh. The squirrel got up and leaped onto Yggdrasil's root, which was running along the wall.

"Did I tell you he breathes fire?"

"It's a dragon. I figured that part out on my own."

"I don't know why you're getting so mad at me," Ratatoskr grumbled. "All I'm trying to do is help."

Henry let out a long breath. "Sorry. I get a little nervous when I'm going to fight a monster."

Ahead, an orange glow filled the tunnel and died down a second later. Henry's throat went dry, and his knuckles went white around the hilt of his sword.

"Why don't you go first?" Henry asked. "The dragon knows you. Maybe you can distract him or something."

"For a hero, you're not very brave."

"Just tell him you have more insults from that eagle."

"He'll ask what they are. What do I tell him?"

Henry raised an eyebrow. "How long have you been carrying insults between those two?"

"Since the beginning of time."

"And after all that time, you can't make up a realistic sounding insult?"

"I can try."

"You do that. When you have his attention, I'll come in. Hopefully, I can take him down before he knows I'm there."

The rodent squeaked and disappeared down the hall. Henry waited a few seconds before creeping after him, but the ground rumbled again. This time, he was able to get a grip on Yggdrasil's root and kept his footing. He moved a little closer and was able to make out the voices.

"Why do you persist in this?" A deep rumbling voice made a tremor Henry could barely feel. "It is obvious the eagle did not send you."

"He said your mother was a worm." The squirrel's quick words contrasted with the slow speech of the dragon.

"I was born of the primordial ice even as he was, and you, for that matter, little friend."

"Yes, well, he said you smell."

"Did he, now?"

Henry rolled his eyes and held his sword and shield ready. He took a step and almost slipped on the obsidian ground. The coin he'd stepped on rolled away, and he was surprised he hadn't noticed the scattered pieces of gold and gemstones lying around. There seemed to be more as he neared the bend in the tunnel. He paused for a second to compose himself. Then, he stepped around the corner and found himself staring at the dragon that lay at the root of the tree at the center of the world.

It lay on a mountain of gold and silver. Other treasure littered the ground, but Henry's eyes were drawn to the beast itself. Four thick muscular legs rose out of the treasure like tree trunks sprouting from a gold-strewn hill. Scales the color of desert sand covered its underbelly. On its body, they became an avalanche of dark gravel, climbing down its serpentine tail, which lashed around and knocked down piles of gold coins. It had no wings, but skeletal ridges ran up its long neck. Its eyes were a solid shade of gray, and Henry didn't even have time to raise his weapon before that deadly empty gaze fell upon him. A forked tongue flickered out from between razor sharp teeth. Henry saw Ratatoskr had been wrong. Even with his head, he'd have no trouble fitting into those massive jaws. A rumbling that shook the whole cavern erupted from the dragon's stomach.

"Well now," the dragon said in a voice that sent chills running down Henry's spine. "Ratatoskr, have you brought me a snack?"

"Ummm...Yes," the squirrel said. "Are you surprised?"

"Very," it said and turned to look at Henry.

Its toothy grin forced Henry back a step. Ratatoskr looked at him and smiled before making a chopping motion with its tiny hand. Henry waved his sword in a manner he hoped looked threatening, but the dragon only laughed.

"What exactly do you intend to do with that, my little morsel?"

"I don't want to fight you," Henry said. "Just let me pass, and no one has to get hurt."

"Only one of us will be getting hurt here, and I very much doubt it'll be me."

The dragon stood, and coins tumbled off its feet revealing claws the same color as charred wood. It moved faster than he would've believed possible. The cavern trembled at its charge, shaking so hard that Henry was thrown to the ground.

It was the only thing that saved him.

An instant later, the dragon's clawed hand slammed down on the spot he'd been standing, sending coins flying. He scrambled to his feet just in time to avoid the dragon lunging with its other hand. Henry lashed out with his sword, and the tip of the dragon's finger came off, claw and all. The dragon roared and recoiled, bringing its bleeding hand to its face.

"You little worm!" It bellowed. "I'll kill you for this!"

Henry had only a second's warning. An orange glow appeared in its mouth, and he raised his shield. The sheer force behind the fiery blast drove Henry back several steps. It was so hot, and for a moment, the fire continued to beat against the shield, but Hephaestus's power held, and the flame turned back and created a firestorm around the dragon's head. The obsidian wall behind the beast became molten slag, and dripped onto its tail, but the dragon seemed not to notice. Smoke drifted up from its nostrils.

"Interesting." Its voice made Henry's skin crawl. "I'd thought you'd only provide a bit of entertainment before a snack, but now it seems I'll have a new treasure to add to my horde. It's been centuries since I've seen anything like that shield."

Too late, Henry realized it was a distraction. The dragon's tail slammed into his back. He stumbled forward, and the beast brought its good hand down, not onto him but onto the top of his shield. For a second, he thought his arm would be ripped from its socket, but the leather strap attaching the shield snapped, and the shield crashed into the ground, embedding itself halfway in.

Henry tugged at it once but had to throw himself to one side to avoid the dragon's strike. Hot blood from the severed finger sprayed on his face, blinding him. He coughed, and an instant later, the air was driven out of him as the dragon's hand forced him to the ground and held him there.

"You hurt me, little human. No one's done that in a long time, but it's time our little game ended."

The beast's great jaws moved toward Henry. The dragon had pinned him down and stopped his shoulders from moving. The angle was bad, and he had no way to put any force behind his swing, but this was exactly the sort of situation for which Hephaestus had forged his sword.

Henry bent his arm at the elbow, and the sword impacted the dragon's hand with the strength of ten men. Two other fingers came off, enough for Henry to free himself. The dragon roared again, and the sound made Henry think his brain was going to explode. Mad with rage and pain, the dragon tried to bite him, but

Henry danced to one side and drove the sword into the dragon's head.

It tried to recoil, but Henry held the sword firm, and the beast's movements tore the sword free of its head. The dragon flailed, and Henry retreated into the tunnel to avoid being hit by its uncontrolled movements. Ratatoskr darted in a second later and hid behind him. Henry took the moment to wipe the blood from his face. The dragon took another two minutes to die.

After everything had been silent for several seconds, Henry crept back into the cavern. The dragon had managed to climb atop its mountain of treasure and lay there staring at him with empty eyes. Blood from its hands and head formed miniature rivers through the gold, and a trickle even found its way into a silver chalice. The squirrel looked from Henry to the dragon and back.

"I take back every mean thing I ever said about you."

Henry looked at him. "I don't remember you saying anything mean about me."

"That's because I didn't, but I wanted to say that just in case."

He knew it should be funny, but his heart was beating too hard for him to laugh. He sat against a pile of gold and felt very tired. Ratatoskr walked up to him and stood on his right foot.

"Are you going to drink it?"

"Drink what?" Henry asked.

"The blood."

Henry wrinkled his nose. "Why would I drink dragon's blood?"

"Because the blood of a dragon you killed provides power."

"It does?"

"Don't you talking humans know anything? Sigrund killed a dragon, and its blood gave him the ability to speak with birds."

"I don't really need to talk to birds."

Ratatoskr let out a long sigh, and Henry could've sworn the

squirrel rolled his eyes. "Dragon's blood is always different, but there are those who would give up whole kingdoms for the chance to drink from one. If I were going up against the gods, I'd want every advantage I could get."

Henry looked at the dragon's corpse. The scent of blood was already making him want to leave, and he gagged even at the thought of drinking it.

"They took Andromeda because I wouldn't drink from the well when I should have," Henry said.

He stood up and walked to the golden hill and picked up the silver chalice and gazed into it. Somehow, it seemed easier to drink if it was from a cup. It wasn't even a quarter of the way full, but he looked at Ratatoskr, and the squirrel nodded. For some reason, the sight made Henry laugh, but when he looked down at the blood in the chalice, he went deadly calm. He closed his eyes and brought it to his lips. For the space of a few heartbeats, he considered throwing the chalice away, but the moment passed, and he threw back his head and gulped down the blood.

FIFTEEN

Heat blossomed in Henry's chest. He tried to cry out, but his voice abandoned him. He doubled over, and his hands went to his chest. His heart was on fire, and when he thought he could bear it no more, the flames raced across his veins until his entire body was burning. His vision blurred, and he barely noticed when he fell to the ground. Abruptly, his face went cold, and that feeling crept throughout his body until the burning had subsided. He lay on the ground breathing heavily for several seconds before he noticed that Ratatoskr had come up next to him.

"Are you all right?"

"I think so. What happened?"

"You drank, then you fell over. By the time I got to you, you were better. What can you do?"

"What?"

"You drank from the dragon's blood, so you have to be able to do something." The squirrel's eyes went wide. "Now can you turn invisible?"

"I don't think so," Henry said. "How do I know what it did?"

"I don't know," Ratatoskr said. "I've never killed a dragon. Oh, I know!"

The squirrel spoke in a series of clicks, and its tail twitched. Henry stared at it blankly.

"Well?" Ratatoskr asked.

"Well what?"

"Could you understand me?"

"No."

Ratatoskr sighed. "I was hoping you could speak Squirrel. I guess not."

"Then, what can I do?"

"I don't know. You're the one who can do it."

"I don't know how."

"Maybe we can figure that out once we get to Midgard."

"Which way?" Henry asked.

The squirrel darted off down one of the smaller tunnels branching out from the cavern. Henry got to his feet and pulled his shield out of the ground. He slung it on his back and walked after Ratatoskr. The ever-present light that had infused the air since they first came under Yggdrasil's branches began to fade, and Henry had to walk slowly. Before long, he had to put a hand on the wall and was surprised to feel rough stone under his fingers instead of smooth obsidian. He paused when he came to a small cavern with four passages forking out from it.

"Ratatoskr," Henry called out. "Are you there?"

He tried again when the squirrel didn't respond. After a few minutes, Henry began to worry the squirrel had left him behind. He considered turning around, but there wouldn't be any point. He could make it back to Yggdrasil, but from there, he'd have no idea where to go. At least here, he had a one in four chance. He was about to go down the second passage from the left when the squirrel darted out from the rightmost passage.

"No!" The little animal cried out. "That goes to one of the elven realms. That's almost as dangerous for you as Asgard itself."

"Sorry, I don't know where I'm going, and you disappeared."

"I just didn't expect you to be so slow."

"Why don't we just go slow for a little while?" Henry asked. "At least until we get to Midgard."

The squirrel let out a heavy sigh. "Fine."

It was so dark that Henry had to navigate by the sound of the squirrel's nails on stone, and more than once, he had to call out to Ratatoskr.

"These all lead to different worlds?" Henry asked.

"Every one."

"I thought..." Henry wracked his mind for what he remembered of Norse mythology, which wasn't much. "Aren't there only nine worlds?"

"There were two, one of fire and one of ice," the squirrel said. "Seven others formed from the void between them, but Yggdrasil touches all worlds, not just the nine that exist here. That's why you should stay close. You don't want to end up in one of the other ones. Not that way!"

Henry froze. He hadn't realized the path had split again. It was the third time he'd almost gone the wrong way. "Can't I just hold on to your tail or something?"

"You could do that," Ratatoskr said, "but then I'd be forced to bite you, and I don't think you'd like losing a finger any more than the dragon did."

He let it drop at that. It was another half an hour before a glimmer of light appeared ahead. Henry started moving faster. By the time he could see the sky clearly, he was running. He leaped out of the cave mouth and breathed deeply.

The scent of wildflowers filled the air, mixed with a faint fragrance of pine. The air felt cool against his face, and he found himself laughing. He was so glad to be out that he didn't even care that the light hurt his eyes. When his vision finally cleared, he saw he was on the side of a flower covered hill. A forest of evergreens covered the nearby landscape. Henry took a step forward and almost fell when something caught his foot. He looked down and realized it was a thin root that stretched out from the mouth of the cave. He bent down and touched its rough surface. It was hard to imagine this was the root of the world tree.

"What are you doing here, rat?"

The words sounded halfway between a voice and a squawk. Henry looked around but saw no one. The hairs on the back of his neck stood up, and he scanned the branches above him. On a thick branch, a dozen feet up, stood the largest crow he'd ever seen. It was almost as big as a hawk. It opened its wings and glided to a lower branch.

"Answer me, rat."

"I'm not a rat," Ratatoskr squeaked, but it hid behind Henry.

"Don't you have a job to do?"

"Not anymore. Henry freed me."

"I did?" Henry asked.

"I can't really carry insults between the eagle and the dragon if the dragon is dead, can I?"

"I guess not."

"This boy killed Nidhogg?"

The squirrel nodded. "Stabbed him through the brain."

The bird squawked a laugh. "A difficult target to hit. I really don't care where you go, rat, but I don't want to see you here, so go before I decide to eat you."

"I didn't know crows ate squirrels," Henry mused.

The bird leaped off the branch and spread its wings in a span that was wider than Henry was tall. It clawed at his face, and Henry cried out and fell back before it flapped up and perched on a low branch. A single black feather floated down and landed on Henry's face. He stood up as Ratatoskr, who'd run to hide behind a tree, scurried out and ran behind Henry's leg again.

"I'm no crow, boy. Don't you know a raven when you see one?"

"Don't you know a squirrel?" Henry asked, not willing to admit that he, in fact, didn't know the difference. Henry looked at Ratatoskr. "Does this mean the dragon's blood gave me the ability to speak to birds like that other guy?"

"No, what makes you think that?"

"Well, I can understand the raven."

"I'm speaking your tongue, human. You could never understand mine," the raven said.

"I wasn't talking to you," Henry said, irritated at the bird. He looked back at his furry friend. "Just how many talking animals are there?"

Ratatoskr huffed. "It's not really that hard to speak your language, but humans hardly ever have anything worthwhile to say, so not many go through the trouble of learning."

Henry sighed. "What do you want, raven?"

"I want that pest to leave so we can talk without him spreading our words to all the nine worlds."

"I wouldn't do that," Ratatoskr said.

The bird glared at the squirrel and cawed. It spread its wings and dove, and Ratatoskr scrambled behind a tree. The raven went after it. Henry's hand went to his hilt, but he didn't draw the blade.

The raven was obviously trying not to hurt Ratatoskr, and he had the feeling this bird was the kind of being one did not want to upset. A few minutes later, the raven appeared back in the branches above Henry.

"You didn't hurt him, did you?"

"Of course not. I just ran him off. It would take more than a fright to hurt Ratatoskr."

"Ok, we're alone," Henry said. "What do you want? Who are you?"

"I'm Huginn. Or you can call me Thought if you prefer."

"Fine, but why are you here?"

"I'm supposed to get you to follow me."

"I don't even like you," Henry said. "Why would I follow you?"

"Men came out of that hole behind you. One carried a golden-haired girl over his shoulder. I saw where they went."

"Where?" Henry asked.

"Not yet. Not until you follow me." It flew to another branch and turned to look at Henry. "Well?"

Henry stayed unmoving for a while, but in the end, he figured he didn't have a choice. He grumbled under his breath at the fact that more and more often, he found himself thinking those words.

"That sword is an amazing thing," the bird said. "Made by a god, unless I miss my guess."

"That's right," Henry said.

"Did you know the gods don't make their own equipment here?" the raven asked. "They have dwarves make it for them, but the gods are greater than they are. It stands to reason that a weapon forged by gods would be greater than anything forged by dwarves. Your sword is quite possibly the greatest weapon in the nine worlds. I'd bet Nidhogg was surprised by it, for as long as he lived anyway."

Henry rested a hand on his hilt. "It's not the only monster I've killed. Where are we going?"

"Oh stop with your thinly veiled threats. Even if I was scared of you, there's someone else I fear a lot more. You're not going to intimidate me. To answer your question though, we're going to where you can get climbing supplies."

"Why would I need climbing supplies?"

"Because they carried the girl to a stronghold on top of a mountain, and you don't have what you need to sneak into a fortress guarded by Idun's finest men."

SIXTEEN

Henry gaped at the raven. "A fortress? You want me to attack a fortress?

"I didn't say attack," the raven said as he flitted to the next tree. "Though, you're the hero. You might be able to pull it off. If you're of a mind to try something a little quieter, consider this. Idun is guarding against armies, not against individuals. If you're careful, you may be able to sneak in and reach the girl before anyone notices."

"She's not guarded?"

"I didn't say that, but Idun doesn't trust the mortals under her command, and she has laid powerful enchantments over her prisoner."

"Magic." Henry shook his head. "I beat Zuab, but she was only mortal. I only survived Circe by running away. How can I go up against the magic of a goddess?"

The raven glided to a thin branch that groaned under its weight. It began to crack, and the bird leaped to another one.

"How can you go up against a witch with an army at her back? How can you oppose a monster so terrible her very sight turns men to stone? You have been doing impossible things for a long time now, human."

"But I couldn't save Andromeda."

"This quest is not over yet."

"You seem to know a lot about what's going on."

"We know many things."

"Is she all right?"

"Idun knows of you. As long as the girl can be used against you, she will not be harmed."

"Ok, so where do we get this climbing equipment?"

"Follow me."

The bird moved from tree to tree, never quite getting out of sight. Occasionally, it gulped down a lizard from a nearby branch or pecked at insects on leaves. They stopped by a brook at midday, and Henry had a little to drink. His pack had been lost when he'd been attacked at the well, but the raven pointed out some berries that were safe to eat. At first, Henry hesitated, but as much as he was already trusting this raven, it seemed pointless to hold back now.

After lunch, the bird flew faster, and Henry had to run to keep up. He'd never been much for running, but he found this to be remarkably easy. He lost track of time, and it was only when the sun touched the western horizon that he realized he'd been running all afternoon. He wasn't even tired. He brought his hand to his brow, but it came away dry. It took him a second to remember that the pants he wore had also been made by Hephaestus. The smith god had said they would allow him to run for a night and a day without tiring. Henry had just never had the occasion to use them before. He'd always had Pegasus when he needed to move quickly. He hoped Valin would bring Pegasus with him when they finally met up again. He really missed that horse.

He was still running when the sun set, though after a few minutes, he lost sight of the raven. He almost stopped to look but caught a glimmer of firelight through the trees. He slowed to a walk and pushed his way through the brush, coming out of the tree line into a large clearing. An ominous peak rose above it, its top covered by clouds. At its base sat a small village, little more than a cluster of stone buildings. A lone figure carrying a torch approached slowly. Henry tensed when the other man grew close enough to make out the staff in his other hand. He stopped about a dozen feet away.

"Are you the one called Henry Alexander Gideon?" the man called.

Shocked by the recognition, Henry nodded, but realized that the man likely couldn't see that in the dark.

"I am."

"Allfather be praised," the man said. "We were afraid something had happened to you."

"You knew I was coming?"

The man's eyes went wide, and the color drained from his face. "I'm sorry, I shouldn't have said anything."

"No," Henry said, "I think you should have. Who told you I was coming?"

"Please follow me."

The man turned and started to shuffle away. After he'd gone a little ways, he glanced over his shoulder. He stopped when he noticed Henry hadn't moved.

"Please, milord." Henry could practically hear the tears in his voice. "We have to go. It's not safe out here."

"I'm not going anywhere with you until you tell me what's going on."

"I swear to you, I will tell you all, but please not here. Surely your questions can wait another quarter hour while we get out of the open."

Henry considered for a second. Though tall and leanly muscled, the man wasn't armed, aside from his staff, which seemed like more a walking stick than a weapon. His left arm quivered a little, though Henry wasn't sure if it was from fear or old age. Regardless, he'd learned enough about defending himself that he should be able to handle one man, provided he wasn't some god or sorcerer or monster just pretending to be an ordinary man which, admittedly, was something Henry was not at all sure of.

"What's your name," Henry asked.

"Please..."

"I just met you, and you want me to go with you. You're obviously hiding something. I'm not coming with you unless you tell me your name."

"Ulrich. Now, please come."

Henry ran the name through his memory, but he didn't recognize it.

"Of course, I don't know Norse mythology," he said under his breath. "He could've told me he was the Norse version of the devil, and I wouldn't recognize it."

He shook his head and drew his sword before falling into step behind Ulrich. They reached the town without saying a word. Everyone went silent as Henry passed. The eyes of the people followed him. Once, a little girl pointed at him and whispered into her mother's ear. The woman, a round-faced midwife, only nodded. Henry started to say something, but Ulrich shushed him.

They came to a building guarded by a pair of rough looking men armed with long knives. They each nodded at Ulrich before stepping out of the way, and Henry's gaze was drawn to a strange design carved on the door. Curved lines intersected each other in ways that his eyes couldn't follow. The pattern seemed to shift as he looked at it. In one second, it looked like an eye, and the next like a tree. Then, it shifted again and looked like a wave moving across the wood. His head started to hurt, and he looked away. The door creaked as Ulrich pushed it open. They walked into a stark room with bare wooden floors. Lanterns lined the wall, and a one-eyed statue that Henry could only assume was Odin stood in the middle of the room. Once inside, Ulrich relaxed.

"We can speak freely now."

"What is going on here?"

"This building was to have been a new home, but when we went into the woods looking for lumber, we found the door already made with a strange carving and a raven perched atop. It said this was the door we were commanded to use for the new building. That night, I had a dream that you would come and that we should give you all possible aid, but that we should discuss nothing outside the walls of this building lest our words become known. In the morning, I discovered everyone in town had been given the same dream."

Henry waited for more, but Ulrich was apparently done. He kept glancing at the door, as if worried about what lay beyond it.

"That's it? Everyone is staring at me because of some bird and a dream?"

Ulrich inclined his head. "A man does not lightly ignore messages from the gods."

"Why are they trying to help me? Or is it just Odin who wants to do that?"

"Milord, they are a mystery. I would not presume to guess at their motives. Such is not for ordinary men."

Henry sighed. He obviously wasn't going to get much useful

information out of Ulrich, but the raven had led him here for a reason. He looked at the thatched roof and imagined the peak beyond.

"What's on the mountain?"

"Hind Mountain? It's only rock and snow, so far as I know," Ulrich said cautiously.

"That's it?"

Ulrich thought for a second. "There's an old stronghold of some forgotten king, but that hasn't been used for as long as anyone can remember."

"Can you send someone to guide me?"

Ulrich shook his head. "It's near the peak, if the stories are true. None of us have ventured that far. We can take you, perhaps, halfway up, but we've had little reason to explore higher. It's cold enough to kill up there. Even treasure seekers and adventurers don't try for that fortress."

"Yeah, I didn't think it would be that easy. How soon can we go?"

"Milord?"

"I have to find this fortress."

SEVENTEEN

The villagers provided him with a hot meal and a warm bed as well as a leatherworker to repair the straps of his shield. The next morning, they gave him a pack of fresh supplies and outfitted him with climbing gear and heavy furs. A burly, fiery-haired man, named Olaf, offered to guide him.

Olaf was practically a gorilla. He was a foot and a half taller than Henry and had to outweigh him by at least two hundred pounds. Even so, the man flinched every time Henry so much as glanced at him. Henry couldn't help but wonder at the dream that had inspired these people to help.

After two days of climbing, he asked Olaf about it. The big man paled and started to shake. It probably hadn't helped that Henry had discarded his heavy furs that morning in favor of the thin cloak Hephaestus had given him. It had protected him from heat once when he'd been thrown into Medusa's cook pot and seemed just as effective at warding off the cold.

Snow began falling on the third day. Olaf started to look down the mountain but didn't say anything. Once, Henry stepped on a patch of snow that he thought was solid, but he slipped and almost tumbled down. Olaf caught him, and they continued the climb. On the fourth day, the weather trapped them in a cave. Henry couldn't help but think of the time he'd been stuck in the middle of a frozen wasteland with a brother who had never been born. That seemed like so long ago. The storm finally let up two days later.

"We should go back, Master Henry," Olaf said.

Henry shook his head. "I need to make it to the top."

Olaf looked up the mountain. The way ahead was covered in snow. The clouds obscuring the peak were still high above. Lightning flashed, and Olaf shivered and shook his head.

"It's too dangerous, sir. This is a bad time to try this. Maybe if the weather were clear..."

"I don't think there's ever going to be a good time to try what I'm going to do," Henry said. "Go back down. I'll find my own way."

"But the gods..."

Henry rolled his eyes. "I'm sure the gods will forgive you. Do you have any idea where this fortress might be?"

"Near the top is all I've heard."

Henry nodded and turned away and began walking away. He looked over his shoulder after he'd gone a few yards, but Olaf was already gone. The only sign of him was a trail of footprints leading down the mountain.

It was a strange feeling to push through the waist high snow. He knew it was cold, but that was an intellectual sort of knowledge, like you might know the snow on TV was cold. He didn't actually feel it. He moved steadily upward, keeping an eye on his hands to make sure he didn't get frostbitten, but the cloak protected him completely from the cold. The wetness of the snow, however, was another matter.

He hadn't gone very far before his legs were soaked, though in the absence of the chill, it was more an inconvenience than anything else. Finding a dry place to sleep was an exercise in futility. The first night alone, he slept under a rock ledge, but woke up around midnight when a light snow started to fall and almost buried him alive. He found shallow caves when he could, but they were increasingly rare. The people of the village below had given him plenty of supplies, and there was nothing to do but keep pressing onward.

Two days later, he came to a sheet of ice at least a hundred feet tall with no obvious way around it. It was the first truly major obstacle he'd faced. He strapped spikes to his hard leather boots and pulled out a pair of ice axes. Slowly, he made his ascent.

The equipment he'd been given was more than equal to hold his weight, but he hadn't anticipated how much sheer strength was required to pull himself up the wall. Before he'd gotten halfway up, his arms felt like they were going to fall off. Every time he jabbed an ice axe higher and pulled himself up felt like he was moving a mountain instead of climbing one. He breathed heavily, but the increasingly thin air sapped the strength from him.

After another ten feet, he saw a small ledge above that looked just wide enough for him to sit and rest for a while. He tried to make his way there, but either the ice was too weak or he hadn't driven the ice axe in deep enough because as he removed one, the other came loose as well. His cry was cut short as a hand shot down from the ledge and closed around his wrist. The gnarled fingers had a vice-like grip, and he thought they would rip his arm out of its socket as they pulled him onto the ledge.

Henry collapsed, breathing heavily for several seconds before he looked up at his rescuer. The man stood at the mouth of a cave that hadn't been visible from below. He was covered in heavy furs, and a long white beard reached halfway down to his chest. His hood shrouded his face in shadows, and the only feature Henry could see was a long nose poking out.

"Thank you," Henry said.

"It's generally not considered wise to go climbing by yourself."

The deep voice spoke slowly and pronounced every syllable precisely. Henry found himself standing up straight and dusting off his shirt before he even realized what he was doing.

"I didn't do it deliberately, but no one else would come this far."

"It would seem your friends are wiser than you."

"I've never really been accused of being wise," Henry said as he pointed up the mountain, "but I do need to get up there."

"It's dangerous up there."

Henry put his hand on his hilt. "I can take care of myself."

The man looked over the ledge. "Evidence suggests otherwise."

"Just who are you?"

Through the shadows, Henry could see the faint hint of a smile. "I am but a simple traveler headed up the mountain."

"Why don't I believe you?"

The man shrugged. "Perhaps because you are not entirely bereft of wisdom."

"Thanks," Henry said flatly. "Why are you headed up? Didn't you say it was dangerous on the mountain?"

"Dangerous for one alone, but I am not alone anymore, am I?"

Henry pursed his lips and looked the hooded figure up and down. There was something about him Henry couldn't quite put his finger on, something unmistakably powerful. Henry knew without a doubt that this man was more than he appeared. Of course, what else could an old man found in the middle of an ice cliff be? For the hundredth time, he wished he knew more about Norse mythology. Maybe then he'd be able to identify this man. In the end, it didn't really matter. If the stranger was offering to help, Henry wouldn't turn him away.

"What's your name?" Henry asked.

"You may call me Bragi."

"Well, Bragi, do you happen to know where this cave leads?"

"To the top of this cliff."

"Let's go then."

EIGHTEEN

The frozen walls were as smooth as glass, and the floor was slick enough that Henry had to walk slowly to avoid falling. Even the ceiling looked more like crystal than ice. Though they left footprints behind them, there were none ahead, which meant Bragi had either climbed down the face of the cliff itself, or he'd just appeared on the ledge. Henry didn't know which was more likely.

Bragi carried a dim white light that looked like an emberstone, though Henry wasn't sure how that could be since Bragi wasn't a dwarf. The light reflected off the tunnel walls and filled the air. Bragi, who seemed to have no trouble walking on the frozen ground, mumbled under his breath as they walked, and Henry caught only the occasional word. Whenever Henry tried to talk to him, Bragi glared at him, and Henry could feel his gaze even through the shadows masking his face. After another hour, they reached the end of the cave. Immediately, Bragi went to a large rock. He paused briefly to brush away some snow and examine the ground. Then he stood up and began walking up a steep path. After a few seconds, he turned to Henry.

"Are you coming?"

"Do you actually know where you're going?"

"To the keep at the top. I assume that's where you're going too, as there's nothing else on this mountain."

Henry nodded, and Bragi turned and continued to walk up the path. Henry went to look at the rock but saw nothing out of the ordinary. Bragi disappeared around a bend, and Henry rushed after him.

The way, while not easy, could hardly be called difficult. In some places, it looked like the ground had been leveled out. They didn't always take the most direct path, but they avoided any steep incline.

"Of course," Bragi said when he mentioned it. "This keep was built by men, and it was built for war, but it had to be supplied. Roads were laid out. When the men left, the mountain started to reclaim the roads, but the marks men leave on the land do not fade quickly."

"How long ago was that?"

Bragi scanned the ground for a second. "Some thousand years or so."

"How is it you know about it, then?"

"I make it a point to know the past."

"Well, that was cryptic," Henry said. "How much longer until we reach the keep?"

The old man pointed up the mountain. As if on command, a cloudbank parted, revealing a fortress of gray stone. Peaked towers rose at two of the corners. The other two looked to have crumbled. One of the walls had a wide crack running through it, and a thin tendril of smoke floated up from somewhere in the building. The remnants of a bridge sat on either side of a gorge before the main entrance, its center having long since fallen. They were still too far to be certain, but Henry thought he saw people moving on top of what remained of the walls.

"How far is that?" Henry asked.

"We could make it to the bridge by the end of the day. There's a small footpath that winds down and then back up to the gate, but it's not something you'd want to do at night unless you had to."

"Like if you're going against a fortress full of enemy soldiers and you don't want to be seen?"

"If you don't want to be seen, why would you go through the front door?"

"Is there another way?"

"It was built for war, but it wasn't built stupidly. The lord who lived here always had a way to come and go without being noticed."

"Doesn't Idun know about it?" Henry asked. Instantly, he regretted his words. He hadn't told Bragi anything yet, and for all he knew, the old man was on Idun's side. Bragi, however, only shook his head.

"She would if she knew to look for it, but she's grown overconfident, and she doesn't see as much as she should."

"You seem to know an awful lot about these things."

"And you know less than you should if you truly want to oppose her."

"You're avoiding the question."

"You didn't ask one. Come, no one has used that passage in a long time, and we'll have to clear out some rubble."

"Why are you helping me?"

"Because you can stop her," Bragi said before turning off the road and heading into the snow.

Henry stared after him for a second before following. The old man forced his way through the snow as if it wasn't there. Henry noted that he didn't seem to get wet, but in light of everything else, that seemed like such a minor thing.

As Bragi had said, fallen rocks blocked the back of the cave. Henry would've thought it was just another cave, but some of the stone in the blocked passageway had definite signs of being worked.

They worked at it the rest of the day, and by the time night fell, they had opened a small hole in the top of the cavern that was just wide enough for them to squeeze through. The passage on the other side was long and dark, but the stones were obviously cut. Bragi's emberstone did little to banish the darkness.

"You know, I was told only dwarves could use those."

"Dwarves are infused with the power of the earth, and their stones feed off that. It's harder for others, but it's not impossible, if you know the way of it."

The gravelly floor crunched under their feet, and in a couple of places, the ceiling groaned and bent downward. They rushed past those places, and in another few hours, the passageway ended in a solid wall. Bragi ran his fingers along it until he found a stone looser than the others. He pressed it in, but nothing happened.

"Sorry," he said as his fingers wandered over other stones. "It's been here a long time, and more stones than the key have shaken loose. Here it is."

The stone beneath his hand clicked. Loose rocks shook free of the ceiling as the wall ground open and revealed an empty cellar. Several barrels had rotted, and their contents had long ago evaporated, leaving only the occasional patch of mold as a sign of their passage. A handful were still whole, and dark liquid dripped from one and ran to a grate on the floor, filling the room with a sour scent. Cobwebs ran from one end of the ceiling to the other, and a trio of spiders fled when the light of Bragi's emberstone fell on them. They moved quietly, but in this silent place, every step sounded like a hammer beating on stone. A loose strand of webbing brushed against Henry's face and he yelped. Bragi turned to glare at him, and though he could see even less of the old man's face than before, Henry shrank back from him.

"This place isn't as empty as it appears," Bragi said in a voice Henry had to strain to hear. "I don't think you want to bring the whole keep down on us."

Henry nodded and took a shaky step forward. They climbed up a stone stairway to a door that had long ago fallen off its hinges. It had to be after dark by now. After all he'd done, Henry knew he should be tired, but the ever-present danger kept his heart pounding.

The empty castle reminded him of the one he'd kidnapped Andromeda's father from once. He'd entered that one through a secret passage too. Of course, the difference was that no one had been there but a pair of men guarding the king. He'd seen more than that walking the walls of this place, and he could only imagine how many people the keep held. They wandered through a maze of halls for the next quarter hour before they saw the first signs of habitation.

"Guards patrolling the hall?" Henry asked as Bragi examined the tracks in the dust.

"So it would appear. It means we're getting close."

They hurried past the tracks. The halls beyond were still dusty, but it was a thin layer of dust instead of the thick carpet that caked the ground behind them. Arcs on the floor in front of doors told them which had been opened recently. Bragi moved past these with casual indifference. Once, when they saw a group carrying torches, the pair dove into a side passageway and Bragi shoved his emberstone into his furs. They waited in silence. Henry had to hold his breath to avoid breathing in the dust they'd thrown into the air.

Unlike most of the warriors Henry had seen since he'd crossed into this realm, these guards were slender and moved lightly on their feet. The guards passed without noticing them, and the pair went on their way. Finally, Bragi came to a stop before a simple wooden door with nothing to distinguish it from those around it. Though firelight flickered beneath it, the dust in front of it said no one had opened the door in several days. Without waiting for Henry to say anything, Bragi pulled open the door, and Henry's breath caught in his throat.

The room contained more treasure than the lair of the dragon Nidhogg. Mountains of gold coins were piled up on either side of the door and ran all the way down a room that could've doubled as a baseball stadium. Fires burned on ornate bronze braziers, though the smell of smoke was curiously absent from the air. Precious stones dotted the area. Jewels and objects made of gold and silver were scattered throughout the room. He'd never seen such splendor. He wanted to reach out and take it.

A dim part of his mind recognized the feeling as the same one that had once almost made him take a bite of a poison apple. He closed his eyes and took several deep breaths, trying to beat back the compulsion. He tried to keep ahold of himself as he opened his eyes. A gleam of red caught his attention. A large ruby, at least as big as his head, sat in the outstretched hands of a statue of a fat man. The jewel cast crimson lights on the wall. Henry found himself staring into it. For an instant, he resisted the urge to go for it, but then the firelight hit it just right so that the stone seemed to glow, and Henry's self-control vanished. He took a step forward and tripped over a jewel-encrusted dagger. The ruby held his attention so completely that he barely felt it when he fell. He got up and walked closer. Bragi shouted something, but it was a distant thing, and Henry ignored it.

Suddenly, a wall of flame roared into existence in front of Henry. He took a step back and threw his hands up in front of his face. The heat washed over him, and he could almost feel his arms blistering. He almost turned away but caught sight of the ruby through the flames. It looked more enticing than ever. He yearned to hold it in his hands. He had to have it. He knew he shouldn't. The fire was obviously hot enough to overcome the protection granted by his cloak, but the ruby called to him. He needed it. The flames would kill him. He had no doubt of that, but neither did he care, and he took a step into the fire.

NINETEEN

Pain blurred his vision, and smoke clogged his nostrils. He didn't even know if he screamed. Only once before had he felt anything like this, when his skin had burned off in a volcano. There was only pain. He fell into the fire and didn't move.

Then, without warning, his body went cold. He felt more than heard the gentle humming, pulsing inside his chest. Something rushed out of him. The crackling of the fire quieted, and for a moment, Henry thought he was dead. Gradually, the pain receded, and strength flowed back into his body. He opened his eyes, slightly surprised to find them intact.

The treasure room had dimmed, and the only sign of the flames was the blackened ground. Henry stood on unsteady legs. The charred line at his feet curved around, and Henry guessed that the fire had surrounded the entire room. He examined his arms and found them free of blister or other injury. Not even his clothes were singed.

Bragi clapped his hands. "I knew it!"

"Knew what?" Henry asked. "Why am I not dead?"

"You're a curse breaker, Henry," he said. "That's what the dragon's blood did to you. No curse can stand before you."

"How did you know about the dragon?"

Bragi brushed it off. "It's not important."

"No," Henry said. "I think it is. How did you know about the dragon, and how did you know that fire wouldn't hurt me?"

"Truth be told, I didn't," Bragi said. "I suspected though. Sometimes, risks need to be taken."

"Risks?" Henry cried out. "I could've been killed."

"You could've been killed when you fought Medusa or when you opposed Zuab. This was no different. In any case, there's still much to do. I suspect the girl you're looking for is somewhere among these treasures. Do you want to find her, or do you want to continue asking me questions?"

Henry scowled at Bragi but nodded. They wound their way through the treasures until they came to a stone slab nestled between two hills of gems and coins. Atop it lay Andromeda.

Her skin was paler than he'd ever seen it, and she wasn't moving. As far as he could tell, she wasn't even breathing. She'd been covered in armor made of interlocking plates of black steel. Runes had been engraved on the metal, though the color made it impossible to see what they were. It might've been his imagination, but they almost seemed to shift and writhe as light touched them. A black helmet hid everything but her face. A thin lock of hair ran down the side of her head. It had changed from golden yellow to fiery orange.

Henry reached out to lay a hand on her forehead, but an inch away, his hand stopped, and his fingers went numb. A chill shot up his arm and raced through his body. He pulled back. His hand came away limp and a momentary panic seized him, but a few seconds later, he could wiggle his fingers. Gradually, feeling returned, and Henry looked at Bragi.

"You wouldn't happen to know how to work this curse breaking power of mine would you?"

Bragi shook his head. "It's never been an ability I've had, but you don't really need to break a curse here."

"I don't?"

"The curse is not on the girl, but on the armor. The gods of these lands are not craftsmen like those of other realms. They rely on the skill of the dwarves, and while items made by such beings far outstrip anything crafted by mortal hands, they can't really stand up to a weapon forged by a god."

Henry nodded and drew his sword. Momentarily, he harbored the illusion of cutting the armor away with a few swift strokes, but he had a feeling that was more likely to gut Andromeda than free her.

He bent down and got as close as he dared to examine the armor. There wasn't much room between the black metal and her flesh. He slipped his blade under the plate joining arm to torso and tried to saw it away, but his curved weapon was ill-suited for that kind of cutting. He pulled it back and took in a breath. Angling the blade slightly upward, he slashed. The sound was a little like aluminum foil tearing. His aim was off, and he only got a small piece of the steel. It fell to the ground and sizzled before evaporating into dark smoke. Henry looked into the thumbnail-sized hole he'd cut in the armor, but darkness hid everything inside.

"At least I know it works," he said as he drew back again.

His aim was better this time, and the entire top half of the plate fell to the ground. The thick smoke billowing from the metal made him cough, but it only lasted a second. When it was gone, Andromeda's shoulder showed between a gap in the armor. Tendrils of black energy reached out from the edge of the hole, but they only extended out an inch. He bit his lower lip and struck again and again, each blow cutting more of the armor free. Eventually, he could touch her arm. Her skin felt cold and clammy, and as soon as he touched her, the black energy squealed and tried to reach for him, but he was far from their limited range. He pulled back and continued the work of freeing her.

It wasn't difficult work, but after a few minutes he was sweating. Andromeda's dress had been cut in several places. Once, he nicked her right wrist. He let out a strangled cry, but the cut wasn't deep and didn't bleed much. When he cut away the iron boots, he saw her bare feet underneath. That wouldn't be good in the snow outside.

"One problem at a time," he said to himself.

Eventually, only the black helmet. He'd saved it for last in the hopes that once enough of the armor had been removed, he might be able to take it off by hand, but when he tried, his fingers went numb again. He laid the flat side of his blade against her cheek and worked it until he fit the tip between her face and the helmet. Carefully, he pushed it in until he encountered resistance. He bit his lower lip and flicked his wrist. The blade sliced through the top of the helmet. All at once, it split and turned to smoke. Andromeda took in a deep breath, and her eyes shot open. She sat up and scanned the room until her gaze fell on him.

"Henry, you're alive!"

She took in her surroundings and wrinkled her brow at the stone slab she was laying on. She swung her legs to one side and stepped off. Her knees buckled, but Henry helped her keep her balance. She gave him a sheepish grin.

"Was I dead again?" she asked.

"No, just cursed."

"How long?" She brought her hand to her head before he could answer. "A few days."

"That's right," Henry said. "How did you know?"

"Soldiers." Her voice was distant, and her gaze empty.

"Yeah, soldiers took you."

"No," she said. "They're coming now. They knew you were here as soon as you crossed the circle of fire."

TWENTY

How do you know?" Henry asked.

Before Andromeda could answer, half a dozen men clad in gold armor rushed into the treasure room. These were the same warriors Henry had seen in the hall. None were very big. In fact, they were all shorter than he was. They wore no helmet and had pale skin and thick hair. They moved with liquid grace and ran so lightly that their armored feet made no sound on the ground. They carried curved swords that more closely resembled Henry's sword than any Norse weapon he'd seen. They encircled Henry and his friends. He looked over his shoulder. Andromeda was still weak from the curse, and Bragi was leaning heavily on his staff.

"I don't suppose there's anything you can do to help," he said.

The old man shook his head. "This is your task."

Henry groaned. "I was afraid you'd say that. Try to keep me between you and them. I'll try to clear a path for you to escape."

"I'm not just going to leave you here. I have too much depending on this."

"I'm not asking you to leave," Henry said, "but fighting these will be hard enough without having to protect you too."

"You can't fight an elf in a straight fight, boy," Bragi said. "Much less six."

"Elves?"

"Yes."

"Great," Henry said quietly. "What can you tell me about them?"

"They're nimble, easily faster than a man, and many have access to potent magic."

"Listen to the old man," a raven-haired elf said. Now that Henry knew what to look for, he could see the slightly pointed ears, and the face was just a little too flat to be human. "We've no desire to kill you. Leave the girl, and you can go."

A few of the elves shifted their weight back and forth on their feet, and a drop of sweat ran down the face of a bald one with gray eyes.

"Is it just me, or are they afraid?" Henry pitched his voice low, hoping those ears didn't allow the elves to hear him.

"You are Henry Alexander Gideon," Bragi whispered. "How many monsters have you destroyed? How many armies?"

"Those aren't exactly everyday things."

"And this is?" Bragi asked. "They'll fight you if they have to, but they're not fools."

"So I can fight them?"

"They'd tear you apart, but they don't know that."

"What am I supposed to do then?" Henry asked. "I'm not leaving Andromeda."

"I'm sorry," Andromeda said loud enough for the elves to hear.

"This isn't your fault," Henry said.

"I wasn't talking to you." She walked up to the raven-haired elf. "Allger, does the loss of your son still pain you?"

The elf's mouth dropped, and his sword fell from his hand, but he snatched it out of the air before it had fallen six inches. He sputtered at Andromeda, and it took a few seconds for his speech to become coherent.

"How do you know my name? How do you know about my son?"

Andromeda's hand went to her head, and she closed her eyes and breathed deeply for a second. When she opened them again, a tear ran down her cheek.

"Idun had no reason to kill him."

"Idun didn't kill Noll. It was a man who crept into our camp and slit his throat along with a dozen other elven warriors. He didn't even have the courage to face him in battle."

"Your party was sent to destroy a village who committed no crime other than bowing to Odin before Idun. She sent you against them for no reason other than petty pride."

"Don't listen to her, Allger," an elf with tan hair and eyes said. "She's trying to lay a spell on you."

Andromeda turned to him. "I've no magic save the truth, Elric. Don't you wish for this senseless war to end so you can go back to Vena and fulfill your promise to make her your wife?"

"How did you..." Elric shook his head. "It doesn't matter. I'll return to her when our task is done."

"Generations of men have lived and died since your task started. How many more before it ends?"

"As many as it takes."

"Do you know the plan Idun divulged to the other gods?" Before he could answer, Andromeda closed her eyes and shook her head. "No, of course you don't. She intends to conquer new worlds as they are being created. She wishes to claim every story as it is being told. Your task will go on so long as one mortal exists to tell a story."

"You're lying."

Andromeda touched her forehead again and bit her lower lip. She looked at the elf standing to Elric's left and told him of his family and of what this war had already cost him. One by one, each elf heard the story of his past and of those he had left behind. None could bear her words for more than a short while before looking away.

"Who are you?" Elric asked.

"I am one who Idun intended to use, and who she might have killed if not for the interference of another. Under Idun, your work will be eternal." She turned to Henry. "You have heard of Master Henry. If anyone can stop Idun, it is he."

The elves exchanged glances. Allger nodded first. He laid his weapon on the ground and walked out of the room on silent feet. The others stared after him for a few seconds before placing their weapons next to his and following. Henry let out a breath he hadn't realized he'd been holding.

"How did you do that?" he asked Andromeda. "How did you know all that?"

"A moment," she said as she looked at Bragi. "Who are you, and how is it that I can't see your past?"

Bragi inclined his head. "I am another who has drunk the waters of the past."

Andromeda's eyes went wide.

"How many of them have there been?"

"Look into the past and find out."

Andromeda closed her eyes, but they shot open a second later. She looked at Bragi and said a word, but her voice was so soft, Henry couldn't make it out. She tried again.

"Odin."

TWENTY-ONE

Bragi let out a laugh and allowed his hood to fall from his head, revealing one gray eye and one covered by an eye patch. The pointed nose and long beard attached to a face that looked old, but it was old in the same way the sky was old. It was a face that had seen more years than Henry could imagine and that would see many more long after Henry himself was nothing more than dust and bones. Even the Greek gods he'd met hadn't radiated the sheer sense of eternity emanating from this being.

"Odin," Henry said in shock.

"Yes."

"The king of the Norse gods?"

Odin bowed his head. "There are some who would call me that, though I don't know how true that is."

"You healed me at Yggdrasil."

Odin looked at Andromeda. "Is he always this dense?"

Andromeda stifled a laugh, and Henry felt his face heat up. "Why?"

"Because if I hadn't you would've died."

"All of a sudden, you're on our side?"

"Hardly all of a sudden." The god lifted a hand and a long spear materialized there. He held it up to show it to Henry. Runes ran along a polished steel shaft and the point glimmered in the light. "Gugnir can hit any target, and not even the creatures that live in the space between worlds can easily survive its strike."

"That thing in the valley we crossed to reach Yggdrasil," Henry said. "You killed it."

"That and more," Odin said. He tossed the spear into the air and it vanished. "Do you recall the pike that drove you into the rocks?"

The image of the one-eyed fish flashed through Henry's mind.

"That was you? Why?"

Odin smiled and approached him. Henry raised his sword, but Odin chopped with his hand and struck Henry on the wrist, sending the weapon clattering to the floor. He'd moved too fast for Henry to see. Odin stopped right in front of him and lifted up Henry's shirt, revealing the wound that still hadn't quite healed. For the first time, Henry realized the slashes weren't random. They didn't even look stationary and seemed to shift under his gaze. They looked exactly like the mark on the door in the village at the base of the mountain. His head even started to hurt if he stared at it too long.

"Eighteen charms I learned which are known by neither man nor gods," Odin said formally. "The last I speak to no one save my sister and the one who shares my bed." He winked his single eye. "And you, I suppose. I learned it from the Oracles themselves. Whatever is marked by that charm is hidden from the sight of Delphi, the Mirror, and Mimir."

"You hid me from her."

"Obviously."

"Why are you helping us?"

"Because I want you to win. My kind has its place in mortal imagination. We were never meant to rule it."

"If that's how you feel, then stop Idun."

"It's not that simple."

"You're more powerful than she is, aren't you?"

"Of course."

"Then, why not?"

Odin gave him a smile that vanished a second later. "Few beings in the nine worlds could ever truly cause me harm. Even among those, there are but a handful that I have need to fear. The rest are like children with swords. Yes, they could technically harm me, but it's not something I'll spare any concern for. Idun, however, has no need to harm me. All she need do is withhold her hand."

Andromeda let out a sharp breath, and her legs gave out from under her. Henry leaped to her side, but Odin was already there and caught her. She opened her eyes.

"The apples," she said, "just like before."

"Yes," Odin said.

"What's wrong with her?" Henry asked.

"Mortals, even those born of these lands, were never meant to drink from the well. Your minds can't handle all the knowledge of the past."

"Can you help her?"

Odin touched her forehead. "Not entirely. Only the Well can do that, by taking what it gave. I can give her a little more time, though."

His fingers made a series of quick gestures on her head. Andromeda blinked and stood up.

"Thank you," she said.

"Now, can you explain about the apples?" Henry asked.

"The apples are a source of life, one that Idun alone can give. Once, long ago before she was corrupted, she was prevented from giving us the apples, and we nearly died because of it. It is a terrible thing for an immortal to see death approaching. No god among the Aesir would oppose Idun directly for fear that she would send us down that path again. I can do little more than what I've already done."

"But you're hidden from her," Henry said.

"Hidden from her vision, but not from her reasoning. If I were to help more overtly, she would know."

"What happened to her?" Henry asked.

Odin looked at Andromeda. "Can you tell him? I've been away from Asgard too long, and Idun will be suspicious." Andromeda nodded. "Oh, one more thing. Though Idun has commandeered it, this is still my keep. I have a steed in the stables." He smiled. "One that I recently obtained. Take him, and he will serve you well."

"Won't Idun know?"

"She will know that you got him from the stable at the same keep you saved Andromeda from. Why should she be suspicious that you stole a horse?"

Odin bowed to each of them and turned to walk away. He rounded a corner and disappeared behind a hill of coins. They went after him, but the king of the Norse gods was nowhere to be seen.

"I knew he wasn't just an old man," Henry said, "but I never suspected that."

"He has a history of going about in disguise," Andromeda said.

"So tell me what happened to Idun."

"Andvari did it."

"The one that turned us into fish?"

Andromeda nodded. "It wasn't his fault exactly. Odin and Loki were going to see King Hreidmar. On the way, Loki killed an otter and carried the body over his shoulder. When they arrived, Loki presented his prize, only to find out, the otter was actually Hreidmar's son. Hreidmar was enraged and trapped the gods."

"How could Hreidmar trap a god?"

"In the heart of his realm, Hreidmar can do whatever he wants, and even Odin can go there only at his sufferance. It's the main reason Idun's forces haven't been able to claim Nidavellir. Hreidmar could've held the gods there forever."

"How did they get away?"

"They made a deal. Odin offered to give Hreidmar whatever he wanted in exchange for their freedom. Hreidmar asked for as much gold as it would take to cover his dead son's hide."

"That doesn't seem like much."

"That's what Odin thought. Hreidmar allowed Loki to go retrieve the gold, but what neither of them realized was that the hide could stretch infinitely. Loki brought more and more gold, but it just stretched larger and larger. Finally, they determined only Andvari's horde would be enough."

She spread her hands out to the treasure around them. Henry's eyes went wide. Some of these mountains of gold went higher than the light reached, and his mind reeled at the effort it would take to transport such a hoard.

"Where did he put it all?" he wondered aloud, but Andromeda went on as if he hadn't spoken.

"Loki went to find him and eventually trapped him in a net. Andvari gave him all this gold in exchange for his freedom. Loki was about to leave when he saw the ring on Andvari's finger. He jumped on him and ripped it off."

"He did that for a ring?"

"Dwarven rings are rarely just rings. In this case the ring,

Andvaranaut, had the power to make gold, but Andvari cursed it to corrupt and destroy whoever owned it."

"I think I see where this is going," Henry said.

Andromeda nodded. "It passed through a number of hands before ending up with those brothers I told you about."

Henry thought for a second. "You mean the Brothers Grimm?"

"Yes, they were here before they were in Argath. They found the ring in some long forgotten treasure horde. When they encountered Idun, Jacob was smitten by her. He gave her the ring before its curse had a chance to work on him and his brother. Idun put it on her finger and hasn't removed it since. The ring's power over gold corrupted her apples even to the point of cursing the tree they come from."

"Hera's golden apples," Henry said, almost under his breath. "The Moirai said they were corrupted."

Andromeda nodded. She walked over to a shield inlaid with gold sitting among half a dozen gems. The image of a tree had been carved on it.

"And the apple tree in Zuab's garden," she said. "You have to understand, Idun is the apples, and the apples are Idun."

"She became corrupt."

"Not entirely," she said. "Odin saw what was happening and used powerful enchantments to stop it. He was almost too late. A bare handful of the apples remain uncorrupted, and it's been those that Idun gives to the gods so that they can sustain themselves."

"Why the uncorrupted ones?" Henry asked. "Wouldn't she want the rest of the gods to be corrupted too?"

Andromeda shook her head. "Idun went from being a gentle goddess of life to a cruel goddess bent on spreading death. She doesn't have the raw power to oppose any of the other gods, and if the corruption were to change any of the gods so they no longer feared death, they might well destroy her, so instead, she rules them with fear."

"How do I stop her?"

"I'm not sure," she said. "I don't think she can be stopped while that ring is on her finger."

Henry's mind flashed back to a much more recent story of a cursed ring, one that had required the ring bearer to lose his finger. It had possibilities. He ran his hand over his hilt, but the thought made him feel sick. He looked at Andromeda. A drop of blood had run out of her nose, and she was holding her forehead again. He clenched his teeth. He could stand to be a little sick if that was what it took. Still, maybe he wouldn't have to. If dwarves made the ring, his sword might be able to cut it.

Andromeda looked up and smiled as she wiped the blood from her face, and she looked at her hand. Her eyes swept over the cut on her wrist and for the first time, she looked down to examine her torn dress.

"It's like the first time, isn't it?"

"What first time?"

She narrowed her eyes. "The first time we met when my wrists were cut by the shackles holding me to the cliff and the rock had cut my dress." She wiggled her toes. "I was barefoot then too, before you gave me those ridiculous shoes." She ran her fingers through her red hair. "Even this is the same color as when you met me."

Henry stared at her for a second. "You remember your hair?"

She raised an eyebrow. "Of course, I remember my hair. It is mine after all."

He gaped at her. While she'd always been able to remember generalities about other worlds, she'd never known that she was different. He wasn't even sure how to ask her about it, but in the end, he put it out of his mind. They had other things to worry about, such as how to get off this mountain.

"Come on," he said. "Let's see if we can find you something to wear that won't let you freeze to death the moment we step outside."

She looked at her dress again. "That's probably a good idea."

TWENTY-TWO

The fortress was deceptively empty. Every once in a while, Henry caught sight of someone darting from shadow to shadow, and occasionally, they found footprints on the dusty ground, but they never actually saw who made them. The first door they opened led to a stark room that had obviously been used recently. A curved sword leaned against a wall, and a full chest of clothes sat at the foot of the bed with a pair of leather boots next to it. Andromeda pulled out a plain green tunic and brown pants along with a heavy cloak. She held them up to herself and nodded. Henry left the room while she got dressed. When she came out, Henry raised an eyebrow at the sword on her belt, but she only shrugged.

"I hope we're not leaving some poor elf without a change of clothes," he said.

Andromeda grinned. "They can live without it. What now?"

"We should find the stables. Odin said there's a horse there."

"Do you really trust him?"

"Not really," Henry said, "but at this point, I'll take any help I can get."

They searched and discovered something strange in the first few minutes. Almost every door in the stronghold was locked and passages that Henry would've sworn had been fine when he'd come in had collapsed. There was only one way to go, and before long, Henry caught the scent of hay and horseflesh in the air.

"I guess you really did convince them," Henry said.

"Convince who?"

"The elves," Henry said, "unless you think someone else led us here."

Andromeda thought about that for a second. Her hand began to move to her head, but she stopped it when she noticed Henry watching. Instead, she nodded.

"Maybe you shouldn't do that anymore," he said.

"Do what?"

"You were looking into the past to find out who collapsed the tunnels and locked the doors, weren't you?"

She started to shake her head but stopped halfway through the movement and nodded.

"We need information. That's why we had to go to the well."

"Maybe, but finding out who closed a bunch of doors isn't exactly the most important thing in the world. If you're not careful, you're going to have an aneurism or something."

She looked at him quizzically. "What's an aneurism?"

"It's..." Henry thought about it for a second. "I actually don't know. It has something to do with the brain, I think. Look, it doesn't matter. Let's just agree that you won't use the Oracle's knowledge unless you absolutely have to. Odin said it wasn't meant for a mortal mind."

She let out a breath and nodded. "You're probably right."

They pushed open the door. Only a single stable was occupied. Henry walked over and opened it. When the horse stepped out, both he and Andromeda gasped. Its coat was the color of storm clouds, and he was as big as any horse Henry had ever seen, but the thing that drew his attention was the legs. There were eight of them.

The horse saw them and whinnied. It trotted over to Henry and nuzzled his shoulder in a way that only one other horse had ever done. Henry's jaw dropped, and he sputtered for several seconds. Andromeda looked from him to the horse.

"Henry what is it?" she asked.

"Pegasus?"

The horse neighed in delight and Henry threw his arms around the horse's neck. For the first time in a long time, He found himself laughing.

"Of course," Andromeda said. "After being a winged horse in Greece and having matchless speed in Argath, who else could Pegasus be but Odin's own horse?"

Henry went silent and stared at her. It hadn't been so long ago that he'd argued with her about the fact that Pegasus had changed. Even when he'd convinced her, she'd forgotten about it a few hours later.

"What happened to you?" he asked.

"What do you mean?"

"I mean you're suddenly remembering things you've always forgotten before. Are you looking into the past?"

"No," she said. "These are my own memories, not something from the Oracle."

"Then why do you suddenly remember?"

She looked away. "We don't really have time for this."

He put a hand on her shoulder and she met his eyes. "Andromeda you don't have to hide anything from me."

"I know," she said. "I just don't want to give you something else to worry about. It won't matter unless we stop Idun anyway."

He stared at her for a second before nodding. He approached Pegasus and the gray horse knelt down. Henry got on, surprised at how much he'd missed riding. He offered Andromeda a hand up, and she climbed on. He threw a glance at the stable doors.

"I guess we should have opened those," he said.

Pegasus reared and slammed four of his front hooves into the door. With an ear-splitting crack, the doors flew outward along with a shower of splinters that had been the door frame a second ago. Pegasus surged forward. He galloped down the rocky path as if it were level ground. Henry screamed when the path took a sharp turn, but Pegasus leaped into the air over the edge of a sheer cliff. It was a full thirty seconds before he realized they weren't falling. Pegasus was running on the air. Henry laughed out loud, and the death grip Andromeda had on his waist loosened.

"You knew he would do that!" Andromeda accused.

Henry shook his head. "If you'll put your hand over my heart, you'll see it's going about a million miles an hour. I had no idea."

Her laughter joined his as they sailed into the sky.

TWENTY-THREE

D o you know where you're going?" Andromeda asked after they'd been in the air for half an hour.

Henry looked around. Clouds stretched all around them. The sun's steady presence on their left told him they were heading south, but he had no way of knowing where exactly they were.

"Nope," he said.

"Doesn't that worry you?"

"It hasn't stopped me so far. Why? Do you have another dad you want to go see?"

Her grip around his waist slacked a little. He tried to turn around to look at her, but it would be impossible without losing his hold on Pegasus. She leaned her head against his back.

"Are you all right?" He spoke so quietly he wasn't sure she could hear over the rush of the wind.

"I'm fine." Her tone said she was anything but fine.

"Is there anything I can do?"

"If you could defeat Idun, I would greatly appreciate it."

"Consider it done," he said.

Henry smiled a bit when Andromeda's arms tightened around his waist, but before either of them could say anything else, Pegasus turned. The horse galloped down some invisible path that descended into the clouds. White washed the world around him. Andromeda shivered behind him, and it didn't take long for them to be soaked. A few seconds later, they came out into an overcast sky.

Below, people ran around like ants. Tents were set up everywhere, and thick columns of black smoke rose from forges carried on wagons. Though they were too far away to see clearly, Henry could tell banners had been set up. Even from his height, he could barely see where the army ended. He had no idea how to even begin putting a number to so many.

They were still fifty feet up when someone noticed them. Gradually, a wave of stillness spread through the gathered people, and Henry felt the eyes of the entire army on him. They landed in front of a large tent. A standard bearing a red lightning bolt flew on the wind. Henry and Andromeda exchanged glances. They jumped off Pegasus and practically flew between the surprised dwarven guards and into the tent.

Inside, startled dwarves stared at them. After a few seconds, Valin cried out in delight, and Fjalar, Valin's grandfather and the king of the Nordi Mountains, let out a hearty laugh. Valin rose and leaped across the pavilion, knocking some maps off the table in front of him. He closed a tight grip around Henry's stomach and squeezed so tight Henry thought he would lose his lunch. Guards rushed in, but Valin waved them off.

"Don't you recognize him?" Valin asked. "This is Henry Alexander Gideon."

The other dwarves looked at him with wide-eyed shock. The guards exchanged glances then nodded. "Of course, Lord Valin. Who but he could come here on that horse?"

They left, and Valin turned back to Henry. "By earth and stone, it's good to see you. We worried after Andvari came back and you didn't. Hreidmar imprisoned and very nearly had him killed for that."

"It wasn't his fault," Henry said. "He offered to take us back, but we refused."

"Yes, I suspected you'd done something like that, and I managed to convince the king. You do have a habit of diving head-long into danger that should kill you and coming out on top anyway. Speaking of which, what's that horse about?"

"Stolen from Lord Odin," Andromeda said.

"Wha..."

Silence blanketed the pavilion. Someone outside must've been listening in because Henry heard the words "Odin's horse" repeated over and over again. Valin and Fjalar exchanged glances. Their mouths hung open for several seconds before both erupted into laughter. Valin pounded Henry on the back.

"You never do things by half measure, do you?" he asked. "Tell me, can we expect an attack from Odin's forces?"

Henry shrugged. "Not for this. He'll hold back as long as he can, but he won't oppose Idun."

"Isn't the Allfather more powerful than Idun?"

"As long as she gives him the apples, he is."

Valin gave him a slow nod. The dwarven generals around the table muttered to each other. Andromeda cleared her throat, drawing their eyes.

"This isn't all Hreidmar's army, is it? What I mean is, I thought I saw men out there."

Valin smacked his head with his hand. "Of course! How could I forget? I'll send for the kings."

He spoke to one of the other dwarves in the tent. The young warrior saluted and rushed out.

"Kings?" Andromeda asked.

"Yes, we met them as we were coming out of Nidavellir. At first, we were worried there would be a battle, but then I saw the banner of King Frederick of Argath."

Andromeda's jaw dropped. "King Frederick?"

"Yes, he was with a king from a land I've never heard of. King Cepheus of..."

He looked up and scanned the canvas ceiling trying to remember.

"Aethiopia," Andromeda supplied, her eyes to the ground.

Valin nodded. "Yes, that was it. Are you acquainted with them?"

Henry gaped at him. "Valin, what are you talking about? The first time we met, you took us prisoner because her father is..."

Andromeda stepped on his foot. He looked at her, and she gave him a slight shake of her head. Henry wrinkled his brow, and she mouthed "Later." Valin looked from one to the other until Andromeda turned to him.

"Yes, we've met them. Henry saved their kingdoms."

Valin's hand went to his forehead in the same way Andromeda had so often done when trying to remember details from another world. Finally, Valin nodded. The generals still seated at the table mirrored the movement.

"Of course. We couldn't have defeated Zuab without you. I don't know how I could've forgotten. If you've done a similar service for Cepheus, then he'll be glad to see you indeed. I take it from all this talk of Idun and Odin that you found your Oracle?"

"You could say that," Henry said. "Andromeda has its knowledge, but it's not something she can get at unless we really need it. How much do you know about curses?"

Valin shrugged and looked at Fjalar.

"Not much," the king said. "It's not something dwarves usually deal with."

"Andvari did," Henry said.

Valin huffed. "Respectable dwarves don't deal in such things."

Henry rolled his eyes. "I know you don't like him, but is there any way you could get into contact with him? He might be able to save us a lot of trouble."

Valin shook his head. "As soon as Hreidmar released him, he disappeared. I went to his lake, but the cave had been cleared out."

"There's no hope of finding him then?"

"No one knows Nidavellir like Andvari. You won't find him unless he chooses to be found. Why are you so interested in him?"

Briefly, Henry glanced at Andromeda but turned away before she noticed. They might be able to find Andvari with Andromeda's newfound knowledge, but he wasn't willing to risk that unless he was sure it would do any good. Instead, he looked back at Valin and related all they had learned of the ring. Valin's face went red.

"Leave it to Andvari to cause all this with a careless word."

"Assuming we could find him," Henry said, "could he break the curse?"

"It's doubtful. Magic laid on metal is meant to endure as long as the metal itself does. It would take a greater power that Andvari has to unravel it."

Henry let out a breath, but before he could say anything else, the tent flap opened, and Frederick and Cepheus walked in. Henry rose. A flash of joy passed on Andromeda's face, but it died a second later. The men looked at her with the affection of a friend they had not seen for a long time, but not with the love of a father to a daughter. Andromeda blinked. If he hadn't known her as well as he did, Henry would've missed the fact that she was holding back tears.

The kings were oblivious to what their indifference had done to her. They each clasped arms with Henry and inclined their heads to Andromeda, but no more. Henry laid a hand on hers and she gave him a weak smile. Everyone sat down around the table. A map of the surrounding area was held down by inkbottles.

"Have you had any encounters with Idun's forces?" Andromeda asked.

"A few here and there," Frederick said. "Nothing of any consequence."

"What's your goal?" Henry asked.

Valin and the kings exchanged glances. The dwarf thumped his finger on the map. Henry looked down. Valin was touching a valley. He dragged his finger to a mountain range six inches away.

"Bifrost," Valin said. "We intend to storm Asgard itself."

TWENTY-FOUR

Y ou can't." Andromeda had gone pale. She blanched at Frederick. "It would be like trying to invade Neustad." She turned to Cepheus. "Like trying to assault Olympus itself."

There was the sound of wings flapping and the air stirred. "Not quite," a voice rumbled from the tent flap.

Henry looked over his shoulder and his breath caught in his throat. The familiar figure of Hermes stood at the tent's entrance. Next to him was a broad-shouldered man with a face covered in pockmarks. A twisted nose dominated his features. He had ears that looked too small, and one of his legs had shriveled. A massive hammer hung by his good leg. Its head glowed faintly red, and he wore armor of shining bronze.

A strangled noise came from Cepheus's throat, and when Henry looked at the Greek king, the man had prostrated himself and was whimpering softly. He pressed if face against tent floor. Henry stared at him for a second and rose to greet the gods of ancient Greece.

"Hermes, Hephaestus," he said.

"It's good to see you again, boy," Hephaestus said. "Tell me, has the equipment I gave you been useful?"

"It's saved my life more than once," Henry said as he extended a hand. The lame god clasped it.

Valin rose from his seat. His gray skin looked more stone-like than ever, and his eyes twinkled like sapphires. Hee spoke with a reverence Henry had never heard in his voice. "This is the forge-master who made your sword and shield?"

Henry nodded. "And who repaired my flesh when that one," he nodded at Hermes, "led me into a volcano."

"How many times do I have to apologize for that?" Hermes asked.

"I don't know," Henry said. "How many times do think would be enough for almost killing me?"

"It's not something I do every day. Sorry again. Now, can we please put that behind us?"

"If the two of you are done, perhaps we can get on with business," Hephaestus said. "I believe introductions are in order."

"Oh right," Henry said. "Hermes, Hephaestus. This is King Fjalar of the Nordi Mountains and his grandson, Valin, the commander of the dwarven armies."

They fell to one knee. "It is an honor," Fjalar said.

"And this," Henry continued, "is King Frederick of Argath and possibly Neustad now that Zuab has been defeated."

Frederick inclined his head. "I'm working on that."

Henry indicated the man with his face to the ground. "And I believe you know King Cepheus of Aethiopia."

"By reputation," Hephaestus said. "Rise, Cepheus."

The king got to his feet, but he still shook in terror. He was drenched in sweat and had left a wet mark on the canvas floor. Color had drained from his face, and he avoided looking at the gods' faces as if afraid they would strike him down for his insolence. He turned to Henry.

"Who are you that you talk to the gods as ordinary men?"

"He is a hero, King Cepheus," Hephaestus said, "and while your reverence does you credit, we are not the gods of these lands. You need not abase yourself before us." He waved a scarred hand at Henry. "Continue."

Henry nodded and grinned. He indicated Hermes. "This is Hermes, messenger of the gods and an occasional friend."

"I said I was sorry," Hermes said, though the half-hidden smile said he was enjoying the jest.

"And this is Hephaestus, god of blacksmithing." Henry's eyebrows shot up. "How much do you know of cursed rings?"

Hephaestus shrugged. "I've made a few in my time. Why do you ask?"

Quickly, Henry related the information about Andvari's ring. Hephaestus shook his head.

"Without having the ring, I can't tell you how to break its curse," he said. He pursed his lips and examined the knife at Valin's belt. "The work of your forgemasters?"

"Yes, Lord Hephaestus."

"May I see it?"

The dwarf nodded and unsheathed the weapon. He handed the weapon to Hephaestus who held it up in the light of the yellow emberstone illuminating the tent. He stared deeply into it, and Henry wondered what he was seeing.

"Tell me, is this Andvari a great deal more talented than the one who made this dagger?"

Valin shook his head. "A fair bit less so, I'd imagine."

"That's what I suspected," the smith god said. "It's very nearly the most impressive weapon I've seen save for those that came from my workshop. It can't stand up to my work though. The sword I gave you should be strong enough to destroy the ring."

Henry sighed. "So I have to fight the enemy leader again."

Hephaestus nodded and handed the dagger back to Valin. "As I said, you are the hero."

"Thanks." Henry glared at him. "Is there anything you can do to help?"

"I don't dare spread powerful artifacts in a world not my own," Hephaestus said. "I can help at the forges though. I suspect there's a thing or two I can teach them that won't unbalance things too much."

"And you?" Henry asked Hermes.

"What else?" Hermes asked. "I can carry messages back and forth between the various elements of your army, and I can do it a lot faster than anyone else."

"That would be a tremendous advantage," King Frederick said."

"Still, that's it?" Henry said. "You came all this way to make a few swords and pass a few messages?"

"It's difficult for us to exercise our power in an area not our own," Hephaestus said. "Doubly so in an entirely different world."

"Then, why did you come?" Henry asked.

"I said it's difficult to exercise our power," Hephaestus said. "I did not say it was impossible." He patted a hand on the head of his war hammer. "When the gods of this world take the field, we will be there to meet them."

"Please don't be offended," Henry said, "but you're not exactly the ideal warrior."

Hephaestus looked down at his withered leg. "This? This is

nothing. I was born like this, and my mother threw me off a mountain because of it."

"Sorry, I didn't mean to offend you."

Hephaestus shook his head. "You didn't, and you're missing my point. As a newborn infant, I survived a fall of a few miles with no injury to show for it save for those I started out with. If the stories I've heard of these lands are true, these gods can be hurt, and they can die."

He hefted his hammer. For a moment, its red light glowed brightly, overpowering the gentle glow of the emberstone. The dwarves around the table got up. Most took a step back, but one stared at the hammer intently, his mouth open in shock. Henry realized this dwarf must be a forgemaster, and he could only imagine what a god's weapon would look like to one of them. After a second, the glow subsided.

"This hammer once split open the head of Zeus," Hephaestus said. "He survived, of course, but if it can do that to an Olympian, I'd imagine it can do much worse to one of these gods."

"We are honored to have your aid, Lord Hephaestus," Valin said.

"What about you?" Henry asked Hermes.

Hermes shrugged. "I can be a spy or a scout. Even if some of them can fly, I doubt they have someone who can keep up with me."

"This is good," Henry said. He turned back to the map and then looked up at Valin. "How long until we reach Asgard?"

"Three days to reach the mountain range," the dwarf said. "Another two to make it to Bifrost."

"Five days," Henry said. He looked at the kings who each nodded. "Then, we end this."

TWENTY-FIVE

F jalar started to speak, but blaring trumpets cut off his words. Two long notes, then a short one. Valin cursed and the kings shot to their feet. Instinctively, Henry stood up and drew his sword.

"What is it?" he asked.

"There's a significant force approaching from the east," Valin said.

"How significant?" Henry asked.

"They have orders not to raise an alarm for less than five thousand," Valin said.

"But we saw your force," Andromeda said. "You have many times that number."

"Zuab had many times our number," Valin said, "and from what I understand, Master Henry here once defeated an entire army by himself."

"Point taken," Henry said. He looked at Hermes.

The messenger god sighed. "Fine, I'll go out and see what I can."

The wings at his heels flapped so quickly they filled the air with buzzing. Hermes darted out of the tent. The wind in his wake knocked down the inkwells holding down the map, but Frederick snatched them up before they'd ruined too much.

"We should get ready," Cepheus said. "No matter what Lord Hermes sees, we'll have to do battle."

There were nods all around the table. They had just started to get up when Hermes burst into the room again, practically knocking down King Frederick.

"Twenty-three thousand five hundred and sixty-two," he said.

The mortals stared at him, but Hephaestus only nodded.

"Is that just soldiers or camp followers too?" Valin asked.

"Soldiers," Hermes said. He pursed his lips and scanned the canvas ceiling for a second. "There were seven thousand forty-two camp followers." He looked at them. "Do children count as camp followers?"

Valin sputtered for a second. "Usually."

"Oh, sorry. Then there are eight thousand three hundred and seven camp followers."

There were several seconds of stunned silence before Frederick spoke. "That's almost half of our combined armies."

Valin cursed again. Henry looked at him.

"What is it? We'll beat them, won't we?"

"Without a doubt," Valin said. "Whether we can beat them and still have enough men to effectively oppose Idun is another matter." He turned to Hermes. "Did they fly a banner?"

Hermes nodded. "There were a few. The one I saw the most was of a flaming hammer."

Valin pursed his lips. "It's not Idun's banner nor one belonging to any of other gods. Unless..." his eyes went wide. "Was the fire blue or orange? I mean, are you sure it was fire and not lightning?"

"It was fire unless lightning comes in red and orange."

Valin let out a long breath. "For a moment, I feared a battle with Thor. I don't know this banner."

"King Budli," Andromeda said. "Budli of Gothia."

"Budli." Henry drew out the name. "That sounds familiar." He quirked his head. "Isn't that the name of your..."

"Yes, I've met him," Andromeda said. "I don't think he's here to fight."

Henry wrinkled his brow, but Andromeda shook her head slightly. He bit his lower lip and nodded.

"Are you sure?" Frederick asked.

"Reasonably sure, yes."

Frederick huffed. "It's been my experience that when people are reasonably sure, in reality, they're not sure at all."

"He can be trusted," she said. "I know that beyond any doubt."

"That's good enough for me," Henry said before anyone could raise any objections.

The last time she'd mentioned Budli hadn't been in reference to some random king she knew. Budli was her father in this world, and she knew better than anyone what he would do. He could only assume that since they were in the realm of Norse mythology, the other kings were no longer her fathers. Budli, on the other hand, still was. Then again, she had changed and looked more like the Andromeda of ancient Greece. Maybe whatever she was hiding had cut her off from this world, though he couldn't imagine what could do that.

The kings and Valin looked at him. Cepheus nodded first. Then Frederick, and finally Valin.

"Just like that?" Henry asked

Cepheus laughed. "Lord Alexander, I've seen you do the impossible enough times to know that word has very little meaning for you. I gather from what I've heard from these that they have seen the same." The others nodded. Even Hermes inclined his head. "If you believe Andromeda, that's enough for us."

"All right," Henry said. "Let's go out to meet him." He motioned at the tent flap. "After you."

TWENTY-SIX

Henry and Andromeda were the last ones out of the tent. As she neared the flap, he grabbed her arm.

"Hold on a second. What's going on?"

"Henry, we don't really have time for this right now."

"You keep using that excuse. It may not get any less busy in the next couple of days, so I want you to tell me now. Why don't they remember you're their daughter? Why didn't you want them to know that King Budli is your father here?"

"Henry, please." Unshed tears welled in her eyes, and suddenly, he felt like an enormous jerk.

"Sorry," he said. "I'll drop the subject." He looked after the departing kings. "You've lost more than I have."

She shook her head. "No, that's not it. I'll tell you, just not now. I really need to not think about this right now."

Henry nodded once and resolved not to bring it up again. He held open the tent flap and followed her out. King Frederick raised an eyebrow, but Henry just smiled and gestured with his hand.

"Lead the way."

The whispers Henry had become all too familiar with followed them, though this time, the focus of their attention wasn't Henry himself. It was the eight-legged horse who trailed him. The name of Odin drifted from the men of Argath and of Greece, in addition to the dwarves, though Henry suspected only the latter group truly knew who the one-eyed god was. Valin made a curt gesture, and a dozen soldiers fell in around them.

The flaming hammer banner appeared over the sea of men a few minutes before the men holding it did. Andromeda missed a step when she saw it but recovered before anyone but Henry noticed. The guards parted, and a huge man wearing a gold circlet stood before them. He looked slightly smaller than a mountain. He had pale skin, though callouses covered his hands. A long-handled axe hung from his belt, and a leather hilt showed over his shoulder, though the sword itself was covered by a heavy fur cloak. He scanned each of the people in Henry's party with a stony gaze. He cracked a smile when he saw Andromeda, but the color drained from his face when his eyes fell on Pegasus.

"Is that..." Words failed him.

"Odin's horse," Henry said.

"Then, the Allfather fights for you?"

"Not exactly," Henry said. "Let's just say he's not against us. I take it Andromeda was right, and you're not here to fight?"

Budli shook his head but never took his eyes from the horse. "The gods have sent elves and dwarves against us." He glanced at Fjalar.

"High King Hreidmar has made his position known," Fjalar said. "Those who went against that are traitors."

Budli nodded. "I heard there was an army moving against Asgard. I gathered every man able to hold a sword and brought them here to join forces." The three leaders with Henry looked at him, and Budli frowned. "They said nothing of a boy leading them though."

Andromeda spoke up. "King Budli, surely you must have heard of Henry Alexander Gideon."

Budli gave a slow nod. He looked Henry up and down, his eyes lingering on the sword at Henry's belt. He looked Henry in the eyes, and Henry had to resist the urge to shift on his feet. Budli took in the army of men and dwarves. A few men were nodding.

"Henry Alexander Gideon. I thought you were a myth."

The ridiculousness of that statement struck him, and Henry erupted in laughter. Andromeda quirked a smile, but the others just stared at him.

"I'm sorry," he said. "It would take too long to explain why that's funny. King Budli, we welcome you and your men to this fight."

Henry extended a hand, and the king took it. One by one, Budli clasped hands with each of the rulers there before turning to Andromeda.

"Andromeda, it is good to see you," he said, "though I must admit, I never thought to find you in the middle of a war."

"We go where we're needed." Her voice cracked. "And we are who we need to be."

"Very true." Budli nodded. "Still, do you know anything of war?"

Andromeda nodded. "My father taught me."

No instant of recognition flashed across his face. He simply nodded. The other kings just shrugged off what she said. Andromeda brought her hand to her face to wipe away a single tear, but even this went unnoticed by them.

"And I take it your father was a great warrior?"

"One of the best," Andromeda said, keeping her eyes lowered. Her voice was quiet, almost consumed by the noise of the camp. Budli, still oblivious to her distress, simply shrugged.

"You know, in all the time I've known you, I don't think we've ever discussed your parents."

Henry thought he should say something to stop the conversation, but without any idea of what was going on, he worried he'd only make this worse. Finally, Andromeda shook her head. "It's not important. If you'll excuse me, I'm suddenly not feeling well."

Frederick nodded at one of the guards who bore the snowflake crest of Argath. "Of course. Brand here will arrange a tent for you."

"Thank you, Fa...Frederick. King Frederick. I'm sorry. I forgot myself."

The king waved off the apology. "You've been through more than most. I can hardly blame you for a little slip of the tongue."

"Thank you," she said again before turning to Henry. "If you wouldn't mind walking with me?"

"Of course," Henry said with a slight bow.

"Tell me, Brand," Andromeda said once they'd walked a little ways. "How does Argath fare?"

"As well as can be expected," he said. "The witch Zuab tried to take over our kingdom and would've succeeded if not for Master Henry here. Now, the threat of Neustad is gone forever, and our alliance with the Nordi Mountains is stronger than ever. The only thing that concerns us is the lack of an heir."

Henry offered Andromeda an arm to steady herself. "An heir?"

"Yes, Master Henry. The king is not a young man."

"He's hardly old and gray," Andromeda said.

"Of course not, milady, but after his disastrous marriage to Zuab, many are afraid he'll balk at finding a new wife."

Andromeda closed her eyes and took in a deep breath. "He won't."

"I certainly hope not."

"Realm before king," Andromeda quoted. "Isn't that what he always says?"

The guard nodded. "As you say."

Andromeda started slowing down. The guard gave Henry a questioning look, but Henry waved him on and Brand moved forward to give them a measure of privacy. Andromeda started to speak half a dozen times, but she always stumbled after a word or two.

"You really don't have to tell me," Henry said.

"How many times have you saved my life?" she asked. "How many times have you saved my family and my kingdom?"

Apparently none, he thought. Not if those men aren't your fathers. "That doesn't matter."

"It's the price the Oracle demanded," she said, making his blood run cold. "In order to drink from it, I had to surrender who I was. I am no longer the princess, and so Kurnugi's influence no longer clouds my memories."

A lump formed in Henry's throat. The Oracle had demanded the same thing of both of them. Only Andromeda had dared pay that price.

"But why?" he asked. "The whole reason you came with me was to save your people. Now..."

"They are still my people," she said. "I remember Aethiopia, Argath, and Gothia, and so many more. From the shining halls of Camelot, to a world inhabited by human mushrooms where my hero is a plumber. You can't imagine the number of worlds I have existed in. I did what I did for them. If Idun wins, they'll all fall, but Henry, I didn't come with you for them. I came for you."

Henry's heart caught in his throat. "Andromeda..."

"You don't have to say anything. One of the first things I looked at was your past. I couldn't see after you were marked, but I know what came before. I understand, Henry. I know where you came from. I suppose you know I dreamed of us being together." She laughed, but a tear glimmered on her cheek. "That's how the story is supposed to go, isn't it? The hero saves the princess, and then they live happily ever after. I'm not even sure I had a choice, but you did, didn't you? You're not of Kurnugi. You may be the hero, but you can choose to do whatever you want."

"I'm sorry," he said. The words sounded poor and inadequate. "I should've drunk from the well, not you. I should've been the one to surrender who I am."

Andromeda shook her head. "What you're doing is a lot more important than anything I've given up. I'm not sure you could have gone on with this fight if you had been the one to drink. It would've taken too much. It's for the best, even if I do cease to exist when this is done."

"What do you mean?"

She smiled, but it was the fake sort of smile people give when they're trying not to cry. "This is a story, and I don't have a role here anymore. Not apart from being your companion. I'm not sure I can exist without you."

"But..."

Andromeda waved off his concern. "When I drank, whatever had been preventing me from remembering the different worlds vanished. I've lived a long time, Henry. Many lifetimes. Maybe more than anyone has a right to."

"We'll go back to the Oracle," Henry said. "Odin said you can give back the knowledge. That should make you the princess again."

"I don't think it works that way." Ahead, Brand had stopped

and was ordering men to set up a tent. Henry and Andromeda stopped a little ways away. "I knew what I was doing when I drank from the well. I've accepted it."

Henry didn't know how to respond to that, and they waited mutely while the tent rose up. Andromeda gave a sad smile before disappearing inside.

TWENTY-SEVEN

The three days it took to reach the mountain range passed without incident. The kings didn't really need Henry's help in planning their attack, so he had no reason to go see them. Andromeda had been trained in warfare in at least one of her lives, but being around the men who had been her fathers was painful for her. As a result, they spent much of their time walking through the army. Though none of the men recognized Andromeda, all stood a little straighter when Henry walked by.

Once, when Henry saw Captain Sholtz, a man who'd been like an uncle to Andromeda in Argath, Henry turned Andromeda away to spare her seeing someone else she'd loved who wouldn't remember her. He wasn't entirely sure he'd succeeded, but if Andromeda noticed the old soldier, she gave no sign. She did find one source of comfort though when they made their way to the picketed horses.

"Oakash!"

The chocolate brown mare whinnied when Andromeda

approached. She threw her arms around the horse's neck, and Oakash nuzzled at her shoulder. Henry had no idea if the horse actually remembered her, or if it only responded to her attitude, but he didn't care. Andromeda laughed out loud, and it warmed Henry's heart to see her happy. A stable boy retrieved her saddle, and they rode for the rest of the day. After that, it seemed like some of the weight had been lifted from her shoulders.

The mountains grew in the distance until their army had reached the base. They split into groups of a hundred, each led by a company of dwarves. Valin's men, better suited for mountain travel than any of the humans, guided them through a series of passes and switchbacks. The smaller groups allowed them to make good time, and in spite of the fact that their ranks had been swelled by King Budli's men, they made it to the top in the two days that Valin had originally estimated.

Bifrost glowed brightly, one end anchored to a ledge on a peak about half a mile away. Its shimmering colors, from red so deep it could've been blood to bright violet that reminded Henry of wildflowers, cast colored lights on the surrounding mountains as well as the valley below. Henry's breath caught in his throat. The valley, presumably the same one they'd crossed before, was swarming with men. They were so far below, he couldn't make out individuals, but the mass stretched out farther than he could see even from the high vantage point. For all he knew, they reached all the way to Asgard.

"How many is that?" he asked, not caring who answered.

"I don't know," Cepheus said. "Hundreds of thousands, maybe millions. That army could swallow us whole and not even realize they'd done it."

Henry turned to Hermes. "You wouldn't still happen to have Medusa's head, would you?"

Hermes shook his head. "I told you that had to stay in Greece."

"Because that would've been too easy." Henry looked out over the army. "What is that?"

Valin squinted until he saw what Henry was talking about. Giant serpent-like creatures moved among the army.

"Lindworms," the dwarf said.

"What?"

"Wingless dragons with a poisonous bite."

"Oh, is that what they are?" Hermes asked. "They attacked Delphi."

"What? When?" Henry asked.

"It was a while ago, before the Moira sent me to you. I always wondered what they were."

"I guess it makes sense that they came from here," Henry said. "What do we do now?"

"They outnumber us many times over," Frederick said.

"I know that," Valin said.

"What are you going to do about it?" he asked

Valin shrugged. "The same thing we did against Zuab, I suppose."

"You don't happen to have an army of ghosts at your disposal, would you?"

"I think you're on the wrong side for that." When Henry cocked his head, Valin glanced at the gathered army. "You said Odin wouldn't oppose Idun directly. If she commanded it, do you think he would fight?"

"Probably," Henry admitted.

Valin glanced back at the army. When he spoke, his voice had gone somber. "They say Odin keeps the souls of the greatest warriors for the battle at the end of time. If this doesn't qualify, I don't know what does."

Henry sighed. "We won't just be fighting an army of elves and dwarves, then. We'll be fighting dead Vikings too. We have our work cut out for us."

Hermes laughed and Henry turned to glare at him. The messenger god smiled. "Henry after everything you've been through, why would you think this was going to be easy?"

"I didn't—"

"Hammer," Hermes said.

"What?"

An electric blue light coming from the army caught Henry's attention. He turned and just barely caught sight of the hammer surrounded by a nimbus of light before it smashed into the rock below him. The sound tore through him, and blinding light filled the air. His bones felt like they had turned to jelly, and he thought his head would explode from the pain. His eyes burned, and he didn't even realize he'd fallen off the ledge until he was halfway down.

The first hint of a scream escaped his lips. Then, Pegasus was there. The stallion galloped through the air with all the speed he'd ever shown as a winged horse. He matched Henry's speed but didn't stop once Henry had landed on him. Pegasus dove down. As Henry's vision began to clear, he saw Valin falling a few feet away. They neared the ground, and Henry screamed, but at the last second, Pegasus veered, catching the dwarven commander.

They landed softly on the ground, with Pegasus running a few feet before launching himself into the air again. Henry's stomach twisted as half a dozen other men crashed into the ground with a sickening crunch. Pegasus's hooves thundered on the air until they reached the ledge the group had been standing on.

Henry's jaw dropped. The ledge was gone. Jagged stone teeth showed where it had broken off. Henry looked down but didn't see any sign of it. It hadn't broken off. It had been reduced to dust. A few, Frederick, Budli, and Cepheus among them, had been thrown clear and were picking themselves off the rock, but most had fallen to their deaths. Andromeda looked up from the mountain, relief painting her face. Pegasus came to a landing next to her, and he got off.

"What happened?" she asked.

Valin hopped off the horse and dusted himself off. "I believe we were just attacked by Thor."

"Where?" Hephaestus said as he forced his way through the crowd.

Henry scanned the area until he caught sight of a lone figure standing at the base of the rainbow bridge. It had to be huge to be visible from so far. He pointed.

"There."

In the same instant, a blue light flickered from the figure. It grew rapidly until it resolved itself as the hammer. Henry tried to back up, but there were too many people. He lifted his shield, unsure if even Hephaestus's magic could defend against such a terrible weapon. A heartbeat before it struck, Hephaestus swung his own hammer, catching Thor's weapon from below. The ring that filled the air reverberated through Henry's flesh and shook some loose rocks free. The attacking weapon flew into the air. Up above, thunder crashed. Hephaestus let out a high-pitched whistle, and a horse cried out from the sky.

Henry looked up and for a second, he forgot to breathe. It wasn't a horse, at least not exactly. Silvery metal gleamed instead of fur, and steel wings resembled Pegasus's original form. Fire burned in its eyes. Henry was fairly certain a metal winged horse should weigh too much to fly, but that didn't seem to matter. It landed so heavily that stone cracked under its weight. Its artificial muscles moved so fluidly they may as well have been flesh instead of metal.

Pegasus sized up his counterpart. The stallion huffed and looked away, which made Henry laugh. Hephaestus climbed on with more than grace Henry would've suspected the maimed god was capable of. The sight of the smile on his pockmarked face sent chills down Henry's spine. Then, the metal horse reared as its wings carried it into the air.

TWENTY-EIGHT

The army threw itself against the mountain like a tide against a cliff. Wherever they found openings, waves of men poured in. They ascended the passes quickly, no doubt aided by dwarves of their own. Valin cried out. Dwarves and men thundered down the mountain. For a second, Henry just stared. Then he noticed the sunlight passing through some of the attackers. King Budli walked up next to him and cursed.

"The warriors of Valhalla, the spirit of every warrior who has ever fallen in battle."

A group of men from Argath ran into a contingent of spirits. The living were consumed like dried leaves before a flame. Each scream caused a tear to fall from Henry's eyes. Somehow, he knew that it wasn't just physical screams he was hearing. It was the screams of souls. He leaped onto Pegasus, and they ran off the cliff, half falling half galloping on the air.

They ran out from the edge several feet before turning and charging a pass as a dozen ghosts rushed through it. They didn't see him coming. Whenever his blade cut into them, the spirits screamed and vanished. A few tried to parry, but his weapon passed through theirs as if they didn't exist. They may have been greater warriors than him in life, but in death, they couldn't stand against a god-forged blade.

In minutes, they were gone, and Henry and Pegasus ran back out over the battle. Dwarves had engaged other spirits in half a dozen places, armed with weapons that had been based on Henry's own. They weren't as effective as the sword Hephaestus had made. The ghostly weapons could turn aside their attacks, but the dwarves were formidable warriors, and for every dwarf who fell screaming in terror and agony, two spirits were dispatched. In a few places, men and dwarves fought more ordinary enemies.

"Since when do Vikings, elves, and dwarves count as ordinary?" he asked himself.

Up above, King Frederick waved down at him. Henry nodded and directed Pegasus up. He landed between Andromeda and one of the men who had once been her father. Aside from Hermes, none of the other leaders were there. No doubt they had joined the battle with their men.

"What is it?" Henry asked.

The king spread his arm over the battle. "You can't fight an army, Master Henry, not one of this size at any rate."

"I have to do something."

"In Argath, you fought until you found their leader. We need you to do that now. In these passes, we can hold them off for a long time, but we can't win. You can."

"If you know where Idun is..." Henry started. His throat went dry and he turned to Andromeda. He hated to ask her, but he didn't see another way. "Can you see her?"

Andromeda grimaced as she met his gaze, but she nodded.

Henry walked up next to her and held on to her arm. She closed her eyes for what felt like an eternity before her knees buckled under her, and Henry shifted his grip to help her stay upright. She opened her eyes and let out a long breath.

"She hasn't left Asgard."

Henry nodded. "I'll take Pegasus and fly over the army. We'll cross the river and find her."

Hermes shook his head. "It doesn't work that way. All paths to other worlds have their rules. The valley itself is the path to Asgard, not the air above it and not the river. You can't just fly over it. You have to go across it."

Henry looked out over the valley. "There's an army in the way."

"I know," Hermes said. "You have to go after Hephaestus."

"What?"

Hermes waved his hand over the army. "Well, you can't go that way. That only leaves the bridge, and there's only one warrior guarding the way to Bifrost."

"That one warrior is Thor," Henry said in a level voice.

"Hephaestus is keeping him busy."

"What about Heimdall?" Andromeda asked. "Isn't he still guarding the other side?"

Hermes shrugged. "Does it matter? Would you prefer to fight an army?"

"Maybe with Pegasus, I could force my way through without having to fight them."

"And maybe Idun will surrender," Hermes said. "Henry, that army stretches for miles."

"He's right, Henry," Andromeda said as she climbed onto Pegasus. "We have to go."

"We?"

She glared at him, but he could tell it was forced. He nodded once and got on the horse in front of her.

"Watch over Oakash if you will, King Frederick," Andromeda said.

"Oakash..."

Frederick drew out the word. Though Oakash was Andromeda's horse, the mare had come from Frederick's stable and had been one of the best. For a moment, he looked at Andromeda, and Henry thought he saw recognition in those eyes. A heartbeat later, it was gone.

"I'll see she's taken care of," the king said.

Henry couldn't see Andromeda, but he felt her arms tense around him. Hermes touched his head with two fingers in an odd sort of salute, and Henry drove his heels into Pegasus's side. The horse tossed his mane before trotting into the air.

Up ahead, blue and orange lights flashed at the base of the bridge. Black clouds swirled overhead, thundering as they spewed lightning. The earth trembled and cracked as great gouts of flame and magma burst forth. Fire and electricity clashed where the two gods battled. The air was alive with power, and waves of heat distorted the fighters. Henry had seen much since he'd come into Kurnugi, but this was something else entirely.

It looked like a man fighting a child. Thor stood as solid as a small mountain. He was nine feet tall and had arms even thicker than Hephaestus's. His skin glistened with sweat, and bruises ran down his bare arms. He wore leather armor that seemed unaffected by the flames his foe threw against him. A long yellow beard was splattered with burns, and rage twisted his face. His hammer was as big as Hephaestus himself, and the earth itself trembled with every step.

For his part, the Greek smith looked to be doing a lot better than his opponent. Pools of melted metal, presumably the remains of Hephaestus's mechanical horse, lay scattered about. Scorch marks covered his bronze breastplate, though the god himself was unharmed. He wasn't even breathing hard. He struck Thor again and again with hammer and flame. Even with his limited training, Henry could see the smith lacked any significant skill in combat. He went at Thor like a blacksmith hammering a piece of iron. Thor struck with his own hammer knocking the smith back a few steps.

The sky rumbled, and a bolt of lightning lanced down, engulfing Hephaestus and filling the air with an electric scent. Hephaestus's face went red, and Henry could almost see the rage coursing through him. His veins pulsed and glowed cherry red like the flames of a forge.

The maimed god raised a hand, and magma washed over Thor. The thunder god slammed his hammer against it. Though there was no reason it should be affected, the magma turned back. Thor twisted his hand and slammed his hammer into Hephaestus's chest. The Grecian flew back and crashed into the rock so hard he sank in. The mountain shook and a geyser of molten earth pushed Hephaestus forward. He slammed into Thor, his momentum adding to the strength of the blow. Thor grunted and a trickle of blood dripped from behind the leather vest. He clenched his teeth, and as Henry and Andromeda neared, the Norseman looked up, and eyes like green fire locked onto them. Hephaestus followed his gaze, and fear flashed in his eyes. The sky rumbled in response to Thor's unspoken command. Hephaestus moved to stop him, but he was too late. The sky screamed. Henry didn't have time to raise his shield before the bolt of lightning ripped through Pegasus.

The power coursed through the horse and into Henry, locking up his muscles. For a moment, he thought Pegasus would stay aloft, but the horse tilted forward and tumbled to the ground near the battling gods. Again, the sky rumbled and lightning flashed, but a wall of magma erupted from the ground catching the bolt.

"Go," Hephaestus called.

"But..."

"I can't fight him and defend you at the same time." He swung his hammer and caught Thor in the chest, but Thor closed his hand around the shaft of the hammer and ripped it from the smaller god's grasp. "Go!"

"Pegasus," Henry said, but the horse didn't move.

"Leave him."

Hephaestus leaped in front of Thor's hammer, grunting at the impact. The blow ripped off a metal plate, but Hephaestus barely budged. The ground shook under Thor, and a chasm opened directly beneath him. He leaped away, but not before the ground spewed molten earth into the surrounding area. Thor roared in pain as some of it splashed on him. Hephaestus took a chance and dove for his hammer. His fingers barely closed around the shaft when Thor kicked him in the stomach, and the weapon clattered away.

"I can't," Henry said.

"Henry, we have to," Andromeda said.

"If we do, he'll die!"

"Remember what he said about falling off the mountain," Andromeda shouted over a blast of thunder. "I'm not sure he can die."

Three quick bolts struck Hephaestus, casting such a bright light that Henry thought the image would forever be burned into his eyes, but when the afterimage faded, Hephaestus was unharmed except for a few more scorch marks on his armor.

Henry drew his sword and prepared to attack, but Andromeda grabbed his arm. Her hand was slippery, and he pulled away without any effort. He paused and looked at her. What seemed like a river of sweat poured from her skin. For a second, he was confused, but then he took in his surroundings. The earth was cracked and broken. Lava bubbled to the surface, and the air was alive with the scent of sulfur and ozone. His cloak protected him from the heat that would undoubtedly kill Andromeda if they stayed much longer. He pulled at Pegasus once more, but the horse didn't move. Henry took one last glance at the warring gods before taking Andromeda's hand and running onto the rainbow bridge of Bifrost.

TWENTY-NINE

It was an odd sensation. The rainbow bridge sloped up sharply, but it seemed to have a gravity of its own which left the earth beneath looking as if it had been turned at an angle.

The battle raged beneath their feet, though looking at it through the multicolored bridge painted it odd colors. The air was curiously devoid of the sound. Even the gods fighting behind them had faded to a muffled rumble. The rainbow itself felt like glass underfoot. Every step gave off a sound that was almost musical. It might've been his imagination, but he thought each color gave off a different note. It tugged at something deep inside, and he found himself moving back and forth between the colors as if trying to reconstruct a song he wasn't sure he knew.

"They look almost like toys from up here, don't they?" he asked as he looked at the armies below.

"No, they don't."

Andromeda's voice was level, and she didn't meet his eyes when he looked at her. He looked down through the bridge again and felt like an idiot. Andromeda may have given up her mantle as princess, but that hadn't affected her memories. As far as she was concerned, her pasts were still very real, and those were her people fighting and dying. From this vantage point, he could see just how outnumbered they were, and he tried to swallow a lump in his throat. Andromeda had already lost so much. He didn't want her to lose her fathers too, but it didn't look like that could be prevented. Their army was holding the mountain against the encroaching tide, but there were too many. One look at the pained expression on Andromeda's face said thought the same thing.

"Let's hurry," he said.

Andromeda pursed her lips and nodded. They walked faster. Before long, they climbed into a layer of clouds and the battlefield faded beneath them. The sky became a shade of dark blue, and stars dotted the sky. Henry wondered if they would cross into space. Of course, he wasn't even sure this realm had space. Before they reached quite that high, though, Bifrost turned. Henry and Andromeda paused for a second at the peak.

The area around them looked more like a map than landscape. The mountains behind them had shrank to small mounds of earth. To one side, a green field went on for miles before giving way to a crystal sea that reached to the horizon. On the other side, an ocean of white covered the ground. Far ahead and to one side, what looked like the top of a tree rose up from the ground. Henry could barely make out the curvature of the earth, and he wasn't sure if he should be surprised that Midgard was round. His logical mind told him it should be freezing up here and that they should have trouble breathing, but Andromeda didn't even shiver, and the air felt as thick as ever.

"This is the top of the world, isn't it?" Andromeda asked as she took his hand. Her voice was quiet, as if she was afraid she'd wake a slumbering world.

Henry nodded. "I think it might be the top of all worlds."

"Are we going to save them?"

He wanted to say yes. He should just say yes if only for the little comfort that would've given her, but he couldn't. In the back of his mind, a sorrowful tune began to play. Their army had come to nothing. They had no great force to storm the gates of Asgard with. Their divine allies had been left behind, and at that instant, Henry couldn't see anything in themselves but a boy far from home and a girl who was no longer a princess.

The music grew louder. It was like no song he'd ever heard, bringing tears to his eyes. When he saw his feelings mirrored on Andromeda's face he almost cursed. The music wasn't in his head. He looked down Bifrost toward Asgard. A lone figure walked the bridge. Each step reverberated through it. The notes that Henry's footsteps had given off were pale imitations. The ones this being gave off could've made stones weep.

As it approached, illuminated only by Bifrost itself, gleaming armor of some incandescent metal covered his body from head to toe, leaving only a small portion of his face. A sharp nose dominated his features, and though his helmet covered his hair, a golden beard spoke of a head that would practically glow in the sunlight. A golden horn hung at his waist opposite a long silver sword. It was hard to gauge size at that distance, but he was big. Henry stepped between the approaching figure and Andromeda and held his sword up. Behind him, the rasping of steel on leather told him Andromeda had drawn her blade.

The man, seven feet tall at least, stopped a dozen feet before Henry and looked out over Midgard.

"Beautiful, isn't it? I fear this will all be consumed before this war is done."

His voice held the deep sorrow of one who had lost much. It reminded Henry of the way his parents had sounded when they learned they weren't going to have another child. The memory brought a tear to his eye, but he blinked it away.

"Heimdall, I take it," he said.

"Yes. Put away your sword, Henry Alexander Gideon. You won't need it."

"Then, you'll let us pass?"

Heimdall shook his head. "Would that I could, but I am charged to guard this bridge, and you will not pass."

"But you care about the people of Midgard."

Heimdall turned to him and smiled. "We all care."

"Thor tried to kill us."

"Don't be misled by my uncle's battle rage. He is a defender of humanity as are we all."

"Then defend humanity," Andromeda shouted. "They're dying on the field below."

"*Humans* are dying," Heimdall said. "Humans die every day. I would change that if I could, but humanity itself will live."

"What do you mean 'if you could'?" Henry asked.

Heimdall shrugged and turned away. He started walking down Bifrost. "If Idun withholds her apples, who will be left to protect the people of Midgard? Turn back, Henry Alexander Gideon. I will not stand aside for you, and you lack the strength to defeat me on my bridge."

Henry took a step forward. "I think you know I can't do that."

The god let out a sigh and lifted his own sword. "Indeed, I do. Would that we could've met in a different time. Goodbye."

Heimdall turned and rushed at Henry, moving so fast as to be little more than a blur. The rainbow roared, and Henry barely caught Heimdall's blade on his. The impact rang through him and the colors of the rainbow momentarily brightened. For a moment, Heimdall pressed his blade forward. Henry's arms burned from the effort of holding the god at bay. Then, a smile spread across Heimdall's face.

"Interesting."

He withdrew the blade and struck, and again, Henry caught the weapon on his own. Heimdall moved so fast. Henry didn't have time to pull his shield off his back and barely had a chance to deliver attacks of his own. Andromeda screamed and charged into the fight, but Heimdall didn't even flinch. His sword darted forward so fast Henry couldn't even follow it. It knocked the sword out of her hand, and with a quick lash of his foot, Heimdall swept her feet out from under her. The whole thing took less time than a heartbeat, and Heimdall renewed his attacks while the former princess was still in the air. Henry didn't even see her land. The only indication was a shrill note from the bridge. All his focus was on warding off Heimdall's storm of attacks. Henry dimly recalled reading somewhere that the clacking of sword on sword would quickly damage both blades, but that apparently didn't matter, not when one sword was made by dwarves and the other by a god.

"You're a fair fighter, boy." Speaking didn't seem to slow Heimdall at all. "You still have much to learn though. You can't win. Turn back. I won't follow you if you retreat."

Henry didn't trust himself to answer and focused all his attention on blocking Heimdall's strikes. Once, he stumbled and lost his balance. It was only for half a second, but it would be enough. A chill spread through his body as he expected a sword blow to his neck or chest, but the attack never came. He met Heimdall's gaze and saw the barest hint of a smile. The god was toying with him.

Did you really think a few weeks of training would be enough to be able to fight a Viking god? he thought.

This wasn't working. He needed to do something unexpected. With every blow, the rainbow bridge grew brighter. Heimdall sent an overhand blow, and rather than parry, Henry threw himself to one side. He slid a dozen feet, crossing alternating bands of hot and cold. He worried he'd just slide off, but he came to a stop inches from the edge. Quickly, he pulled out his shield. Heimdall covered the distance between them in two great strides and Henry lashed out, not at the god himself, but at the band of blue light at his feet, intending to cut it out from under his opponent.

The sword passed through the bridge like it was made of water. The minimal resistance threw Henry off balance, and Heimdall slammed his weapon against Henry's shield. He slid another couple of inches. Behind Heimdall, Andromeda's still form stirred. Desperate to keep his opponent's attention, Henry followed Heimdall's attack with a thrust of his own, knowing it would leave him open. Heimdall grinned. He flicked away Henry's attack and touched him on the shoulder with the flat of his blade. Henry felt his face heat up.

"You have heart, boy. I'll give you that, and no one can fault your courage, but there is nothing more you can do here. Turn back. Take the girl with you."

As if on cue, Andromeda leaped on his back. The distraction would only last a moment, and Henry thrust with all his might, trusting the sword to enhance his blow. It sank into Heimdall's armor an inch.

The god reached back and plucked Andromeda off him. He looked at Henry and sighed before he tossed her at him. The edge was right behind him. He couldn't dodge. Instead, he braced himself, not to catch her, but only to keep them both from falling.

She slammed into him far harder than he expected, and the impact lifted him off the ground. Desperately, he grabbed her with his left arm and tried to jam the sword into the bridge, but it passed through as easily as before, and Bifrost vanished into the clouds above them.

He didn't know how long they tumbled through the air before they finally broke through the clouds. Snow blanketed a frozen landscape, and they were heading right for a deep canyon. For a second, he thought they would hit at the edge, but they missed it by a few feet. He had only seconds. The canyon was thinning, and the sloping wall rushed up to meet them.

"Hang on to me," he cried out as he let go of Andromeda and gripped his hilt with both hands.

A moment later, her arms closed around his chest. The wall came closer. He lifted his sword overhead and jammed it in. Shards of ice flew everywhere. They started slowing down, but the freezing air numbed his fingers, even through the protection of the cloak. He tried to use his legs to keep himself from running into the frozen wall, but they hadn't slowed enough, and he slammed into it.

Cold like he had never felt raced through him. Ice tore at his face and chest. His fingers threatened to slip off of the sword. Andromeda screamed as the canyon wall tore her arms. They came open, and for a moment, Henry was afraid she would fall, but his head jerked back as she grabbed his cloak. Choking and freezing, it was all he could do to hang on. They were going slower now. He thought he could see the metal of the blade bending, but he knew it wouldn't break. Like his shirt and cloak, it was god forged.

The cloak. The cloak that was supposed to protect him against heat and cold which, according to Hephaestus, only the strongest magic could counter. Panic shot through him, overriding the pain, but there was nothing he could do. He looked on in horror, and the metal groaned. They were only about a hundred feet from the canyon bottom, and he began to hope they would make it when the blade snapped. He barely had time to scream before crashing into the frozen ground.

THIRTY

Henry woke to pain. Everything that wasn't numb from the cold hurt. Even breathing sent pangs of pain through his chest, and the frigid air burned his lungs. He had to wipe away the frost on his eyelashes before he could open his eyes. Andromeda lay unconscious next to him. Both huddled under the protection of the cloak. Aside from the gentle rising and falling of her chest, she wasn't moving. He didn't know if he had managed to go to her, or if she had come to him. The hilt of his broken sword lay on the snow a few feet away, but he saw no sign of the blade. His shield was nowhere to be found. Wordlessly, he unclasped his cloak and left it on Andromeda while he went to retrieve the weapon.

As soon as he was free of the cloak, the cold hit him like a knife. He yelped, and rushed over to the sword, but he didn't anticipate how slippery the ice was, and lost his balance. The ground slammed into him. The impact reawakened parts of him that had gone numb. He grabbed the hilt, which burned his hand with cold. He refused to let go of it and scurried back under the cloak. Andromeda opened her eyes to him lying beside her, breathing hard and clutching the hilt with both hands. The blade was only six inches long and ended in a sharp edge. Frost crystals had formed along the break, and part of the guard had broken off. Henry just stared at the hilt.

"How can that be?" Andromeda asked, her voice unsteady from shivering.

"It's this world," Henry said. "Wherever we are, it's destructive enough to overcome Hephaestus's power."

Andromeda looked around and took in the frozen area. She let out a long breath that steamed in the air before nodding. "Jotunheim."

"What?"

"Jotunheim is the home of the frost giants, the greatest enemies of the gods."

"Frost giants," Henry said with a raised eyebrow, but then he nodded. "Why not? We've certainly come against everything else on this journey. Why not frost giants? You wouldn't happen to know how to get out of this world, would you?"

Andromeda closed her eyes for a second before nodding. "If memory serves, Jotunheim shares a border with Asgard."

Henry shrugged. "That's something at least. Do you have any idea where that is?"

Andromeda shook her head. "I've never heard any specifics about Jotunheim except that it was a terrible place."

Henry looked around. "Yeah, I think I got that. Can you walk?"

"I think so."

"Good. Let's stay under the cloak."

They leaned against each other as they stood. Fortunately, the cloak didn't seem to need to cover their skin to protect them. As long as they were under it, it blunted the cold. They picked a direction at random and headed off.

It was a struggle to walk. Every step brought fresh pain. Every once in a while, one of them would lose their footing and fall. More often than not, the other would fall trying to keep them up. Henry lost all sense of time and moving forward became a real effort.

"We have to keep going."

Andromeda sounded like she was trying to convince herself more than him. Her eyes were unfocused, and she barely lifted her feet as she walked. They slowed and huddled closer together as they walked. Even their shared body heat seemed almost nonexistent next to the cold pressing in on all sides, but she was right. They had to keep going, but the canyon wound ahead with no end in sight.

Wisps of snow danced across the ground in response to the biting wind. Andromeda stumbled and groaned as her weight shifted to him. The cold had sapped most of his strength, and he collapsed under it. He shook Andromeda but she didn't move. Panic mingled with the pain and exhaustion, but it was a dull thing, more an echo than an actual emotion.

"Please get up."

His words came out as hardly more than a whisper, and he realized he didn't know if he himself had the strength to rise anymore. She didn't even stir. He grabbed one arm and dragged her to the edge of the canyon, hoping that the frozen wall would provide some measure of protection. He threw the cloak over them, but it was a meaningless gesture. No one was coming for them, and if they couldn't press on, this cold land would swallow them, and Idun would conquer all of human imagination. What little strength he had left was focused on keeping him alive and awake. If he lapsed into unconsciousness...

He shook his head and tried not to think of Andromeda's still form as the sky darkened and the temperature dropped. Henry tried once more to rise, but there was no point. He fell back down and prepared to die.

"Mom, dad," he said. It seemed like there should be tears, but they didn't come. His parents deserved at least a few tears. "I'm sorry for leaving. I hope you have that other kid. Maybe he'll be a better son than me."

A pale blue light appeared behind him and, for a moment, he thought it was the light at the end of the tunnel. He turned around and got ready to go into the light, but it wasn't just one light. Dozens of tiny blue stars shone in the ice. He stared at them dumbly for a second trying to decide if he was imagining them. Then, much deeper in the ice, a new cluster of stars appeared, much dimmer than the others. Before long, the ice was alive with them. Hope blossomed in him, giving him strength he didn't know he had.

His numb fingers closed around the hilt of the broken sword and he jabbed it into the ice. He wasn't sure if the ice itself was weak or if some portion of magic still inhabited the metal, but it went in easily. Over and over, he chopped at the wall, but less than a minute later, his newfound strength had deserted him, and he leaned against the wall. He didn't even feel the cold anymore. He tried to stand, but his bones creaked and groaned under the effort. He pushed himself up just as a white crack spider-webbed from one the holes he'd made. He started at it uncomprehendingly. A loud crack filled the air, and his arms pushed through the ice. A shout escaped his lips just before his body impacted the wall, but he broke right through and fell onto the floor of massive cavern made of ice.

A wall of warm air greeted him, and he breathed in with an almost delirious joy. His skin began to tingle, and he actually laughed. Half a second later, he remembered Andromeda. Panicked, he turned toward her. Her skin had turned blue, and he dragged her in and pulled her away from the hole he'd made. It was only then that he allowed himself to take in the cavern.

In the fading light, he couldn't see much. Snow covered the frozen ground. Scattered around, he saw clusters of blue light in the ice itself. They didn't provide much illumination, but it was enough for him to see sharp stalactites hanging from a high ceiling. He turned back to the hole. Other lights were in the ice above it, and a few wiggled around in the broken pieces at his feet. He bent down to examine them. They had already begun to disappear into the ice.

"Glow worms?" he said.

Andromeda groaned nearby, and he rushed over to her. Her skin was still discolored, but she opened her eyes.

"Henry?" She blinked several times. "Where are we?"

"I'm not really sure," he said. "I think we're still in the giant's realm, but it's warmer in here. At least it's enough for the cloak to make us think that."

"I'll take whatever I can get."

"Can you walk?"

"I think so."

"Good. Let's head that way. It seems to be where the heat is coming from."

They walked slowly into the interior of the cavern. The glow-worms did little but allow them to see vague shadows. After a few minutes, the ice gave way to slush, and a little while after that, to rock. The faint light revealed wisps of steam. Henry almost fell when he stepped into a puddle. The water was warm. He stared into the darkness and could just make out a number of pools. A stray glow worm fell from the ceiling and plopped into one of the pools. It flickered and died as it sank in.

"We should rest here," he said.

"Do we have any food?"

Henry shook his head. "I lost my pack when we fell off Bifrost, and I haven't seen anything we can eat since."

"I was afraid of that," she said as she sat down on a rock next to him, and he joined her a second later. "What are we going to do, Henry? We can't survive out there, and for all we know, we could be going deeper into Jotunheim."

"Maybe you could look into the past and find out if we're going the right way."

"Look for what?" she asked. "Unless someone has gone from these springs to Asgard, I can't exactly ask how to get there. Maybe if I could freely scan the past without my head exploding I could find something, but short of that..."

"I think there might be another option," he said.

"What's that?"

"Have you ever heard of a place like this in Jotunheim?"

"I told you all I know about Jotunheim..."

"I know, just a few stories. This is supposed to be the land of the frost giants, right? It doesn't make sense for there to be hot springs in the middle."

"What are you saying?"

He looked out over the water, and took in a deep breath, taking in the steam. The warmth in his chest felt wonderful.

"I think this cavern leads to another world," he said.

"What world?"

"I'm not sure, but it has to be better than here."

"What about Idun?"

"We can't fight her if we freeze to death."

He couldn't see her face in the darkness, but he imagined her biting her lower lip. She didn't want to do this. Neither did he, for that matter, but he didn't see any other option. Jotunheim had nearly killed them. It would finish the job if given half a chance. She had to see that.

"What about Cepheus, Frederick, and Budli?" she asked. "What about their men who are dying trying to reach Asgard?"

"How long do you think they can hold out?" he asked. "They could already be dead."

She leaned against him and laid her head on his shoulder. When she spoke, her voice was so quiet he could barely make it out. "I know."

He put his arm around her. "Look we don't have to decide right now. We're not going anywhere until we get some rest. Let's talk about this in the morning."

He felt her nodding against his shoulder. A few seconds later, she was snoring soundly. It wasn't long before the efforts of the day caught up with him, and he fell into darkness.

THIRTY-ONE

The ground rumbled, and Henry opened his eyes. Light from the hole illuminated the cavern, revealing an area smaller than he'd thought. It was perhaps two hundred feet across and twice as wide. Frozen spikes hung from the ceiling, and a dozen steaming pools littered the rocky center. A narrow river flowed to the back of the cavern and disappeared through a thin crack in the stone. Two wide openings stood on either side. The ground rumbled again. He shook Andromeda awake, and her eyes opened slowly, but another rumble made them go wide.

"Something's coming."

She nodded, and they stood up. He lifted his stump of a sword just as a shadow appeared in one of the openings. It looked like a man but was at least twenty feet tall. It carried a club in one hand, and when it stepped out of the entryway, Henry saw blue skin and white hair. The club was the bone of some huge creature. It wore a breastplate of black metal, and its eyes were pearly white with no color at all. Henry stepped in front of Andromeda and lifted his weapon. The giant gave a great booming laugh that shook the cavern. Icicles fell around Henry and Andromeda. One sliced into his arm, but the rest shattered against the stone or splashed into a pool.

"Put away your broken knife, little man," he said.

"If we follow the river, he won't be able to follow us," Henry said quietly.

"That path leads to another world, doesn't it?"

"I don't know, but that would be my guess," he said, "but even if it is, we should be able to come right back once he leaves."

"Should?"

"Hermes told me that not every path goes both ways."

"Maybe I can look into the past to see if this one does."

"If you pass out, I won't be able to carry you out of here."

There was silence for several seconds before she said anything. "We can't take that path."

The giant took a step toward them.

"Are you sure?" Henry asked.

"Yes."

"Then, go. I'll be right behind you."

A second later, footsteps came from behind, and he turned to follow. The giant roared, and the ground shook as they made their way between the pools. Ice fell from above with loud splashes as the giant crossed the center of the room. Henry almost lost his balance when they moved from rock to ice, but they made it to the other opening. It sloped upward, and it was a struggle to climb. The giant was right behind them. Henry pulled Andromeda into a smaller side passage hoping the giant was too big to follow, but it forced itself in.

The passage groaned and shifted. Abruptly there was a loud crack, and chunks of ice crashed to the ground. The walls each moved back a foot, and the giant's steps resumed. It was getting closer. Henry spotted a crack in the ice, one far too small for the giant to fit. He and Andromeda dove in. It only went back about a dozen feet. The entrance darkened as the giant bent down and looked into the hole. Henry threw his hilt at the giant's eye, but even when it had been whole, the sword had never been meant as a thrown weapon. It bounced off a wall and skidded under the giant's face. The creature chuckled, and when it spoke, Henry realized it was male.

"You have spirit, little man," he said, "more than most of your kind."

"Heimdall said the same thing," Henry said.

The giant growled, and Henry took an involuntary step back.

"Talk to it," Andromeda whispered.

"What?"

"Reason with it."

"How do you expect me to reason with that?"

"Come out," the giant said. "It won't be nearly as pleasant for you if I have to dig you out."

"The giants are the enemies of the gods. We're not exactly their favorite people right now. Convince it we're on the same side."

"It's worth a try," he said under his breath.

He walked up to the entrance. The giant's eye had to be half the size of Henry's face. The snowy white eyelashes were covered with a layer of frost.

"We're friends," Henry said.

The giant laughed so loud Henry had to cover his eyes. "I like you, but I have no human friends, particularly not those favored by the gods."

Henry gave a laugh of his own, but it sounded strained. "You think they favor me? Heimdall told me that after we fought, just before he threw us off Bifrost."

"You spin a good tale."

"How do you think we got here, in the middle of your land with nothing to protect us from the cold? This is where we landed."

The giant blinked and backed up a second. Something crashed, and Henry realized the creature had sat down.

"All right. I'll listen. Come out here and tell me your story."

"How do I know you won't kill me?"

The giant chuckled. "You don't, but you know I will if you stay in there."

Henry looked at Andromeda and she shrugged. "It's not like we have very many options right now."

Henry nodded. His throat felt dry, and his heart raced in his chest. His knees felt like jelly as he stepped out of the cave. He glanced at the broken sword but didn't pick it up. He sat in front of the giant, the icy breath not quite overcome by his cloak. The air smelled like rotten meat. Andromeda sat beside him a few seconds later. He would've preferred for her to stay behind, but he had no way to tell her that without letting the giant hear too.

"Well?" the giant asked.

"The gods, some of them at least, have been trying to kill me for a long time. I'm sure they thought they succeeded when one of them threw us off their bridge."

"And what were you doing on Bifrost? Were you coming or going?"

"We were going into Asgard, hoping to catch them by surprise."

"To do what?"

"To stop them from trying to kill me. I've heard that in these lands, the gods can be killed. I don't like having to look over my shoulder. I just wanted it to end."

"So you thought to attack the gods in their own home," the giant said between laughs. "Bold. Stupid, but bold, but you are still a human in the middle of Jotunheim, and your kind are not welcome here."

"We're trying to leave," Henry said. "I understand your realm borders Asgard."

The giant drew back and stared at them. Henry resisted the urge to shrink from that gaze. Once again, the giant's laughter shook the cavern.

"You were thrown off Bifrost by a god, and landed in one of the most hostile worlds to mortal life and your next idea is to go in the realm of the ones who did that to you?"

Henry shrugged and tried to look nonchalant about it. "Like I said, I don't like people trying to kill me."

"All right, little human, you've convinced me."

"You'll let us go then? Or can you show us the way to Asgard?"

"It's not up to me. You'll go to Thrym, king of the frost giants. He'll decide if we'll give you aid or grind your bones to make our bread."

THIRTY-TWO

The giant led them through a network of frozen tunnels. The dim sunlight filtering through the ceiling told Henry that this cavern wasn't just some feature of the land that had frozen over. It was made entirely of ice. As they walked, the light faded. The giant didn't say anything, but once they got deep enough, he lit a large torch. The ice almost seemed to recede from the dancing flames.

"It's almost like the time we were captured by Valin, isn't it?" Andromeda asked.

"I don't think Valin would've eaten us, though."

"Do you think he was serious about that?"

"I don't think he had a reason to make that up."

They had to jog to keep up with the giant's long strides as he led them through a number of passageways. A couple of the caverns they passed through had other tunnels leading out. Henry considered trying to use one to escape, but he had no idea where he'd go if he succeeded. For now, at least, the giant king was their greatest hope.

They walked for hours. Unlike the path leading to the dwarven city of Kerat, which lay under the Nordi Mountains, the way the giant took them on eventually sloped upward. Light shone through the ceiling again and steadily grew brighter. The giant never slowed, and before long, Henry's legs began to burn and the cuts on his stomach reopened. From Andromeda's wheezing beside him, he could tell she wasn't doing much better.

"How much longer?" Henry asked.

The giant sniffled. "You tire after such a short walk and yet you expect to defeat the gods?"

"Unless I've seriously overestimated them, I'm not going to beat them by walking so just answer the question."

The giant chuckled. "We're nearly there."

True to his word, they soon rounded a corner. The slope became a little steeper and passed through an opening in the ceiling. The wind howled, carrying a chill from outside that pierced the cloak. Instantly, he moved to Andromeda's side and threw the cloak around her. They huddled together as they came out of the tunnels.

For the first time since entering this world, there was a clear sky, and the sun reflected so brightly off the snow that Henry had to shield his eyes. A castle stood in the center of a field of blazing white. Frozen towers surrounded a large central spire. Walls of blue ice glimmered in the sunlight. A path of packed snow wound through the landscape. At first, Henry thought it was similar to the other castles he'd seen, but as they came close, he realized just how much bigger it was. It wasn't just scaled up from human size. It was a hundred times the size of the Hreidmar's castle in Nidavellir, a thousand times bigger than King Frederick's palace in Argath.

As they neared the towering walls, they could make out the individual bricks of ice. At random, blocks sank into the wall, and by the time they'd reached it, a wide doorway had opened. The giant passed through it without breaking stride. Eager to get indoors, Henry and Andromeda rushed in, thankful for the protection from the elements. It was still cold inside, but it was nothing next to the deathly chill they'd just come out of.

The ice forming the floor was slippery, but not just because it was ice. It wasn't wet at all but was perfectly smooth. It felt like walking on glass, and it was just as clear. Henry found himself gazing down into it. Blurry figures sat within, and he focused on one as they passed. His eyes went wide, and he took in a sharp breath.

"Is that a skull?"

The giant paused and looked down. "Of course. All our enemies rest there. Thrym's throne sits on the skull of Baldur himself, and you walked over Hod's skull when you passed the threshold of this castle. Your skull will join them if Thrym isn't satisfied with what you say."

"Well that's a pleasant thought."

Another giant in heavy furs stumbled into their guide. He smelled like he hadn't taken a bath in a month and couldn't seem to keep his balance. The giant leading them didn't bother to ask questions. He just slammed his bone club into the other giant's head. There was a loud thump as he fell to the ground. The sound echoed through the building until Henry was sure the entire castle had heard. The giant spit on his fallen companion as they passed. Henry and Andromeda went around him by a wide margin.

"Why did you do that?" Henry asked.

The giant shrugged. "He was in the way."

He plodded on without saying another word. They rounded a corner and came to a solid wall. The giant banged his club against the wall three times. A few seconds later, a seam appeared, and the wall split. Instantly, all heat was sucked from the air. Someone cried out, and Henry wasn't sure if it was him or Andromeda. He fell to the ground, his lungs burned by the cold air. He looked at his fingers and saw the tips turning black. The *thunk thunk thunk* of giant footsteps moved away from him. Henry was shaking hard, and it was all he could do to turn his face in that direction. His eyes couldn't focus, and he saw a vague blob of color moving around inside the room that had opened.

"My king." The giant's voice was perfectly calm.

"Litr," a raspy voice said. "Why have you brought humans into my hall?"

"They claim to be enemies of the gods. I thought they might give you some amusement."

"Really?" The giant king drew out the word. It would've sent shivers down Henry's spine if he hadn't already been shaking. "What are their names?"

The giant hesitated. "I don't know. I didn't think to ask."

"Sloppy, Litr. Very sloppy. Well, mortals, what are your names?"

The cold receded to a level similar to outside. Henry's vision cleared, and he tried to get up. He was still shaking, and his arms couldn't seem to support his weight. Andromeda was barely moving, and he crawled over to her and covered her with his cloak. She stirred but didn't rise.

"What weak beings these mortals are," the king said.

The temperature shot up so fast Henry almost expected the floor to melt, but of course, it didn't. It was only warm in comparison to the bitter cold that had filled the hall a second ago. Now, it seemed to be within the limits of the cloak. It was still a struggle to rise, but he managed it, making sure to keep Andromeda protected as well.

The giant king looked like a blue-skinned human, if humans

grew to be thirty feet tall. He had a long, pointed nose and beady white eyes. His beardless face was smooth, and his hair looked like spikes of ice. He reminded Henry of the Jack Frost character he'd seen in some Christmas movie, and his mind flashed back to when he'd first entered Kurnugi, when Virgil had said they were near the home of the ruler of winter. He couldn't help but wonder if he was close to that spot.

"I'm Henry Alexander Gideon." His breath steamed in the freezing air.

"Hmm, I have heard of such a mortal," the giant king said.

"Yeah, I'm getting used to that. Does what you've heard tell you that Idun wants me dead?"

"It does indeed. It also says you led an army intending to storm Asgard itself, and that you brought strange gods as your allies."

"Then, Heimdall threw me off the bridge, and I ended up here," Henry said. "You're well informed."

"Excuse me, Lord Thrym," Andromeda said. "Is that battle still going on?"

The giant king glanced at her then turned back to Henry. "So far as I know, your army is still there. It's no easy thing to defeat an army with so many dwarves while they defend a mountain. They can't win though."

"Not without help."

"Henry no, we can't unleash these..." her eyes darted to Thrym, and when she spoke, her voice was so soft even Henry could barely hear her. "We can't send these *things* to Midgard."

"Why should I care if one mortal army lives or dies?"

"I'm not asking you to care about our army," Henry said. "I'm asking you to care about the one we're fighting. If the gods win, they'll be even more powerful than ever."

The king leaned forward on his throne. "And what do you propose to do about that?"

"Send me to Asgard so I can deal with this threat."

Thrym laughed. "Tell me, boy, in the fight that saw you thrown off Bifrost, how many gods were you fighting?"

"One," Henry said. "Just Heimdall."

The giant gave him a level look. "One. You couldn't even defeat one, and you want to attack the heart of their realm."

"With respect, Lord Thrym," Andromeda said, "the gods fear Master Henry. Maybe he can kill them. Maybe he can't, but in either case, you risk nothing by letting us go."

"Unless the gods see this as an attack. I've no desire for open war with Asgard just yet."

"Asgard is engaged in a war on..." Andromeda thought for a second before shrugging. "I have no idea how many fronts. They're attacking every world they can reach. They won't be eager to start one with you either. You don't actually have to help us. You just have to not kill us."

"An interesting proposition. Asgard already counts you as an enemy, and there would be nothing odd about you attacking them." He tapped his finger against his chin. "Yet your chances for success would be much better with my help than without it, and I would gain a powerful ally."

"We don't want to lead an army of frost giants into Asgard," Henry said.

"No, that would be a trifle obvious, wouldn't it? I was thinking of something else. You are unarmed."

"My sword was broken when I fell, and Andromeda's was lost."

"He tried to attack me with this."

Litr opened his hand. The broken hilt looked like a toy. Henry's face reddened when the king laughed.

"Did he now? Let me see that." The giant walked over to his king and deposited the broken weapon in his outstretched hand. Thrym turned it over a couple of times. "Yes, I believe I can work with this."

He closed his eyes and a blue nimbus surrounded the hilt. A few seconds later, what remained of the blade collapsed to dust. Thrym's breath began to steam, and that steam swirled around the hilt.

"What..."

Henry's words caught in his throat as a new blade began to grow out of the hilt. Unlike the steel gray of Hephaestus's weapon, this one was ice blue and mildly translucent. The blade was straight and looked paper-thin. After a few seconds, the giant king opened his eyes and idly tossed the weapon at Henry. The blade sank a foot into the floor. Henry just stared at it.

"Take it," the king said.

Henry put his hand on the hilt, half expecting it to be cold. Instead, warmth suffused him. The sword came out of the ground easily. It was much lighter than it had been before. He swung it experimentally. The sword felt like an extension of his arm. He felt strong. With this, he could do anything.

"This won't melt, will it?"

"Oh no. It can stand temperatures far hotter than those that would melt steel. It'll also protect you from this land. I doubt it's the equal of the blade you had, but it's more than enough to accomplish your task."

"And what task it that?" Henry asked as he swung it a few more times. It felt natural in his hands. The way light gleamed off the blade mesmerized him.

"With this, you can slay the gods."

THIRTY-THREE

"Litr, kill them," the king said.

"What?" Henry cried out.

The giant roared and thundered toward them. His club came crashing down, and Henry rolled out of the way just as it smashed into the ground. Chunks of ice went flying, and a frozen sheet fell from the ceiling and shattered on the ground. The giant lurched at him, and Henry dove between his legs, slashing with his sword. The blade sliced across the top of the giant's boot but didn't go deep enough to wound him.

"What are you doing?" Henry shouted, but the giant king just stared impassively while his underling attacked.

Litr's club tore through the air toward Andromeda, but she was moving too fast and ducked under it. Henry leaped at the giant. He swung high, and his blade cut into the back of Litr's knee. Blue blood sprayed out, steaming as it landed on the ice. The smell of rotten fish almost made Henry gag. Litr cried out and stumbled.

He launched a meaty fist at Henry, but Henry raised the frozen blade and allowed the giant to impale himself. Litr drew back and screamed something that Henry could only assume was a curse in the language of the giants. Andromeda had retreated to the door that had sealed itself again.

"I thought you were going to help us," Henry shouted.

"Litr, if that human is still alive in thirty seconds, I'll have your head."

The giant swung wildly at Henry. He danced out of the way and slashed at the club, lopping off three feet of it. The lighter weight threw Litr off balance, and he stepped on his wounded leg a little too hard. He tripped over his own feet and crumbled to the ground. Henry rushed over to him and put his sword on the giant's neck. The giant froze, though Henry could see fear in his eyes as he looked at the king. Suddenly, this creature seemed like a sad and pathetic thing.

"What's going on here?" Henry asked.

"You failed, Litr," Thrym said, shaking his head. "Very disappointing."

"No, my king," Litr stammered. "Forgive me. I underestimated him. That sword..."

"Sword or no, he is only a mortal."

"No!"

He screamed. The ground under him writhed, and a thin tendril formed from the ice and wrapped itself around the giant's torso. Heedless of the blade still at his neck, Litr struggled against it, but though it was no thicker than Henry's little finger, it was apparently strong enough to hold its prisoner. Henry could only gape. The giant flailed but other tendrils reached up and held him prone. Slowly, he began to sink into the ground. Frozen tears fell from his cheeks. A few seconds later, he'd vanished. The ice where he'd lain looked as solid as ever. Even the cracks from his attacks were gone.

"What happened to him?" Henry asked.

"His skull will join those beneath us."

"I thought that was only for your enemies."

The giant king shrugged. "Weakness is as great a threat as anything else. That is enemy enough for me."

"But why did you order him to attack in the first place?"

"As I said, weakness will not serve me. If you're going to go into Asgard bearing a frozen blade, I intend to see you have at least a chance of success."

"You mean it was a test?"

"Of course."

"What if I had failed?"

"Then your skull and your friend's would be the ones beneath my throne room."

Henry tried not to look afraid. "Then we're done? You'll help us?"

"I'll send someone to guide you to Asgard."

"We haven't had good luck travelling outside through your realm."

"The sword will protect you."

"What about Andromeda?" Henry asked.

The giant king shrugged. He reached into his chair, and his hand sunk into the ice. When he brought it out again, he held a small crystal hanging on a frozen chain. He tossed it to Andromeda. She caught it and dangled the crystal by its chain. It seemed to glow with a faint inner light.

"That will melt as soon as you leave Jotunheim, but it'll keep you from freezing while you're here."

"Thank you," Andromeda said.

"Thank me by succeeding or at least by dying without revealing your connection to me."

"We'll see what we can do about that." Henry said.

THIRTY-FOUR

The giant who led them out of the castle didn't give a name and never spoke a word. Henry found himself wondering if he'd be able to fight this giant if he had to. The thought held a peculiar joy, and his hand moved toward his hilt almost of its own accord. He forced himself to put that thought away. It refused to disappear entirely though, and he couldn't help but imagine the giant whimpering before him like Litr had at the end. It was a strangely satisfying thought.

True to Thrym's word, the cold didn't touch Henry. Even with the weapon sheathed, he never felt anything more than a mild chill. Andromeda was having an easier time of it as well. It still hurt to move, but that was only as a result of falling off of Bifrost and not of this land slowly killing them.

"Have you given any thought to what you'll do once we reach Asgard?" Andromeda asked.

For some reason, the question annoyed him, and he sneered. "Find Idun and stop her."

"Just like that?"

"Just like that."

"Have you considered that Asgard is a world every bit as large as Midgard. You can't just assume you'll find the way."

"I've found the way so far," Henry said.

"And look where it's brought us."

"It hasn't always been so bad."

Andromeda stopped in her tracks and gaped at him. She had to run to catch up. "Henry, we were just thrown off a bridge between worlds and landed in one of the worst realms in all of existence."

The giant grunted. Andromeda glanced at him but otherwise ignored him. Henry's hand twitched toward his hilt, but he stopped himself. The giant just plodded on, and Henry gave Andromeda a sidelong glance. She smirked, and though the giant gave no other obvious response, Henry could've sworn he picked up the pace a little.

Before long, they came over the crest of a hill. A wide river ran from horizon to horizon. A thick bank of fog obscured the opposite shore. The water churned so much that the entire surface was white with foam. Jagged rocks poked out of the water at irregular intervals, any one of them could probably split a man in two if carried by such a strong current. It was as if the river had a set of mismatched teeth just waiting to chomp down on human flesh.

"Asgard lies on the other side of the Ifngr," the giant said. Then, he turned to go.

"Wait, how are we supposed to get across that?" Henry asked.

"That's not my problem," he said as he disappeared down the hill.

Henry's hand closed around his hilt before he realized he'd done it. He took a step forward before Andromeda put a hand on his arm. He almost pulled away and ran after the giant, envisioning thrusting his sword through the creature's back. He shook his head free of the idea and nodded.

"Well, he sure was helpful," Henry glanced at the departing giant before looking at Andromeda. "Any ideas?"

"Let's go down," she said. "Maybe we can ford it."

The hill was steep enough that they took ten minutes to reach the bottom. Henry could see a lot of other ways the giant could've brought them that would've been easier, and he began to suspect they'd been brought this way because of resentment over Andromeda's comment about how bad this realm was.

As it turned out, the river was even stronger than it had looked from atop the hill. Henry put his foot in ankle deep. He very nearly lost his balance to the strength of the current.

"So that won't work," he said.

"How deep do you think it is?"

Henry drew his sword and knelt down. He stretched out his arm and sank the blade into the water, but the blade didn't reach the bottom of the river. He looked at Andromeda and shrugged. He started to pull out the sword but stopped. A small island of ice had formed where the blade met the water. He pulled the sword out another inch, but ice remained where it was, growing ever larger. It reached about two feet in diameter before the growth stopped. About an inch of the edge closest to him had anchored itself on the shore. He drew the sword out.

"Well, that's interesting," he said.

He stood up and pressed against the ice with his foot. The edge broke away, swept up by the water. It smashed against a rock a little ways away. Henry put the sword over the water and looked at Andromeda.

"You can't be serious."

For a moment, the comment annoyed him, but he forced it to the back of his mind. "I don't see you offering any better ideas."

Andromeda scanned the shore of the river, but there was snow as far as they could see. There was nothing to build a raft or boat from, no bridge in sight. Finally, she met his eyes, let out a long breath, and nodded. Wishing he were as confident as he was pretending to be, Henry drove his sword down where water met shore.

Again, ice formed. Once it had stopped growing, he moved his sword through it. The ice gave no more resistance than water, and his blade passed through it without damaging it. Once he had a line six feet wide, he moved the blade into the river and put one foot on the slowly growing ice bridge. He pressed down several times, but it seemed solid. Holding his breath, he put his full weight on it. He half expected it to crack, but it held. He took a step forward and Andromeda followed him.

Water spilling onto the surface of the ice made it slippery, and they proceeded with agonizing slowness. The shore behind them disappeared into the fog before the one in front of them was visible. Andromeda yelped, and he turned just in time to see the frozen amulet Thrym had given her melt, wetting her clothes.

"I guess we're out of Jotunheim. Are you cold?"

"A little." There was the slightest hint of steam in her breath. "I won't freeze to death, though."

He took off his cloak and handed it to her. The sword probably wouldn't protect him against heat, but it served well enough against the cold. After pressing on for another fifteen minutes, he thought he saw a shadow on the horizon. It took another few minutes for him to be sure.

"Finally," he said, pointing at the shore.

As if it had been waiting for that moment, the ice behind him cracked. The bridge shuttered. Henry forced the sword forward, trying to reach the shore, but it was too far, and the sword could only freeze water so fast. A section of the bridge ten feet across came loose, and they shot down the river. The current sent them into a spin, and Henry didn't notice the large rock until they'd slammed into it. The ice shattered, and they plunged into the water.

Swimming was impossible. The current was too strong, and it twisted him too fast for him to gather his bearings. He couldn't tell which way was up and started choking on the water. He held his sword with a death grip, willing it to freeze more water to give him something to hold on to, but he was moving too fast.

A shadow appeared, though he wasn't sure if it was above or below. Needle-like claws gripped his arm and pulled him. He tried to struggle against it, fearing it would drag him under, but it held fast. Just when he thought he would pass out, his face plopped onto the muddy ground of the shore, and the claws released him.

Coughing, he managed to sit up and wipe the water from his eyes. He had to blink several times to clear his vision. Andromeda was lying next to him. A black bird half as tall as Henry himself perched near Andromeda's arm. Henry closed his eyes and searched his memory for the name.

"Huginn?"

The bird's caw sounded somehow angry, and Henry found himself backing away until he bumped into something. He turned around and saw a second bird, just as big as the first. It cocked its head.

"Are you sure these are the right humans, Huginn?" the first one asked. "This one doesn't even know the difference between you and me."

"They're only humans, Muninn," Huginn said. "You can't

expect too much of them. You have to admit that was a clever way to cross the river."

"I don't see how drowning is clever," Muninn said.

"That part wasn't deliberate," Henry said.

"Yes well, it never is. Still the idea was clever. It almost worked. Where did you get an ice blade anyway?"

"Where do you think he got it from, Huginn?" Muninn asked. "They did just come over from Jotunheim. I swear you're as bad as humans sometimes."

Muninn squawked, but Huginn chirped in a way that sounded almost like a laugh. Henry got up and walked to Andromeda. She was unconscious again. Grimly, he wondered how many times he had saved her life. He shook her gently, and she opened her eyes and smiled.

"I guess we made it."

Henry smirked and offered her a hand up. "It was close there for a second. Are you all right?"

"I think so."

"Good," he said as they turned away from the river and looked into the home of the gods.

THIRTY-FIVE

A sgard was beautiful: a verdant garden that looked like it had never known a rough hand or harsh weather. Flowers of every size shape and color were arranged in neat rows according to their type, and they filled the air with a mix of smells that made Henry feel light-headed. Butterflies as big as hawks floated from flower to flower. Nearby, stood a tree with golden leaves that glimmered in the sun. A gentle breeze rustled the leaves giving the impression of music. Behind the tree stood a massive castle of yellow stone. One great tower rose on the side nearest the river, and a wall that had to be a hundred feet tall surrounded the castle. A gate of black iron stood open, and a stone path wound from it, leading deeper into Asgard. Henry took one step toward the castle, but one of the birds landed in front of him.

"I would not go in there if I were you, Mortal," Huginn said. "Once one crosses the threshold of Valhalla, he may not leave save at Odin's call."

Henry's jaw dropped. "That's Valhalla?"

The raven nodded, which was a peculiar gesture for a bird. "Where fallen heroes do battle against each other until the day Odin summons them to war. It's empty now, in any case."

"They're still at the battle against the kings," Henry said.

Once again, the bird nodded. "No one expected them to last this long. Your allies are to be commended. I take it you want to go see the gods."

"If that's where Idun is," Henry said.

They passed a few other castles, which the ravens identified as halls belonging to various gods, but Asgard itself seemed empty save for the occasional bird and butterfly. The wind carried a gentle heat. As they walked through the garden, it was difficult to believe so much hatred and suffering had come from such a serene place.

"It reminds me of Zuab's garden," Andromeda said.

"It makes sense," Henry said. "The ones who came to help Zuab probably came from here. If we looked around, I'd guess we'd find the way to Argath, probably under Idun's apple tree."

"What makes you say that?"

Henry shrugged. "It's obvious. The Moirai told me Hera's apples of immortality had been corrupted, and that they could as easily kill as grant life. Zuab had a tree of apples that were practically death given form, and your past memories said the Brothers Grimm had given Idun a ring that corrupted her apples. My guess is they were all the same tree."

"You see, Muninn," Huginn squawked. "He does have a thought in his head."

"Maybe, but it's just the one."

Henry turned to Andromeda. "I think what the crows are trying to say is that I'm right."

"Ravens!" they squawked in unison.

Henry shrugged. "What's the difference?"

Andromeda quirked an eyebrow. "Are you feeling all right?"

"Yes, why?"

"You've been...unkind recently."

Henry huffed. "I'm just tired. Can you blame me?" He looked up at the birds without waiting for her to respond. "I am right though, aren't I?"

Muninn bobbed his head. "The apple is a thing of power in many stories. You need it, or something like it, to cross into as many worlds as Idun intends to conquer."

"Maybe we should just chop it down," Andromeda suggested.

"I'm not sure that would do it. Maybe Idun could just grow another one. If she couldn't though, it would lead to the death of all the gods here, and I'm not sure that's something we want to do."

"After all the death they've caused, how can you be so squeamish about bringing about theirs?"

"Because I'm not sure the stories will survive the gods' deaths," Henry said. "The Oracle of the Present said there are few things that are not in my power to destroy. If I understand Kurnugi correctly, even if something is killed here, it still exists in other stories, but I got the feeling the Oracle was talking about something more permanent than that. If I destroy the gods, they might not exist in any story."

"They wouldn't be missed," Andromeda said.

"Are you sure? Would this world even exist without Odin? Would King Budli or the rest of the people of Gothia?"

Andromeda grumbled but didn't say anything more. They continued following the birds. A gentle quiet had fallen over Asgard. Even the birdsong sounded muted. The smell of flowers faded, and the vibrant colors seemed to dull.

They passed near a vast hall that, according to the ravens, was Odin's home. Though they said it was made of silver, the metal was dull as, if it had sat out in the elements untended for a long time. Given how mild the elements were in Asgard, Henry thought that unlikely. As soon as they passed the hall, the wind stopped. A thin cloud floated in front of the sun, and all the butterflies and other insects landed on flowers and didn't rise again. It was as if all of Asgard was holding its breath, waiting for something. Henry had the uncomfortable sensation that it was waiting for him.

He saw the rainbow first, its top appearing just over the horizon. Henry found his pace quickening. They crested a gentle hill. Beyond, perhaps a hundred yards away, the ground ended in a cliff. Past that, an army spread out across a valley that terminated at a mountain range. Lightning flashed in the distance followed by a surge of orange light, and he froze in his tracks. He looked at the birds.

"Thor and Hephaestus? Are they still fighting?"

"Did you think a battle between gods was a simple matter?" Huginn asked. "Such things can last for weeks or months. Even years. I suspect they'll be fighting long after all the mortals beneath them have grown old and died. Legends are born of such things."

"We're almost there, aren't we?" he asked.

"Very close, young human. The end of Bifrost lies at the edge of that cliff, and the gods await nearby."

Henry nodded. With every step, a dozen fears ran through his mind. For all his bravado, he wasn't really sure what he was supposed to do, especially not if he had to deal with all the gods to get to Idun. One had been more than he could handle, and he wasn't even sure how many gods there were. He didn't think he could count on Odin's help either, regardless of what he'd said.

When they approached Bifrost, his blood went cold, and he drew his sword. Heimdall stood on the rainbow bridge only a few feet from Asgard. His armor shone with ever-changing light, and he carried his sword in his right hand. When he saw Henry, he inclined his head and motioned at a path that went down the cliff.

"Your adversary waits just over there."

"You're not going to try to stop me?" Henry asked.

Heimdall grinned. "I am charged to guard this bridge. I would be a poor guardian if I left my charge to go indulge myself in a battle, wouldn't you say?"

Henry nodded slowly. He looked to Andromeda. She had gone a little pale but smiled when she met his gaze.

"I guess it's time," she said.

THIRTY-SIX

H enry and Andromeda walked down the path. Sheer walls rose up on either side of them. Through the opening ahead, he could see the peak where Bifrost ended, where Thor and Hephaestus fought. Fire and lightning flashed atop it. Henry and Andromeda came out on a large ledge overlooking the valley between worlds.

Wingless dragons moved through the sea of men toward the mountain. If Henry squinted, he thought he could see a couple dead on the field. Dozens of men and women stood on the ledge looking out over the battlefield. They were talking softly, and none noticed the two intruders.

Henry tried to move quietly but kicked a loose pebble. It skidded across the ground and clanked into the armored leg of a one-handed god. Instantly, conversation ceased. As one, the Norse gods turned to look at him.

Henry's hand fell to his hilt, but he let it fall away a second later. There was no way he'd be able to fight all of them. There was the sound of rasping steel as the gods drew their weapons. Henry took a step back. The crowd stirred and parted. Odin stood in the center. He carried a long spear in one hand. Flowing robes covered his body, and he wore a hood that didn't quite hide his one-eyed face.

"It seems we have guests, my friends."

"Impossible!" someone cried out.

"They couldn't have defeated Heimdall!"

Other gods shouted, and their voices blended together into a thundering roar. Henry's head felt like it was going to explode. Dimly, he realized his hand had closed around his hilt. Odin banged the butt of his spear into the stone. Though it was only a gentle tap, the whole mountain shook at the impact. Most kept their balance, but a few fell. When those had gotten up, the gods went silent and looked at their king.

"They did not defeat Heimdall. The boy is hidden from my sight, but the girl is another matter. I see her being thrown off Bifrost. Judging by the tattered condition of the boy's clothes, he was with her. They survived Jotunheim itself to reach us."

A gasp rippled through the gods. A woman who was little more than a girl stepped out next to Odin. Unlike the others, she bore no armor or weapon. She wore a pure white dress that shimmered as she moved. Patterns of woven gold ran across her bodice, and her golden hair was tied in twin braids. Her alabaster skin looked like it had never seen a day of sun, but her face was red with anger. Henry had seen her before, when he'd asked the magic mirror who was responsible for the war. Idun, the holder of the golden apples.

"Allies of the giant king," she shrieked.

"No, Idun," Odin said. "Enemies of yours do not mean allies of Thrym."

"Have you gone senile, old man?" she asked. "He bears a frozen blade. How else would he get one if not from the giant king?"

"The boy's recent past is obscured, but what transpired before he crossed into this realm is not. He once turned an army to stone with the head of a vanquished foe. Given what else I see of him, I could well imagine that sword as a prize won from an enemy rather than a boon from an ally."

"Foolishness," she said. "I can see the past as well as you and—"

"Then you know the path he's walked is hidden from us."

"His past is but Thrym's is not. I see that beast of a king bestowing a blade and testing its bearer to make sure he was capable of killing us. I see the girl there too. Who could it have been but this boy?"

The gods grumbled. A woman with snow-white skin and icy hair raised a bow. A faint blue tinge colored the arrowhead and several of the gods backed away, but Odin raised his hand.

"Lower your weapon, Skadi. I can see that as well, but this would not be the first time a hero obtains spoils from an enemy with trickery."

Skadi looked from Odin to Idun. For a moment, Henry thought she wouldn't listen, but Odin cleared his throat. Skadi released the tension on her bow and lowered her arrow. Idun grew even redder. She stamped her foot, but it seemed a pitiful thing after what Odin had done.

"Enough of this," Idun said. "These are the ones I've been looking for since the beginning. I preserved the girl for her knowledge once, but not again. Kill them, old man."

Odin's expression never wavered. "No."

Idun's jaw dropped. It took several seconds before she could find her voice. "What?"

"I said no, Idun. I'll not fight your battles for you."

"I'll forbid you the apples," she said. "You'll grow old and die."

"We'll see."

Idun gaped at Odin as if unable to accept his defiance. Odin just stared at her, his face devoid of any emotion. Eventually, she looked away, as if unable to bear the weight of that one-eyed gaze. It took her a second to recover, and she turned to the other gods.

"Kill the mortals!"

Two gods leaped forward, one was the one-handed man Henry had seen earlier, looking no less fierce for his handicap, and the other, a man in a chain shirt and an iron helm. Both carried long swords. Henry lifted his weapon, but he knew he couldn't stand against two of them. For a second, however, he didn't care. The sight of them filled him with a cold rage. Before he could do anything, Odin's voice rang through the air.

"Tyr, Hermod, hold!"

The command in those words was absolute. Even though it hadn't been directed at him, Henry found himself lowering his weapon. The pair of gods paused for a second, but took another step forward, though it obviously required great effort. Odin banged his spear against the ground again, and the armored gods struggled to maintain their balance as the ground shook. When it calmed, the pair glanced at Idun. Rage had twisted her expression so much Henry could hardly recognize her.

"What are you waiting for?" Her screech made her sound more like a little girl than a goddess. "I said kill them."

Odin stepped between the gods and Henry. He threw back his hood and shifted his shoulders. His robes fell to the ground. The figure beneath them was anything but an old man. His arms were thickly muscled, and he wore armor of interlocking scales. It glowed a faint orange. Long white hair had been tied in a single braid. He set his legs wide, and his knuckles whitened as he tightened his grip on his spear. The tip of the weapon gave off an angry red light. The mask of the wise old man vanished, and all signs of frailty melted away. This was no longer Odin the Wanderer who Henry had met on Hind Mountain. This was Odin, warrior king of a race of warrior gods, and as his gaze fell on the assembled deities, each one shrank back. Finally, he turned to Idun.

"No, Idun. They will not touch these mortals."

"You would dare?" She turned back to the gods. "Any who does not attack will never taste another apple. Die with the Allfather!"

The crowd took a hesitant step forward, but Odin simply shook his head and moved his spearpoint from god to god. They stopped and looked at each other.

"If they disobey you, they will die eventually. If they disobey me, they will die today."

"You can't fight them all," she said, no longer sounding sure of herself.

Odin smiled. "Are you so sure? Well, you may be right at that, but I wonder how many I could kill. It could be any one of them, and they know it. These are not your pet mortals, Idun. We have all lived for ages and still have an eternity before us. It is not so easy to risk that for the sake of one girl's tantrum."

"Tantrum?"

"Well, what else would you call it? You are one of us, Idun, and we do not shrink from combat. This is your battle. Face it yourself."

Idun glared at the gods. Most avoided meeting her gaze. A few glanced at Odin before shaking their heads. Idun was breathing heavily, but Henry felt himself calm down. Idun shrieked again and grabbed an ivory hilt at her belt that Henry hadn't noticed. She drew a long thin blade and held it steadily before her. The silvery metal hummed as she moved it back and forth through the air.

Henry's mouth went dry. He'd always assumed that if it came

down to a fight, he'd be able to beat Idun, but he'd underestimated her. She was still a Norse goddess, and the gods of the Vikings were warriors all. Henry's sword hissed as he tightened his grip on the hilt. Steam swirled around the blade. Without needing to be told, the rest of the gods formed a wide circle around them. Odin took Andromeda's hand and led her to the circle where he stood next to her. A tall blond woman stood at her other side. The one-eyed god nodded to him, and Henry set his feet and prepared to fight a goddess.

THIRTY-SEVEN

Idun darted at him. Henry raised his sword, but she struck low, cutting a shallow gash across his leg. He tried to strike back, but she'd already danced out of the way. She gave him an evil grin and he took a step back. In the same instant, she lunged. Henry swung his sword in a desperate arc, knocking her sword away an instant before it skewered him. He slashed, but Idun slammed her blade down on his. The tip touched the ground, and she brought her foot down on it. He felt the sword slipping from his grasp, but she hissed and drew back. He withdrew his sword.

A circle of ice had formed on the ground and a layer of frost had crawled up Idun's leg. She looked down at it, and Henry lunged, but Idun moved like a snake. She twisted out of the way and tried to strike, but her frozen leg threw her off balance. Henry lashed out at her left side, and she batted the attack aside. Their swords rang against each other, the anger inside Henry growing with every blow. Idun made it through his defenses several times and delivered a number of shallow cuts. Henry's sword only made it past her parries once, but even then, his sword bounced off armor that had been hidden by her dress.

He couldn't keep it up. The wounds Idun gave him piled up on top of the injuries he'd taken in Jotunheim. He felt himself slowing. He had to do something risky and hope it ended better than his fight with Heimdall. Idun thrust and Henry pushed forward. Her sword pierced his shoulder, but his sank into her arm. Ice spread from her wound until her hand froze, and frost crept up her blade. Henry pulled back and slashed at her weapon. It shattered under his blow, and Idun fell back. Henry stood over her and held his sword at her neck.

"It's finally over," he said.

He pressed the sword into her neck. A thin trickle of blood ran down to the ground. It froze a second later. This was the one who had caused so much fear and pain. She was the reason he'd been trapped here. It would be such a simple matter to end it here and now.

"Henry, no!" Andromeda called.

He clenched his teeth. "She deserves it."

His sword pulsed with every word. It thirsted for her blood. Out of the corner of his eyes, he saw a group of gods surge forward, but again, Odin banged his spear on the ground. Without removing his sword, Henry looked up. Several of the gods gaped at Odin, as if not believing he would stop them from saving Idun. The woman on the other side of Andromeda whispered something, but Odin shook his head and looked at Henry.

"You must not do this," he said. "Idun alone can give the gods the golden apples that maintain their life. They will shrivel if any hand but hers picks them."

"They were on her side," Henry said. "Thor tried to kill me, and Heimdall threw me off Bifrost."

"Did I not save your life and guide you when you journeyed to rescue Andromeda from Idun's grasp?" Odin said. "Did I not hide you from her sight?"

"It *was* you!" Idun cried out.

Henry glared at her and put pressure on the blade. She recoiled and went silent. He blinked at her. Her skin had turned blue, and she was shaking. The area around the tip of his blade was covered in frost. Henry sneered at her before looking up. Odin's single eye had never left him.

"Will you kill me too, then? I could no more survive without her apples than the rest."

Henry paused, but his hesitation only lasted a second. "You were her king. If you'd done your job, none of this would've happened. I never would've had to leave home. My parents would have never thought I was kidnapped. Andromeda would still be..."

There was a soft clinking. Henry looked down just as a frozen tear fell from his cheek and shattered on a ground covered in frost. The pain in his shoulder had gone numb, and he was dimly aware that the blood that had spilled from his wound had frozen.

"Henry."

Andromeda's voice was quivering. For the first time, Henry realized the entire ledge was covered in frost. The skies above rumbled with dark clouds and a light snow began to fall. Andromeda was shaking, the cold apparently more than Hephaestus's cloak could handle. Even some of the gods shivered.

"Stories do die, sometimes," Odin said quietly. "I know this. Thrym knows this. Even Idun begins to understand. If you kill her today, no story will ever come from this realm again. We are the memory of an entire people. Will you destroy us and give our place to Thrym? I doubt he'd be kinder than we, and I'm not sure what it would do to your world."

Henry looked at the gods. Suddenly, they didn't seem so fierce. More than one drew back at his gaze. Though they still towered over him, he couldn't help but see them as small.

"How many have you killed?" Odin asked.

"What?"

"Not monsters, ghosts, or beasts. How many humans have you killed?"

In spite of the cold, Henry started to sweat. "Idun isn't human. She's an idea someone came up with a long time ago."

"So are you," Odin said. "So is Virgil."

A chill that had nothing to do with the weather shot through his body. Virgil was the first person Henry had met when he'd crossed over into Kurnugi. If not for Virgil, Henry would have died long ago. More than that, Virgil was his brother who had never been born. He had existed only as a dream in the minds of his parents, but that had been enough to give him life in Kurnugi. Virgil had died keeping Henry alive.

Henry tightened his grip on his hilt. Idun squirmed under the blade. He drew back and the gods gave a collective gasp. He swung but turned his blade at the last instant. The side slammed into the ground with a sound like breaking glass. The blade shattered. Its fragments scattered across the stone. They liquefied and evaporated. The ice where the blade had struck melted and the frost vanished in an ever-growing circle. Idun's frozen limbs thawed, and color returned to Andromeda's skin.

Henry collapsed, breathing heavily. The rage that had slowly been building in him since he received the sword vanished. Idun hissed and got to her feet. She stormed over to the gods and held out a hand.

"Give me a sword."

"No, Idun."

Odin spoke softly, but the stones resonated with his voice. None of the others moved to help her. The goddess let out an ear-piercing shriek and leaped through the air. She crashed into Henry, making him roll over on his back. She set a knee against his chest and closed her hands around his throat. His vision went dark, and he clawed at her hands, but it was no use.

Andromeda screamed, and he heard sounds of a struggle. He kept hoping Odin would intervene, but Idun tightened her grip and started banging his head against the stone. Desperate, he ran his hands along her arms until he found her fingers. His fingers brushed against a metal band on her right hand.

Henry's body pulsed. An energy he hadn't realized was there flowed out of him, and his body went cold. There was a sound like thunder. A force pressed Henry into the ground. Idun was thrown aside. It passed after a second, and Henry sat up, gasping for breath. He felt something hard in his hand and looked down. The ring in his hand was split in two. Brilliant orange lines ran through it, though their light was fading. A second later, they had gone dark. The ring crumbled to dust, and the wind carried it away.

"Curse breaker." Odin's words were carried on the wind.

All around, the gods looked at Henry with awe. Odin released his hold on Andromeda, and she ran to him. A few feet away, Idun picked herself off the ground. The same orange lines glowed on her skin. Tears streamed down her cheeks, each one glowing brightly. The light vanished when they hit the ground. With each tear, the lines on her skin dimmed.

"What have I done?" she cried.

"Now, it is over," Odin said.

THIRTY-EIGHT

peak to the generals. Tell them to cease their attack on the mountain," Odin said to Huginn and Muninn. The two ravens flew out over the battlefield as the god turned to a blond woman wearing a feathered cloak. "See to Thor and the foreign god."

The woman nodded. Her cloak rustled in the wind. A second later, a large yellow-feathered falcon rose from where the woman had been. It streaked through the air toward the mountain that still flashed with fire and lightning. Then, Odin walked over to Henry and offered him a hand up.

"Well done," he said.

"Now what?" Henry asked.

"My ravens will end the battle, and Freya will stop the fight between Thor and Hephaestus."

Andromeda put a hand to her head and took in a deep breath. "What about the other worlds? Idun sent men to many of them."

"They will be withdrawn. We have no need to conquer other

lands." He looked Andromeda up and down. "There is one more thing to do, however."

"What's that?" Henry asked.

"The knowledge of the Oracle of the Past was never meant for a mortal mind." He turned to Idun. "It wasn't even meant for you, for that matter."

Idun nodded first, and Andromeda mirrored the motion a second later. Henry took her hand.

"Does that mean Andromeda will be the princess again?" he asked.

Odin shook his head. "What was paid for the knowledge cannot be easily regained."

"But it is possible?"

"Perhaps, if she has the strength and the will."

Henry turned to Andromeda. "If anyone can do it, you can. I can stay and help you if you want me to."

"No," she said. "You've done enough. I can't ask you to do more."

He looked into her eyes for a long time. There was so much he wanted to say, but the words wouldn't come. Hermes had once told him that Andromeda wasn't human, and that he shouldn't think of her as one, but he couldn't help it. They'd been through so much together. It was hard to believe this was the end. More because he didn't trust himself to speak than for any other reason, he nodded. Tears blurred his vision, and he wiped at them. He looked away from her. The gods had already begun to depart. The last of them disappeared up the path. Only Odin and Idun remained. Henry nodded at him, and the four of them walked up the path and to the rainbow bridge.

"I thought this went to Midgard," Henry said.

"Bifrost goes to both Midgard and Yggdrasil, but it is the same bridge."

"We decide to which one we're going, and the bridge takes us there," Henry said. "Virgil mentioned something like that about travelling between worlds."

"It's more or less the same thing," Odin said.

Before he could lead them on, three man-shaped figures came into view with a horse behind them. It only took a few seconds for Henry to recognize Hephaestus's limping gate. As they neared, the features of the other two became clear: Hermes and Heimdall. The horse, naturally, was Pegasus.

"Then, we won," Hephaestus said once they'd come within earshot.

A single plate of his armor remained on his chest, sporting a wide crack. For all his talk of being indestructible, a bruise covered half his face. Gold blood dripped from a wound in his chest. Hermes looked none the worse for wear. He grinned and slapped Henry on the back.

"Good job! I knew you could do it."

"Thanks," Henry said dryly. "It's amazing what you can do when no one leads you into a volcano."

"You're never going to let that go, are you?" Hermes asked.

"It wasn't Hermes that led us into a frozen world," Andromeda said.

Henry's face reddened, and the gods laughed. Odin nodded at the Olympians.

"I have opened the ways to your world. The mountain at the other end of the bridge will lead to your Olympus, and the caves within will lead to the Nordi Mountains. Frederick can find his way from there."

Hephaestus nodded. "We will leave as soon as we can. You'll see that Henry gets home?"

"I will."

Odin extended his hand, and Hephaestus took it. Hermes did the same a few seconds later. The Greeks nodded at Henry. Pegasus walked up to him. For a second, his form blurred. Then, instead of one horse, there was two, one the eight-legged steed that rightfully belonged to Odin, and the other the winged stallion Henry had found in Greece. He looked at Odin.

"He was the hero's horse, and he became what you needed according to the world you were in, even to the point of becoming something in Argath that hadn't existed before. The hero's journey is over now, and he must return to where he comes from. Part of that is in Greece, and part is here."

Henry nodded and felt an odd lump in his throat. Pegasus had been a faithful companion, but one that couldn't follow him home. The Greeks walked back the way they came, with the winged version of Pegasus trailing after them. Though Henry's group followed a second later, they didn't see the Greeks. After a few minutes, a large tree appeared in the distance, and they came under Yggdrasil's branches. Odin led them to the cave containing the well. Idun stared into it. Her skin glowed brightly for a second before the light flowed into the water. Idun let out a breath.

"I never knew having knowledge could be such a burden." She looked at Odin. "I don't know how you do it."

Odin grinned. "I've had a lot of practice. Now, for Andromeda."

The same thing happened, and once the light had faded, she seemed weak. Henry went to her side. She smiled at him but didn't take his arm.

"Thank you, Henry," she said, "for everything." She hugged him and brought her cheek to his. He could feel the tears on her face, and a lump formed in his throat. She pulled away and didn't look at him. "Goodbye."

Henry nodded and turned to Odin. The god nodded once and motioned for Henry to follow. They went deeper into the tunnel. The air grew colder, and Henry started to shiver. The cave branched off, with a thin portion of Yggdrasil's root running down it. Odin pointed.

"Yggdrasil touches all worlds including yours," Odin said. "This will lead you home."

THIRTY-NINE

T he cave walls closed in around Henry, and he had to get on his hands and knees. Yggdrasil's root ran along the ground, and Henry kept one hand on it at all times. A faint scraping sound came from ahead. Henry paused for a second but pressed on. After all that had happened, he didn't believe Odin would send him down this path unless it was safe.

The scraping grew louder. A gentle breeze caressed his face, and he smelled fresh cut grass. He crawled faster. Abruptly, the ground gave way under him. Only the root remained, and he clung to it as he fell. His armed jerked as he swung, not from a root, but from a branch, and he found himself staring through a window into his own room.

It was dark, only illuminated slightly by light coming from the hall. He gaped, not quite sure if he could believe it. He looked up. Instead of Yggdrasil, he was hanging from the ash tree in his back-yard. The full moon shone brightly overhead, and stars twinkled in a cloudless sky. He dropped to the ground and ran his fingers through the grass. Someone had mowed the lawn recently. Henry jumped when the sprinklers came on, but after a few seconds, he realized he was laughing.

He was home.

He ran up to the back door and banged on it. The porch light came on, and the door opened. His dad stood in the doorway. His hair still looked like it had never been combed. His eyes were puffed up and a little red, and his shirt was wrinkled. He looked at Henry, and his brow arched in confusion.

"Henry?" His face lit up. "Henry!"

Henry threw his arms around him and laughed again. They held each other tight. Water dripped from Henry's clothes to his dad's, but neither one cared. A petite woman with dark brown hair poked her head around the corner. When she laid eyes on Henry, a sound halfway between a gasp and a squeal escaped her throat. Henry freed himself from his father's grip and ran to her.

"Mom!"

He wasn't sure how long the three of them embraced, laughing and crying in each other's arms. It was midnight before they sat down in the living room. Henry had a glass of water in his hand with actual ice cubes floating in it. He hadn't seen an ice cube in a long time. He found himself staring at the ceiling fan. It was such a simple thing, but the people he'd been with the past several weeks would've considered it a miracle.

"What are you wearing?" his mom asked. "You look like you just came from a renaissance fair."

Henry looked down. He still wore the shirt and pants Hephaestus had given him as well as the boots he'd gotten in ancient Greece. The rips had repaired themselves, though Henry didn't know if that had happened before or after he'd crossed back into his world. He wondered if they still had the power Hephaestus had given them.

He shrugged. "I didn't exactly have a lot of choice about what to wear."

"We got a note that you'd been kidnapped," his dad said. "How did you get away? Where have you been?"

Henry almost choked on his water. He'd spent so much time trying to get home he'd never stopped to consider what he would say when he got there. If he tried to tell them the truth, they'd think he was crazy.

"I don't know," Henry said, spitting out the first words that came to mind. "I was in a room. I broke out and just started running. I didn't stop until I made it to the backyard."

"Who took you? How did they get you out of the school with no one seeing?"

"I don't know, dad," Henry said. "I'm sorry. I just don't remember."

"It's fine son. Don't worry about it. We'll call the police in the morning. Don't worry. They'll catch whoever did this."

Henry had apparently been gone almost a month. He stuck to his story about not remembering. He gave only vague details. He could tell the police were frustrated, but there wasn't much he could do. They left after a few hours with instructions to call if he remembered anything else. He promised he would.

It was Sunday, and apparently news of his return spread fast, because they received a steady stream of visitors. Friends and neighbors stopped by. Even family members they never saw except for Christmas and Thanksgiving showed up. His mom made a big lunch, and though it wasn't as fancy as the kingly feasts he'd had, it was, in its own way, much more grand.

By early afternoon, the constant well-wishers had exhausted him, but it was a pleasant sort of exhaustion, instead of the bone-deep tiredness that came from being afraid for your life. He plopped down on the couch. People constantly tried to pry the story out of him, but he never gave anyone more than he'd given the police. Hours later, they sat down for dinner, another big meal to feed everyone who happened to be there at the time. They laughed well into the night, though he was ready for bed by the time the last person left.

His alarm buzzed in the morning, and he just stared at it for several seconds before turning it off. How strange the real world seemed after Kurnugi. He got dressed but wasn't looking forward to another day of smothering by his parents, so he dug under his bed looking for his backpack until he remembered it had been lost somewhere off the shores of ancient Greece. He got his old one from his closet and went into the living room. His mom was making pancakes and looked up when he came in.

"Oh," she said when she saw his backpack.

"Yeah," Henry said.

"Wouldn't you rather stay home?" his mom asked. "You've been through a lot."

"Mom, after everything, I just want to do something normal," Henry said. "I promise I'll come home right after school. I'll even run if that'll make you feel better."

"Fine," she said, not sounding quite sure of herself. "Just be careful."

"I will, I promise."

He walked to school as he had so many times, pausing briefly at the spot where he'd first met Hermes. It had all started here. He drew every eye as he walked through the doors of Twain. A lot of people had been at his house the previous day. Others were just now learning he was back. People actually clapped when he walked into Mr. Adam's class. He sat down next to his friend Daniel who had a silly looking grin on his face.

"Glad you're back," Daniel said.

Henry smiled. "Me too."

It took a while for the class to calm down, but Mr. Adams didn't seem to mind.

"Welcome back, Mr. Gideon," the history teacher said. "We're all glad you're back. I'm sure we'll have you up to speed in no time." The class groaned, but Henry only laughed. The teacher shot him a grin. "We have another surprise. You may have heard that the United States agreed to grant sanctuary to a group of refugees. Some of them will be attending Twain."

Henry dimly remembered seeing a news report about that before he'd left. Two guys and a girl walked into the classroom. Henry's heart raced. The girl had bright red hair and emerald eyes. She carried herself like a princess, though she wasn't one anymore. She met his eyes and smiled. Mr. Adams was making introductions, but he didn't notice. The three moved to find desks, and the girl sat next to him.

"How did you get here?" Henry whispered.

"I surrendered my role as princess."

"But Odin said you could've gotten it back eventually."

"As a princess, I couldn't be anything else, but when I gave that up I gained something more."

"What's that?"

"A choice. I followed you because I choose to live a human life."

They talked throughout the day. Though neither understood how, apparently she had appeared in the midst of the refugees before the three had been brought to the school. There had been enough people that no one had noticed a girl who hadn't started the journey with them. However it had happened, she was now ready to start a new life here, no longer as a story, but as a real human girl.

The rest of the day passed quickly. After school, he invited Andromeda over, but she insisted he spend some time alone with his parents. Reluctantly, he agreed. He gave her his phone number and promised to teach her how to use a phone the next day. As promised, he ran home, but when he went inside, his heart skipped a beat. His parents were seated at the dining room table with grim expressions on their faces.

"What's going on?" he asked as he closed the door behind him.

His mom bit her lower lip and his dad took her hand. "We got a call from Dr. Thomson."

Henry searched his memory for the name before it hit him. Dr. Thomson was the fertility doctor they'd been using. He smiled so hard his face hurt.

"Are you having a baby?"

"Yes but..."

"That's fantastic!" Henry said as he threw his arms around her. "I'm going to have a little brother!"

Henry's parents exchanged glances before looking at him. "Henry, we don't know that. It's too early to tell."

"I know it," he said.

"Then you're not upset?" his dad asked. "Last time..."

"I'm excited," Henry said. "Just don't start going back and forth about his eyes again."

His mom laughed. "I can't wait to look through all those baby name books."

"You don't need to do that," Henry said.

"Oh?"

"Virgil. His name is Virgil."

About the Author

Gama Ray Martinez lives near Salt Lake City, Utah. He moved there solely because he likes mountains. He collects weapons in case he ever needs to supply a medieval battalion, and he greatly resents when work or other real life things get in the way of writing. He secretly hopes to one day slay a dragon in single combat and doesn't believe in letting little things like reality stand in the way of dreams. Find him at http://gamarayburst.com/ and http://www.facebook.-com/gamarayburst.